HER QUIET LEGACY

K T BOWES

Before You Read This Novel

I'd already written half of Jack Jethro's story when a glass of wine and a tentative suggestion found me laughingly committing to taking a neurodivergence assessment.

It didn't matter because I was the right side of normal, whatever that was. So, I went into it glibly, firing my answers from the hip and feeling strangely understood.

Until I saw the results.

It shouldn't have come as such a shock to have my neurodivergence confirmed. I mean, I'd always sensed that I was different to everyone else but I'd learned to live with it. We all have flaws and talents. I figured I just kept mine hidden deeper than most people.

I'd written *Her Quiet Legacy* because it struck a deep chord in my soul, but I didn't imagine Jack's story would ever see the light of day. It was private, personal, and probably the most honest thing I'd ever written. The novel flowed with frightening ease and the test results provided the reason I'd found it so cathartic. Jack made sense to me in all his agonising complexity.

But seeing the results written down in language which concluded I was very likely on the broader autism cluster caused a crisis in my understanding of myself.

Who was the woman in the mirror who faked joviality during stressful social gatherings? Behind her smile lurked the knowledge she'd checked the lock on the front door seven times before she left for her appointment. She worried she'd left the iron on, even though she hadn't used it. The urge to drive home and check felt overwhelming. So, she did. Too many times to count.

Finding patterns no one else probably noticed provided some escape. It's incredible how much light relief a carpet design or a particular sound can produce in someone seeking a focal point to cling to when they're drowning. Those same factors can also cause intense misery.

My stress tells were many and varied but I hid them behind a mask of affability. Influenced by peers and authority, I became the view of myself which most satisfied society's picture of a neurotypical female. It's easier to raise a smile if the screams stay inside your own head.

The test results forced me to take stock of my self-image and make peace with myself. In the cold light of day it brought relief because it depersonalised my struggles with scientific labels. I found understanding in a colourful graph which demonstrated my unique shape within humanity. I'm different but that's okay.

And so, I'm sending Jack out into the world to fend for himself. He's talented and wonderful and impossible all at the same time. But his story deserves to be told in his own voice and I'll leave him to do that.

I have a feeling he'll be just fine.

For my friend, Dorothy Rico.
For your unwavering faith in me.
Thank you from the bottom of my heart.

1

A Broad Brush:

Used to Cover Large Areas Not Requiring Detail

"I live by two simple rules." I flicked the beer mat with my thumbnail and it flew into the air, spiralling twice before I caught it between fingers and thumb. The kid next to me pushed his baseball cap further back on his head and eyed me as though wisdom might miraculously grace him. Twenty something and skinny, I knew of his reputation for hitting women. Roddy, the local cop, told me that fact four months, five days, twenty-three hours and four seconds ago. I remember because he breathed beer fumes into my ear and I'd tried not to flinch. I would have remembered anyway.

"What are they?" the kid demanded. "What are your fancy rules?"

I shrugged and let a smirk play across my lips. The barman stopped wiping the counter and waited, already knowing the answer. "Don't play unless you can win." My customary stammer on the last word lulled the kid into thinking I was stupid.

He frowned and shifted in his seat. Pushing out his bottom lip, he considered the cash he just lost on the card table behind us. I sensed the cogs of his brain ticking through their rotation as he paused. *Fail one.* "What's the second?" he snarled.

"Never hit a woman."

Roddy let out a snort at my elbow, spraying beer across the counter in front of him. The barman's face creased in disgust as he moved over to mop up the mess. The kid swallowed, his fingers straying to the red and purple hickey beneath his jawline. *Fail two.* "What if they deserve it?" he asked.

I bit my lower lip and shrugged, tension easing from my shoulders and ebbing back through the muscles either side of my spine. "They never deserve that," I replied, adding menace to my tone. My interest waned, and I didn't want to talk to him anymore. I'd mapped out this hour as my social time, structuring it so I could sit next to Roddy and watch him grow drunker as the clock hands moved towards the magic moment of my escape. The kid's interference threatened my routine. The large hand ticked past the twelve and the small hand moved too far over the nine for comfort.

Roddy nudged me with his elbow, slopping beer into his sleeve. "Leave the kid alone," he wheezed. "If I don't understand you after ten years, he sure as hell won't after five minutes." I jerked away from his mess, not wanting it to touch me. Not wanting him to touch me.

I reached for the bottle of ale in front of me and almost knocked it flying. Monday, Wednesday and Friday I turned up at the club and bought the beer. I took one sip and Roddy drank the rest after I left. Now I'd touched it twice, and the realisation sent a coil of dismay firing through my brain. My hand rested back on my thigh and I clamped it with the other one to stop it from trembling.

"You hit on my girlfriend." The kid balled his fists and spoke through gritted teeth. I figured the friendly chat might be over as he climbed off his stool.

"Which girlfriend?" Roddy set his bottle on the beer mat and I saw the barman reach for his phone.

"Tahlia!" He spat her name with more bile than sentiment. "And he hit on her." His dirty finger jabbed close enough to my cheek to contaminate my air space.

I pursed my lips to halt the smart ass reply I'd learned from a squad member in the army. To stop it tumbling out, I took a decent inhale of the bar's fetid air. Discarded slops and cigarette smoke from the beer garden's open doorway filled my lungs. Roddy shook his head. "This guy's been the hottest bachelor in town since before you wore long pants. He doesn't want any of them."

I slipped off the stool and faced the kid, watching his eyes narrow in determination. He slid sideways and blocked my exit. The clock's large hand moved onto the five and my nerves jangled. His expression shuttered, and I saw he expected me to lie my way out of trouble. "Excuse me," I said, and waited for him to move aside.

My mother's voice echoed in my head. *'Be polite, Jack. Use your words, son, but only the kind ones.'* Like a navigational reference point in my mind, I focussed on the memory of her favourite blue scarf. It smelled of lavender because of the vibrancy of the colour, convincing my brain of its presence like visual onomatopoeia. I liked lavender. It pained me I couldn't speak to Mother. Not until tomorrow could I obtain her wisdom on the skinny kid's behaviour. We spoke on Thursdays. I wasn't sure what might happen if I rang her on a Wednesday night after nine o'clock. Bad things. Awful things. She wouldn't answer, but someone else might. My mind sparked with possibilities, and I shut it down before it could get into the swing of informed tragedies.

"Blonde. Blue eyes." I drew myself up to my full height and dwarfed him. Conversation at the card table ceased. Lifting one hand, I patted the air as though measuring his girlfriend's height. The kid's nostrils flared like a bull's and he squared his shoulders.

"What?" he snarled.

"Your girlfriend." I patted the air again. "Blonde. Blue eyes. Sometimes black eyes if she upsets you. Your girlfriend." My attention wandered to the swathe of ugly carpet meandering towards the door. Twenty-one yellow squares and twenty-two blues made up my route. Odd and even. Wednesdays were odd days. Usually. One shoe per square. If I messed up, I needed to think of a plausible reason to walk back and repeat the exercise. Roddy liked it. I often used the excuse of buying him another beer.

"You'll be sorry you ever noticed her." The kid took a step towards me.

Behind me, Roddy let out an unpleasant swearword. Despite being our local cop, he didn't hop down off his stool. But his foul language made me want to add another rule. The barman brought the local police station's number up on speed dial, his fingers working on the keypad while he kept his gaze fixed on me. Clever guy. Dialling without looking. I angled my body sideways to the kid's, attempting to diffuse the situation before he blew a gasket and hurt himself. Forty three steps to safety called to me from behind him and the large clock hand moved to cover the ten. "You've got the wrong guy," I said.

2

—··—

SPECK IN THE PAINT:

CAN BE INTENTIONAL AND USED FOR TEXTURE

The kid let me walk away, though I'm not sure why. Perhaps the sight of Roddy hauling himself from his stool and staggering across the carpet made him think twice before picking a fight with the biggest guy in the room. Roddy sprayed beer from his lips as he addressed the kid. "Let him go, Nathan. Look at his muscles, dude. He'll crush you like a bug."

Nathan looked me up and down before jabbing a knobbly forefinger into the wall of defined pectoral muscle, which created a plate across my chest. "Stay away from Tahlia!" he growled.

I ignored him, tilting my head at Roddy as a silent farewell. The neat cravat tied around my neck seemed tighter as I moved, tension swelling my blood vessels until it became a noose. He jerked his chin upward before reaching for my full bottle and drowning his life in hops and foam for another evening of small-town fun. The alcohol negated his memories of a wife he lost through neglect and a son who crossed the street to avoid him.

The forward motion of walking eased my nerves, each touch of my soles to the sticky carpet providing comfort and the solidity of routine. Twenty-one yellow squares. Twenty-two blue. I passed over the threshold, paying lip service to the fallen soldiers commemorated on a verdigris plaque on the lobby wall. My fingers knew their names with the accuracy of braille, and I paused to touch the third one down in the right column. *Jonathan George.* He'd died in Normandy generations before mine. We shared no connection other than his placing on the memorial board. Acknowledging his name with a touch satisfied another of my compulsions and kept the monsters at bay. I'd work through the entire list in five years, top to bottom, left to right. Then, with anticipation and a faint sense of thrill, I'd start again at the top left like a snail traversing a wall. I liked to think of it as progress. If the patrons of the Returned Services Association bar thought it weird, they kept their opinions to themselves. The medals nestling in the safe at home rewarded bravery during active service, but the ghosts in my mind betrayed a body count I'd buried beneath routines and habits designed to suppress them.

Roddy's drawl carried through the open doorway, and I paused as I heard my name. "Don't pick a fight with Jack.

That guy can strip a gun in half the time as any normal human. Show him a map and he'll know the terrain after five seconds." His cackle accompanied the scrape of my abandoned glass bottle across the wooden bar and the hiss of the bubbles as he poured it into his glass. "Hell, he'll even correct it for you and put in routes you never noticed."

"Shut up, Roddy!" The growl of an older patron rebuked him. No one in the RSA talked about their service. Those who boasted brought suspicion to themselves, their bravado tales alienating instead of ingratiating them with the locals. Real warriors didn't tell war stories. They showed up each night, played Housie or dominoes and drank to forget.

Four steps took me into the car park and the fresh winter air. Sixteen more would take me to my truck on the road, but my phone vibrated in my pocket before I could begin the familiar count. I let it ring five times and then answered, my reply curt. "Jack Jethro."

"Hey Jacques." Her Parisian tones filled my ear like syrup, enticing me towards a life I'd rejected. She whispered my name, embracing it with her tongue.

"Yeah." As always, she stripped the words from my throat and left me with nothing but a grunted acknowledgement. Julia knew me well enough not to bother with niceties.

"I have a contract for you, mon amour." She left the sentence hanging, waiting for the information to percolate through my brain and perhaps encourage a different answer from last time.

"No more." The two words elicited her dramatic sigh which whooshed into my ear. I'd said them twice in recent months and four times the previous year. "You said you understood." She'd said that last time, accompanying the sentence with a promise. It caused a physical ache in my chest that she'd lied.

"I know." Her tone became conciliatory. "I do. But you'll want this one. I need to see you again, anyway." She paused. "I want to see you again."

"No." A stabbing index finger disconnected the call. I knew what would happen when we got together. The pattern was always the same, but one which grabbed a hold of me and took control. I couldn't afford to engage with habits and patterns over which I had no authority.

The phone slid into my back pocket with ease, but my fingers twitched. As though given a mind of their own, they formed around an imaginary cylinder and the auditory centre of my brain joined them in their conspiracy. I heard the hiss of a spray can and the tinkle of the ball bearing at the bottom. The heady scent of Acetone, Xylene and Toluene returned to haunt me, and I shook my head to shuck off the lure. Thirteen steps and counting took me almost to my truck.

"Hey, you!" The skinny kid raised his voice as he left the safety of the lobby and crunched across the car park.

I turned to face him, obliging him with a reaction he expected. My arms hung by my sides in a non-threatening manner, and I schooled my features into an impassive mask. His steps quickened as he moved towards me, growing in confidence with each stamping step. My fingers twitched, changing the imagined sensation of the paint cannister for the deep ridges surrounding a grenade. I pictured releasing the pin and filling the kid's mouth with the hard metal object. Messy, but fun.

"Don't walk away from me when I'm talking to you!" He added a bullishness to his tone, assisted by the alcoholic fuel he'd imbibed at a discount in the RSA. Dilated pupils occupied the space where cobalt irises should have glittered under the glare of the street lamps. Something else accompanied the beer to tickle his sense of righteous indignation.

"I'm not walking." I stated the obvious, my most infuriating gift in life.

His eyes bugged, the whites like boiled eggs in the darkness. "Smart ass!" he growled. He ground to a halt before me as though his thought processes hadn't taken him beyond this moment. "Go near Tahlia again and I'll kill you."

"Right." I remained stock still, weighing the possibilities of his next move. The laws of probability activated, filling my brain with ratio and percentage as I trawled through scenarios. When his fist rose and headed towards my chest, a wave of disappointment exhaled with my sigh. The sum of the probabilities for all outcomes is one.

I blocked his fist with my forearm, the fingers of my other hand closing around his throat. "There were better options," I mused. My thumb and middle finger constricted the arteries on either side of his neck, and his hands clawed at my sleeves. I held him at an arm's length, reducing the effectiveness of his feckless kicks. "Leave. Me. Alone." The words ground from my throat, and I hardly recognised the guttural tones created by my frustration. A hard shove set him on his backside in the road. I shaped my fingers into an imaginary gun, levelling them towards his face. He leaned on the asphalt with his arms splayed behind him, feet still lifted in the air. "Boom." I whispered the word, filling it with the venom of a kill shot before pulling my keys free and unlocking the driver's door of my truck.

"Weirdo!" he shouted. "You'll get what's coming to you. I know something you'd rather I didn't. You're gonna pay." The diesel engine roared to life, and I counted to four before slipping the gear lever into reverse. The kid scrambled sideways on his hands and knees, perhaps realising he'd fallen outside my range of interest. Backing over him would cause a heap of issues, not least a wasted hour of pressure-washing the tyres in the dark. I spun the vehicle in an impressive U-turn before wincing as I travelled in the wrong direction. That wasn't meant to happen. It wasn't how I ended my evenings at the RSA. I'd allowed the kid to get to me and he'd spoiled my routine. I drove to the main road and all the way home before returning and starting again. When I parked my truck for the second time that evening, the kid was gone.

3

COUNTERFEIT;

A COPY OF AN ORIGINAL

Instead of arriving home at ten minutes after nine, I breached the incline to my mountain hideaway an hour late for the ultimate time. Julia's call rattled me, muddying the usual routine which corrected mishaps in my timetable. I went through my series of actions without relief. Locking and unlocking the truck seven times led to walking back and forth to the porch steps in equal number. The security light strobed on and off with my activity. But by the time I'd unlocked the front door for the seventh time, my hands shook, and the keys fell to the lobby floor with a loud clang. I squatted in frustration, resting one knee on the floorboards while I fought for equilibrium. The roundness of one key in particular drew my attention, my fingers smoothing its worn edges as I kept my eyes closed. It helped, the familiar sensation of the smooth metal soothing my soul. The key to Julia's house. I inhaled and exhaled seven times before rising.

Seven.

The number of completion or divine fulfilment.

Something I would never achieve.

"Enough now." I spoke to myself out loud, my voice echoing in the empty house. They were Mother's words, her familiar cadence a balm to my battered soul and the only constant in my turbulent childhood. She'd tried to help me cope, strategising structures to carry me into adulthood. The education system left her no choice. Her pleas for assistance were disregarded. Anyone capable of labelling me as a dot along the sliding scale of a behavioural spectrum declined. I didn't throw desks or disrupt other children. Silent and friendless, I presented no obstacle to others' learning and sucked up information like a sponge. I became one of life's Grey Men, invisible but dangerous.

The rounded key slipped through my fingers and a fast wrist action caught the bunch in my open palm. The bothersome evening threatened to fry the tentative synapses which kept me connected to reality. It dictated evasive action. I rose to my feet, not needing to switch on the overhead light. The satisfying clicks of my cowboy boots against the floorboards dulled as I crossed the doormat and snatched another key from the dresser.

The front door closed behind me and I locked it once. "No more, Jack," I repeated, terminating the number seven's hold on my actions through a sheer act of will. My truck still cooled on the driveway, a random click issuing from beneath the bonnet. The fingers of my left hand caressed the new key as I strode to the detached double garage which crowned the hill. The man who built it thought me foolish for blocking the panoramic view from the ground floor windows of the house. He said I'd regret it, but I proved him wrong each day. I ate and slept in the renovated 1950s house, but I spent my life in the building disguised as a garage.

The ground floor housed my gym. I enjoyed owning my own equipment, able to work as little or as much as I pleased. Thirteen years in the army demanded peak physical condition, but I'd resented the sweat stained plastic and hand prints decorating everything at the public gyms. I'd spent too many years feeling dirty in my own skin.

The Wellington builder installed a bathroom at the rear of the structure and learned after the first few weeks not to question my plan. I paid for his flights, his food and his time, allowing him the free use of a granny flat behind the main house. The previous owner had secured planning permission for a similar structure but never followed through on the design. It was the reason I purchased the house after leaving the army. I paid the builder in cash, dug the holes for the footings and hired any heavy equipment required from a haulage firm in Hamilton which delivered to the house. The town gossips didn't notice my project or make it the subject of their speculation. A bank of well-placed trees hid the structure from across the river and an automatic gate at the bottom of the three-kilometre driveway meant it remained my greatest secret.

I hung all my keys on their peg next to the door and flicked on the lights. A satisfying click sounded as the fluorescent strips paused before lighting up across the ceiling, powered by a generator hidden in the bushes behind the garage. Lifting my phone, I made a call to the power company. The woman who answered yawned before speaking. "Welcome to Zenith. I'm Bobby. How may I help you?"

I cleared my throat. "I live at 250 Hakarimata Road. I registered my bills to Dexarn. The power supply to my property is out again. I have a generator, but I'd like you to fix the issue, please."

"I'll just check to see if there are any other reports." Her voice gained a sing-song quality as she got into her stride. A keyboard tapped in the background. "I'm seeing nothing yet. Can you estimate when it happened?"

I ground my teeth against her mouth-breathing, the sound amplified in my ear by the connection. "I arrived home a few minutes ago and the front gate worked, but it has a back-up battery. The house is out, but I just heard the generator start."

She hissed through her teeth, and I yanked the phone away from my ear. "Ah, I'm sorry Sir, but I think it's just you. There's a charge for visits relating to a single property. We have a crew in your area, I'll dispatch them now to at least administer a temporary fix. They'll check the junction box on the boundary, but I'll ask them to call if they need access to your property. Is it okay to give them this contact number?" She mouth-breathed again as she read from the caller ID unit to confirm my contact details.

"That's fine." I exhaled, knowing the engineers would find the problem at the junction box they'd replaced less than six months earlier after a season of unnatural surges and outages. It's why I'd invested in the generator. Bobby closed out the call after assuring me the engineers would text or call with their inspection report. She promised they'd add the surcharge for the visit to my next power bill. Unless their equipment proved faulty, which she doubted.

My body pulsed, aching for the satisfaction of exercise, and I obliged it. A cupboard at the end of the room disgorged a clean tee shirt and shorts, socks and trainers. Relief filled my chest as I stripped and folded my clothing into a neat pile and set it on a shelf. My tan cowboy boots slipped into place next to it, the left sole butted against a stray twenty-cent piece. I removed the cravat at last, smoothing out the creases and pressing it into a square. It had done its job, hiding the tracheotomy scar which marred the skin at my throat. A jagged knife wound in my left pectoral rose like a pink and white craggy mountain of ruined flesh. The army field medics aimed for survival. They weren't plastic surgeons.

Fourteen kilometres later, I slowed the treadmill to a walk and hit the weight bench. Silence hissed around me as I subdued the compulsions raging through my brain, beating them into submission through exhaustion. My biceps bulged as I lifted the bar, my lips moving in whispered counts as I stilled the monster in my soul. The wind blew across the mountain as the evening progressed, throwing leaves and twigs at the roll doors at the end of the structure.

My phone vibrated on the floor, and I almost dropped the weight bar onto my head. I remained lying down as I answered the call. Moving leaves and the roar of a passing car formed the backdrop for the engineer's baritone. "Hey, mate." He shouted into the phone, forgetting his surrounding noise didn't affect my hearing.

"Hello." I kept the greeting short, not wanting a long explanation for the fault.

"It's a horrible bend and I know the last engineers moved the pad-mounted transformer on your boundary higher, but it's possible a truck clipped it with a wing mirror again. The casing is hanging off and rain is going into the unit. We've made it safe for now, but another crew will come back tomorrow morning and replace it. The management might need to think again about where to site it if it gets hit again."

"Thank you." Rain pounded against the roof of the structure, and I wrinkled my nose, sparing the unfortunate man a moment of pity for his commitment to duty.

He ended the call at the same time as a shout coincided with the squeal of wet tyres. I heard the words, "Bloody truck almost hit me!" and pursed my lips.

Hours passed unnoticed, and I only checked my wristwatch as I smoothed shower gel over my forearms. The big hand marked the three, but the short hand grazed the twelve with a lengthy caress. "Thursday." My voice echoed back to me from the tiles, and I crossed my arms over my chest to push the hot water from my shoulders. The awfulness of Wednesday had passed beneath me without notice and moved aside to allow the emergence of a fresh new day. My heart lightened, and I dried and dressed myself in clean underwear from the cupboard. Julia's intrusive phone call nipped at the edges of my resolve, and I pushed it aside with an aggressive mental shove. I couldn't allow her to affect my hard-won state of calm. Not now.

I took the twenty-cent piece from the shelf and turned it in my fingers. Like the key to Julia's house, I'd smoothed its edges through constant contact. Despite my aching arms, I reached around the side of the cupboard as though preparing to haul it forward out of the way. Instead, the coin slipped into a metal slot between its back panel and the wall, causing a gratifying click. The Wellington builder had signed a non-disclosure agreement in his crabbed hand, but it hadn't proved necessary. He died in a car smash six months after finishing my building and returning home. His alcoholism hadn't hindered his competency in the same way it affected his driving.

The planning officer had shrugged at the finished structure and signed the paperwork to legitimise it in the council's Land Information Management system. But he hadn't seen its beauty behind the ugly roll doors and boxy, cedar wood facade.

The cupboard swung forward to reveal the Wellington builder's greatest work. I fixed the cupboard in place and stepped onto the ladder leading to the lower level. He'd called it a panic room. It offered the exact opposite to me.

4

ABSTRACT:

ART THAT IS NOT REPRESENTATIONAL OR BASED ON EXTERNAL REALITY OR NATURE

At the bottom of the narrow staircase, a wall of solvent hit me. The hydrocarbons I'd released into the air hours earlier still lingered, their scent both sugary and chemical. I flicked on the light switch and another button next to it. A fan whirred to life in the back wall, filtering the air and venting the noxious chemicals through a pipe which led into the darkness. The strong air currents on the mountain would snatch the particles and hurl them away to be diluted and subdued. And my secret room would remain my own.

An oil painting rested against an easel, the colours muted in a sepia, 1960s style. A music stand next to it contained the photograph I'd painted from. The client emailed it to my business address with the request for a quote. A woman bent to pick roses in a garden rich in tone and shadow. Behind her, a 1900s era villa nestled at the bottom of a hill. I'd stuck to the original photo until almost the last brush stroke, subduing my urge for drama. The woman's skirt hung to her ankles in swathes of rich auburn fabric, her head bowed and covered by a wide brimmed straw hat. I stood back to admire the textures captured in the two-metre-wide painting and nodded with satisfaction. The vintage hues diminished the leafy greens and the reds of the brick house, giving them a washed-out effect. It held the elusiveness of a revived memory, and I liked it. The woman's fingers clutched a single rose, her trophy for persevering in the harshness of colonial New Zealand. Blood red tones gave the petals an ethereal appearance, standing out against the rest of the painting like a beacon of hope. I didn't care whether the new owner approved of my creative licence or not. The twenty-thousand-dollar price tag gave me permission to interpret the photograph in any way I wished. And the scrawled 'X' in the bottom right corner made it mine. I often wondered if signing my single initial on canvas and auctioning it would produce the same interest. On lazy days when the demons whispered their threats in my mind, I wished it was that easy.

With the oil paint still tacky for another week, I'd already turned my attention elsewhere.

A glass screen hung from the ceiling, one side splattered with paint and stained by escaped coloured mist. My protective mask and suit hung on a wall peg just inside the sliding door. Built from the remnants of a greenhouse, the cubicle kept the oil canvasses safe from drifting. 'A room within a room,' the Wellington builder called it. The metal door squeaked on its sliders as I moved it aside and stepped through the gap.

Spray paint dried within seconds, adding a versatility I'd discovered late in life. One colour could blot out another in seconds, unlike oils and watercolours. I'd secured my place in the art scene with unsolicited murals on prominent businesses in Auckland, favouring the anonymity of Banksy with all his sarcasm but none of his political commentary.

'X' brought me notoriety and more money than I earned in the army. Jack Alexander Jethro. I plucked the 'X' from my middle name, calculating it as the eighth letter in my full signature. The number eight represented creation and new beginnings, and that's what 'X' gave me. It also held the place of the twelfth letter from the end of my name. Twelve brought perfection, entirety, and order. It added the irony in relation to my constant state of flux. I became 'X', dotting my signature on murals around the Auckland scene and promoting my brand through secrecy. Each installation meant something to me, communicating my love for the paradise of New Zealand against the backdrop of a war-torn world. I should know. I'd seen both sides.

My latest work featured a yellow kowhai bud bursting into bloom. The iconic national flower took centre stage in a riot of ochre and sunshine hues. Behind it, a sludgy green tide betrayed the fruits of decades of ignorance and mismanagement. I closed my eyes and let my fingers coast across the original work. I'd spent the afternoon slicing out a stencil, which would expedite the spraying process once I'd chosen the desired location. The spray paint held a different texture with every stroke. While it appeared uniform from a distance, each squirt of the can communicated its personality. Though I'd continued with commissions for oil and acrylic paintings, I hadn't sprayed for over a year. Not since last time.

When my mobile phone rang upstairs, I closed the sliding door and jogged up the steps to answer it.

"Jacques." Her tone held frustration. Instead of her usual smooth J, it held a sharp clang. "We need to meet, mon amour."

"No more murals." She couldn't see my frown, but I sensed she felt it, anyway.

"You've never been precious about your work. Why start now? Auckland City Council painted over five of them before you became famous, and it didn't bother you. Why did that one in Wellington affect you so much?"

"She paid for it."

"You keep saying that, but who is *she*?"

"It doesn't matter anymore." It didn't. The painting had been her final request before the dementia stole her personality and her ability to care about the past. I'd done as she asked, and they'd obliterated it with a wall of cream emulsion and normality.

"I put the refund back into the account like you requested." Her tone held a familiar disbelief. I balled my fists and hoped she wouldn't probe, the wish futile, as she took a breath and continued. "Five bucks, Jacques. A night's work for five dollars and you refunded it. I just don't understand."

"But I do." My index finger trembled as I ended the call and closed up the secret room. The cupboard seemed heavier than usual as I pushed it over the gap and waited for it to click shut. The cool wood soothed my warm forehead, but not the war waging beneath my skull. I contemplated starting something else, but a glance at my watch showed the small hand nudging the one of Thursday morning.

My body ached for sleep and my brain concurred. I turned my phone onto silent and left the garage, carrying it on top of my folded clothes. A cool breeze nipped at my exposed skin as I padded across the driveway in my boxer shorts and entered the silent house. Julia's disappointment settled over me like a mantle, and I knew she'd call again. The key turned in the lock and I pushed my dirty clothing into the basket in the laundry, retrieving my phone at the last minute and setting it on the counter. Heavy steps carried me upstairs to the king size bed, which allowed my long legs to remain beneath the covers, and I sighed as I flopped face down on the mattress.

It was Thursday. Mother would call later. The electricity generator would last as long as I fed it diesel, meaning the landline would accept her call. I'd ask for her advice about the skinny kid. It would give her something else to think about.

5

Expressionism:

Means by which an artist communicates ideas and emotions

Army life filled my dreams. Despite my mother's frustration, lack of a label enabled me to enlist on my seventeenth birthday. I forged my social worker's signature and left two months later, bound for Waiouru Army base and twelve weeks of intensive training. I loved it. Structure and routine filled my world from dawn to dusk and all the other hours on either side of them. I did everything they asked. Nothing more. Nothing less.

I woke from sleep with my fingers twitching. During my dream, I'd stripped, cleaned and rebuilt a 7.62 Minimi, the army's light support weapon of choice. No one yet had beaten my record.

Birds rustled in the trees near my window, calling to each other with an irritating shrillness. My wristwatch displayed the time as just after nine, but my aching body begged to stay in bed. I rose, using my stomach muscles and planted my feet square on the floorboards. Yesterday had been an odd number day. The narrators decreed today would be too. The coolness of the wood grounded my first thoughts of the day with their solidity. An urge to paint sneaked into my mind like thread veins and I stretched my arms above my head, enjoying the satisfying crack of my joints.

The stairs creaked as I took them two at a time. The Thursday-odd-day demanded I step only on the odd ones and I gripped the banister rail to make sure I didn't screw up the first five minutes of my day. Two more commissions demanded my attention, and I didn't have the energy to go back to bed seven more times.

For breakfast, I ate three wheat biscuits. On less busy days, I favoured rice pops, but only when time allowed me to count out one hundred and forty-four into a bowl. Today was not that day. I sat at the counter to eat, rejecting the stained milk once I'd pushed the last spoon of wheat strands into my mouth. Flecks dotted the milk's surface and reminded me of the debris floating in Hamilton's Rotoroa Lake. Nausea bubbled into my throat and I ran the bowl under the tap seven times before dumping it on the top rack of the dishwasher. Rain pelted the kitchen window, mist drifting from the mountain to engulf the house in its precipitous embrace. Foreboding squeezed my heart, and I glanced at my watch. Mother would phone in less than half an hour.

I retrieved my phone from the laundry and checked the camera at the front gate. The black and white static of a snowstorm betrayed a fault which appeared in the night. Tutting, I walked to the fuse box and flicked the switch back up into position. The system reset and the camera flickered to life, displaying a clear image of the space in front of my gate. Sheet rain spread across the asphalt road beyond it, the hiss of a passing vehicle exacerbated by the echo through the speaker. I continued my journey upstairs, dodging the even steps. Eleven missed calls from an unknown number had depleted its charge and I plugged it in after deleting Julia's five texts. I shampooed my hair and soaped my body in the shower, eager for my Thursday ritual to begin. A successful start would cement a satisfactory day, one in which I could paint without distraction.

My phone screen lit up as I shaved off the rough beard, which grew during the previous week. I stopped the electric razor and stared at the number strobing across the display. My watch showed I had five minutes remaining until Mother called, so I ignored it and hoped they stopped. A text message told me the engineer had been the unknown caller and that he'd replaced the green dome and reconnected the wiring. I wrinkled my nose and winced. Good manners dictated I text back to thank him.

Wearing the aftershave Mother gave me five Christmases earlier, and a shirt and trousers she liked, I settled on the reclaimed pew in the lobby and waited for her weekly call to the landline. A blue and white checked cravat hid the scar and stopped the curious questions, which burst like staccato gunfire from the lips of strangers. The aftershave held a strange, funky scent. It had arrived a few days before Christmas with a card in Mother's handwriting. It seemed rude to question its composition when she'd gone to so much trouble to procure it. I'd Googled the term *prison aftershave* and not liked the conclusions.

My phone had gleaned a thirty percent charge, and I bounced my knee in time with the flashing dots from the digital clock. With less than a minute to go, I forced my body into a state of calm to avoid jiggling the device onto the rug. At one minute past ten and twenty-three seconds, the receiver for the landline rang. I snatched it up and held it against my ear, holding my breath and waiting for her gentle cadence to sweep over me.

But the voice wasn't hers. Anger surged in my chest like a flash of fire and I pulled the receiver away from me to stare at the smooth brown plastic. The old analogue phone couldn't show me the identity of the caller. "Don't hang up!" the voice urged, loud enough to carry from the device and boom into the empty hallway. "She said you might."

I forced my dry throat to swallow and lifted the phone to my ear. "Jack Jethro." The change in routine had thrown me for a loop and I resorted to the familiar, beginning again at the start.

"Mr Jethro, my name is Doctor Tyndale and I work at Auckland Region Women's Corrections Facility. I'm calling on behalf of Alexandra Jenssen. I understand she's your mother?"

An invisible hand glued my teeth closed, and I struggled to grunt a reply. The demons in my head threw paint and brushes in the air, screaming about disaster as the doctor destroyed my routine in less time than it took me to climb the eleven odd steps up to my bedroom. He continued as though I'd acknowledged him. "Your mother's health is a little worse this week. She doesn't remember why she's here. The Alzheimer's has accelerated, and it's possible she suffered a stroke in the night." His tone changed to one of consolation. "But she remembers you and that she needed to call you at ten o'clock this morning. I've tried your mobile number a few times but couldn't reach you. She insisted I use this number at ten o'clock."

My teeth ground in my head, my mind empty of answers. I'd never managed passing conversation or meaningless chatter and no words arrived to assist me. "Mother?" I asked for her, a plea in my voice.

"Okay." He admitted defeat. A cacophony of sounds carried through the connection as he bumped the handset with the clank of a wedding ring and whispered just out of earshot.

Breathing filled my ear and my head. "Jack." Her voice sounded strained and distorted, as though she spat the word through only half her mouth. "Gain," she managed, the word hissing with force. "Ain."

I swallowed and pursed my lips. "Mother? I wanted to ask you about a man at the bar last night." I launched into the conversation I'd planned, not able to cope with the thought it might not happen.

The doctor cut off my sentence, his voice louder than Mother's and more jarring. "We'll transfer her to Auckland General mid-morning for tests. You'll need to contact the prison governor for permission to visit her. It shouldn't be a problem." The call ended without giving me the chance to reply. The phone hung limp in my fingers as the coiled cord swung as though pushed by an unseen hand. I closed my eyes to block out the sensation of floating on the river like flotsam, but the sinking feeling grew worse.

This wasn't how Thursdays must begin.

6

POINTILISM:

CREATING AN IMAGE USING A SERIES OF DOTS

I spent the morning bouncing around the prison switchboard without success. In desperation, I drove my truck to Auckland and took a room at one of the less expensive hotel chains. Larger establishments proved too busy to fuss over single occupants. They took my cash, gave me a view of a brick wall, and left me alone. Most guests wanted a view of the ocean. They didn't tend to look so thrilled at the idea of counting bricks for the next twenty-four hours.

Julia phoned again as I dumped my overnight bag on the carpet and checked the sheets for marks or stains. I found nothing and celebrated by taking her call. "Leave me alone!" I barked. "Mother's sick and they won't tell me where she is."

"You're in Auckland?" Hope infused her tone and her voice rose. "Let's meet, mon cher. Where are you?"

Emptiness gnawed at the edges of my psyche. The need to repel her vied with the desire to transfer my security to her. With my mother missing in action, it left me vulnerable. Despite my better judgement, I conceded. I wouldn't tell her my location but agreed to meet her in a restaurant at the Viaduct.

Showering and dressing again restored some of my equilibrium and activity stilled the twitching of my fingers. I arrived at the restaurant before her but loitered across the street until she got settled. Julia's fiddling with everything from the tablecloth to her cutlery drove me insane. This Thursday had already gone as wrong as Wednesday. Adding an argument to its catalogue of disasters wouldn't help.

She alighted from a taxi with the grace of a swan, gliding up the front steps in a long coat which hid a shimmering cocktail dress. The stirring of an unnamed emotion woke in my chest and I fought to douse it. My fingers ached for her ebony ringlets to run through them like water, and I closed my eyes to dispel the fog of desire. Even a glutton pushes food away when his stomach hurts, but Julia's claim made me eager to feast until I exploded. I counted to one hundred and forty-four before using the odd steps to the front of the hotel. A waiter approached me and I jerked my head towards Julia. She'd picked the seat facing the door and her long lashes fluttered as she spotted me in the entrance. Her gaze drank in my muscular build, stroking me from toe to forehead with a lascivious smile across her lips. A sensible voice in my head urged me to turn around and go back to my hotel. I ignored it in favour of the one suggesting I book a room upstairs and stop resisting.

"What do you want, Julia?" I paused while the waiter hauled my chair from under the table and waited for me to sit. His eyebrows knitted in response to the tension swirling around my head. It entered with me, creating a dark cloud of protection and cloaking me in disdain.

"Just sit down, Jacques." She sighed, indicating the seat and glancing up at the man whose hands hovered over the leather backrest. "A fruit juice for me and whatever he's drinking, s'il vous plaît."

"Water." I gave him a cursory nod and allowed him to push the seat behind my knees. He left my ass hanging in mid-air a moment too long and the brewing rage in my chest bubbled. Hitting him seven times over the head with the chair might help, but I didn't do it. Instead, I glared at Julia, venting my instability on her. "I don't need a menu. I'm not staying."

She released a sigh of exasperation. Her pretty lips drew together in a pout, although she'd lost some of the tension from her delicate olive features. Her eyelashes fluttered, and dark shadows beneath her eyes made her appear tired. "Can we have a sensible conversation for once?" she asked, and it sounded more of a plea than a demand.

I shrugged and bit my tongue as the waiter poured water into tumblers and set one before each of us. "Will the lady require a menu?" he asked, and the smirk rose to my eyes before I could stop it. I glanced across at Julia and saw her shake her head.

"No. Thank you."

My right index finger strayed to the glass and halted a bead of condensation as it tracked an eager path towards the tablecloth. Julia leaned forward. "Thanks for not saying something cutting," she said. Her expression held sincerity, and I nodded, making a gruff sound I hoped would stop her venturing along paths ruined by rubble. "When he called me a lady." She licked her lips, and I saw longing in her unguarded hazel eyes.

"What do you want, Julia?" I demanded, needing the conversation finished so I could visit Auckland hospital again and trawl the corridors on my quest.

She exhaled and sat back in her seat. "I have a commission for you."

My gaze rolled to the ceiling and back again, exasperation bursting through to the surface despite my best efforts. I shook my head. "I said no. How can you not understand?"

Her pupils dilated, and I realised my mistake. "Understand you?" she mused. "There's no hope of that, mon cher."

"Goodbye, Julia." I rose and pushed my chair back. The waiter halted on his reluctant trajectory and made a swift about face. I saw him shake his head at another server and annoyance sparked in my chest. Public displays of emotion weren't my thing, and yet the guy looked at me like I was a serial loser. "Don't contact me again."

"I wanted to see you." She sniffed and her eyes watered. Injustice lay over her shoulders like a cloak. "I knew you'd reject the commission, and I wanted to explain it to you myself."

My head shook from side to side and I shrugged. "I don't have time for this. And don't even think about leaking anything to the media because my lawyer will trash you."

"I promise I won't." Her tone surprised me and didn't contain the edge of spite I'd expected. She'd threatened it last month. Something else lurked beneath her request and I paused, my feet pointing away from the awkward meeting, but my head turned towards her. Curiosity set up a nagging beat in time to my raised pulse. "Please stay." She patted the neat place setting I'd abandoned and appealed with her eyes. "Jacques, please. We both know how much you hate regrets and if you don't do this, it'll haunt you for the rest of your life."

I sat.

I heard her out.

And I discovered she was right in her assumption. I would have turned it down and I would've regretted it.

7

ALLOVER PAINTING:

**COMPOSITION WHERE EDGE TO EDGE HAS
EQUAL SIGNIFICANCE**

I'm not sure how Julia always got her way. It's one of the many mysteries I could never solve. No spiritual wrangling or mathematical equations compared to her energy or the manner in which she infected me with her thrill of just being alive. She awakened the thing I dreaded most, leaving me with an emotional kraken to slip back into its box. We rolled around in the hotel's king size bed until dawn, Julia wearing nothing but her wedding ring and me in my socks. Daylight brought solemnity for her and the insipid sadness, which crept in with the end of something enjoyable. I just wanted to find my mother and go home.

Her nails tickled as she dragged her fingers along my sternum and I released a shudder of discomfort. With the bloom of sex dissipating, our intimacy waned. I fought the urge to move away from her, knowing from experience it caused offence. Instead, I forced my body into a state of rigid acceptance as her inky curls bounced against my shoulder.

"Do you ever regret this?" She rested her chin on my biceps, the bone ridged beneath her delicate skin. She'd shown little interest in my battle scars after the horror of the things she'd seen in her short lifetime. Perhaps she considered my wounds trivial compared to those.

"No." I counted to seven in my head and when she sighed, began again at number one.

"You're meant to ask if I regret it." Irritation entered her tone, but left just as quickly. "You won't ask. You never do. But for what it's worth, I don't."

I grunted in reply but continued to ground myself in the familiar numbers parading across my inner vision like playing cards. She tilted her head and her cheek flattened against my arm. "I finished paying the mortgage on la maison last week." I glanced down at her in surprise and missed number five. The others tumbled over their fallen comrade in my brain, creating a mess instead of order. Julia pushed herself upright in the wide bed. Her mocha toned breasts bounced like ripe peaches as she folded herself in half and clasped her arms around her knees. Glittering brown irises peeked from behind her curtain of lashes. "Do we need to change the agreement now?"

I swallowed, and any response fled in the face of her nakedness. Stunning last night in the lowered lighting of the restaurant, she gained added beauty from the speckled dawn through the bedroom window. Satisfaction had reddened her cheeks and added a glow which burned from inside her. My lips twitched for more of her kisses.

Her eyes narrowed as she smiled at me from behind the crest of her knees. Skin as soft as silk created pits and troughs along her thighs to the downy junction between her legs. She'd done it on purpose, playing on my weakness as my brain stuttered and stumbled over incoherent thoughts. I had nothing, not even when she slid across my thighs and lowered herself against me. "I love your appreciation for numero sept." Her words purred from between ripe lips. "You have so much energy for your age." She delivered the insult, though only five years separated us.

I closed my eyes and smoothed my fingers along her spine, counting the joints until their conclusion at the back of her neck. The scar from a bull whip left a raised ridge which snaked around her torso and finished with a flourish beneath her left breast. My exhale deflated my chest, and she smoothed her body over mine as though designed to fit. "Why do you fight me?" she whispered. Butterfly kisses murmured over the tendons in my neck. "Stop resisting the inevitable." A hard nip startled me, awaking my demons until their screams blocked out the gentle hum of the air conditioner and the sounds of other guests jabbering their echo in the hall. I opened my mouth to speak and her lips covered mine, robbing me of my words and silencing the demons.

The sun rose higher against the backdrop of Julia's moans, bathing the Auckland rush hour with a blanket of its glare. Once satiated, she sat sideways on the mattress, a love bite turning purple on the arch of her breast. She'd demanded it, anticipating her enjoyment later at the way it would peek from beneath her blouse as a suggestion. But only in the privacy of her home. Never in public.

She sighed and stretched her arms above her head, lifting her feet from the carpet to inspect the pink nail polish dotting her toes. "You always leave me unable to sit." She turned her head to face me and smiled at my blank expression. I studied her lithe form as she walked around the bed towards the bathroom, her chatter muted by the echo of the tiles. "What should I do about la maison?"

I exhaled and counted to three. "I don't want it. You paid for it. Take my name off the title."

Water slapped against the sides of the shower cubicle, and Julia poked her head around the door. "I can't. You should stay registered to my address until I gain New Zealand citizenship. The officials must believe our marriage is legitimate." Her face disappeared and the shower door creaked. The cadence of the spray changed to admit her body, and I ground my teeth, unable to leave her comment hanging. I slipped from the bed and removed my socks, joining her in the shower. A mouth full of warm water halted my protest, and Julia's soapy palms on my chest almost made me forget. She washed me, her experienced fingers pressing acceptance into my tight muscles until I became subdued and submissive. Then we sat side by side on the mattress in fluffy white hotel towels, our thighs touching but our hearts distant.

"We agreed you would divorce me. But you won't, will you?" My words clanged against the silence.

Julia's eyelids fluttered closed. "How did you guess?"

I lifted my gaze to stare at a picture on the wall. Hotel maintenance had screwed it in place to prevent theft and it irked me they hadn't used a spirit level. A vase of gaudy flowers lurked within an ochre frame, marred by a mahogany mount. I wondered why someone would steal it and allowed my subconscious to process Julia's question. I swallowed. "The evidence. You hoped when you signed the marriage certificate that I'd change my mind. You're stalling, but you know I never wanted a wife."

Julia's head bowed as though a hod of bricks balanced on her crown. "You're an honourable man, Jacques Jethro. You've done everything Grey asked of you and more." She sighed, regret lacing her tired love for a fallen soldier. The army captain had delivered his last instruction to me as the blood pumped unhindered from the stump where his leg once hung. He'd promised her an escape from the war-zone but his plan had backfired. "I hoped you might grow to love me." Julia lifted her chin and sadness cast glitter across her irises. "Do you not believe just a little that we could make a marriage between us work?"

I exhaled and my shoulder bumped hers through the towel. The confident, demanding woman from between the sheets had diminished behind feminine fragility. It tugged at my core, urging me to cherish and shelter her vulnerability.

It was a pattern.

My pattern.

One I'd grown tired of following. "I can't live with others." The statement tasted like worn leather in my mouth. "I follow routines and set tasks. Having someone else in the house forever would disrupt that."

Julia closed her eyes and gave an almost imperceptible nod. She'd already known the answer. I'd given it eight years ago when our hasty wedding gave her residency. The goal had been citizenship and her permanent safety from the overlords in Iraq who wanted her blood spilled on the unforgiving sand. She'd picked a side in the relentless war. And lost.

"Then, we continue as we are," she concluded in a whisper. "Like this." Her fingers snaked from beneath the folds of her towel and rested over my thigh. "I will act as your agent and filter commissions. And you will behave as my husband when I need you."

I shrugged. Her proposal presented no threat to the equilibrium. I dipped my chin in acceptance. Julia had formed part of my pattern and routine. We'd somehow fooled the immigration officials, her bubbly personality making up what I lacked during the intense interviews. I'd bought the house in Ngaruawahia under an anonymous trust associated with my professional brand of Xander, holding the two parts of myself within manageable parameters. I'd messed up the letters to create Dexarn. The townsfolk believed I rented the house from an unnamed landlord. A need for privacy dictated I stay away from listings of my name or address.

I frowned and shuttered my eyelashes. "When will you get notification of your citizenship?"

Her fingers formed claws on my thigh and the pink polish stood out against the snowy towel. The French accent slipped to betray a Persian lilt. "I became eligible last year. But you've avoided meeting and we need to fill in the application together."

"Okay." I rose and stripped the damp towel from my shoulders. Her proximity created a fog around my thinking processes, bathing me in lust and base instincts. Julia destroyed my reasoning.

She snatched at the towel, mischief making her irises sparkle. "Aren't you forgetting something?" Her lips tilted up at the corners. "Lucky numero sept."

I hadn't forgotten, but I'd hoped to distract myself from our shared and familiar compulsion.

I needed patterns.

Julia was insatiable.
Together, it spelled trouble.

8

AESTHETIC:

CONCERN FOR THE VISUAL QUALITIES OF AN OBJECT

My phone call to the prison garnered no further information. I dropped the device onto the mattress with a sigh.

"No luck?" Julia dipped forward and used a towel to squeeze the moisture from her damp curls. They hung like coiled snakes waiting to spring. I shook my head in reply and focussed on the delicate red lace framing her underwear. She danced away with a giggle as I reached for her. "We both have places to be," she chided. "Perhaps we should meet more often to continue the ruse?" She spoke the sentence as a question and I nodded, powerless against the clean floral scent emanating from her body. Her skin shimmered like silk as she moved to an armchair and gathered her dress. With a co-ordinated shimmy, she disappeared beneath the fabric and emerged as the respectable, high-class art dealer of the previous night.

Adding pantyhose and high-heeled boots which hid her ankles, she completed the image.

"What's the matter?" She smoothed her palms over her stomach and offered me a smile. Her head cocked in readiness for my response. "I can see the cogs turning behind your eyes."

I shrugged, the furrow in my brow causing a headache to blossom. It seemed more than skin deep, the confusion scoring it to the bone. "Which is the ruse?" I swallowed, realising I could no longer recognise the difference. The mattress dipped as Julia sat next to me. She peered over her knees and tucked her feet beneath the folds of her dress. Her sharp heels clicked together.

"Our marriage was the ruse, but even though it's no longer necessary, I wish to keep it." She took my chin and turned my face towards her. "This is the real me." I tasted the chemicals in her red lipstick as she planted a kiss over my mouth. "This is the real you." She kissed me again, and I inhaled, hungry for more of her. Disappointment tamped down the urge to devour her as she pulled away and dropped her hand. "The only falsehood remaining is the art you hide behind, Jacques. Why don't I set up an exclusive media interview? The exposé will cause the final ruse to die."

The notion filled me with horror and her hazel irises flashed as she saw it burst into flame in my mind. Her pink fingernails dug into my wrist as she clamped a hand over it and squeezed. "Don't panic. I wouldn't do it without your permission."

My head shook from side to side as though a mysterious hand controlled my neck. My brain denied me the words to convey the reasons I'd hate the world knowing my identity. Julia's grip relaxed, and she patted my sleeve. "It is perhaps best for my finances to maintain your anonymity. The commission on your last painting paid off the remainder of the mortgage." She smiled, genuine admiration drawing up the corners of her lips. "Everyone wants a piece of you, mon cher. They all want a painting by 'X' hanging in their lounge."

I nodded and my mind stretched to the canvas propped up in my studio. "I've finished *The Woman in The Garden*. It's drying."

Julia nodded, the movement quick and business-like. "I'll use the van from the gallery to fetch it when it's ready. The courier asked questions last time which makes transportation a risk to your privacy. We must take more care over such details now that your work has become such a sought-after commodity."

I pressed my lips together in reply, not wanting to know the machinations of keeping my secret. Julia would handle it as she'd done for the last eight years, running the gallery and auction house in Auckland and enjoying her role as my agent. She rose and dug in her handbag for her phone, wrinkling her nose at the sight of whatever she found on the screen. "Four texts and three calls from Gordon. He wants to know if I'm working today."

"Are you?"

She gnawed on the inside of her cheek and shrugged. The fame and accompanying fortune of 'X' had fast tracked her into a directorship at the struggling gallery. A thirty percent stake had propped it up and delayed the owner's bankruptcy. Only she knew how to reach me. Only she could commission and sell my paintings. It robbed the owner of recourse if she chose not to turn up for a day's work. He was powerless, and he knew it.

I pressed my fingers into my eyes until it hurt, seeking to dismiss Julia's issues from my head. "I need to see Mother. The prison confirmed she's in the hospital, but the doctors won't tell me where they're keeping her."

"Would you like me to find her with you?" Her voice softened and her desire to help me washed over the distress occupying my chest. I almost nodded, changing it to a shake of my head at the last second. I kept my eyes covered to avoid seeing the disappointment on her face. Mother didn't agree with my rescue of Julia. She thought it risky and underestimated my ability to act as the dutiful husband for five years. She didn't know we'd progressed to secret assignations in hotel rooms or that we'd learned to meet an unspoken emotional need within each other. A part of me acknowledged I'd dreaded the prospect of divorce while at the same time craving it. Julia presented a loose end in a neat, predictable pattern. I imagined a life in which someone else tumbled with her in a wide hotel bed and balled my hands into fists. The loose end had become a permanent graft, and I liked it.

I pushed myself to stand and lifted my jacket from its hanger in the wardrobe. The second day clothes irritated my sense of cleanliness and I longed to get back to my own hotel room and change. "I'll find her," I asserted.

Julia nodded. "When will I see you again?" A catch in the back of her throat showed how much my answer mattered to her.

I crossed the room and dug my fingers into the silky soft coils at the back of her neck. My kiss smudged her lipstick but offered a promise. "Soon. You can fetch the painting and stay the night." My tongue grazed her top lip, and I closed my eyes and dominated the intimacy, pulling away as her arms lifted to wrap around my neck. "I'll phone you," I whispered.

"And you'll do the other commission?" Hope blossomed in her eyes. "Will I email you the contract?"

"Yes." Our foreheads touched for a moment as I nodded. "I'll need time to plan and good weather. Cordon off the wall and set up a scissor lift. I can do it in a night."

Julia grinned. "What is the cost?"

I snorted and pleasure warmed my chest. "Make up a number that hurts. Get the money up front and make the contract water tight."

9

—·—

WATERCOLOUR:

PIGMENTS GROUND TO CREATE AN AQUEOUS SOLUTION

Julia made a call to an Auckland politician who'd bought an expensive painting from the gallery. She turned away from my blank expression as she asked him to contact the prison governor and locate Mother. I slipped into the bathroom while they made uninteresting small talk, not wanting their cluttered speech to fill the vacancy in my head.

My hands gripped the sides of the sink as I stared at my image in the mirror. Wide blue eyes looked back at me, a fringe of dirty blond hair bouncing against my eyelashes. Julia said I was handsome, but the word meant nothing. "It's just a face," I told myself. A functional face with useful parts, eyes, nose, mouth, and ears.

Yesterday's cravat refused to twist in the right places. The fabric remembered the previous knot and protested as I wrapped it around my neck. I closed my eyes to block out the mess and tied it from memory. It didn't cover the scar, and I snatched it off and tried again. Julia pushed open the door on my fifth attempt. "Let me." She shoved away my fingers and released the fabric. "It needs an iron," she soothed. She disappeared with it dangling over her fingers like a dead creature and I waited in the bathroom while she clattered around with the hotel's ironing board. Minutes later, she returned with it pressed flat and slipped the cravat around my neck. It held the heat and burned as she folded the edges and pushed them inside my shirt collar. "Very chic," she commented, stepping back to admire her work. "Very French. Loop it like a necktie. Don't wrap it around your throat like a pirate."

I frowned at my image in the mirror and stopped myself from agreeing with her. "People stare at my scar. They ask questions. I don't like it."

Julia cupped my scratchy cheek in her hand. She lifted herself onto her tiptoes and placed a kiss over my lips. "You're beautiful," she whispered. Her thumb coasted across my mouth, removing the red lipstick in a practiced movement. "The only person who doesn't see it is you."

I trusted her. If she said the sky was green, I'd believe her. She'd never lied to me before, and I suspected it wasn't in her nature. But I didn't care about the face I saw in the mirror each morning when I shaved. Its symmetry pleased me, but I didn't crave the attention of others. I just wanted to be left alone to paint, and count, and ease my way into processes and patterns that allowed me to breathe from one moment to the next.

Julia turned towards the door and gave me a smile. "Go home, Jacques. My friend will phone when he has news. Take my calls this time." She glided from the bathroom and retrieved her long coat from the armchair. Emptiness licked at the edges of my psyche and I ached to call her back and forge something more wholesome from our association. But the narrators in my head robbed me of words and kept me pinned in place, screeching warnings of the unpredictability she threatened in my carefully crafted life. They didn't release me until the door clicked shut in her wake.

Julia had settled the account for the room and I drifted back to my own hotel with the outlook of the brick wall. The neatness of the red rectangles offered a pleasurable security, but I resisted counting them, leaving that enjoyable task for later. I longed for another shower, but Julia's cravat nestled comfortably against my throat. Unsure I could replicate it, I sought to preserve it a while longer. Later, I would reverse engineer it and figure out how to do it for myself. My hotel provided a decent buffet breakfast, and I examined the various food offerings laid across a hot plate in the dining room. A man with a paunch hanging over his pants leaned across a tray of bacon. He continued talking with his companion as he used the tongs to scoop up four pieces, and I dismissed that option.

Apart from Mother and Julia, I found myself unable to tolerate the bodily fluids of others. Not just the actuality, but the mere potential. It proved one of the less appetising memories of my army career, the notion of brotherhood and the sharing of food and drink during scarcity. My natural repulsion surprisingly superseded the desire for survival, and I went hungry many times during pooled rations. I turned aside as he released a blustering laugh, fancying I saw the spit droplets cascade across the waiting tray.

The milk jugs held a significant threat, the creamy liquid poured from their bottles by human hands to increase the risk of contamination. I chose cereal from an original container and carried my bowl and a black coffee to a corner table to eat. It took an effort to disregard the hands which had wrapped the warm cutlery in a napkin. I'd waited for a fresh batch straight from the dishwasher, hanging around the tray as a server dumped them into their compartment. "They're still hot," he warned, and I smiled and nodded.

A boy at a nearby table watched me with interest as I lifted out the dry flakes of puffed wheat one at a time. The activity of counting drowned out the noise of his curiosity in my brain. I sat back with a sigh of satisfaction and aspirated puffed wheat number two hundred and ninety-nine. The napkin hid any uncouthness, but my wheezing coughs invited attention. A concerned server approached, and I waved him away, hiding the retrieved and soggy ball of wheat in the folds of the tissue. Friday seemed as doomed as Thursday, and I didn't know how to wipe the slate clean. I stared at the remains in my bowl and ran through the scenarios. I could replace number two hundred and ninety-nine with another sugary ball and continue my operation, or abandon it. The thought of eating the real number two hundred and ninety-nine caused nausea to rise into my gullet. But I needed to finish the process somehow.

Despite the scratchiness of my throat and watering eyes, I selected two smaller balls of puffed wheat and ate them with more care. Mission accomplished. I'd saved Friday.

Julia phoned as I settled in my room to count the bricks. The activity proved less fulfilling than I anticipated, as several of them had blunted corners and the bricklayer's incompetence left blobs of cement in random places. "Hello, Julia." My tone held depression as I answered her call.

"Your mother is still in the hospital but unable to receive visitors. She has suffered another stroke and is in intensive care. The prison authority will phone you with an appointment once she is more stable."

My palm scraped against the stubble on my chin as I ran a hand across my face. My mouth emptied of possible responses. Julia's sigh reached my ears with the same clarity as if she sat next to me. "Je suis désolé, Jacques. Is there anything I can do to help?"

I cleared my throat, the sensation from the puffed wheat choking me anew. "No," I managed. "Get the contract for the mural to me by the end of today and check the weather forecast. I'll do it next Tuesday night."

Julia made a sound of disbelief, and I heard the confusion in her voice. "But it takes weeks for you to plan and to prepare the stencils."

"I can do it." I swallowed in a gulp. "This one is easy. I have the plan in my head already."

"Oh, be careful mon cher. This contract is not for trifling with and if he doesn't like it, he'll bury you."

The first genuine smile of the day spread across my lips, and I examined a shaft of sunlight which sneaked between the buildings and dappled the surface of the bricks. For a moment in time, they shone and glowed, a hidden beauty contained within their dull facade. I exhaled, and the grin remained, even as the sun shifted enough to remove its glory. The bricks returned to their mahogany shadows. "Only you and Mother know my real identity," I breathed. "So, let him try."

10

--·--

Juxtaposition:

Placing things for comparison or contrast

I checked out of my hotel room and drove home, navigating the drama associated with a two-car shunt on the southern motorway. A police officer waved me through the broken plastic and glass debris on the asphalt, exhaustion and veiled temper in his eyes. I gripped the steering wheel in white-knuckled fingers as I crunched my truck tyres over someone else's ruined Friday. Images of broken bodies wrapped in camouflage filled my mind's eye. Exploded flesh replaced the shards of red reflector and I blew out puffs of strained breath, which made my chest muscles ache. "One hundred and four, one hundred and five." I named the numbers aloud to dull the shouts of pain and anguish leaking from my memories.

Turning right onto the back road to my house allowed the tightness in my chest to loosen. I lowered the driver's window as I crossed the Tainui Bridge to connect with the sounds and smell of the Hakarimata Ranges. The familiar bird calls and the tang of damp foliage soothed my fractured mind. The Waikato River trapped the winding rural road between the foothills of the mountain and its watery depths. It forced the asphalt to follow its lead as I counted the tips of the range before my house. The right turn into my driveway presented several life ending hazards, and I prepared myself for the usual routine. Checking my rear-view mirror, I ensured no other traffic followed me for at least a kilometre. But a people mover joined me on the road as I passed a string of houses and I cursed aloud. Needing to make the turn after a blind right-hand bend, I couldn't risk it without the following vehicle running into my rear at a speed touching one hundred kilometres per hour. The driver wouldn't see my indicator until too late.

With my shoulders slumping in defeat, I powered through the second of two hairpin bends, intending to continue into town and make my turn at the entrance of the nearby quarry. My series of processes allowed for the contingency of backtracking and, while it frustrated my goal of getting home sooner, it didn't cause concern.

I flicked my gaze towards the end of my driveway as I straightened the steering wheel after the bend. The closed automatic gate safeguarded the steep road to my privacy, but I blinked at the sight of a car parked in front of it. Long and sleek, it perched on the slope with exhaust fumes progressing from its rear. A man in a matching jacket and trousers pressed the buzzer and leaned in to listen for an answer. I gaped at the car in shock at the same moment the driver glanced in his side mirror. His dark features sharpened as he recognised me. He leaned forward to watch me blast past my own gateway.

Unable to turn at the quarry due to an emerging aggregate truck, I continued into town and slowed for the fifty kilometres per hour limit. The people mover rode the rear bumper of my vehicle and honked in anger as I indicated and made the turn in front of the bus depot. Sweat beaded on my palms as I contemplated waiting it out until my visitors grew tired and left. I needed to paint, seeking an expression for the confused emotions which Julia always brought to life. It didn't matter what they were selling, I wouldn't buy.

I took a deep breath and pulled back onto the road with care. Scenarios flew across my mental cork board as I drove towards my driveway. My home called to me like a siren, promising a caress which muffled the world's noise. I slowed before reaching the back of the vehicle blocking my entry and eased my truck onto the narrow strip of gravel next to the post-box. An approaching car flew around the hazardous bend just beyond it, a squeal of tyres displaying the driver's difficulty in staying on the road. I watched the dawning of terror in his expression as he noticed the police car nestled in front of my gate and I imagined his gratitude that I'd blocked the patrol car in, preventing it from chasing his retreating ass.

Roddy emerged from the driver's side and slammed the door behind him. "Geez, they come round there fast." He tucked his blue shirt into his uniform trousers. "I wondered why you drove past and then the detective saw that people mover on your tail." He jerked his head towards the man in the suit. "This is Detective Sergeant Henare."

The man approached me with considered steps. The loose gravel outside the gate had left a layer of dust on his shiny shoes. He lifted his hand and offered it to me, bony fingers and a protruding wrist bone emerging from his jacket sleeve. Blonde hairs covered the backs of his fingers and I stared at his bitten fingernails. After a moment of awkwardness, he dropped his hand.

Roddy winced and narrowed his eyes at me in warning. Thirteen years in the same platoon had taught him what to expect, but he couldn't buffer me against the detective's superior rank. I gritted my teeth as he spoke to me like he would an imbecile. I wasn't the one who'd got so drunk I'd worn someone else's underwear on my head like a hat and paid a hooker for a good night's sleep. But I kept his secrets to myself, just like I always did. "Detective Sergeant Henare wants to ask you a few questions, Jack."

"What about?" My fists balled next to my sides, and I spread my legs as though at-ease. I stared at the detective, drinking in every last detail of his mousy hair and mismatched blue eyes. One widened even as the other squinted, his head like an oddly formed duck egg. A quarry truck barrelled towards us, its engine brakes whooshing out warm air as it slowed for the bend. Mere millimetres of air stood between the detective's sleeve and the filthy chassis as it navigated us at speed. The man's hair lifted like a toupee before settling back in a series of disturbed flaps.

"Let's get off this bloody road!" Strain leaked through the command. He jerked his head towards the gate but addressed Roddy. "How far is it up to this guy's house?"

Roddy swallowed and looked at me for the answer. When I remained silent, he glowered at me for leaving him hanging. "Not sure," he ventured. "I've never been invited." He slid into the driver's seat and slammed the door.

I climbed back into my truck and ran through my options. As another truck passed and almost clipped my side mirror, I limited my choices to one. The gate slid open at the press of the button on my key fob and after a worrying backward roll as he removed the handbrake, Roddy's patrol car started up my sheer driveway to the house.

11

MALLEABLE:

CREATE COMPRESSIVE STRESS TO ALTER A MATERIAL'S SHAPE

Roddy edged the patrol car next to the bottom step of the porch. He climbed from the vehicle and stared at the house while hauling his trousers up over his belly. The detective also emerged and looked around my driveway as though studying an enclosure at the zoo. I pushed my truck as close to the roll doors of the garage as I could manage without blocking Roddy's exit. I had no intention of letting the police officers into my home.

"We're off the road now." I dug my fingers into the front pockets of my trousers and puffed out my chest. "What do you want?"

"Can we come in?" The detective gave a pointed glance at the steps and back at me.

"No." I answered with honesty and Roddy's eyes widened. He made a cutting motion across his throat in warning.

Detective Sergeant Henare leaned his weight on one leg and fought to maintain a casual stance. He didn't know how to respond. I knew the signs. "Can you tell me what you know about Nate Watson?" He folded his arms across his chest to create a visible barrier between us.

I frowned and ran the name through the extensive data banks stored in my brain. It didn't surface. "Nothing, officer. I don't know him."

Roddy made an inaudible sound in the back of his throat like a growl. Henare's eyes narrowed, and a satisfied smile lit his lips. "That's not true, is it, Mr Jethro? You had an altercation with him in the RSA on Wednesday night."

I blinked and cocked my head to the side. My gaze slid towards Roddy. "The skinny kid in the bar?" I frowned. "Nate Watson. That's his name?"

"That *was* his name." Detective Sergeant Henare took a step towards me. "His body washed up on the riverbank at Mercer last night."

"Right." No emotion crossed my face. I didn't care. It removed a problem for me. I didn't need to ask Mother to analyse my conversation with him. It wouldn't be repeated, so it lost its importance.

"I don't know him."

Henare jerked his head towards the patrol car. "I'd like to hear your explanation down at the station, Mr Jethro. You can come with us now of your own free will, or my colleague can arrest you."

The colour rose into Roddy's cheeks. He didn't stand a chance, and he knew it. His audible gulp drew Henare's attention, and I used the moment to stuff my keys into my back pocket. Mother would have gone with the officers, tucking her lavender scarf around her neck and clambering into their car without fuss. She'd done exactly that. She relinquished her freedom with relief and settled into the back seat with a valiant wave at her watching son. The image remained carved into my eyeballs. *'It's what I expected,'* she'd whispered across the kilometres between us, our maternal bond reduced to a once-a-week phone call. *'We knew life would be different.'*

"I'll come with you."

Roddy's shoulders slumped as tension drained from his face. His expression relaxed into its usual florid state. He hurried around the vehicle and fumbled open the rear door. "In you get, Jack." His attempt at joviality fell to the ground like discarded marbles. He still winced when I stepped towards him.

The car stank of disinfectant with the faint overlay of vomit. I fastened the seat belt because it followed the rules and not because I wanted contact with the bugs and germs its surface contained. Silence filled the vehicle as Roddy steered to the bottom of my driveway. Both men looked back at me as we stopped in front of the gate. "Can you open it?" Henare spun around in his seat, but Roddy studied me through the rear-view mirror. The fob dug into my backside, but I couldn't touch it without washing my hands seven times after handling the dirty fixtures of the vehicle. I shrugged and favoured the other option.

The door made a horrible creak as I flung it open. The downward angle of the vehicle on the steep driveway threw it forward on its hinges. My biceps tensed as I wrenched it back into place with a click. My downhill stroll must have seemed too casual, because I heard Henare's dramatic sigh. Leaning over the hedge at the side of the gate, I pressed the access code into the keypad. The metal structure slithered sideways on its runners, the mechanism smooth and well maintained. I waited until Roddy eased the vehicle off the driveway before clambering into the back seat and repeating the process. The gate slid closed behind us, an obedient sentry protecting my secrets.

Roddy drove on the wrong side of the road for thirty metres, leaning forward to check his side mirror and ensure no one flew around the blind bend and collided with us. His trajectory wavered enough to betray his activity the previous night. I hoped he wasn't drunk enough to crash the car before I washed my hands for the last time.

The worn fabric rumpled beneath my grip as I kept my hands away from my clothing. The cleanliness compulsion became worse after I left the army, bringing with it an ache in my soul. I couldn't rid my skin of the sand of Helmand Province, or the fine dust of the plains of Iraq, my fingers still coated in the blood and brain matter which settled after the initial pink bloom. My mental processes no longer distinguished one tour from another, melding them all into a bitter nightmare of boredom and blood. My trigger finger itched, and I squinted through my right eye, picturing the side of Henare's head exploding. A crawling sensation indicated Roddy's gaze coasting across my reflection, and I sought his wary brown eyes in the rear-view mirror. He gave the slightest shake of his head. Another warning.

The tiny police station in Ngaruawahia smelled of leftover pizza and sweat. Henare used a keypad to unlock a door in the waiting room, flicking on lights as he led the way along a narrow corridor. The original property served as a house and the cheap conversion into a police station left the period features in place. Henare stepped into an office still decorated as a child's bedroom. He waved his hand at a seat opposite an empty desk. "Sit down, Mr Jethro." He walked around the other side and slumped into an office chair. It rocked as it absorbed his weight.

Roddy closed the door and stood behind me, his tension settling over the room like a suffocating cloud of concern. The skin on the back of my neck tingled at his proximity.

"That's all thank you, Sergeant." Henare dismissed him with an insincere smile, which didn't reach his eyes. "I can take it from here."

I didn't need to turn around to sense the impact of the dismissal. Roddy floundered, his protestations incoherent. The question rose into my mind, presenting the facts. Yet still I couldn't discern whether his worry was for me or for the Inspector.

12

MERZ:

ART FROM SCAVENGED FRAGMENTS

I eyed the visitor's chair with a practiced eye and deigned it safe for me to sit on the worn plastic. The standard issue seat screamed its institutional identity and reminded me of the army. So, I sat, placing my knees in perfect alignment and resting my fists over them as though for a platoon photograph. Henare stared at me from the other side of the desk. "Where were you last night, Mr Jethro?"

I studied a long hair protruding from his forehead and wondered if he knew of its existence. His muddy hair spiked from his scalp to create a forest of disarray. I breathed in and out and my trigger finger twitched in muscle memory of taking a shot. "I stayed in Auckland overnight." My voice held no emotion. "I arrived at my hotel just before two o'clock and checked out this morning."

Henare leaned forward. His pen leaked ink onto the inside of his middle finger as he scrawled in a notebook. "Why did you travel to Auckland, Jack? Can I call you Jack?"

I tipped forward to inspect the toes of my shoes and shifted them so they created a perfect formation in front of my knees. "My mother is sick. No."

"No?" He frowned and lines appeared across his forehead.

I exhaled, frustration persuading me to hit him seven times before leaving. I fought the impulse, but the uninvited notion reminded me I needed to wash my hands. A spasm started somewhere inside my chest wall and radiated out as a tremor in my fingers. "No. Don't call me Jack."

"Right." Henare blinked and jerked backwards. "What's the nature of your mother's illness?"

"It's private."

Henare sighed. "Can she verify your visit for me, Mr Jethro?"

I frowned and my left eyebrow started its familiar compulsive twitch. Balling my fists, I rose and the detective's eyes widened as he shoved his chair back from the desk. "I didn't see Mother. She's in ICU and not allowed visitors. I'm waiting for a phone call about her condition."

"Okay." Henare rose to match my stance. He dropped his pen onto the desk and frowned at his ink-stained finger. "So, the hotel can confirm your stay?"

"Yes."

"And if I check their security footage, I'll see you entering the property and staying there until this morning, won't I?"

"No."

A smirk lit on Henare's lips. "And why is that Mr Jethro?"

I pushed my left hand behind my back and tapped out a series of three beats against the waistband of my trousers. "I went out for dinner and didn't sleep in my room."

"Please sit down again, Mr Jethro." Henare jerked his head towards the grey plastic chair. "I need to account for your whereabouts from the moment you left the RSA on Wednesday night until an unlucky dog walker discovered Nate Watson's body floating face down in the Waikato River this morning. The coroner will determine a time of death, but until then, it's my job to line up all the facts. You were the last person to see Nate alive. Witnesses saw you arguing. The CCTV from outside the bar shows you speaking to him again before you left in your truck. I want to know what he said to you, Mr Jethro." He kept throwing my name onto the end of his sentences as punishment for being unable to call me Jack.

Sitting created the sensation of ants crawling beneath the skin on my legs, so I remained standing. I spread my feet and clasped my hands behind my back as though at-ease. The opportunity to offer facts subdued my anxiety, and I listed them in a robotic tone. "He thought I hit on his girlfriend, but I didn't. I left, and he followed me into the car park. He repeated his accusation, and I refuted it. His words were, '*Hey, you! Don't walk away from me when I'm talking to you!*' He called me a '*Smart ass,*' and said, '*Go near Tahlia again and I'll kill you.*' He followed me to my truck and tried to hit me. I blocked his fist and held him by the throat."

The colour drained from Henare's cheeks to leave him pale and sweating. He'd overplayed his hand and knew it. I sensed in that moment he didn't really believe I'd killed the skinny kid when he invited me into his office. My revelation made him regret the civility, and he wished he'd taken me into the back bedroom disguised as an interview room and recorded my confession. His hands shook as he reached for the telephone on his desk, changed his mind and fiddled with his blotter.

"I left him in the street. When I looked in my rear-view mirror, I saw him return to the bar. He called me a *Weirdo* and went back to his beer."

Henare slumped into his chair. The seat rocked on its spindle. "He did," he conceded. "The security camera picked him up as he walked across the car park. He went back inside the bar and complained you tried to throttle him."

"Self-defence." I gave a nonchalant shrug. "He followed me and I had nothing to say to him."

Henare leaned forward and rested his elbows on a stained blotting pad. He retrieved his pen and the hairy finger joints showed white through his skin as he rolled it between his fingers. "Do you care that he's dead?"

"No." I inhaled through my nose. "I'd never met him before Wednesday night and I won't meet him again."

"Right." Henare scratched at his eyes with the backs of his knuckles.

A knock shook the door and Roddy poked his face through the gap. He glanced at me before addressing his superior. "I brought coffee." His shoulders edged the door aside, and he proceeded into the room with a battered tray. Two glass mugs sat on it. Coffee, the colour of river water, sloshed onto the tray as he walked with increasing confidence. Scratches caught the light and made the surface of the mugs glitter. I knew I wouldn't drink from either of them. Henare lifted his chin in acknowledgement, but his gaze tracked to me.

"Where did you have dinner on Wednesday night and if you weren't at your hotel, where did you sleep?"

My heart sank like a stone and settled on a precarious ledge in my stomach. Any movement would send it pitching into an abyss. I made a poor liar and Mother always advocated for the truth. She hated liars. It was ironic that she'd allied herself with one. Counting to seven in my head, I released my truth. "I ate at the Red Dragon Hotel on Ponsonby Road in Auckland. I slept upstairs in Room 42."

Roddy clattered the mugs onto the desk and left brown rings on Henare's blotter pad. He rose and clutched the tray to his chest as the detective wrinkled his nose. "You booked one hotel room and slept in another." His left eyebrow hiked. "I'm guessing you met someone for dinner and the party continued." I didn't reply because he hadn't asked a question and he sighed. "Am I right?"

"Yes."

Roddy stared at me and gave a series of rapid blinks. He appeared stunned by the revelation, and I imagined the pistons firing in his brain.

Henare leaned back in his chair and clasped his hands behind his head. "A woman, Mr Jethro?" Tiredness leaked from his tone. "Can she vouch for you?"

A lump rose into my throat as I realised I'd failed my mission. '*Protect Julia,*' he'd said, blood burbling from his lips as he gripped my forearms. I'd tried. Until this moment, I'd believed the captain would have celebrated my achievement. Julia was safe and free. The skinny kid had ruined Wednesday and Friday of my week, undoing a decade of careful planning and subterfuge with his arrogance and now his death.

I bumped my fists together behind my back in an imperceptible movement and dug my nails into my palm. The skinny kid had undoubtedly ruined his poor girlfriend's life, judging by his possessive accusations. But he wouldn't destroy Julia's from the grave. I cleared my throat and spoke with clarity so Henare wouldn't misunderstand. "I met my wife, Detective Sergeant Henare. And I spent the night in her hotel room."

Roddy released a gasp of disbelief and the tray hit the floor with a clang.

13

--

DADA:

AN EXPRESSION DEFYING CONVENTIONS OF ORDER AND LOGIC

"When did you get married?" Awe and wonder filled his tone. I watched a flush creep up his neck and into his cheeks as his mind ran through scenarios.

Henare ignored him, flapping his hand towards the tray on the dirty carpet. A shard had separated from the wooden handle and Roddy's fingers shook as he bent to gather up the debris. "Why did you say nothing?" he muttered under his breath. Then the actual issue. "Why didn't I get an invitation?"

"Am I able to speak to your wife, Mr Jethro?" Henare put his hands on his hips and rose. He glared at the telephone on his desk. "Is she at home now?"

My mind raced through possibilities and settled on the story we crafted with care eight years earlier. It held enough truth for me to carry it with conviction. "She works at a gallery in Auckland. We have a house in Mission Bay. I rent the Ngaruawahia house because I enjoy the peace. We split our time between the properties."

Roddy gaped. His jaw slackened, and he stared at me through bleary eyes as though seeing me for the first time. I'd dragged him into my patterns and habits over the last eight years without either of us realising it.

"So, she's at work now?" Henare lifted the receiver of his desk phone. "What's the number?"

I turned to face Roddy and forced my lips into a smile. "May I have a drink of plain, boiled water?" I asked.

His lips parted, but he remained in place, glued to the carpet by reluctant feet. Henare lifted the phone to his ear and checked the dial tone. "Number, Mr Jethro!" he snapped. "And we'll need to put all this on record." His gaze drifted to the peeling wallpaper and a length of coving which attempted to vacate its corner of the ceiling. "We might need to travel to Hamilton."

Roddy clutched the tray to his chest and splinters of the damaged wood spread across his police issue navy pullover. Henare glanced up at him and sighed. "Get the man a drink of water!" he snapped, his patience with Roddy's fumbling gone. Roddy swallowed and shot me a glance, which warned of a forthcoming deluge of questions he knew I wouldn't answer. Still, he'd try to force me to divulge my secrets, convinced our shared combat made us blood brothers. It didn't. That brotherhood ended when they all denied a dying man's request to protect the girl he'd rescued from her abusers. He'd turned to me in desperation and the irony amused me. The last soldier he'd invited into his confidence had been the one to do what he asked. Had he understood my nature, he would have asked me first.

Rescuing Julia had shattered my belief in the brotherhood and fractured my nerves. I resigned at the end of my last tour, not wanting to breathe the same air as my platoon. The squad's guilt hung over us like a stifling blanket and as I worked to smuggle Julia from country to country using false documents, I no longer shared their burden of a war that didn't interest me.

"Mr Jethro!" Henare depressed the call button again as the waiting dial tone grew bored and morphed into a shrill wail. "I want to speak to your wife!"

I gave him Julia's mobile phone number and watched him dial. His protruding hairy knuckles bothered me. A bulbous index finger stabbed at the keypad, rapping out the precious threes and sevens which made up her number.

"Julia Jethro." Her light voice rang through the handset as though trying to reach me through Henare's skull. "How can I help you?"

Henare cleared his throat and glanced at me. I recognised the moment he wished he'd made the call from elsewhere. Anger made him sloppy. "I have your husband here," he began.

Julia interrupted, her voice tinny by the time it reached me. "Jacques? Where is he? Why can't he speak to me? Is he ill?"

"Nothing. Nothing is wrong." Henare flapped his hand in the air and swallowed. "I'm Detective Sergeant Henare from the Waikato police."

"Mon Dieu!" Julia's voice gained a shrill quality. We'd crafted a blueprint for every situation, but I hadn't foreseen this one. Her finding herself at the mercy of the local constabulary had always formed a possibility. Me being held by them wasn't on the list. I sat in the plastic chair and spread my sweating palms across my knees, trusting Julia to act her part. It occurred to me that in our eight years together, I'd asked for nothing in return for her rescue. Admitting to myself that I needed her help caused a warmth to spread across my chest.

"He's fine, Mrs Jethro. I need to ask you some questions."

"Can I speak to my husband?" Steel entered her tone. "I'd like to satisfy myself of his wellness."

"In a moment." Henare took a deep inhale. "I'm investigating an incident in Ngaruawahia. I understand you work in Auckland and I need to check when you last saw Mr Jethro." He turned aside from me to avoid my study of his features. His pink ears told me how much he hated being the one under scrutiny. Julia's voice became a muffled vibration. I used my thumbs to exert pressure on my inner knee joints, alternating with the fingers clutching the outside. The rhythm grew from somewhere inside my soul, soothing and overriding my angst.

I jumped as Henare sat the phone receiver back in its cradle. "You're free to leave, Mr Jethro," he said, his tone flat. "Your wife corroborated your story. Happy anniversary. I might need to speak to you again once the coroner gives me a definite time of death for Mr Watson."

I rose without speaking and tucked my chair with the front legs nestled against the desk. After a moment's hesitation, I dragged it back a few inches to a more acceptable position. Henare watched me, his eyes narrowed and his expression thoughtful. "Bye, Mr Jethro," he said with a sigh.

Mother hadn't filled my repertoire with futile chit-chat and so I ignored him and left the child's bedroom disguised as an office. The door clicked as I pulled on the handle, punctuating my visit with a loud full stop. The heels of my cowboy boots tapped against the rimu floorboards in the hallway of the old house. After a brief wait for assistance and a glance in his direction, the officer at the desk helped me exit the security door. I'd registered the push button to unlock the heavy door, but chose not to touch it, letting him finger the bacteria on the shiny plastic. The door closed behind me and I glanced back to see him pushing a sandwich between his lips.

Roddy met me in the car park. It housed a few civilian vehicles and a patrol car emblazoned with its vivid colours. He dumped his cigarette on the ground and rushed towards me. A white haze continued to rise from the lighted end. "What the hell, man?" he demanded. His face contorted into a series of lines and ridges. "You got married!" I towered over him as he postured in front of me, but his anger overshadowed us both. "You sit next to me at the RSA every Monday, Wednesday and Friday and you said nothing!"

I shrugged, his ire irrelevant. Glancing around the car park, I remembered my truck still sat on my driveway. I wrinkled my nose and fantasised about washing my hands seven times and indulging in a lengthy shower to rid me of the bacteria gained by my unanticipated outing. My fingers patted the seam of my trousers as I contemplated washing them or just throwing them into the recycling bin in the centre of town. '*Burn them*,' a voice whispered in my head. '*The other options take too long.*'

I dug my fingers into my trouser pockets and hunched my shoulders against Roddy's barrage of questions. "See you tonight," I murmured.

"No, you won't." Roddy's tone held an unfamiliar hardness. I turned to face him, my frown drawing my brows so far down my forehead ached.

"But it's Friday." I swallowed, my statement obvious. Friday was our night to sit at the bar of the RSA and follow our usual pattern of companionship. My mental processes rolled forward like an invading tank, too heavy to manoeuvre along a different route. Heaviness tugged at the soles of my shoes, gluing them to the floor. "It's Friday," I repeated.

Roddy shrugged. The action suggested a borderline between irritation and nonchalance, but his flashing eyes betrayed his extreme fury. "The inspector will keep me working until we catch Nate Watson's killer." He puffed up his chest as though suggesting he played a bigger part in the crime solving than a glorified chauffeur.

"How did the kid die?" The question bubbled up from curiosity and not from any notion of caring.

Roddy pushed his lips into a pout and glanced over his shoulder as though expecting to discover Henare watching him through a window. "Not sure," he admitted. "Broken neck or drowning. We're waiting for the coroner to give us those details."

"Right." I turned away from him and began my treacherous walk home along the country lane. Ten minutes to the edge of town and ten more of dodging traffic on the fast road to the end of my driveway. A broken neck or drowning. Neither of the limited options sounded like a fun way to depart from life. It couldn't have happened to a nicer bloke.

14

LANDSCAPE:

AN IMAGE WHICH HAS NATURAL SCENERY AS ITS PRIMARY FOCUS

My phone vibrated as I stepped off the last section of pavement before leaving the town behind me. Julia's number flashed onto the screen. Rain slapped the grey concrete, leaving dark polka dots and swishing beneath the tyres of passing cars. "Jacques?" Concern filled her voice. An odd echo accompanied it and traffic noises moved around her location. "I'm on my way."

"Where?" I halted by the gates to the quarry, choking on the dust kicked up by my sudden stop.

"I left as soon as I finished the call with the detective. Gordon sent me home because I feel unwell, Jacques." Her voice wobbled as she spoke the lie, desperate to communicate the terror lodged in her chest. We never shared details over any communication system able to relay our conversations to others. She wanted to meet and discuss this latest threat and its ramifications in person.

"I'm almost at the house." I tried to infuse my tone with gentleness. "Why didn't you text and I could have met you at home."

Julia paused, latching onto my use of the label for her Auckland house. We'd gotten sloppy, letting the facade of married life slip. This latest spotlight boded trouble for both of us, but more for Julia. Deportation for her would be a death sentence. A deep dive into her credentials would uncover our subterfuge, though it would never reveal the truth. Only three people ever knew her proper story, and one of them lay six feet under the soil in a plot in Dunedin. Well, some of him, anyway.

She exhaled. "You have important work to do and I crave some time away from the city." A low chuckle accompanied her next statement, her words bright and tinkling. "I missed you, Jacques. We will spend some quality time together and you will look after me." She disconnected the call, but the warmth of her voice remained.

I stuck to the sliver of verge on the left of the rural road, half expecting Roddy and Inspector Henare to appear and ticket me for jay walking. It seemed less risky than hugging the correct lane facing the traffic and then dashing across the apex of a blind bend to the bottom of my driveway. Julia's imminent arrival threw me into a spiral of anxiety and I flew through my forensically clean home after discarding the clothing worn in the police car. I set the washing machine onto soak out the bacteria and got the fire roaring in my lounge.

Julia phoned as her Mercedes cruised the last hazardous serpentine bend and I opened the gate from the keypad in the hall. Her tyres kicked up spray on the wet gravel as she slewed her car to a stop in front of the garage door. She hauled an overnight bag from the back seat and met me on the porch. Our fingers touched as she let me take the strap from her wrist. "Are you okay?" Her ebony lashes shuttered her irises, a line of concern forming between her brows.

I nodded in reply and lifted one side of my mouth. "The detective's arrival stopped me from exercising." I gnawed on my lower lip. The heavy bag bumped against my thigh as I hoisted it and clasped it against my chest. My head gave an involuntary twitch to one side and Julia's brow furrowed deeper.

"Go." She waved her hand towards the garage and my gym equipment. "I brought lunch. I'll call you in an hour." She hefted a baguette from the back seat of her car. Tan crumbs sprinkled the black upholstery and cascaded from the ineffectual paper wrapper onto the ground beneath her high-heeled boots. My eyes widened in horror and she laughed and slapped my biceps with her free hand. "I'll clear up after myself." Her left eyebrow rose. "I know the rules."

My feet pointed in the garage's direction and the gym equipment, which would enable me to silence the narrators in my head for a few hours. I frowned as they disobeyed the order to move. My shoulder dipped, warmth spreading outward from Julia's jovial contact with my body. I turned towards her and forced my lips to say the words screaming in my head. "Julia."

"Yes?" She cocked her head in expectation, her chocolate irises dancing and sparkling in the greyness from overhead.

"I've missed you." My lips clamped shut over the words and I turned, my body rigid as I paced to the garage and let myself into the cavernous room. The door clicked shut behind me and I leaned against it. I hadn't opened and closed it seven times, the compulsion strangely absent. Julia's presence offered both the crisis and the cure. I'd estimated the weight of her bag at less than seven kilogrammes, not even meeting the limit for a flight bag. My heart both soared and ached. Staying for one night or seven, she promised to disrupt my routine with her arrival and send me crashing to earth with her departure. It's why I'd avoided her for the last forty-five days, six hours, twelve minutes and fifty-five seconds.

I closed my eyes and pressed my cheek against the smooth plaster wall, seeking the building's solidity and pattern of regularity. By the time my fingers had tapped out a beat of one hundred and forty-four, I'd collected my fragile nerves into a manageable bundle and prepared to exercise until I found my equilibrium.

My feet pounded against the belt of the treadmill with force and determination. The regular rhythm stilled my frantic mind as I concentrated on my breathing. In. Step, step, step. Out. Step, step, step. It left no room for other confusing thoughts and the activity banished all but my body's demands. Julia, Mother, and the skinny kid. They couldn't get to me behind the safe wall of exertion.

Except Julia could. She'd shared the gym in the years before we purchased the Auckland house for her. She'd done her own healing here, sweating out her trauma and screaming at the self-inflicted pain which overlaid the wounds delivered by others' cruel hands.

I strained through the final repetition, pushing the weights against the tug of gravity and locking my lungs with the effort. The bar slammed into the cradle above my head and I inhaled a ragged breath. Weights clanked on either side. The threat of Julia's crumbs had pervaded my peace and nagged in the back of my mind. Would she clean them up as she'd promised? What would I do if she didn't? Mother's advice circled in my brain, offering solutions and sentences to smooth over the impending disaster. *'Be nice.* Her sensible whispers filled my psyche as though she sat next to me. *'It's not the end of the world.'* I knew that. I'd seen the end of the world in several war zones. Humans always recreated what they'd lost, adding the unseen timer which began its relentless ticking in the background on a perpetual countdown to the next destruction. And then the next.

"Hey." Julia's soft voice sent my heart into the roof of my mouth and I choked. She patted my back as I sat up and wiped my lips. "Sorry. I didn't mean to frighten you, chéri."

I snorted out a laugh at the notion of her tiny frame causing me physical fear. The emotional stuff proved something very different. She grinned at me and wiped her hand on her skirt. The action confused me, perplexed by her spreading of my sweat over her clothing without repercussions. "I stink." The statement clattered into the silence.

"I don't care." She tossed her ebony curls and gave a shrug. My lips parted with the same reverence as the moment I'd watched a mother suck a child's dummy after its trip onto the floor before placing it back into the child's mouth. It seemed incredible that Julia might gloss over my bacterial content with such disinterest. It made no sense to my logical mind.

"I cooked lunch." She stroked a slender index finger over the handle of the exercise bike next to the weight bench. "Are you hungry yet?"

"Yes." I answered without consulting my stomach, but a cursory mental examination met with its agreement. "What are we eating?"

"Roast chicken, cheese from the shop in Ponsonby and garlic bread." Her index finger slipped inside the collar of her shirt and stroked the silky skin which bore the love bite. Her irises glittered, and she cast her gaze over my sweat soaked tee shirt and shorts. "But first, I'm craving a shower, and perhaps a little dessert." Her hips swayed as she moved towards me, the outline of her thin waist and full breasts revealed through the delicate weave of her favoured, expensive fabric. The buttons popped open on her shirt and I swallowed, seeing she'd already removed her bra. Ripe breasts spilled forward as she dipped to wriggle free of her skirt.

My muscles tightened, the tendons taut and ridged beneath my skin. I balled my fists and my eyelids fluttered closed. My body bore the scars of cruel schoolboy pranks and open violence, yet nothing compared to my terror of the monster Julia awoke in my soul. I'd survived war zones and covert military operations. But one day, my confused feelings for Julia would stop my heart stone dead.

15

DIPYTCH:

WORK OF ART ON TWO HINGED PANELS

Julia had cleared up any evidence of stray crumbs in the kitchen, and I again experienced gratitude at the seamless way she meshed with my life. We ate in companionable silence, her considered trip to the supermarket providing a feast. I loaded the dishwasher while she sipped a mug of fruit tea. Frustration seized my fingers and turned them into fists when the gate buzzer sounded from the lobby. Julia jumped, and I hated the visitor just because of her frightened reaction.

"Who's that?" she demanded, wiping spilled pink liquid from her wrist.

"Just someone at the gate." I showed no intention to answer the second round of buzzing and she moved before I could tell her I always ignored it. The susurrations of her white dress created a soothing whisper across my soul as she passed me. Her ebony curls stroked her shoulders in a gentle caress and she glided into the lobby. Julia always walked on her toes, and her graceful movements fascinated me.

Buttons clicked, and she pressed three before the outside noises intruded on our peace. "Oui?"

A voice crackled through the speaker. "I'd like to speak to Mr Jethro." The sound of a car speeding past drowned out the rest of his sentence.

"Jacques." Julia appeared in the doorway. "I recognised the voice of the police officer from his earlier call. He stands at your gate." Her teeth worried at her lower lip. "What should I do?"

I offered what I hoped was a reassuring smile. She dropped onto her heels, and I wasn't sure if that was a good sign. My stomach muscles tightened and I tucked my shirt into my pants before approaching the intercom. The security monitor gave Henare a comic appearance as he dipped to speak into the intercom without noticing the camera. The angle produced an enlarged chin on a tiny head. An engine purred in the background, and as Henare moved sideways, I squinted at the sight of Roddy behind the steering wheel. Unable to formulate a suitable sentence with Julia watching, I hit the switch to open the gate. The camera captured Henare's peculiar downhill run as he barrelled back to the car and flung himself into the passenger seat. The whirring of the gate mechanism echoed in the lobby until the vehicle passed through and the camera closed the connection.

A compulsion rose like an itch in my chest and threatened to burst free. I closed my eyes and tapped the wall seven times. Then I turned to break the news to Julia. "You need to prepare for the arrival of the police officer," I warned. "There's a problem I don't have time to fix."

Julia's eyes widened, and she glided along the hall and upstairs to the room she'd claimed as hers eight years earlier when we set about fooling the immigration department. She hadn't stayed at my house for over two years, but I knew her clutter still lurked out of sight behind the wardrobe doors. The door closed with a click behind her and the weight of her fear pressed down on my skull. I walked to the porch and leaned my forearms on the balustrade, readying myself for the visitors.

The patrol car laboured up the steep hill, the engine straining through the gears. It rounded the final turn and Henare leaned sideways to speak to Roddy as they noticed me waiting for them.

"Hey, mate." Roddy slammed the driver's door and stuck his thumbs into his waistband to haul up his trousers. He performed a curious twisting action as he walked to the bottom of the porch steps and looked up at me. His trousers settled back below his stomach as though he hadn't bothered. His gaze studied me with more clarity than earlier, the previous night's alcohol having run through his system. I jerked my chin upwards in acknowledgement of his greeting, but Henare beat him to the first step and skipped onto the deck. I sensed a different mood surrounding him, a combativeness which hadn't been there at the police station. He squared his shoulders as he waited for me to turn towards him. A flicker behind his eyes showed the moment he realised his inadequacy. I looked down at him from my six feet and three inches, taking the time to crack my neck twice on one side and once on the other. The lack of symmetry in the movement irked me, but I corrected the imbalance by joining my fingers and reversing the stretch to produce a series of satisfying pops.

Henare took a step backwards and Roddy's outstretched hand against his spine stopped him from falling off the deck. "Mr Jethro." He gathered his courage with a glare at Roddy. "I have a few more questions." He jerked his head towards the open front door. "I don't want to get difficult and start requesting warrants but I can."

I inhaled and addressed Roddy, seeking safety in familiarity. "You can come in to talk, but you're not searching my house without following the legal process."

"That's okay, isn't it?" Roddy spoke to the back of Henare's head as he looked up from the second step. The detective nodded and waited for my invitation as though under starter's orders. A shallow nod of my head sent him over the threshold at a dash. He didn't stop to wipe his feet on the doormat. Roddy hung back, twisting his hands in apology. "Sorry about this, mate," he whispered. "I know you didn't do it but he's under pressure. The kid's uncle is a Hamilton city councillor, and he's kicking up a fuss about his nephew's death."

"City councillor?" I hiked my right eyebrow in wonder. "The skinny kid didn't have two brain cells to rub together."

Roddy made a low growl in his throat. "It runs in the family. The uncle isn't too bright either, but he's got the ear of the press. Haven't you seen the media reports?"

I shook my head in reply. "I don't watch TV."

"Right." Roddy nodded. He didn't ask why, and it negated the need to tell him how the effects of such visual disturbances robbed me of sleep and increased the power of my compulsions. He just remembered I showed no interest in cinema visits while on leave or movie nights while deployed. I never made excuses. I just didn't show up at the appointed time. My platoon learned not to take issue with my peculiar behaviours. My gun and my fists supported them in the field, and that's all that mattered.

Henare stood in the lobby and inspected the art on my walls. A two metre high painting on the right occupied all his attention. "This is stunning." He reached up with eager fingers, which stopped just short of the canvas. "It's like a photograph. Where did you get it?"

Roddy gave me a wink of approval, as though Henare's appreciation of my home made any difference to his desire to blame me for the skinny kid's murder. I stepped over the threshold and frowned at the painting which had grabbed the detective's interest. My spine stiffened as he scrutinised it. His hairy fingers pulled a pair of wire-framed spectacles from his top pocket and he slipped them onto the end of his nose.

"This looks like a painting by 'X'," he breathed. His head moved as he scoured the canvas for the tell-tale signature. I grunted and closed the front door with an exaggerated click, hoping to move him beyond the massive clue to my identity. Stupidity made me hang it, not able to part with it after completion. Julia's image stared back at me, constructed from layers of sepia toned oil paints. A hijab covered her head, the folds of the scarf depicted through light and dark shadows. Her wide eyes and long lashes betrayed her fear as she looked over her right shoulder, her lips drawing into a pout. Ebony ringlets sneaked from beneath the scarf to kiss her shoulders in a curled caress. Desert sand covered her toes, glittering like sparkles over the hem of her robe. I'd used real sand in the image, projecting the third dimension and adding to the realism.

The painting had graced the wall of my lobby for the last eight years. Declining all visitors except Julia meant no one but her had ever seen it. But I realised my colossal error of judgement as Roddy took a step forward and released a ragged breath. "She looks like a girl I once knew in Iraq," he whispered. He swallowed and his gaze tracked to me and then back to the painting. Guilt radiated from his hazel irises, and so it should. Others in our squad were better equipped to rescue Julia from her peril. I was the last resort for our dying captain, his pleas given in secret, hushed gasps when the others refused his last request. "Angelica. Wasn't that her name?" He scratched his chin with a greasy finger as suppressed memories surfaced as a silent conviction. "The rebels killed her family and forced her into an arranged marriage. Weren't her parents Persian nationals working for some Christian organisation? "He cocked his head and stared at Julia's image. Wasn't it Iraq?" His shoulders slumped. "I've often wondered what happened to her. "His eyes darkened with the inner haunting of regret and I glimpsed the void in his soul. Guilt like tar spread across his decisions and tainted his world.

Henare lifted his glasses and placed them on his forehead. He squinted at the bottom right-hand corner of the canvas. "It's definitely by 'X'," he persisted. "I recognise the distinct brush strokes. He does this sideways, downwards stroke to create shadow. This must be worth a fortune." Admiration laced his tone and his body language changed as he regarded me with fresh interest. "I wonder why he didn't sign it."

I kept my silence because I had signed it. Not once, but fifty times. The tiny crosses at the hem of Julia's robe were a variation on my usual signature, weighing down the fabric which pooled at her feet, and protecting her modesty. It was a declaration of my commitment to a lifelong mission. No one would ever hurt her again. Not on my watch.

16

Fauvism:

Bold colour and brush strokes

Henare anticipated a welcome I didn't intend to give, threading his way through the house to the lounge. He clasped his hands behind his back and stared through the bay window at the Waikato River beyond the bush. The squeal of distant tyres betrayed a vehicle taking the first of many bends too fast.

I leaned against the door frame and set my focus on the craggy branch of a bare oak tree in the distance. Autumn had stripped the branches, and I sympathised. One conversation with the skinny kid had flayed my privacy to the bone.

"Your wife is here?" Henare jerked his head towards Julia's high-heeled boots peeking from beneath the sofa. I ground my teeth and gave a cursory nod. "May I speak to her?" He raised a dirty blond eyebrow, and it disappeared beneath his flapping fringe.

"Not today." I inhaled through my nose. "She came home sick."

Henare flattened his lips into a line. "But she felt well enough to answer my call from the gate?"

I shrugged. "Count yourself lucky. I ignored you."

Roddy gave a hiss of shock and shot me a frantic glance. His eyes widened to convey his angst, and he gave the merest shake of his head in warning.

"Fine!" I growled. "Wait here."

Hurried steps took me to the bottom of the stairs and onto the landing. Panic robbed me of the knowledge of whether it was an even or an odd day and I tripped in my haste. I tapped on Julia's door and waited for her reply with growing impatience. "Come in," she called, her voice muffled.

I slipped through the narrow gap I created and stood at-ease, my brow furrowed and the words fluttering free of my tongue. She reclined on the floral bedspread with a paperback clutched in her hands. The spine rested on the gentle curve of her stomach. She studied my expression with her characteristic wisdom. "You didn't kill the boy," she said, her tone dismissive. "Answer their questions and they'll go away again."

I swallowed and closed the door tight against the frame. "That's not it," I whispered. "The other cop knows you. He served with me in the army and he was there when we liberated you and the other women." I winced as she dropped the book and pushed herself up on her hands. We never spoke about the other women. One had killed herself and the other got lost in the system and ended up deported back to the place she'd escaped.

"He knows me?" Her buttocks spun as she placed her feet on the rug. "You never said."

"Error of judgement." I admitted my mistake without shame before adding the clincher. "He recognised your portrait in the lobby. What shall I do?"

Julia groaned and her back arched as she dipped forward. "Oh, Jacques! That damn painting." She ran a hand over her face and her lips turned down in sadness. "Send him in to see me."

"Roddy?" My eyes widened in horror. "No!"

Julia shook her head. "The detective. What did you tell him?"

"I said you came home sick."

"Good." She nodded and leaned forward to snatch a fluffy blanket from the armchair next to the bed. "Tell the detective I will see him here."

I kept my fingers on the door handle and watched as she drew her feet back onto the bedspread and shook the blanket over her knees. She retrieved her paperback from beneath the folds and offered me a reassuring smile. "Go, Jacques. Keep the other one occupied."

Half way down the stairs I remembered it was Friday and the narrators had designated it an even day. I almost did the splits trying to avoid the next odd step. My elbow clattered against the banister rail, and Henare met me at the lounge door with a frown. I jabbed a finger up the stairs. "Walk past the bathroom and it's the first bedroom on the right. She's unwell, but she said she'd see you."

"What kind of unwell?" Roddy's nose crinkled, and he glanced up the stairs.

I blocked his exit as Henare slid past me. "It doesn't matter. She won't see you."

"Oh." His eyes narrowed to slits. "Why? What did you tell her about me?"

"Nothing." I pushed past him into the room and turned my back on him. Digging my hands in my pockets, I took Henare's place by the bay window and searched the landscape through his eyes. Roddy's shoes clicked across the floor boards until he joined me.

"Why have you never invited me here?" His tone contained petulance. "Why didn't you tell me you got married?" His disappointment bounced off me and fell to the floor between his feet. "I thought we were friends," he concluded when I didn't answer.

Ngaruawahia sprawled across the landscape on the other side of the river, mansions interspersed with wooden villas held together with Number 8 wire. Appearances were deceptive. Poor men lived in the mansions, bowing beneath the choke hold of debt. The villas teemed with children and families, getting by on very little, but without fanfare. I sighed. "I married Julia eight years ago in Australia. Her work in Auckland means she stays away during the week."

Roddy's laugh startled me. "And it gives her a break from your neat-freak tendencies." He said it as a statement rather than a question. No one wanted to bunk with me in the army. The squad's disorganised clutter lit a fuse in my brain.

"Yeah." I accepted the excuse he'd offered and wondered if it could be true. Did my rules and strange habits drive Julia away? My shoulders slumped. Did I care? Our current arrangement suited both of us. Didn't it?

Roddy exhaled through his nose and slumped onto the sofa next to the roaring fire. "What did Nate say to you outside the RSA?" he demanded. His gaze slid to the doorway and back to my face. He lowered his voice. "I can't help you unless you tell me the truth."

I pulled my hands from my pockets and clasped them behind my back. Spreading my feet as though at-ease helped me to think. Voices rumbled overhead and Julia's soft laugh drifted to my ears. "He repeated what he said in the bar, that I hit on his girlfriend. I told Henare."

Roddy nodded. "He said you confessed to pushing him in self-defence. That fits with what Nate said when he walked back into the RSA. Why would he think that, Jack? Do you even know his girlfriend?"

I nodded and turned to face him. "Yes. I met her when I almost ran over her son on the road to Hamilton."

"You what?" Roddy rose and his belt strained at the effort of containing his stomach. "Did you tell Henare?"

I shrugged. "He didn't ask."

Roddy blew out a breath and covered his mouth with his hand. "Jack, this is bad. This is really bad."

17

MIDDLE GROUND:

THE PART OF THE PICTURE THAT IS BETWEEN THE FOREGROUND AND BACKGROUND

Henare clattered down the stairs and entered the lounge with his lips curving upward in a smile. He flipped his notebook closed and placed it into his inside jacket pocket without looking. "Your wife has corroborated your statement," he concluded. "The approximate time of death for Nathan Watson is after you left the RSA and before you drove from your property to travel to Auckland yesterday." His irises sparkled. "You stopped for petrol in Huntly at the start of your journey. The security cameras at the garage show your vehicle still covered in ice. I'm satisfied you'd driven for less than ten minutes."

He turned to leave and Roddy cleared his throat. I saw the mental dilemma in his eyes. Did it matter anymore that I'd given the skinny kid a different reason to pick a fight with me? He glanced at Henare's retreating back and relaxed as the brotherhood's unspoken loyalty won the silent battle. His footsteps pattered after Henare's, reminiscent of an obedient puppy.

The detective halted again below the portrait of Julia. He squinted up at the stunning eyes peering from beneath the moving folds of the hijab. "Remarkable," he breathed. "Where did you get it?"

"Julia." It wasn't a lie. My confusion for her had driven every brush stroke as I sought to exorcise her presence from my soul. A tsunami of sand surrounded her, each speck a testament to the disaster which threatened our coexistence. Her refusal to divorce herself from our sham relationship made real the prophecy in the painting. It would bury both of us beneath the relentless sands of time. "It's wonderful." Henare nodded and pulled open the front door. "I'd like to visit her gallery." He halted on the doormat and glanced up again, unable to tear his gaze from the image. "Are you sure it isn't an 'X'? It bears all the characteristics."

I shook my head. "No," I replied. "It's not an 'X'."

Henare shrugged. "I hope you have it insured."

Roddy gave a feckless wave as he took care on the steps of the porch. An icy breeze had brought ice from Antarctica and spread it over my elevated property. I closed the door and leaned against it, measuring the speed of my heart in groups of seven and waiting for my peace to return. A sound at the top of the stairs drew my attention. Julia sat on the top step with her chin resting in her palms.

Her slender fingers covered her mouth, and she appeared tentative. The folds of her dress covered her legs in an angelic swathe of light. "It's not an 'X'," she repeated. "It's a Jacques Alexander Jethro." Her accent mangled the consonants in my name, adding a softer edge than my mother intended. She exhaled and smiled from behind her fingers. "We should speak about the commission," she said, fracturing the last of my quietude. "I am sorry I asked you now. I fear you might betray yourself to the world."

My exhale escaped the realm of extreme pain. I lifted my palm and ran it across my face. "Come to the studio." I jerked my head backwards towards the room hidden beneath the gym. Julia's eyes glinted with pleasure at the rarity of the invitation. She jumped to her feet and glided down the stairs.

I watched the patrol car through the gate camera. It slid out during a gap in traffic, hugging the wrong side of the road until Roddy was sure no one powered around the hairpin bend to rear end him as he crossed the centre line. As Julia fetched her coat and boots against the damp air outside, I flicked through the footage from the past week. I watched my truck leave for my regular stint at the RSA on Wednesday night, the tail lights flickering as I paused to judge the road. Fast forwarding through the images, I tutted as static occupied the screen at the moment the power outage occurred. It hadn't recorded my subsequent six arrivals home. The switch across to the generator caused the surge which tripped the connection.

The insatiable compulsions which drove my actions seemed able to accept the overriding survival instinct. But my alibi now appeared shakier than I realised, the need to do the journey seven more times after the skinny kid ruined my exit threatening to mark me as guilty. Henare might have noticed the camera buried in the box for the intercom and could demand to see the footage. I tapped my lip three times before deciding not to offer it ahead of his request.

"I'm ready." Julia appeared next to me, her hazel irises flashing with excitement. A dimple in her cheek twitched as she worked to suppress her grin. With a nod I hoped appeared gracious, I snatched up my keys and opened the front door.

A bitter wind clawed at my forearms, slicing through the thin fabric of my shirt as though it didn't exist. The trip across the driveway to the garage proved hazardous, and Julia wedged her fingers into the crook of my elbow to avoid slipping on the gravel. She blew out a cloud of condensation and stamped her feet as I turned the key in the lock. The overhead lights bloomed over the gym equipment as I slammed the metal door and took a moment to catch my breath. Julia wiped her feet on the doormat and winked at me as though proving her good behaviour entitled her to progress.

Her heels rapped against the wooden floor as she hurried towards the cupboard which disguised the entrance to my studio. I'd allowed her to visit my private space twice before, the first time by accident when she'd come looking for me and the second when I needed her help to extract a canvas via the ladder. An aura of anticipation swirled around her as she tapped an impatient foot on the floor. "Hurry, Jacques. I wish to see *The Woman in The Garden*. Perhaps I could take it back with me?"

I shook my head. "It's too big for your car. Come back with the gallery's van. It still needs time to dry."

She drew her shoulders up to her ears and flapped her hands to hurry me along. "You frustrate me, Jacques! Walk faster!" I halted half way across the gym, her excitement reaching the reactive part of my brain and causing angst. She observed my reticence and calmed herself, forcing her fingers behind her back. "Sorry," she muttered. Her throat constricted as she swallowed, perhaps remembering how I'd shot her abductor for less erratic behaviour. She stepped away from the cupboard and pushed her chin beneath the folds of her coat collar.

"Turn around and cover your eyes."

Julia complied, knowing I wouldn't access the entrance with her watching. Her fingers shook with anticipation as she clamped her palms over her face and turned her back on me. Her collar muffled her words. "What will I do if anything happens to you?" she demanded. "Your work will remain buried here forever with no one able to see it."

I used the coin to turn the catch and pushed the cupboard aside. "I've written a will." My words echoed in the space between the gym and the studio. "It contains instructions." I sprang down the ladder with ease and waited for Julia. When I didn't offer her assistance, she rested her hand on my shoulder to descend, too used to my quirks to show offence when I pulled away as soon as her feet touched the floor. The coin went into the back pocket of my trousers and I surveyed the neat space with a critical eye. Bulbs mimicking daylight flared from the wall sconces when I flicked the switch.

Julia gasped and almost ran towards *The Woman in The Garden*. "J l'aime," she breathed. "She is parfait." Her fingers twitched in front of the canvas, but she resisted the urge to touch the tacky oils hugging the woman's skirt. "When can I take her?"

I exhaled and sighed. What Julia judged a masterpiece filled me with irritation. But for the vibrant flower, I'd painted a replica of the image in the photograph, yet the lack of symmetry irked me. My art rebelled against the order and control in my life, forcing me to abandon my compulsions and habits in favour of some other quality I couldn't name. The paint brush unleashed the same monster which Julia aroused in me, driving me towards pleasure and pain in equal measure. I'd learned to hate what I couldn't control but succumbed to it like an addict. "It's still drying." I reiterated the words and let her draw her own conclusion. A dehumidifier whirred in the corner, sucking out the damp Waikato air to leave the perfect conditions for oils.

"I don't trust you." She narrowed her eyes and cocked her head at me. "You'll decide you hate some part of it and destroy it. Like before."

I clamped my teeth over my lower lip and winced. She knew me too well, her concerns legitimate. It had happened once, and I'd forced her to return the deposit to the client. If something about the painting offended my fragile rules, I couldn't correct my mistakes and produce it again. My mind wasn't wired for do-overs.

"I promise not to destroy it." Speaking the words made them true somehow, though I'd need to face the painting away from me to avoid the critic in my head.

"Okay." Julia's shoulders dropped as she relaxed. "I know you'll keep your word."

My lips twisted, and I frowned. "What about Mother? You promised."

She nodded. "I did." She drew her mobile phone from her coat pocket. "There's no signal down here. I'll call him again from upstairs."

"Thank you." The glass screen which contained the drift from the spray paint drew my interest. A blob of red had created a bloom of pink mist, which stuck to the surface like blood. Images appeared in front of my inner vision as though vomited from a hidden vault in my mind, brain matter mixed with shards of bone and granular white flesh. I inhaled a ragged breath and my fists clenched in front of my eyes. The army trained me to become the perfect killing machine, driven by their goals and guaranteed to complete them to the last without fail. But they hadn't factored in the other toll to my person, the rolling images of death and corruption which stained my fingers and burned into my eyeballs. I would never be clean.

"Jacques!" Julia's sharp rebuke shocked me, and I gulped as I returned to the studio. The chill air bit through my shirt and I shivered. I glanced at the glass again, surprised to see blue paint and not red speckling the translucent sheet. My body rocked as Julia gripped my elbows and shook me. Peppermint tingled against my nostrils from where she'd brushed her teeth after lunch. "Jacques." She spoke my name again, her version of it containing a familiar softness. She inhaled and dropped her chin. "How do you work in this dungeon without going mad?"

I snorted, the laughter bubbling in my chest containing sincerity. "I'm already mad."

"You and me both." Her lips parted in a sad smile. She shivered and withdrew her hands. "We have much to discuss. The client is demanding a completion date for the dock mural. Are you sure this is a good idea?"

A genuine smile flickered across my lips. "Yes. Do you have the dimensions of the wall he wants painted?"

Julia's delicate nose wrinkled and her eyes resumed their haunted look. She wrapped her arms around herself. "It's in the email I sent you early this morning. But it faces the harbour, Jacques. Every boat entering the dock will see it. The world will view it through the high-profile sporting events filmed there. And the America's Cup is due to be held on the water next year. If you try to make a statement, he will destroy it." She touched my arm with tentative fingers. "It upset you that the council accidentally painted over the five-dollar commission. You need to consider this piece with care because it affects us both."

I nodded and forced my teeth to unclench. My words stuttered free. "I didn't care about the mural." My next swallow created an audible gulp. "I created it for someone. They took away my gift."

Julia tutted and exhaled a minty breath. "I hope you know what you're doing, mon cher."

18

BAROQUE:

A TERM MEANING COMPLEX, DRAMATIC AND EXTRAVAGANT

We discussed the logistics of the job, but not the content. Julia's surprise would be as genuine as those who intended to view the reveal. I never occupied myself with thoughts of who might attend because I wouldn't stick around for the final curtain. My mind strayed to the early days of my art career when I'd decorated walls around Auckland city like a criminal. Early morning commuters admired my handiwork, pondering my identity and entertained by media speculation. I loved the freedom of those works best, their transient beauty fragile at the behest of the elements. It didn't matter that others defaced them because I never returned to view their fading colours. They remained etched in my memory forever, a visual expression of my torturous thoughts. They featured in my inner vision as the army redeployed me on another peace keeping mission which inevitably ended in someone else's death.

"Jacques?" Julia's teeth chattered. "Can we go back to the house?"

"Yes." I set my pencil on the notebook so it sat perpendicular with the binding. "You'll organise the heavy equipment and the scaffold?"

She nodded and stammered her words. I hadn't noticed the drop in temperature as we'd mused over proportions. "The company will insist that an operative accompanies you on the scissor lift. It's their health and safety policy. How will you ensure he isn't able to identify you in the future?"

"I'll wait until we're back on the ground and then kill him."

Julia's jaw dropped and her eyes widened. The stark overhead lights cast lines and shadows over her face from her eyelashes. "What?" She exhaled and stamped her foot. "Your jokes are not funny."

"I wasn't joking." My lips quirked upwards. I'd spent my existence unintentionally riling every authority figure in my life without understanding how. Knowing I could press Julia's buttons at will amused me. She slapped my arm before extricating herself from the curtained area. Her heels clicked against the concrete floor.

Images and possibilities played on the canvas of my mind as we ate leftover chicken for dinner. I laid on the sofa in the overly warm lounge and closed my eyes. The rattle of the ball bearing in the bottom of each spray can created the symphony for my planning, my ear buds funnelling Beethoven's *Moonlight Sonata* to soothe my soul. Julia unearthed the TV and watched it with the sound turned low, snoozing on the sofa opposite me.

A phone call disturbed our reverie and she sat up straight to take it. Her tone sounded clipped as she snatched her mobile from the coffee table and listened to the speaker's message. "Merci. I'll tell him." She blew out a ragged breath as she ended the call, staring at the darkened phone screen for a while before looking up at me. Her sudden change of mood had banished the comforting rattle from my mind and forced me to focus.

"Something is wrong." I pushed myself upright, using my stomach muscles. My ear buds fell to the floor and disconnected themselves from my phone. An atmosphere of dread shrouded her and her irises glittered with a peculiar light.

"Jacques, I'm so sorry," she began. "There's no easy way to say this, but my friend has discovered that your mother died this afternoon at a few minutes after three o'clock. The prison authority is remiss for not informing you." She set her phone on the cushion next to her and gave it a push with her index finger. It shifted sideways as though accepting responsibility for bearing the awful news that I was now completely alone.

My feet hit the rug, and I shifted them to sit square. No useful words presented themselves in my empty brain, so I kept silent.

"He said you can make a formal complaint." Julia's words faded as she recognised their futility for herself.

I rose on wobbling knees and forced my feet to carry me across the room. I needed to spend time alone, to indulge in the compulsions and numbers which would carry me through this new war zone. Mother's voice filled my head with her laughter as though she walked next to me. But she hadn't done more than sit opposite me for years, hugging the table which separated us. Prison guards had listened to our conversations with impassive stares, ready to rebuke physical contact or halt the passing of drugs or weapons. She walked with me only in my memories of childhood, her bright disposition and illimitable faith acting as the guiding light in my grey world.

I took myself to bed and laid in the darkness with my eyes open. Shadows played on the ceiling as the bush outside continued with its busy cycle of life. I hadn't cried for years, though I wouldn't have rejected the tears had my body created them in tribute. She'd done her very best for me and I owed her more than words could express.

My mind turned to thoughts of my father. He'd beaten and subdued my mother without mercy behind closed doors while shining in the spotlight of public approval. He wounded her in the comfort of a penthouse with a sea view, but it made no difference to the bruises she hid beneath silky scarves and department store makeup. The welts and broken bones hurt just the same as if he'd beaten her in a hovel.

He'd hit me once. I'm sure he regretted it every time he looked in a mirror.

The bedroom door slid open and light from the hallway created a yellow triangle on the floor. "Jacques?" Julia spoke with softness. When I didn't answer, she widened the gap and entered my safe space with her germs and bad news.

"I'm sleeping." Uncharacteristic petulance entered my tone. With my arms and legs stretched out like those of a corpse, I might have been telling the truth.

Julia snorted. "It's twelve minutes past seven in the evening and you're a grown man." She stepped across the rug and slumped onto the edge of the bed. "No one sleeps this early, not even you."

"You gave me bad news." Accusation drifted between the words and she brushed it aside with ease.

"That's the other reason I know you're not sleeping." She exhaled. "Je suis désolé, mon cher. But perhaps it's best you hear it from someone who cares for you."

I grew silent as her words swirled around in my mind. Was it better? Did it matter who pronounced the judgement? My shoulders relaxed and some of the tension filtered from my chest to pool beneath me as a puddle of grief. "No more Thursdays at ten o'clock."

"Perhaps I can call you instead?" Julia dropped her voice to a whisper. "Would you wear a smart shirt and tie for me?"

My hair shuffled against the pillow as I shook my head. "You'd get busy and forget."

The light refracted off Julia's black curls as she nodded in acceptance of my judgement. "Oui. And besides, I prefer you naked." She released a laugh filled with tiredness. I squinted as clothing rustled and the light turned her white dress into a blaze of yellow. It clicked with static as she cast it onto the floor. Her underwear followed, and she padded to the other side of the bed and lifted the covers. A cool draught accompanied her, sliding over the mattress and wrapping its icy fingers around my limbs.

Julia's hair tickled my skin as she pressed a gentle kiss against my shoulder. "We still have each other," she whispered. She rolled onto her side and slithered her body over mine, moulding herself to fit my shape. The coolness of her skin and its silken quality acted as a balm to my inner fretting. Numbers rose and fell again with a futile bounce as they lost their essence in the face of her ethereal pull. They evaded me, supplanted by a more powerful force.

Julia's toes brushed the tops of my feet in a gentle stroking motion, and I closed my eyes and pictured her breasts against the fine hair covering my chest. My fingers cracked the casing of the fists holding them hostage and snaked their way through the covers to rest in the curve of her spine. Warmth blossomed through me and I wrapped my legs around hers, pinning her to me so I could pour my whole life into this moment. My lips found hers in the darkness, our tongues dancing in a hungry duet of need.

Dying beneath the subtle ecstasy of Julia's tongue and fingers would be a hell of a way to go. I prayed it would be excruciating. I hoped she'd take her time.

19

CANON:

A GROUP OF ARTISTIC, LITERARY, OR MUSICAL WORKS THAT ARE ACCEPTED AS REPRESENTING A FIELD

I slipped from the bed while darkness still shrouded the mountain, driving to the small township for bread and milk. Familiar faces smiled in recognition as I wandered the aisles of the tiny supermarket in search of something nice to give Julia for breakfast. I settled on fresh eggs with organic, wholegrain bread and added a bunch of lilies to my basket on the way to the counter.

"Freezing out there." The cashier jerked her grey head towards the doors sliding open to admit another early customer and a following breeze. She shivered in her store branded duffel coat as she pushed the bread across the scanner. "It's tragic about that young man dying in the river, isn't it?" The brown eyebrow she raised in question didn't match the steel curls on her head. I frowned and my mind spun off in distractions of wondering which was the fake. A dot of pencil near the bridge of her nose gave the game away. She'd coloured in her fading eyebrows and missed. "You didn't hear about it then?" She shoved the flowers across the scanner and plastered a smile onto her face. "These are fresh today. Are they for someone special?"

I ignored her question and paid using my card. She waved me off like an old friend, anyway, as though I'd taken part in her barrage of quizzing without reluctance. My phone rang as I climbed into my truck and I connected the call without thinking. Henare's voice filled my vehicle. "Mr Jethro. It's come to my attention that you drove Nathan Watson's partner and their two children to the Women's Refuge safe house in Hamilton last week." *Roddy*. I closed my lids and let my eyes roll beneath them in ghoulish paroxysms of frustration. "I'm giving you the benefit of the doubt, Mr Jethro. Did you forget to mention it?"

I stared at the wall in front of my truck, focussing on the bricks and judging them perfect enough to count. I reached seven before Henare cleared his throat in an indication of his impatience. A gulp issued from my throat as I swallowed. Nine, ten, eleven, twelve. I could stop. "You didn't ask," I offered. "I'd never met her before. Her son ran out in front of my truck. She came to my window and asked for a ride to Hamilton."

Henare exhaled. "Let's get this straight. You almost killed her child and then she asked for a ride and you gave it?"

"Yes." I saw her face in my mind's eye, tears streaking her porcelain cheeks. A split lip and a black bruise beneath each of her vivid blue eyes betrayed a woman who'd had enough.

"What did she say?" Henare demanded. "Thanks for not killing my kid and can you give me a half an hour ride out of your way?" Sarcasm laced his tone.

"She didn't say that." Her daughter's sobbing filled my head. "She said she needed to get to safety, or he'd kill her. Her girl cried all the way to the refuge but her boy remained silent." An eerie silence. I remembered the need to stuff my own head with distraction, the numbers arriving to file past my inner vision on bodies created by dancing playing cards. They filled the void occupied by the violence and I'd kept them. I'd wanted to communicate my gift to the stony-faced boy but a glance in my rear-view mirror told me he'd found his own distraction techniques. They'd last until he stumbled across something better, something chemical and able to produce highs scalding enough to block out the hopelessness. The animalistic cries of a battered parent never left the eardrums, no matter what distance the hearer put between them.

I exhaled. Henare didn't like me. I'd witnessed his attitude in classmates, teachers, and army captains who wrote me off as stupid or weird. I'd followed orders to the final full stop and instead of endearing myself to my superiors, it generated suspicion instead. Henare coughed into the phone, a jarring, fluid sound which seemed deliberate. "You need to add to your statement," he concluded. "Can you come to the station now?"

A drop of water glistened on the white petal of a lily, the bunch of flowers nestled against the eggs to stop either of them from catapulting off the passenger seat. "I'll come later," I agreed.

"No, I need you to come now, Mr Jethro. Be here in ten minutes and don't make me come looking for you." A click ended the call and the fizz of static tickled my ears. The truck's digital dashboard displayed the moving image of a receiver being replaced on an old-fashioned telephone by an unseen hand. A curly cord dangled out of view.

I toyed with the notion of disobeying him. I'd noticed how my adherence to rules and regulations deviated at the point I considered my own safety under threat. He viewed me as an anomaly on the canvas of his workmanship. If he could smudge out my existence, I imagined he'd take the chance to hide me away in a prison cell. I glanced at Julia's lilies and winced. The droplet of water slid from the petal as I touched it with my index finger. How would I know if they were thirsty?

Julia had never visited Mother in prison. I used that fact to deduce the unlikelihood of her visiting me, either. It helped with the choice to drive the five hundred metres to the police station and park on the narrow street opposite the front door. I left my shopping on the front seat and tucked my phone into my back pocket.

"Can I help you?" A blonde woman behind the counter shuffled paperwork before clipping it together with a staple. I pursed my lips to hide my grinding teeth. Her carelessness stopped the pages sitting straight, the bottom one sticking out, proud of the rest. I imagined Tahlia's daughter showing more intelligence in compiling the bundle. A twitch tapped in my cheek below the scar from a stray shard of wood blown from a building in Helmand Province. Her question stymied me. She probably could help me. Why else would she spend eight hours sitting behind the desk in a police station. My mind strayed into a cul-de-sac, and I blinked and stared at her.

She shifted in her seat in discomfort and reached for something beneath the desk. I pictured her fingers seeking the panic button located near her right knee and pressing. My brain opened a passage in the cul-de-sac and my thoughts plunged through with possibilities and scenarios of what might happen. I wanted to see, but then Julia wouldn't get her lilies. And she wouldn't visit me in prison.

"Ah, Mr Jethro." Henare burst through the security door and nodded to the woman behind the counter. "Come with me."

I plastered what I hoped was a conciliatory smile onto my lips, but the widening of the woman's eyes suggested it didn't look as I imagined. My body turned like a plank of wood as I followed Henare through the door and into the dull hallway behind it. He guided me back to the child's bedroom and I halted in the doorway, not wanting to be trapped in the paradox. "I don't like it in here." A faded yellow sticker of a floating balloon revealed itself next to the window as the curtain moved in the breeze. Bars on the outside of the frame deterred enthusiastic burglars. The rusting metal cast long diagonal shadows like railway tracks across the mustard carpet.

Henare nudged me in the spine, causing me to move away from his touch. "You and me both, buddy," he answered with a sigh. "I can't quite believe my promotion involved moving from a nice open plan office to this."

"Leave the door open," I growled as Henare fixed his fingers over the brass knob. Though I'd been in the room just the day before, an oppressive quality had taken up residence during the intervening hours. I wanted no part of it.

Henare tutted and his shoulders slumped in defeat. Realising that unless he arrested me without just cause, he couldn't force me to occupy the battered plastic chair opposite his desk. He waved his right hand in dismissal and sank into his creaky office chair. "Fine," he sighed. "I'll ask you questions, write the answers, and you can sign them. If I still worked in Hamilton, I'd have recording equipment, a willing constable and an air-conditioned interview room."

I frowned. Henare spoke of promotion with enough irony to convey the actual issue. His move to Ngaruawahia was less of an elevation and more of a punishment. Closing the case involving the skinny kid might redeem his career. My mind set to wondering what Henare had done to get sent to the boonies. A list of possible infractions scrolled past my inner vision.

"What are you grinning at?" he snapped, looking up from his empty refill pad. A ball-point pen pivoted between his middle finger and his thumb.

I hadn't realised my facial muscles had done their own thing and schooled them back into their safe, impassive mask. "You had an affair," I blurted.

His eyes widened, and he threw his pen on the pad. It bounced twice before rolling between a green stapler and a plastic package containing a sandwich from the dairy around the corner. Egg and beetroot, the packet read. I swallowed, recognising the sudden urgency to get this process finished. The claustrophobia induced by the room and Henare's dissatisfied air wouldn't improve after he'd released the sulphur from his sandwiches.

"Bloody Roddy!" He thumped the desk and the sandwich packet toppled over sideways.

"No." I jerked my head at his fists. My body slipped into the natural at-ease posture, finding solace in the pose's familiarity. It increased my confidence as my mind panicked over Julia's wilting lilies on the front seat of my truck. "You have a tan line on your ring finger from a recent separation. Your shirt is the same one from yesterday and rumpled. I suspect your partner ironed them for you, so you never bothered to learn. A broken marriage wouldn't alarm the chief constable enough to deploy you here, so you crapped on your own doorstep somehow."

Henare released an expletive which I hadn't heard at such proximity since leaving the army. I winced and considered the shower I'd take when I got home. Maybe with Julia after I gave her the lilies. "Just answer the questions," he snarled. Unable to locate the pen lying right under his nose, he reached in his drawer for another, yelping as the mechanism caused it to slide shut over his finger. Anger rolled off him in waves and I closed one eye as he bowed his head to the pad of paper, imagining a single shot putting him out of his misery. If I timed it just right, the curtain would lift in the breeze and his brain matter would fill the faded yellow balloon sticker.

"Mr Jethro!" His shout caused my limbs to jerk. "What date did you pick up Nathan Watson's partner?"

I blinked. "I didn't pick her up."

His jaw dropped. "So, why are you here?" he screamed. It couldn't be healthy, all that blood pooling in his face. *'One kill shot would do it,'* the narrating voice in my head informed me. But then it changed tack. '*The lilies are dying; the lilies are dying.*' it wailed.

20

CARICATURE:

A RENDERING, USUALLY A DRAWING, OF A PERSON OR THING WITH EXAGGERATED OR DISTORTED FEATURES

The blonde woman's face appeared in the doorway, and she eyed my prone stance with concern. "Is everything okay, Detective Sergeant?" she asked.

"Yes." Henare choked out his reply and searched in his drawer for another pen, his fingers returning empty. "Please, can you fetch me something to write with?"

She trotted away on sensible flat soles, her mid-length hair bouncing against her white shirt. "Obviously your broken legs mean you can't get it for yourself," she muttered under her breath, her words in time with the staccato beat of her steps.

Henare released a long breath and leaned back in his seat to observe me through narrowed eyelids. "Did you give Nathan Watson's partner and children a ride to Hamilton?" he growled.

"Yes." I nodded as I affirmed his statement.

He swallowed and closed his eyes. "So, why did you just tell me you didn't pick her up?"

I frowned, deciding Henare was probably as stupid as I'd first concluded. Mother said initial impressions were usually correct. At the thought of her smiling face when she said it, my shoulders drooped. "My mother died yesterday." My mind fretted over the lilies again and I wanted to go home to Julia.

Henare paused and his teeth closed with a snap. "I'm sorry." He spoke the words, but he didn't mean them. The obligatory condolence allowed him to push on with his pathetic interview. I'd seen interrogations conducted using methods that would ensure he couldn't touch his egg and beetroot sandwich with the same enthusiasm after viewing the results of decayed brain matter. "Then let's get this over with and you can go home to your wife." He sighed and rubbed a hand over his face. "What am I not understanding, Mr Jethro? Did you, or did you not give Tahlia Hendry a ride to Hamilton?"

"I did." I studied his fingers as the knobbly knuckles bunched and released. The blonde woman returned with a handful of pens and dumped them on the desk. The pile collapsed like a disaster in a logging yard. Two more dashed for the edge of the desk and bounced against the mustard carpet. Needing to rescue the lilies, I dug for words to end the impasse. "I gave her a ride, but I didn't pick her up. Married men shouldn't pick up girls."

Henare exhaled hard enough to lift the top sheet of paper. "Right," he sighed. "Just describe what happened please, Mr Jethro. In your own words."

I lifted my gaze to the ceiling. The stained surface morphed into a sheet of white canvas and I mapped out my movements on the previous Monday, spreading it before me as a time line. The details proved trickier than I'd first imagined, involving a delivery of art supplies for 'X' from an overseas company. Local stores showed too much interest in projects involving anything over a hobbyist's volume, but the American corporate didn't care as long as they received payment. I glanced down at my feet and moved my right cowboy boot parallel with the left before starting my explanation. Henare's pen wobbled in anticipation.

"I missed the delivery of a parcel because I didn't hear the gate buzzer. The courier driver took it back to the depot at 32 to 36 Gallagher Drive in Hamilton." I waited for Henare to finish writing before adding the postal code. He raised his eyebrow but copied it onto the page. "I drove along Great South Road towards the eighty kilometres per hour sign at twelve minutes past two, and a child ran into the road. I braked and stopped, but the truck left two black lines of rubber on the road."

"You got out of the vehicle?" Henare spoke without looking up at me.

"No. I noticed the tracks on the way home."

He blinked. "I mean, you got out to check on the child?"

"No." I shifted my gaze back to the ceiling. "His mother put her arms around him and took him back onto the verge. A girl waited there, clutching a teddy bear with a single button eye and a kerchief with red spots on white fabric." My fingers lifted to touch the cravat at my neck. It wasn't as good as Julia's, but I'd reverse engineered her loop to create something similar. I swallowed. "The bear had the single button eye and the kerchief. Put the comma after 'there' but not after 'teddy bear,' or the girl will have those attributes."

A glance at Henare showed him biting hard enough on his lower lip to create a white welt in the space beneath his teeth. *Frustration.* I recognised it and steered my mind back to sift through the information. "The woman opened the passenger door and apologised. She kept looking back at a house behind her."

Henare nodded. "Nathan Watson shared a house with her. Blue with a white picket fence?"

I frowned at his ridiculous test. "No. Next door. Paint peeling off the window frames and a hole from a kick in the green front door."

"Right." He sounded happier and his slanted writing lost its flat quality. Swirls accompanied the description of the house. "Continue." He waved the pen at me.

"She asked if I was travelling to Hamilton. I said the address of the courier service but she wasn't interested. She pushed the children into the back seats and climbed in. Kept apologising."

"What were her exact words?"

I closed my eyes to picture her frightened expression, the tears streaked under the bruises and her shaking fingers pressed together in her lap. "She said, *'I need to get away from him or he'll kill me. Do you know anywhere safe I can go?'* I suggested the Women's Refuge in Hamilton and drove her there."

"Why did you know the location of a refuge for battered women?" His tone held incredulity. "Those places are secret."

I licked my lips before responding. Aside from Mother's distaste for lying, I found it used too much mental energy and veered away from it as a life choice. Telling lies involved too many potential loose ends and sent my internal narrators into a whirl of speculation. It was something best avoided. So, I stuck to the truth. "Mother and I lived there from 12th June to 15th September 1996."

Henare's silence made me glance at him. A deep frown gouged lines in his pasty forehead. I didn't want to tell him anything more and weighed up the probability of his asking. Curiosity would make him want to, but it held no direct relevance to the case. He didn't need to know that we'd lived there twice more after that, each time dragged back to Auckland by my father's minions. Happy times in my memory, they provided spaces of peace and silence before the inevitable rages which punctuated our homecoming.

"Okay." Henare tapped his pen on the paper. "Did you know Tahlia Hendry before that day?"

"No." I shook my head, and he seemed satisfied. It seemed irrelevant to add that I'd seen her with the skinny kid, but never spoken to her before the day of the near miss.

"Have you seen her since?"

"No." I turned to stare along the hallway. The blonde woman sang in the front reception. She warbled a pop song in a pitch too high for her vocal cords. It reminded me of the straining of a fan in hot weather.

"Okay." Henare pushed the paper and the pen towards me. "Sign this and then you can leave."

I blanched at the thought of touching the pen he'd handled, and my upper lip curled over in disgust. My mind performed a quick calculation of the potential contaminants on the surface of the other pens the woman left on his desk. She'd smelled of hand soap and perfume and I risked Henare's offence by reaching for one which had rolled next to a wilting potted plant. I speed read his crabbed notes and scrawled my name at the bottom. He'd already added the date.

"Rhona!" Henare yelled for the blonde woman, and I jumped at the unexpectedness of his shout. The singing halted, followed by a ringing expletive. She reappeared in the doorway. He didn't wait for her to question the summons, flapping my statement in the air between us. "Photocopy this and give the duplicate to Mr Jethro," he instructed. "Then type it up and add it to the system."

She cocked her head and frowned. "I'm a desk attendant, not a personal assistant." Her tone held a bite, which Henare ignored. She left the room with a flounce, the vibration from her angry feet sending two more pens from the desk to the floor.

I turned to follow her and Henare's next sentence stalled me. "Does the camera at your gate make recordings when someone activates the system?" he asked. "Either by pressing the buzzer or by you opening the gate?"

"Yes." I shoved my right hand behind my back and tapped out beats of three with my thumb and middle finger.

"Can I get a look at the footage from Wednesday?" He raised an eyebrow in speculation. "It'll give you a stronger alibi."

I schooled my face into its characteristic blank mask and shook my head. "Sorry. A truck clipped the box at the edge of the property that night and wiped out the electrics. The generator surged and killed the camera. The gate mechanism is on a separate fuse and I went straight to the gym in my garage. I didn't realise until the next morning that it had tripped."

Henare wrinkled his nose. "You don't mind if I check with the power company? I take it you reported it?"

"Yes." I gave a confident nod and turned towards the hallway without looking back at him.

"Did you have a nice anniversary?" His question left the air molecules vibrating. Unable to think of a decent answer, I kept walking, my heels clicking against rotten floorboards in desperate need of replacing.

21

CHINE COLLÉ:

A TECHNIQUE, USED IN CONJUNCTION WITH PRINTMAKING PROCESSES SUCH AS ETCHING OR LITHOGRAPHY

The sun pushing through the grey clouds had doused my truck with heat. It seemed determined to punish my frivolity by concentrating its super-heated rays on Julia's unfortunate lilies. I sat in the driver's seat and lifted the bunch in careful fingers. The heavy bulbous heads bobbed within the plastic wrapper, their stalks arched and lolling like the necks of dead swans. Rage mingled with sadness to create a suffocating potion in my chest. I lacked the energy to drive back to the supermarket and replace them.

Settling the flowers on the seat with the tenderness of a parent, I drove home to my eyrie in the mountains.

A dry patch represented the space where Julia's Mercedes had sheltered the driveway from the overnight rain. Sunshine glittered on the aggregate showing through the gravel. She'd gone.

A curious vacancy opened up in my chest and I tapped my sternum one hundred and forty-four times while I waited for the pain to alleviate. No Mother. No Julia. The eggs, the lilies, and the special bread nestled on the passenger seat with an air of rejection. I didn't know what to do with them in Julia's absence and acknowledged a sense of confusion settling over my head. I didn't know what to do with myself, either.

The empty house shrouded me as I stepped over the threshold. I carried my shopping into the kitchen and focussed on reviving the lilies. It seemed important to nurse them back to health, dredging up an old trick of Mother's. A drop of bleach went into the bottom of the makeshift vase, a jam jar from the recycling bin stepping up to accept the challenge. I filled it with water to just beneath the lip and unwrapped the flowers, poking their stalks into the liquid one at a time. They lolled like drunks over a toilet bowl, shuffling from side to side as I set the jar on the counter. Their helpless state reflected mine with more parallel than I could bear, and I found a ball of string in the cupboard over the microwave. I used it to tie the bunch together, forcing their heads upright and growing frustrated when they listed to one side as a unit.

"It's no good," I whispered to the empty kitchen. Bending at the knees, I bobbed up and down seven times. Scenarios filtered through my mind, each resulting in the death of the flowers and the emptiness of the jar without them. The presence of the lilies turned it into a vase. Only their existence had salvaged it from the waste.

It occurred to me that Julia turned me into a husband. Without her, I was a strange man hiding on a mountain, producing priceless paintings in anonymity.

She answered on the first ring and I stuttered my sentence without a greeting. "Come back," I asked, the second request in our eight-year marriage.

"Sorry." She lowered her voice. "I left a note upstairs on your pillow. Gordon called. He's complaining about my absence yesterday. I needed to get back for the exhibition starting tonight, but I don't know how much longer I can take this." Her inhale betrayed exasperation, and I cocked my head, the fresh problem occupying my busy brain.

"You don't like it there?" I'd bought the thirty percent share in the art gallery because she'd seemed interested. But on reflection, it suited me to have someone on the inside distributing my work. Mother said it would all blow up in my face. Was this what she'd meant? It sounded as though Gordon had turned his powerlessness into spite.

Julia exhaled into the phone. "I don't know, Jacques. He wants more of your paintings to sell. His wife has picked out a mansion in Devonport and you're his ticket to success. I told him *The Woman in The Garden* is almost ready. Now, he wants to know when the next one is coming. And the next and the next. He's never satisfied."

Tiredness laced her tone, and I imagined her scrubbing at her eyes and spreading Kohl across her high cheekbones.

"I'll find another solution to my distribution issues." The decision galvanised me, and happy endorphins flooded my blood cells.

Julia turned aside from her phone and she whispered to her assistant. "What do you mean he's playing golf today?" she demanded. "The exhibitors arrive in half an hour." For a moment, she forgot about me as Gordon's nasal voice rang out in the echoing open space of the gallery.

"You took yesterday, so I'm taking today and tomorrow." Petulance carried across the distance. "I've told the client he can have *The Woman in The Garden* by Monday, so you need to phone him and organise delivery." The tapping of Gordon's patent leather shoes grew closer and his hissed threat extended further than he imagined possible. "I want to see more paintings coming through from now on, and we're taking a bigger commission. Whoever 'X' is, he or she has enjoyed a cushy ride until now, with forty percent commission. Other galleries charge fifty. We need to raise ours to match theirs."

Julia exhaled. "We can talk about that later, Gordon. Please stay for now. I'm unwell and Mandy can't cope alone with the set-up of the exhibition."

Her words left my lungs stuck in an inhale. It was the second time she'd claimed a malaise, and I realised I'd assumed the first time was a ruse to defend me against

Henare. Gordon's voice burred in the background like a knife sharpener and I tapped beats of three on the floorboards with the toe of my cowboy boot and waited for the fear to subside.

"Jacques? Sorry." Julia exhaled. Gordon's steps thrummed away into the distance.

"You're unwell." The statement held a harshness I hadn't intended. "What can I do?"

Julia's swallow didn't bother me in the same way as Henare's. "I should go," she sighed. "He's gone to the golf club, which leaves Mandy and I coping alone across the weekend. I'll call you later, Jacques." The line cut and a static ringing replaced her hazy tones.

Mother's death crowded into the silence, my inability to contact her slicing like a cleaver through my mind. Julia represented the last anchor in my precarious world. Our bond changed because she'd helped me with Henare's suspicions. She'd done something other than ferry and sell my art to strangers. She'd perjured herself for me. Henare had wished me a happy anniversary, but our ninth year of marriage loomed ahead on the horizon in two months, four days, twelve hours and twenty-five seconds. I wracked my brain for clues and wished I'd asked Julia what fictitious reminder she'd conjured for the detective's benefit. Running through the calendar built into my mind produced nothing.

Instead, I turned my interest towards the prison I'd inadvertently created for Julia. Walls built from kindness in place of barbed wire. But obligation still at its centre.

22

CITYSCAPE:

AN IMAGE WITH URBAN SCENERY AS ITS PRIMARY FOCUS

The lawyer phoned me straight back. He earned too much from my retainer to ignore me for more than a few hours. "How can I help you, Mr Jethro?" he asked, his tone jovial. His open question added a level of safety not experienced with the receptionist at the police station. It gave me room to move, and the words tumbled free with more ease.

"Shortland Gallery." I didn't bother with niceties, grateful he didn't expect them. "Instruct an agent to sell the thirty percent interest owned by the Dexarn Trust."

"Ohkay." A pen scratched on paper. "When?"

"Now." I exhaled, relief causing my fingers and toes to tingle. "Value it at today's equity. Give the majority shareholder the chance to buy us out but put a limit on the time he has to pull the money together."

Mouth noises issued into my ear, and I pulled the phone away with a grimace of distaste. I switched the phone to speaker and placed it on the counter, catching the end of his sentence. The lawyer's voice echoed off the kitchen cupboards as he resumed the conversation. "There's a ten-day option on the initial contract. It didn't matter back then because the turnover wasn't much. He could have scraped that together with a payday loan." He snorted at his own joke and I blinked, grateful the sound hadn't ricocheted around my eardrum. "It's a bit of a different story now, though," he surmised. "I went to an exhibition there last month. It's become the vogue place to snag art by up-and-coming New Zealand talent. The buyer there has a real eye for what's hot. Being an exclusive retailer for 'X' has catapulted the business into art history. You might need to relax the terms of the original contract, or the other guy won't stand a chance at raising the money." Fingers tapped on a keyboard. "Rossie. Yeah, Gordon Rossie. It looks like he doesn't own the property. The building is on a lease, so he'll have to leverage any mortgage on the viability of the business itself."

"I don't care." A New Zealand falcon soared over the mountain behind the house, its tawny colours camouflaged against the vibrant shades of green. It captured my attention and my fingers twitched, aching for the solidity of a paintbrush. "Get it done. You can call him now and then follow it up in writing."

The lawyer hissed in discomfort. "Do you know if he has an exclusivity clause with 'X'? That might cause difficulties, as I understand from the media that he only deals with that gallery."

"There's no exclusivity clause." A smile broke out across my lips. "X can sell wherever he likes."

"Okay. Then Gordon Rossie better hope he doesn't. I'll activate everything now." A swishing sound indicated the lawyer rubbing his hands together, perhaps at the thought of his extra fee. "Do you want to invest the profit into anything else?"

"Maybe. I'll let you know."

If the man had ever guessed my identity as the painter, he knew better than to join the dots for the media. The lawyer who leaked JK Rowling's pseudonym had learned the lesson for everyone in the legal industry. He exhaled. "I'm about to ruin someone's day." A wistfulness entered his tone. "I might have to ask him to sit down first."

My eyes narrowed as the falcon swooped at an unseen point on the floor of the bush, bored with tracking its prey and intent on a kill. I shrugged before remembering the lawyer couldn't witness my indifference. Gordon had forgotten who pulled his ailing gallery full of wonky pottery and vanity pieces into the limelight. He'd underestimated Julia's skill as a saleswoman and connoisseur of beauty. I'd remind him just as he approached the first tee with his Fair Isle sweater and matching socks. But it wouldn't be my voice he heard.

Killing the conversation without a goodbye, I figured Julia deserved a warning. She ignored my call and her phone sent an automated text, promising she'd phone back later once she became free. I responded with a curt message.

'It's over. Get out before he comes back. He'll be angry.'

The phone rang as I balanced it in my palm and considered sending Julia another message. Imagining her soft tones whispering into my ear, I connected the call and waited for her to speak. Henare's voice boomed from the device. "Mr Jethro?" He spat my name like a curse.

"What?" I jerked in surprise at the failure of the Caller ID function, which showed him phoning from a private number.

"I owe you an apology." He didn't sound sorry, his tone brash and bucolic. "The body fished from the river wasn't Nathan Watson's." He cleared his throat. "False alarm."

Confusion stole my words, running around the room with the essence of my irritation and disappearing into the lobby. It left me in a shroud of silence. Henare moderated his tone. "He's still missing and we're searching for him, but he's not dead."

"He's not dead." I repeated the words as though I believed their implications.

Henare continued. "It seems this kid fell into the river on Wednesday night and washed up at Mercer. Watson's girlfriend gave a positive identification based on the clothing, but we drove the mother up to look this morning. The chief just phoned me. Case of mistaken identity. Nathan Watson had a birthmark on his right thigh and this kid doesn't."

"He's not dead." The fate of the skinny kid didn't bother me, but it meant Henare couldn't stop me returning to Auckland and rescuing Julia. "Okay."

He tutted. "Bit embarrassing. Are you satisfied with a verbal apology?"

I had no words, so I ended the call without replying.

"This isn't how Saturday should go." I spoke into the silence as I sped along the new expressway between Huntly and Auckland. The steady vibration of my tyres against the fresh asphalt created a sense of peace. It washed over me and I drove on autopilot, my mind still and blissfully empty. It wasn't how Saturdays usually looked, but my routine for the sixth day of the week paled in importance against the need to liberate Julia again. The notion of being useful provided me with a contented background hum.

Downtown traffic snarled my progress, reducing my speed to a frustrating crawl as I neared the gallery. I hadn't visited for years and the dereliction of buildings in the city centre took me by surprise. No longer meeting the requirements for earthquake safety, the old stalwarts wore boarded faces as committees decided their fate. The surviving businesses hid their struggles beneath bright facades, but an air of dejection hung over the street. An inexplicable nervousness infused my blood, and I parked and stayed in the truck for longer than I'd planned.

My fingers dropped coins into the parking meter as a traffic warden ambled along the pavement on the other side of the road. Cars lined up bumper to bumper, and I wondered where their owners had gone. They weren't in any of the shops. They'd paid for parking and then disappeared like leaves on a breeze.

As my boots stepped over the threshold of the gallery, busyness and chaos hit me in the face. Reams of black cloth covered the concrete floor. The beamed ceiling took the cacophony of voices and scattered them into the air as disjointed echoes, which made no sense. A man crawled on the floor, draping the cloth over a series of wooden boxes. A tray of blown glass ornaments rested dangerously close to the heel of his shoe.

Artists filled the vacuous space, arranging their creations in designated areas with the tenderness of a parent. My last work hung from a rail on the supporting wall between the two rooms used by the gallery. A red dot displayed its status as already sold. I studied the rustic farm gate in the image with a critical eye. My fingers itched to paint over the lichen on the bottom rung of the rotten wood. Immortalised in the painting, it no longer existed in real life. I'd taken the photograph of Julia on a visit last year, but included her image only from the waist down. Her skirt hung over her knees and my brush had captured her sense of freedom as she pivoted on the top of the gate. The photo captured the laughter in her body language and I'd used the light and textures to convey that without the viewer seeing her face. She'd worn black ankle boots to walk with me up to the lookout, frustrating me with her desire to touch and absorb everything on the way. I'd used my phone to take the snap, and painted it after she left for Auckland.

"Can I help you?" That question again. It assailed me from the lips of a young woman who'd crept up on me while I gazed at the painting. With a complexion the texture of a ripe peach, she stared up at me through trusting eyes still not jaded by life. Spinning around, she jabbed her finger at the painting by 'X'. "That one's sold, but Julia's the agent for the artist." She blinked and smiled, leaning forward to share the secret. "I think 'X' is a man. Julia won't say but I'm sure of it." Her grin widened. "You can always leave your details and if something else comes in, we'll phone you." Her nose wrinkled. "Things get snapped up pretty fast."

I took a step back from her and shook my head. "I don't like it."

Her jaw dropped at my brutality and her eyes narrowed. I'd spoken the truth. The whole composition offended me in a bone aching irritation. Julia's skirt occupied too much of the canvas, a swathe of white fabric interlaced with line drawings of navy flowers. I hated the gate. Running up to the lookout as an alternative to the treadmill, I'd failed to notice how dilapidated the gate had become until Julia seized on it for the photograph. After she breezed back out of my world, I'd grown to detest the sight of the rotten wood and the lichen. Its lack of symmetry caused me genuine anxiety.

It seemed rude to tell the girl I'd torn the gate from its rusty hinges and chopped it up with an axe. Its carcase fed the wood burner for a day during the coldest part of the winter months. A metal one replaced it. Symmetrical. Galvanised. Perfect.

"Everyone loves it." She drew her lips into a pout. "It sold within hours of Gordon hanging it on the wall."

I imagined the sullen gallery owner grumbling about the wasted effort of climbing up the ladder, and the curve of my lips betrayed my inner voice. "I'm here to see Julia."

"Oh." She leaned forward as though inspecting me through a microscope. "Who can I say is calling?"

"I'm not calling." My blank expression drove her backward and out of range of whatever she saw in my face. "I'm standing here."

"Okay." She spun away, her black skirt swishing over her ample thighs. Everything jiggled as she walked with purpose, even the floorboards carrying her vibration to safety. Two women accosted her before she could reach the partition into the second room. One waved a staple gun in front of her face and peered at her with expectation.

Mandy. I realised as she walked away that I'd just met Mandy, Julia's newest assistant. A flicker of guilt snaked up my spine. The forty percent commission on works by 'X' probably paid her wages. Lifting a hand, I brushed off the crumbs of airborne recrimination trying to settle on my left shoulder. I couldn't save everyone. Just Julia.

Mandy disappeared behind a screen into the gallery office. Julia emerged at her shoulder, her left hand raised to stifle a yawn. Mandy conveyed the message without disguise and I deciphered her expressive phrases from a distance, employing my ability to lip read. "There's a guy here to see you. He's really hot but a bit weird." She dipped her glossy head closer to Julia's. "He doesn't like the painting of the woman on the gate."

Julia frowned as she looked up and her gaze sought me as I waited on the doormat. She gave a long blink and her lips curved into a smile. One perfect ebony eyebrow rose in acknowledgement and her quick footsteps rapped on the floorboards. A floor length grey skirt swished around her ankles, the covering a remnant of the burka they had forced her to hide behind as the slave of a prominent terrorist.

A shiver of anticipation snaked up my spine until she glanced up at the painting. Uncharacteristic laughter filled my eyes, though none of it passed the joviality on to my rigid stance. I fancied she glowed as she walked towards me, resisting another look at the painting as she stepped below it. "Jacques." Her palms pressed against my chest as she rose on her toes to kiss me on the mouth. "Don't look at it." Her right hand cupped my chin, and she brought my head lower to remove my gaze from the picture. Her hazel irises danced with amusement. "I don't trust you not to smash it to pieces the day before the buyer collects it."

"I hate it."

"I know mon cher." Noticing Mandy's obvious interest, Julia turned her back on her assistant's ogling and swallowed. "Come to the office with me, Jacques." A furrow marred her brow. "Are you in Auckland to see to your mama's affairs?"

My lips twisted in response to her mention of Mother. I shook my head. "Her corpse is in the system. They can't tell me when she'll be available for cremation."

Julia's body jerked at my matter-of-fact delivery of the truth. She paused for a moment and her full lips parted and then closed as she considered a response. Her delicate fingers snaked through mine and she tugged my wrist. "Come with me," she insisted. "I'll make us coffee."

23

Collage:

Derived from the French verb coller, meaning "to glue."

We didn't make it as far as the office. Gordon Rossie blasted through the automatic doors as though pursued by a tsunami. A ridiculous pair of plus fours flapped at his knees over the Fair Isle socks I'd imagined but never guessed he'd actually wear. He'd abandoned his spiked golf shoes in favour of a pair of trainers in order to drive to the gallery in a rage. Spite filled his ruddy face, contrasting with his wispy, grey-flecked hair and the pretentious goatee beard glued to an undershot chin.

He barrelled through the gallery, fear and fury blinding him to the many obstacles littering his route. Shouts and squeals rose like echoes as artists pulled their masterpieces away from his stampeding feet. My mind reduced his speed and trajectory to a series of scenarios and possibilities, switching his golfer's attire for a mental silhouette of a suicide bomber. My cheek sent a twinge of pain as a reminder of what happened when shrapnel hit flesh. 'No mercy.' Captain Grey's words whispered through my memory and Gordon Rossie walked into the relentless knuckles of my right fist before he'd even noticed my presence next to Julia.

A woman behind him screamed as he listed backwards, dragging a tray of delicate ceramics out of range of his projected landing. She grappled with the box, rolls of flesh rippling like bat wings beneath her arms. Silence shrouded the gallery like the hush which followed a bomb blast, a moment of nothing as though time had stopped. Rossie continued his flailing backward pitch, his eyes wide and his mouth open. My bunched fingers seized the front of his diamond patterned vest and I rescued him from his fall. Lifting him almost off his feet, I snarled into his shocked face, "Never run at my wife like that again!"

He swallowed and a line of spit snaked like a tributary to join the blood trickling from a split lip. Aiming for his nose, I'd underestimated his height in the split second of decision and planted my fist into his mouth instead. The marks from his front teeth left grooves in my second and third knuckles.

Rossie raised both hands to his face and clutched his bleeding mouth. Words gushed from his lips but shock and anger rendered them incomprehensible. I released the fancy knitted vest and gave him a slight push for good measure. He listed like a flagpole and I turned my back on him, focussing my attention on Julia.

All colour had drained from her face to leave her cheeks a waxy grey. Her irises darkened to the colour of fear and I sensed her withdraw into the brutal space in her mind where our shared horror converged. Tears filled her eyes as she looked up at me, their glittering orbs of saline spilling over her eyelashes and plunging over the crests of her cheeks.

"What the hell's going on?" The man with the box of blown glass had ventured close enough to witness Julia's distress and the blood staining Rossie's chin. "I'm calling the cops!"

"You don't want to do that." The chill in my words stopped him in his tracks and his lips made futile flapping actions. I narrowed my eyes and gave him the full effect of my most sinister expression. My height and bulk intensified the threat and his community spirit evaporated into the heavy air.

He lifted his chin and picked his team. "I saw him running at Julia." He shrugged. "I'd have hit him too if I'd been closer."

A snort issued from behind him as the women collected their wits about them faster than any of the other soft handed men. "Yeah, right," the ceramics owner hissed. She clapped her chunky palms together. "The show is over. Let's get this exhibition set up. Does anyone have more staples for this thing?" She jerked her head towards the empty staple gun. The volume of the murmuring among the artists hiked to its normal hum and someone provided a fresh box of staples.

I shielded Julia's shock from them, using my body to screen her from their scrutiny. I'd seen her catatonic once before and dreaded the consequences if I'd inadvertently put her back there. Just like last time, I dipped my body and scooped her into my arms. Her limbs held a more wooden quality, and I found myself hoping it boded an argument and not a week of silence. "I'm sorry," I whispered against her temple. The words felt strange on my tongue. Mother had trained me to say them as a boy, offering them up as a consolation for some incomprehensible offence. The army had stripped them from my armoury, my training officer not impressed by the prospect of an inadvertent admission of guilt.

Julia's arms looped around my neck and the relief weakened my knees. I headed towards the back of the gallery and the office, Rossie following with the hem of his ruined knitted vest stemming the blood from his lip.

"I wonder if my Reggie would pick me up like that," the ceramics owner sighed.

I frowned, contemplating a portly husband eating chicken strips from a bucket each night with his overweight wife. "I doubt it," I replied, my voice loud enough to carry back over my shoulder.

"Mon Dieu!" Julia groaned, and I took it as a good sign that she hadn't descended into the frightening stupor Captain Grey had instructed me to rescue her from.

I bent to place Julia in the plush office chair angled sideways from a wooden desk. She cringed in discomfort and the action told me it wasn't hers. The pressure from her fingers around my neck increased, and I shook my head. "Sit here," I commanded. Rising, I took in the office I'd never visited before today. Another desk behind the door bore a photograph of us on our wedding day. In the picture, my lips tightened into a line at the crime I'd just committed with a cheap pen moments earlier. Julia clutched her flowers to her stomach within the frame, the darkness of her eyes fathomless. The presence of the photo took me by surprise, our marriage no longer under such harsh scrutiny from the immigration department. I couldn't take my eyes off the picture, seeing the things I'd missed at the time.

Gordon Rossie collapsed into the second office chair, which gave a disturbing groan at his weight. I ignored his complaints, frowning as I read Julia's discomfort eight years earlier. Was it because she'd just married a stranger or because she still wasn't used to having her head uncovered in public? Unable to decide between the two, I resisted the urge to smash the frame over Rossie's ungrateful head.

I exhaled and set my legs into the at-ease position, figuring if I fixed my hands behind my back, it might stop me from hitting him again. My palms itched to send his nose cartilage backwards into his brain. As I linked my fingers, the knuckles of my right hand complained. A tiny bone clicked when I moved it and I winced. Good job I could paint with both hands, but I still wished I'd hit him with the left.

Subdued, Rossie bent forward and wiped his nose across his sleeve. "I could press charges for assault," he mused. A nasal quality gave his voice an irritating whine.

I snuffed out a sarcastic sound. "You could," I admitted. My gaze never left the photo, wondering why I'd turned up to marry Julia wearing a chest full of medals. It occurred to me I'd wanted to impress her. She'd spent eight months travelling across the world to marry Captain Grey, unaware he'd died in another sortie on a different continent. Her expression still held shock in the photograph, her frightened smile a grimace against the backdrop of the realisation she had no choice. I peeled my gaze from the revelation and focussed my ire on Rossie instead. "Do it." I goaded him, a primeval urge to make him squirm, superseding all other niceties. I moved my feet together. "Just let me make it worth your while."

Rossie winced and jerked backwards in the chair. He appealed to Julia's better nature. "Why are you doing this?" he whined. As his lips curled away from his gums, I noticed how his front tooth had cracked in a perfect diagonal and set my compulsions to the task of deciding if it looked more like a scalene or an isosceles triangle. While the narrators busied themselves with the safety of the assignment, they left me free to concentrate on the interaction between Julia and Rossie.

"I don't know what you're talking about." Her shaking fingers fumbled for the clip holding her bun on top of her head. Curls cascaded over her shoulders in an ebony deluge, which made me want to dip my fingers into its waves.

"The business!" Rossie rose from the creaky chair, balling his fists at his sides. His lower lip wobbled as he saw the flare of interest in my eyes and he forced his fingers to release their futile threat. The chair rolled far enough to hit the wall with a gentle thud. He swallowed and began again. "Your lawyer called me just as we got to the back nine." He gave a dramatic blink and his fingers twitched. "Ruined my freakin' game!"

Julia exhaled and shook her head. Looking up at me, she searched for answers. "Jacques?"

"Why does he have the best chair?" My question threw them both for a loop, and Rossie answered before Julia. I saw her wince at his reply.

"I own seventy percent of this bloody business!" His voice rose, and I ground my back teeth together to mute the overwhelming desire to respond to his antagonism with violence. Mother would have been proud at my restraint. I fixed a sickly sweet smile on my face and cut across Julia's feeble attempt to smooth over the situation.

"Well, now you own seventy percent of nothing."

"Oh, Jacques." Julia groaned. She bowed and her forehead pressed against my wrist. "What have you done?"

24

NASTALIQ:

A TRADITIONAL FORM OF CALLIGRAPHY USED MOSTLY FOR PERSIAN, URDU, AND MALAY MANUSCRIPTS

Julia sent Rossie from the office while she collected herself enough to make coffee. I refused it, but she made me a cup anyway, setting it onto the desk next to where I still stood like a soldier at-ease.

"Explain." She slumped into the tattered chair which Rossie had vacated and straightened the frame bearing testament to our sham marriage. Her fiddling offered time for me to order my thoughts into a viable explanation, and the words moved across the screen in my mind. I abandoned four different options, sweeping them sideways and out of view as though swatting mental flies.

Julia cleared her throat. "He could call the cops and get you arrested for assaulting him." She kept her tone soft and placatory.

I shrugged. "He's a twat."

Julia sighed. "Is that the best you can do, Jacques? You destroy my business with a single phone call and then walk in here and smack my boss?" Her voice rose at the end, her Parisian accent returning with full force. I realised I liked it and schooled my lips away from their desire to smile like a schoolboy. "This isn't funny!"

My knees jerked at the sharpness in her tone and my humour dissolved into irritation. It bothered me that my body refused to obey me around Julia. "He isn't your boss. I heard how he spoke to you on the phone." Petulance oozed from every pore. I jabbed my index finger towards the torn fabric of the seat, which hugged her slender body. "He gives you the ripped chair and a discarded computer unit from his child's bedroom." My eyes narrowed, and I dipped my head to deliver the force of my wisdom. "You shouldn't sit behind the door."

Julia's eyes widened, and she placed a protective palm over the makeshift desk. Her coffee vibrated with the movement. She tutted and her shoulders slumped. "I forget how you notice everything." Her fingers fluttered over her lips. "I shouldn't have inferred that I didn't like it here." She closed her eyes. "It was ungrateful."

"Ungrateful?" I tasted the word on my lips and wrinkled my nose at its sourness. "I've never asked you for gratitude."

Julia exhaled and bent double as though preparing to vomit. I stiffened, but only frustration emerged as a whoosh from between her lips. "You've never asked me for anything!" The threatening tears bulged over her lower lids before plunging south. The folds of her skirt absorbed them. She sniffed, a guttural, disgusting sound. "The call from the detective was the first time in eight years I've proved useful to you." The flood erupted from her eyes, surging along tracks in her makeup and streaming through the dent in her jawline. She gave a shuddering inhale. "It made me feel needed."

She dipped her body and grappled in a basket beneath the table. Her fingers drew out a box of tissues and she thudded it onto the plasterboard surface. She reached into the hole with a tentative movement, snagging one of the flimsy pieces between finger and thumb. It looked half empty, and that told me perhaps she cried at work a lot. I softened my stance. "You're unhappy here." I presented it as a statement, rather than a question.

Julia shrugged. "I love the art and I'm great with people. It was an incredible opportunity for someone like me."

There it was, the qualifier.

"Someone like you?" I blinked. "Julia Jethro?" My voice contained a more robotic tone than I'd intended. I regretted it but couldn't swallow the words and bury them back where they'd come from.

"But I'm not, am I?" She lowered her voice to a hush and glanced at the door. Rossie hadn't closed it behind him and I fancied he listened on the other side. I imagined myself pulling the trigger in a fast two-tap and blowing his face through the adjoining wall. It might be worth the trouble.

"We can't talk here." I took a step towards her. "I'm hungry."

Julia closed her eyes and pressed another tissue over her nose. "We can't talk anywhere," she muttered from behind it. The sound of her nasal excavation turned my stomach, banishing all hopes of bacon, eggs, fried bread, and tomatoes. Julia could order them on separate plates for me so they didn't touch. Waitresses thought me weird, but she seemed able to get away with it somehow. Her French accent and ready laughter smoothed over my anomalies with frightening ease.

"I'll have rice pops." I changed my mind. "In a bowl."

"Right." Julia rose and tucked her chair beneath the desk. She exhaled and straightened her shoulders, displaying the backbone which had helped her survive her ordeal.

Rossie leaned against the wall in the corridor and Julia frowned as we exited the office. He shot a wary glance in my direction before addressing her. He turned his body as though to pretend I didn't exist and his tone became wheedling. "We can work out an alternative," he insisted. "There's no need to sell your portion of the business." A smirk lifted my lips. He'd spoken to his accountant or lawyer in the few minutes between leaving the office and changing his attitude. When he placed his fingers over Julia's wrist in a half-hearted attempt to delay her progress, my blood super-heated from indifference to rage in a millisecond.

He squawked as I snagged the back of his collar in my left hand. His scrawny neck sunk into the folds of his shirt and knitted vest, leaving his head as a mound reminiscent of Humpty Dumpty's egg headed tale as I lifted him off his feet.

"Put him down, Jacques." Calm radiated from Julia as she turned and raised an eyebrow at me. Malevolence gave her irises a shiny hue, as though she meant the opposite. It left me in a state of confusion as Gordon Rossie dangled from my outstretched arm. I set him down in response to the satisfying ache in my biceps, and not because I cared about his comfort.

He seemed to shrink before my eyes, his wispy hair losing its lustre and his spine bowing earthward. "I can't afford to buy you out," he admitted, his tone deferential. "I've overreached, so if you persist with the sale, I'll need someone else to buy into the business." He swallowed, his Adam's apple bobbing beneath his goatee. "They'll find out that you're the agent for 'X' and not me."

Julia hissed in disgust. She tossed her head and her ebony curls bounced in their replaced clip. I focussed on the way the overhead bulb caught their highlights and started counting. "You let everyone think 'X' dealt with you?" The shock in her voice suggested she hadn't realised. She shook her head again, and I lost count and started over, beginning with the glimmers of amber near her crown. "I should have known. You kept me away from all opportunities to speak to other owners." She clicked her fingers. "You put off the journalist who wanted to interview you until he grew bored. This is why."

Rossie swallowed. His shallow nod jammed his chin deeper into his collar. "I'm sorry."

"You're sorry?" Julia took a step away from him, her lips curled back in disgust. "You've left me to do everything for the last six years. And now you're just sorry."

He clasped his fingers together as though praying, the knobbly knuckles reminding me of Henare's vile finger joints. Instinct forced me to take a step back, and I clattered against the wall. Julia put out her left hand and rested it on my arm, five centimetres above my elbow. Her touched warmed through my jacket and sent heat spiralling along the muscle to my shoulder. "You're disgusting!" She spat the word at Rossie, satisfaction in the set of her jaw as he crumpled. He bent double and blew out a breath of genuine agony. No amount of physical torture could hurt him in the same way as the two simple words.

"We've run out of staples again. The ceramics girls used them all." The slender man who blew liquid glass into animalistic shapes stood in the narrow gap at the end of the hallway. He held the orange stapler in delicate fingers. His lower jaw shot forward to create a childish expression. "Oh. Did you hit him again?" He addressed me with more interest than concern.

I shook my head and acknowledged a modicum of regret. "I would have liked to, but it wasn't necessary."

"Oh, well. Staples!" Disinterested, the artist shook the empty gun at Julia and she jerked her head towards Rossie.

"He'll get some for you," she replied, her tone sickly sweet. Despite my limited perception of other's emotions, even I burned from the effect of the hot caramel in her voice.

The artist edged away from her and tapped Rossie on the shoulder with the staple gun. "I have less than two hours to set up my display. This really isn't good enough."

"Two hours?" I inhaled and prepared to question how it might take one hundred and twenty minutes to sit a collection of glass animals and pots on a length of black cloth.

Julia's fingers closed around my arm in a hard enough grip to induce pain. "He's a perfectionist," she said, a bite in her tone. It silenced me. After all, it took me three days to paint the red rose in the hand of *The Woman in the Garden*. And I still wasn't happy with it.

"Thank you, Julia." The artist took her observation as a compliment and creases covered his face like a map as he smiled. "It's wonderful to be recognised."

As my lips parted with another unfortunate comment, which refused to be silenced, Julia hauled me into the gallery. She called over her shoulder, "We're nipping out, Gordon. The floor is all yours."

25

ZIGGURAT:

A TERRACED PYRAMID FORM COMPRISING SUCCESSIVELY RECEDING STORIES

"You're such a jerk, Jacques." Julia shook her head and released a dramatic sigh. She lifted a mug of steaming Earl Grey tea to her lips and breathed in the aroma. Too hot to sip, she set it down on the table.

"I disagree." A fried egg floated in a sea of grease on the bottom of a cereal bowl. I pointed at it, my fingernail not quite touching the length of translucent goop clinging to the edge of the yolk. "I don't like egg-snot."

Julia exhaled and ignored me.

Chastened, I pulled the plate of sausages towards me and examined them for flaws. My stomach growled, and I closed my eyes and tensed every muscle in my body as though in pain. A bullet through the shoulder and a wood shard embedded in my cheek didn't touch the agony of my confusion.

"Jacques." Julia's soft voice broke through the noise in my head. "Eat the saucisson."

"Saucisson. Saucisson." I whispered the French word for sausage, letting it roll through the turmoil and occupy my tongue. I opened my eyes to find her leaning forward and frowning.

"It's getting worse," she concluded. "You have less control."

"Less control." I repeated her words like a trained parrot, aware I did it but unable to stop. "Less control."

"Eat the saucisson." She lifted a knife and fork from a terracotta flower pot in the centre of the table, and my eyes widened in horror. "Arrêter!" she commanded. "Stop! Eat the saucisson."

"Eat the sausage." I sighed and accepted the cutlery. I was out of my routine and out of my depth. "Mother's dead." I winced as the compulsion gripped my knees and the fork dropped to the table with a clang. I couldn't touch it now. Its contact with the contaminated surface reminded me of the hands that took it from the dishwasher and placed it in the flowerpot. Perhaps other customers had touched it too, shoving it aside and reaching for another. *Hands. Hands. Dirty fingers.*

Julia reached into the flowerpot and retrieved another, waiting until I gripped it before releasing her hold. "I know," she whispered. "Everything is clean. I come here often and am friends with the owner."

I made the mistake of glancing at the egg and the snot seemed to hail me from the greasy yellow of the yolk. My eyes widened and Julia snatched up the bowl and moved it onto the table behind her. "Now, eat the putain de saucisson." Her use of the vulgar swear word caused a tickle to begin in the back of my brain. I laughed and her shoulders tensed. "See what you did." She waved her hand. "I have said your F word and now I cannot look at the sausage."

Another giggle bubbled in my chest and I grinned. Deft movements cut the first sausage into seven parts and it became acceptable. I repeated the action with the second and took a bite. My stomach growled again. "You keep the photograph at work."

Julia sipped her tea and observed me. "I have another copy at home."

I stopped eating and stared at her. My hands dropped until the cutlery touched the edge of the plate with a dull clang. The piece of sausage rolled back to its mates. "Should I have one?" An ache filled my chest at the thought I had somehow transgressed and hurt her.

Julia shrugged. "I don't know, Jacques. It helps me to remember how far I've come and how fortunate I've been."

I squeezed my eyes shut against the narrators which shouted negative thoughts into the cavities in my skull. Why would she want to remember any of that? How could she consider herself fortunate? She sighed, and I opened my eyes to find her watching me. She leaned forward and clamped a hand over my wrist. The handle of the knife scraped against the cheap crockery and the sausages wobbled.

"I am lucky, Jacques," she whispered. Tears budded in her eyes. "Rebels murdered my parents in front of me because they could. I don't have to recount to you the horrors I saw and experienced at their hands. But there are still women in that same position all over the world. I think of them every day. But you rescued me and I will be forever grateful."

I squirmed beneath her gratitude. "Captain Grey rescued you." My stomach growled, but it rebelled against queasiness and no longer in hunger. "He led the operation to liberate your camp. He paid for your passport and organised your trip. Not me." I tugged at my wrist, but she didn't let go, her knuckles whitening in the futile tug of war. I could sweep her off her chair with one hand, but never would. Not Julia.

Her lower lip wobbled. "You met me at Sydney airport holding a painted sign with my name on it." A tear plunged over the lip of her right eyelid and splashed off my plate. "You were there for me."

"But you came for Captain Grey." I kept my tone light, repeating the familiar mantra like a lifeline. "But he died. He asked me to take care of you."

"And you have." The pressure from her fingers increased more, her nails digging into my skin. She was making me say it. I didn't want to say it, but she left me no choice.

"Captain Grey had a wife and three children." I blew out a relieved breath. "And a dog, and a cat, and a budgerigar called Fred."

"And a budgerigar called Fred." Julia's sad smile tapped on my iron heart, creating a booming sound in my chest. "So, you married me, Jacques." She withdrew her hand, and the sausages jostled together on the plate like mothers gossiping at the school gate. She delivered the blow without even touching me. "I will divorce you, like we agreed. The facade is making you ill. You don't deserve my selfishness. I'll speak to the lawyer." She rose and pushed the chair beneath the table. Her eyes glittered with tears as she turned and left the shop.

———⬡———

I drove back to Ngaruawahia, not turning off towards the Tainui Bridge but staying on the Great South Road until I reached the town. The notion of home offered me respite from the confusion, but my brain resisted the emptiness of my house. I found myself at The Point, a local gathering place which sported a pavilion and a canon left over from the Waikato Wars. The canon reminded me of the army, infusing me with safety and regimental routine. The Waikato River surged past, its confluence with the clay stained Waipa River creating smears of orange within the sinister green depths. I could see the upper levels of my house on the other side of the river, my bedroom window poking above a clump of native pittosporum trees. Dense bush hid the garage and its secrets from all but aerial views. I forced my shoulders to relax and locked into the security its presence offered. A fragile thread extended from the house to me, holding onto me and providing stability. I exhaled, and the tension lessened.

Other houses dotted the foothills of the Hakarimata Ranges, plush lawns meeting the riverbank without consideration for the vigorous undertow which stole its foundations from beneath them. A man sat on an orange ride-on mower, leaving fluorescent lime stripes in his wake. I watched him travel up and down the slope, waiting for him to move the wooden bench at the crest of the hill overlooking the river. My mind filtered through the sequence he might use to complete his task as, oblivious, he continued to create his stripes.

My anticipation grew as he mowed nearer to the bench. Up and down. Up and down. I imagined the laborious process of getting off the mower, moving the bench, mowing beneath it and then replacing it. The bench provided an obstacle, and I wanted to know how other people dealt with such things. Tension increased in my mind as I recognised he might not put it back in the exact same space. Perhaps he moved it a little every week.

I jumped at a knock on my passenger window and frustration built in the back of my neck. Roddy tried the handle and yanked the door open. Before I could object, he clambered into the seat next to me, bringing the aroma of pastry, steak, and cheese. He smiled at me and I recoiled from the blob of mince stuck between his front teeth. "You didn't notice me." Satisfaction leached from his voice at having taken me by surprise. "You're off your game, sunshine."

"My mother's dead." I said the first words which entered my head and fixed my gaze back on the mower. The man altered its trajectory to skirt the bench, and I winced. "Julia is divorcing me."

"Wow!" Roddy turned to face me. "That's why you didn't come to the bar last night. Henare let me go early so I waited for you. Sorry for your loss, mate."

I lifted my left hand and jabbed it at the mower in the distance. "He's not moving the bench."

Roddy leaned forward and squinted. "So?"

"It won't look even." My upper lip curled in disgust. "He's making a mess of it." Unaware of our scrutiny, the man on the ride-on circumnavigated the bench. It rocked as the rear wing of the mower clipped it in the turn and the gardener got the front wheel stuck between the bench's front and rear legs. "I can't watch." I covered my eyes, but the mental images replayed across my retinas.

Roddy burped and sighed. "You're a weirdo, Jethro." I kept my eyes closed and leaned my crown against the headrest. I hugged the label to me, turning it over in my mind. The army had dictated a neat orderliness which suited me, but not Roddy. I'd flourished while he'd drowned. My inability to let him take me down with him had saved him, creating a bond which meant more to him than it did to me. He exhaled and jabbed his left index finger at the sprayed signature on the low wall surrounding the skate park. "Did you see that guy from Wellington City Council on the news last night? He's appealing for that graffiti artist to get in contact with them. They've made a public apology for painting over the mural he did on the side of the citizen's advice bureau." He snorted. "They've put the wall back to how it was and want him to do it again." He released a breath full of exasperation. "We arrest the little gits down here and confiscate their spray cans. Why would you encourage someone to graffiti a public wall? It's stupid."

Tiredness gripped me in its vice, robbing me of the energy to throw Roddy out of my truck. I imagined starting the engine and picking up speed before giving him a shove. The radio attached to his Kevlar vest fizzed, and I figured I probably shouldn't.

Roddy cleared his throat. "Henare said he phoned you." A lightness in his tone betrayed his enjoyment of the detective's humiliation. "The kid who died lived in

Cambridge. The dental records finally came back with an identification. He went missing weeks ago. Divers searched the river as far as Mercer but didn't find him." I cracked open one eye to see him staring at the inky green depths of the Waikato. He sighed. "The taniwha doesn't always give them up, does it?"

I neither knew nor cared. His lunch scents had polluted my truck and spoiled my enjoyment of the fragile peace. "Get out," I said. "I'm going home."

Roddy tutted. He swung his legs sideways off the seat and his rubber-soled shoes clunked on the runner board. "See you on Monday?" he asked. "The first round is on me."

"Yeah." I started the engine and waited for him to close the door. He waved and climbed back into his patrol car. The stained bucket from a junk food outlet sat upright on the passenger seat as though accepting a lift. Pie wrappers and an empty drink can nestled inside its cardboard walls. I pondered what might happen if I let Roddy buy the first round of drinks at the RSA and shivered. The skinny kid's disruption of my routine seemed to have no end.

I averted my gaze from the uneven stripes beneath the bench, grateful for the foliage which obscured the abomination from the front windows of my house. As I reversed out of my parking space, the gardener appeared with a weed whacker and set about churning up the earth beneath the wooden legs of the bench.

26

VIRTUOSITY:

GREAT TECHNICAL SKILL OR CAPTIVATING PERSONAL STYLE

Closing my front door for the seventh time, I became aware of the click, which echoed in the cavernous space. I'd been responsible for myself since the age of seventeen and grateful for the peace it brought. Captain Grey had used many trite words to enthuse his squad of hand-picked killers. His voice reverberated in my mind. *'You are who you are when you're alone.'* It sounded poignant when he first said it, and ironic as I shouldered his coffin and walked it past his sobbing wife and children.

The compulsions fretted at my nerve endings, not letting me be until I'd expended the energy which drove their insanity. Whirling around, I left the house and made my way across to the garage.

After an hour on the treadmill, I phoned my lawyer. The middle knuckle of my right hand had swollen and prevented me from lifting weights or using the punch bag. I winced as I closed my fist and waited for him to answer.

"Mr Jethro." Mouth noises issued from the speaker as he swallowed something wet and messy.

"I've changed my mind about selling the thirty percent." I left the sentence hanging as I bent to loosen the laces of my trainers.

"But I've put the sale in motion." The lawyer's voice sounded hoarse, as though he'd swallowed too fast and couldn't catch his breath. "I phoned the other owner and informed him of your decision."

"Then phone him again." My right shoe lace consumed my attention, snagging into a knot as I fumbled with the slippery fabric. I sat down on the end of the weight bench and grunted as I bent to fix the mess.

"So, you're no longer selling?" The lawyer swallowed and bolstered his courage. "And you want me to tell him today?"

I sat up straight with a whoosh. The shoe lace required thought. And both hands. "He's selling." My gaze drifted to the hidden stairwell, to my studio. My mood ticked upward at the thought of finishing the delicate fronds of the kowhai leaves. "He's selling and I'm buying. I want it all. He's on the verge of bankruptcy, so don't let him haggle." I named an amount which Rossie would attempt to inflate and finished my instructions. "Then I want ownership of the building and any of the others you can secure in that street."

"You need a real estate agent for that, not a lawyer." He added a chuckle to his tone, but I sensed his eagerness to drop the project.

"Then find one." '*The shoe lace is stuck. The shoe lace is stuck.*' The narrator-voice went into overdrive and I couldn't leave it any longer. "Julia is divorcing me." I rapped out the ultimate reason for the call. "Let her have whatever she wants." I tapped the screen to end the conversation and set to work extracting myself from the tangled lace. I missed the army boots which had encased my feet and ankles, wearing them for weeks at a time on deployment without trouble. My middle finger ached, the bone grinding as I picked apart the knot with difficulty. I'd need to paint with my left hand for a while, and the thought of the challenge sent a bubble of excitement up the back of my neck.

I showered and changed into overalls before descending the ladder into my studio. The heady scent of chemicals hit me like a wall and I paused to enjoy the mixture of oils and solvent before banishing it with the extractor fan on the far wall. The vibrant yellow kowhai bud called to me, but I changed my mind as I headed behind the glass sheet. It didn't feel like a day for sunny yellow and burnt umber.

A sullenness settled over me and I directed the negative energy into the end of a soft pencil. This commission would be the last for 'X'. My lips curved into a smile of satisfaction as I sketched out the images I would later spray onto the dock wall. I'd spoken the truth when I told Julia I didn't need to practice, but Mother's death had infused me with the desire to get it perfect. I imagined her horror at the plan and then her ready laughter. '*Do this for me, Jack,*' she whispered. I nodded, the promise containing a certain poetic justice.

I jumped as my phone rang again, hauling me from the safe solitude of my art. I'd forgotten to mute its irritating cry. The pencil lead snapped beneath the pressure of my fingers. Drawing left-handed created no difficulty, but laziness meant I'd got out of practice. Cursing, I stepped from behind the partition and snatched up my phone. "Jethro!" I barked, hoping to send the caller scuttling away from contact with me.

A male throat cleared, a discomfiting sound. I pulled the phone away from my ear and activated the speaker button. Glancing back at my sketch through the distortion of the glass, I sensed the Muse abandoning me for other minds. She hated interruptions as much as me. The voice sounded tentative. "Hi, Mr Jethro. I'm calling on behalf of the prison governor. He wishes to extend his sincere apologies for the confusion surrounding your mother's death." I swallowed and stared at the phone, the air molecules hissing in the gaps between the man's words. "Are you there, Mr Jethro?" His tone held an element of fear. Julia's friend, the politician, had given someone a kick.

"Yes." Hostility oozed from the back of my throat to create a growl. "Where is my mother?"

The throat cleared again, and I released an audible sigh. "She's on her way to a funeral home in Huntly. We understand you live nearby. I can give you their phone number so you can make arrangements for her burial."

I memorised the number he gave me, revelling over the digits which proved divisible by three. A rebellious compulsion made my finger jab at the icon, which ended the call as he launched into more apologies and platitudes. I didn't want them. They served no purpose.

The receptionist at the funeral home picked up after three rings. Another positive sign. Her voice held a silky smoothness, which reminded me of Julia. "Mr Jethro." My name slid off her tongue. "She'll arrive here in half an hour. Would you like to be here to greet her?"

Would I? The words wouldn't come, stuck somewhere between my brain and my mouth. I floundered, and she covered the gap for me as though used to clients going to pieces over the phone.

"Why don't you let us get her settled and you can drive up in a couple of hours? We'll make her beautiful for you, and then you can chat with our funeral director about the arrangements. Does that suit you, Mr Jethro?"

"Yes." I didn't want to hang up first, hoping she'd keep speaking to me. The compulsions pushed behind my eyes, causing pressure in the blood vessels. The narrators wailed into my mind. '*I love you, Jack.*' Mother's dead. '*I love you, Jack.*' Mother's dead.

"We'll see you later, then. Bye for now." She killed the call first and left me staring at the darkened phone screen. My sketch paper fluttered in the air from the extractor fan and I imagined the Muse slipping from beneath it and leaving me alone. I didn't want to go to the funeral home. I didn't want Mother to be dead. It wasn't Thursday, so I didn't know if I could talk to her. Words might not come out of my mouth, and then what?

I showered again, convincing myself that the grey lead coating my fingers and the side of my left hand warranted seven all over scrubs and seven hair washes. My skin tingled as I dried myself and dressed. The view from the bay window in my bedroom showed the river and part of the garden of the man with the ride-on mower. A wave of gratitude infused me that I couldn't see the abomination of the bench or the grass beneath it. I lifted my binoculars from their case on the tallboy just to make sure. His roof shielded it from my scrutiny. I need never look at it again, but I knew I would. My truck would find itself sitting across at The Point just so I could check it like another compulsion springing from nowhere. I'd work out his mowing schedule and force myself to watch him butcher the grass, over and over again until I died.

Instead of my usual cravat, I covered my scar with Mother's lavender scarf. Knotting it at my throat in Julia's clever pattern, I mastered it enough to create a passable effect, though it took me twelve attempts. I got it right on the ninth, but released and retied it another three to create a sense of completeness. I matched it with a lilac shirt Julia gave me the Christmas before last and some navy trousers. It took time to polish my cowboy boots as I delayed the inevitable departure. The safe hidden beneath the stairs disgorged the box containing my service medals, and I shoved them into my jacket pocket before turning to leave.

The gate buzzer's shrill tones shot through my nerves as I handled my keys. Checking the camera, I groaned at the sight of Roddy sitting behind the steering wheel of the patrol car. Henare lifted his finger again and pressed the call-button a second time.

27

VIEWPOINT:

THE POSITION FROM WHICH SOMETHING IS VIEWED OR OBSERVED

I didn't bother letting Roddy drive up the long lane to my house. My truck cruised the treacherous downward slalom with ease and I arrived at the gate to find Henare climbing back into the police vehicle. He stopped to observe me with his right foot already in the foot well, the sound of my diesel engine alerting him to my approach. His body twisted as he extracted his foot.

I secured the handbrake but left the truck idling, opening the driver's door and standing on the sill. "What?" I gave the patrol car a pointed glare to indicate they blocked my route.

Henare cleared his throat and approached the gate again. The stainless-steel poles bisected his face. "We need another chat, Mr Jethro." He shifted from one foot to the other and I imagined how Mother might interpret his behaviour. Or Julia. *Shifty*, they'd both say.

Roddy slid from the driver's seat, the hinge creaking as he shoved open the door. "It's okay, Jack," he called. Henare turned his head just enough to make his colleague blanch at whatever he saw there. Roddy's fingers twisted in front of him as his loyalty stretched to a breaking point between the army brotherhood and the oath he swore as a police officer.

"My mother's waiting for me."

Roddy cocked his head and frowned. "Where, mate?" His eyes widened in the same way they did when a squad brother once lost the plot and shot up a derelict hut with every weapon on his person.

I gave him the address and watched the realisation crawl across his features. "Ah, the funeral home in Huntly. You know where that is?"

I nodded and glanced at the screen in the truck. The satellite navigation system still waited for my instructions, but I could punch them in once I got rid of Henare. "Huntly." I let the name of the town drag across my lips. "They're making her beautiful."

Roddy winced and flapped his hand towards Henare. "Let him go, man," he pleaded. "His mum died."

Henare ground his teeth and turned his rigid body towards the car. "Fine!" he snapped. "But I need to see you. Nathan Watson's body turned up an hour ago."

I blew out a sigh of exasperation. Of course, it did. The skinny kid seemed determined to ruin my routine, even from beyond the grave. I slipped back into my seat and slammed the door. The press of a remote control caused the gate to shudder to life and begin its slow journey sideways. Roddy started the patrol car's engine and screwed his neck around to back out of my driveway and onto the hazardous road. As I waited for their departure, I locked the gate open and punched the address for the funeral home into the sat nav. The map on the screen spun to show my location and created a route towards a red pin on a Huntly back street.

The police car slid backwards onto the road and headed north, not because Henare wanted to check my destination but because the sharp bend dictated their direction. After selecting Beethoven's *Moonlight Sonata* on my phone and directing it to play through the stereo, I released the handbrake and drove my truck through the aperture. Another click of the remote and the gate slid shut behind me. I checked the road and turned left.

I didn't see the patrol car during my journey, so figured Roddy hadn't doubled back to Ngaruawahia. The robotic voice of my sat nav led me to a converted villa near Huntly lake. I parked in a car park carved from what was once the front lawn and prepared myself for visiting Mother. The music helped to empty my head and twelve taps of the steering wheel offered back the preferred rhythm of my existence.

A receptionist looked up as I entered the building, crafting her features into something resembling respect and sympathy. I'd noticed her seconds earlier, laughing at something on her computer screen. The change in her expression made me blink and robbed me of my prepared sentence. She rose from behind her desk and stepped towards me, offering her outstretched hand for me to take. Her fingers appeared clean, the nails painted a demure light pink, but I opted not to touch them and kept my hands by my sides. It threw her and it amused me that we'd stymied each other. The way she tilted her head to observe me reminded me of Julia at our first meeting. She'd wanted Captain Grey and got me. She hadn't known what to say either.

The name badge, which sat wonky against the pattern of her blouse, said 'Leoni' in a cursive font. I absorbed that information and dug the lost words from where they'd sunk into the pit behind my Adam's apple. "Alexandra Jenssen." I said Mother's name in the hope it might stop the woman staring at me. She'd given me her mother's maiden name at birth. It proved to be a good thing in the end.

"You're very tall." She blinked at her own forwardness and her olive cheeks pinked. Her body dipped at the waist enough to convey her discomfort. "Sorry, sorry. Your mother is such a tiny lady, I expected someone smaller." She flapped her hand towards me, compounding her awkwardness. "You have such a gentle voice on the phone, I conjured up an image of you that wasn't correct." She pressed a pink nailed finger over her lips to stop her verbal diarrhoea. I attempted an encouraging smile, knowing what it felt like to have my innermost thoughts dragged from my chest by an unseen magician's hand and flung to the corners of the room.

"One metre and ninety-two centimetres," I offered. "Six feet and three inches tall."

"Yes." She scurried behind her desk and fiddled with the papers there. "You're very handsome." Her eyes widened in horror. "Sorry, it's the Asperger's. They didn't think I could do this job and so far, I'm proving them right." Her fingers twitched against her pile of papers. Three slid from the top and cascaded onto the floor. She blinked and forced her mind back to my errand. "Alexandra Jenssen." Back on safer ground, she exhaled with relief. A flush had tracked from her open necked blouse to her throat. She re-emerged from behind the desk and started again. "Your mother is in St. Peter's chapel of rest. Follow me." She teetered in front of me on her high heels, her ankles giving a painful twist with each staccato step.

I trailed behind her, my body moving with a calculating ease born of practice. Stealth and silence had become my friend as a child, helping me to fly beneath the radar of notice and potential danger. Perfecting it had started as a mental challenge and then a habit. I couldn't stop if I wanted to and I put my energy into walking only on the odd carpet squares. Saturday was an odd steps day. It made me miss the ease of deployment. The relentless sand of the desert required no special steps. Wind and the violent storms which blew up from nowhere did the work for me, smoothing over the squad's footprints as though we never existed.

Leonie stopped at a doorway marked by an image of the saint. After giving a soft knock, she pushed the door open and stepped inside. My heart trembled in my chest. *I want to see Mother. I don't want to see Mother.* A substandard job with the carpet squares had created a hiatus of half squares which gave me cause to falter. I couldn't decide whether to count the two bits as a single even one or separate them into odd and even. Leoni poked her head back into the hallway and I followed her with a giant step which stretched the seams of my trousers. Over compensating, I cleared the fragmented mess and missed the first of the squares in the new room. My boot landed in the centre of an even square and I looked up to find Mother lying as though sleeping on a gurney.

"What do you think?" Leoni smiled at me, offering me the opportunity to take part in admiring her work.

I clasped my fingers behind my back and settled into the at-ease position. A white sheet touched the underside of Mother's chin. The knuckles of her fingers and toes showed through the thin fabric. Someone had crossed her arms over her chest and rested her hands on her sternum. Her ready smile no longer disguised the sunken cheeks or hollowness around her eyes.

Leoni touched her own cheek, her skin peachy and alive. "We added a little foundation and rouge," she whispered, her tone deferential. It explained the absence of the familiar creases which I usually counted during rare visits outside our Thursday phone conversations. The makeup robbed me of the road map on which I relied to navigate the maternal relationship.

I shook my head. "It's not her."

Leoni's eyes widened and her lower jaw dropped to reveal tiny bottom teeth. "It's not?" Horror infused her tone, and she snatched at a piece of paper resting on a nearby sideboard. "Alexandra Jenssen." She tapped the name with her index finger. "She arrived this morning." Her face creased into lines. "But you're saying it's not her?"

I closed my eyes and swallowed. The effort required to explain myself seemed greater than the desired outcome. I weighed the problem in my mind, wondering whether to bother. I should. Mother deserved it. My eyes snapped open, and I discovered Leoni in a state of heightened nervousness. The paper shook in her fingers. "It is my mother," I concluded. "But she doesn't wear makeup anymore." She had once. She'd used it to disguise the bruises and the cuts administered to her body by the narcissist she loved. Prison had separated her from him and from her former life. She said she could be herself in there.

"Oh." Leoni's torso collapsed inward, and she hunched herself around the knowledge. "We can fix that."

"I'll do it." I held out my hand in expectation.

"Right. Yes. Not a problem." She clip-clopped from the room on the heels too high for her build. Returning seconds later, she held out a packet of perfumed wipes. "Would you like help?"

I shook my head, and she withdrew from the room and from me, perhaps grateful I had declined her offer.

The wipes smelled like jasmine, with a faint scent of antiseptic beneath the heady floral tone. I set my phone on the sideboard to continue the first movement of the *Moonlight Sonata* it had begun in the truck. "I wanted to ask you about the skinny kid," I began, tugging a wipe from the packet. "But I guess there's no point now." So, I worked in silence, stripping away the tanned powder from her face and restoring the crinkles to their previous state. I counted the gentle strokes to distract me from the strangeness of her skin through the thin wipe. The muscles on the right side of her face pulled her lips and cheek down into a grimace and I realised too late what the makeup had meant to disguise. My fingers moved the wipes with delicate strokes as though I painted her on a canvas, reaching one hundred and forty-four movements until Mother emerged like a spring bud from beneath the snow.

Relief settled over me, my mood shifting in time with the comforting waves of piano music composed by a deaf man.

Standing back to admire my work, I mapped the familiar dents and contours in Mother's face with my eyes. A gentle tap on the door heralded the arrival of Leoni. "Is everything okay?" she whispered. Her gaze tracked to the dustbin by my feet, wipes cascading from it like a waterfall. She pushed her way through the gap and closed the door behind her. "Did you bring her some clothes?" she asked. "She arrived wearing a hospital gown."

I took a step back, my head already shaking. "I have nothing for her," I confessed, my voice shaking at my failure. My fingers tapped the scarf at my throat. "Just this."

"I'll see what she came with," Leoni whispered. Her heels tapped from the room, along the hallway, and back to the comfy reception area. I slipped into the at-ease position and braced myself for her return. I heard the plastic bag crackling before Leoni re-entered the room. "She just had these with her." Her heels dug into the plush carpet as she spun to lay the bag on the sideboard. She withdrew a folded white blouse and a pair of grey trousers. The clothing balanced on her palm as an offering.

"Her prison clothes," I concluded. "She liked prison. Can she wear them?"

"Yes, of course." Leoni took a step towards the bed. "Would you like to dress her?"

Synapses fired in my brain at the thought of seeing Mother naked. I shook my head and backed away from the gurney and the abhorrent suggestion. "No!" My answer sounded too rough, judging by the defensive flare which appeared in Leoni's brown eyes. "No, thank you. I'll come back another time."

I spun towards the door and took giant strides into the hallway. In my confusion, I shouldered the wall like a blind man seeking an escape.

"Mr Jethro." Leoni's worried face appeared behind me. "We need to speak about the funeral. Where do you want it and how many people might attend? There's lots to still discuss."

Twelve times twelve is one hundred and forty-four. I used maths equations to drown out her plea. My mind turned to Mother's last word and the confusion it caused. *'Gain.'* I escaped to my truck as a smile spread across my face. Twelve taps of the steering wheel consolidated my understanding. Not *gain*, but *again.* The stroke had robbed her of the ability to form the full word. She wanted me to do something again, and I knew what it was.

The engine rumbled to life, and I drove onto the main road, comforted. "I'm already on it, Mother," I promised her ghost.

28

SCALE:

THE RATIO BETWEEN THE SIZE OF AN OBJECT AND ITS MODEL OR REPRESENTATION

A storm rumbled closer overhead, crossing the Hakarimata Ranges and preparing to drop its wrath on the river snaking through the valley. I crossed the Tainui Bridge in my truck, the tyres loud over the metal plates the council had installed to protect the crumbling asphalt. The road repair crew crowded together to wait for the storm to pass, rain bouncing off their orange safety helmets and pelting the road in waves. The metal plates created an interesting three beat at the legal speed and I liked it enough to make a complete turn around the roundabout and drive across it again. Speeding up destroyed the rhythm and, disgusted at having ruined something good, I headed for the Great South Road and drove the long way towards Ngaruawahia instead.

I parked at The Point for the second time that day, not because I needed time to decompress from my time with

Mother, but because my compulsions forced me to look at the mess the gardener made of the grass beneath the bench. His efforts with the weed whacker had chunked up the soil along with the grass. The seat sat at a weird angle, as though he'd tried to correct it too late. I blew out an exasperated breath and, like many things in my life, wished I'd never seen it. Imperfection presented like smelly socks in my brain. I knew they stank but kept lifting them to my nose just to check they were as bad as I believed. Now I'd seen the bench, I couldn't just leave it. Horrified over and over again, I'd be unable to stay away from the sight.

Feeling as though I had no choice, I drove across the Waipa Bridge towards home and turned right before the last of the houses flanking the river. Rain drenched my hair as soon as I stepped from the truck, soaking through my jacket and eking into my shirt. Mother's lavender scarf flattened against my throat like seaweed strangling a swimmer.

The hammering of my fist on the front door echoed inside the house. Noises came from within as someone thudded a door closed and shuffled along a bare hallway. I stood at-ease on the narrow path and waited. The door whipped open and one of the old soldiers from the RSA presented himself in the gap. Stubble graced his pointed chin, and he narrowed his bushy eyebrows into a line. "What?" he snapped. His irises flared with recognition, and he cocked his head. "Lieutenant Jethro. What's the problem?" He took a step nearer the threshold and looked down at me. Even with us both retired, he outclassed me by enough ranks to make me uncomfortable with my mission. "Speak up, man!" he barked. "My lunch is getting cold." A gnarled, arthritic finger jabbed at me, the nail yellow and ridged.

"You didn't move the bench." I held his gaze with determination. "Your lawn is a mess."

His mouth opened and closed. Salt water swam in his rheumy eyes. He lifted both clawed hands up for my inspection. "What do you want me to do about it? My pension doesn't allow for a gardener."

I gave a decisive nod. "I'll drive my mower round every Thursday at eleven o'clock." Bringing my heels together, I felt my fingers itch to perform a salute that wasn't required.

He gaped at me and I sensed his gaze burning into my back as I left his property. Rain dripped from my hair into my eyes and blurred my vision. My truck roared as I floored the gas and headed home. I'd be old one day and unable to mow my own grass. Shaking my head, I made the first of many relevant decisions. "I'll tarmac the bugger," I whispered to the empty passenger seat.

⸻✠⸻

I turned off my mobile before entering the gym and found my ear buds in the cupboard where I kept my exercise gear. Two hours of running satiated my need for busyness and stilled my soul enough to paint. The gruelling workout on the treadmill made up for my inability to use the weights. My knuckle joint smarted from the exercise of cleaning Mother's face. If Julia was there, she would have strapped it, but she hadn't contacted me after her announcement in the cafe. My mind sifted through the evidence and I concluded the episode with the sausage had been the deal clincher. I wondered how many other men had found themselves alone because of their eating habits. A tiny voice in the back of my skull whispered that it rather enjoyed having Julia as a wife. I silenced it with seven ice cold showers as punishment.

The preparatory sketches for the mural reminded me of Julia and Mother, and I couldn't face trapping myself behind the screen. I donned a clean set of overalls and stood before an empty canvas for a while, letting the weave of the fabric percolate my creativity. The image of the bench plagued my mind, and I chose acrylic paints to wrestle it from the grip of my compulsions and turn it into something beautiful. Lime green and burnt umber morphed the canvas into a garden, the paint drying fast enough to allow re-coats but not too quick for blending the colours of the winter scene. I painted from memory, using a wider brush than the oil paintings demanded. After four hours on my feet, the canvas bore the riverbank, the grass, an outline of the weather board house in the background and the mountain.

In a moment of mischief, I added a splash of white to designate my house in the background. It overlooked the canvas like a benevolent queen, the roof and bedroom window peeking from between the convergence of two ridges. By the time I'd formed the base colours for the river in the foreground and sketched the offending bench onto the slope, my eyes ached and my ear buds had run through the *Moonlight Sonata* too many times. As I cleaned my brushes with warm water and washing powder at the sink behind a plastic curtain, it irked me how I'd lost count of exactly how many of Beethoven's movements had passed through my ears. Julia threw back her head in my mind's eye, laughing at my need to control everything. *'Of course you forgot!'* she jibed. *'Isn't that the point?'*

Darkness shrouded the driveway as I secured the door to the gym, and tiredness bowed my shoulders. I'd dressed in my street clothes and carried my sweaty gym wear in my outstretched right hand, navigating the short distance to the porch. The security light flashed on as it picked up my movement and I unlocked the house and flicked on the hall light.

The gate intercom flashed its red light to inform me I'd missed a caller. I waited until I'd set the washing machine cleaning my gym clothes and the ones I'd worn earlier before I checked the identity of the visitor. Henare's face appeared in the camera five times across the previous six hours, as though he'd made a mission out of hunting me down and talking at me. The day waned with each visit, the time showing the last as ten minutes earlier. My body tensed as the buzzer sounded shrill in the silence of my house.

Exasperated, I dipped to speak into the intercom. "What?"

"You can't put this off, Mr Jethro. Speak to me now or I'll get a warrant and leave you no choice." He stepped away from the camera, his image growing grainy in the speckled glow from the headlights behind him. I jabbed my index finger at the button to unlock the gate and counted to one hundred and forty-four. That's how many seconds it took me from the road to the house, but only if I encountered no unforeseen obstacles and kept the truck in second gear.

Henare's ascent held no perfection and nor did the man himself. He arrived at the top of the hill with the patrol car still in first gear, the engine whining loud enough to send the birds scattering from the bush in alarm. I blinked in surprise as he climbed from the car. Leaning sideways to stare into the passenger seat, I saw it empty. He breached the three steps to the porch and held out a hand, which I ignored. I folded my arms across my chest because the stance often worked to repel unwanted conversations.

Henare smiled. "We're having this chat inside, Mr Jethro." His voice held a note of authority, which he ruined with a jibe. "The heating in that car is crap and I've hung around waiting for you for hours."

I stepped aside to allow him entry and winced as he closed the door behind him. Conjuring up the mental list of tasks needing attention before I crawled into my bed, I added washing the front door handle. Again, Henare drifted to the painting of Julia and he peered along the bottom of the canvas. "Are you sure this isn't by 'X'?" he demanded.

My jaw worked against my cheek, and a huff of irritation escaped from my throat. Henare turned to face me. "I'm sorry about your mother," he said. A vein pulsed in his right cheek, showing through the dirty blond shadow which coated the lower half of his face. "My sergeant phoned the funeral home, and they said you left hours ago." His eyes narrowed. "I've been waiting to speak to you."

I shrugged and dug into my back pocket for my phone. My brows knitted as the screen lit up to show four missed calls from a private number, twelve from a mobile I didn't recognise and one from Julia. I spun the screen to face him, demonstrating he wasn't the only person I'd ignored. He shrugged and leaned against the wooden wainscoting which lined the lower half of the lobby. "I had to wash Mother's face." The words emerged stilted and filled with a pain I hadn't sensed hiding beneath them. "The girl covered her in makeup and she wouldn't like it." I shook my head and my fingers twitched with the remembered motion. My right knuckle ached, and I pushed my hand behind my back, figuring Henare didn't need to know how I gained the injury.

"I'm sorry." He said the futile words again by rote, trotting them out in the same way Mother taught me to cover my crimes. They meant many things, but not that he felt genuinely appalled for me. He jerked his head towards the open lounge door and raised his left eyebrow. "Can we sit down for this chat, please? It's been a long day."

I schooled my face into its most sinister glare, but he ignored me, stealing permission and stepping into the lounge, anyway. Light flared from the chandelier in the centre of the room and I squeezed my knees together and closed my eyes to internalise the silent scream. I wanted to yell at him to stop touching stuff, but knew an outburst wouldn't hasten his exit. It would just delay my enforced cleaning spree, and I needed to get it done before I forgot all the things he'd contaminated. *Gate buzzer, door handle, light switch.* I smudged the gate buzzer off the list. It didn't need to be there because I never touched it. The remote kept me safe from visitors' germs. I blew out a breath and removed my boots before joining Henare in the lounge.

He stood in the centre of the rug, still wearing his shoes, and my nose twitched. I dug my hands into my pockets to stop myself from clamping them around his neck and squeezing. He cleared his throat as though hinting he'd like a drink, and I returned his ignorance with some of my own. His shoulders dipped a little in unspoken defeat, giving his thin chest a concave appearance behind his oversize grey shirt. "You have good taste," he mused, waving a limp hand at the chandelier and the expensive wallpaper featured behind the fireplace. "Did you employ a decorator?"

"No." I growled the word and released a yawn that would have horrified Mother with its intentional rudeness. A glance at the digital watch on my wrist emphasised the point.

"You renovated the house yourself?" Surprise laced his tone.

"With Julia." My tongue tripped over her name and the stutter crawled from the dark recesses of my brain to threaten my speech. I bought the house after our fake marriage and we'd holed up here for two years while she recovered from her journey, her trauma and her disappointment.

"Ah, your lovely wife." He inhaled and took a panoramic view of the lounge before turning to me. "Sergeant McAllister mentioned your divorce."

Sergeant Roddy McAllister needed a smack in his big mouth, but I kept the sentiment to myself.

Henare shrugged. "She spoke about you the other day with genuine fondness." He cocked his head. "Perhaps it's a blip."

"Blip." I repeated the word, liking how it sounded on my tongue. The narrators seized it and danced in my chest, repeating it over and over in a series of strange voices which made me want to scream and cover my ears. I should have ignored it and not repeated it aloud. Now, they'd torture me with it.

Henare bent his knees and sunk into my sofa. I lost all hope of banishing his essence from my home now he'd contacted something fabric. I wanted leather for its ease of wiping clean, but Julia insisted on plush cream fabric which contrasted with the forest green of the wallpaper. We'd bonded in our own silent way over the decorating, putting on a show for the visiting immigration official. We'd learned to trust each other. I thought we had, anyway.

My brain fixated on a replay of the day we'd parted company. It took two years for her fake holiday visa to convert to something which allowed her to stay. Permanent residency gave her the same rights as me but they could still deport her. Captain Grey had organised her passage across the world and used government contacts to provide falsified documents. He'd made her promises he couldn't keep, so I'd kept them for him. We'd driven to Auckland to pick up her visa from the immigration office and she'd told me she wasn't coming home. She said I didn't need her, and I'd believed her.

Henare cleared his throat again, and I jumped. I pursed my lips and focussed on his pale complexion beneath the scattered light from the chandelier. "I'd like to look at the footage from your gate camera," he said. "Is it on a memory card?"

I pulled my phone from my back pocket without answering and brought up the app which displayed activity from the camera feed. He rose and stood next to me, his warm breath coating my fingers and turning my stomach. "So, you get notifications when someone buzzes the gate?" His voice lowered, a man on the hunt.

I shook my head and jabbed my left index finger at the notification bell which showed as greyed out with a line through it. He gave a nod of acknowledgement. "Pull up the footage from Wednesday night, please. Does it only work when someone presses the buzzer?"

I pushed my phone into his hands and took a step back. The risk of inhaling his fetid breath while speaking proved too much for me and I abdicated responsibility for the phone. Removing myself to a few steps away, I watched his fingers scroll across the time line at the bottom of the screen. I added the phone to the list of things requiring a clean. He raised his eyebrows and gave a nod. "I see, it picks up movement." He stroked the screen as images reflected across his irises. "You exited the gate here." Scroll, scroll, scroll. "It shows you returning at nine fifteen." His shoulders dropped. "Then nothing until the next day when it picks up a passing car."

I nodded.

"You mentioned before that the fuse blew and you switched it back on the next morning."

I nodded again.

Henare exhaled. He handed the phone back to me and I stared at it nestling in his palm. It tilted as I watched and so I took it, wiping the screen on the thigh of my trousers. His eyes widened and his lips parted, though he didn't comment on my obviously disgusted view of him. "I checked with the power company. They confirmed you made the call later that night. You have a generator?"

I nodded, noticing the twitch speed up in his cheek as I offered no further information to punctuate his monologue. His jaw flexed, and he leaned his weight into his left side, pushing the toe of his right foot forward as though in an unspoken challenge. "Is there another entrance to this property?"

I frowned and stared at the ceiling. "Via the Hakarimata summit." My eyes closed as I traced the route in my mind. "Across two paddocks, through two farm gates, along the bush line, through some forestry and onto the track from the old reservoir."

Henare's lower jaw dropped. "So, not with a vehicle then?"

"A tank could do it." I thought about the mess and the narrators went nuts behind my eyes.

Henare blew out a breath. "The coroner says Nathan Watson died before ten o'clock on Wednesday night. The food he ate at the RSA was undigested in his stomach." He shrugged. "Your camera footage shows you arriving home at fifteen minutes past nine, which is ten minutes after you left the bar. I don't think even you could traverse a mountain and home again in less than forty-five minutes." The bristles rustled against his palm as he dragged a hand across his chin. "Can I have a copy of that footage, please? For my record of investigation?"

I lifted my phone and downloaded the relevant section of footage to my files. The Bluetooth picked up Henare's device, and I allowed it to sync while I sent the brief video clip. I closed the connection as soon as it finished and wiped his phone's ID from my settings. He nodded with satisfaction at the beep of confirmation. "Thank you," he said. He turned his body towards the doorway and I dared to hope it indicated his imminent departure. But he stopped and turned back towards me, finding me wiping my phone screen on my trouser leg again. "Where were you this afternoon?" he demanded. He jerked his head towards my phone. "I checked today's footage, and it shows you arriving hours ago. Did you ignore me on purpose?"

"No." My expression held no guile. "I worked out in the gym and took a shower."

He glanced up at my damp hair and his lips parted. His gaze coasted over the bulging biceps straining at the sleeves of my shirt and I saw in the widening of his eyes the moment he judged my physique worthy of six hours of lifting weights. He reached the front door and touched the handle again, his protruding knuckles rolling with the movement of his fingers. "Why did you join the army, Mr Jethro?" he asked, turning the knob.

The simple question gave me hope as I delivered my answer. "My social worker said it would give me structure."

"Right." Henare stepped onto the porch and the security light bathed him in a yellow glow. I didn't wait for him to leave, pressing the button to open the gate and then jabbing another to lock it in that position. By the time the detective reached the bottom of the long driveway, I was enjoying a date with a bottle of cleaning fluid and a cloth, wearing only my boxer shorts.

29

ABJECT ART:

A TERM USED TO DESCRIBE ARTWORKS WHICH EXPLORE THEMES THAT TRANSGRESS AND THREATEN OUR SENSE OF CLEANLINESS AND PROPRIETY

Sundays were even days and provided a modicum of relief for my mind. I'd stayed up late cleaning, the initial desire to expunge Henare from my home spreading to a general gutting of every room except Julia's. Sinking into my mattress after two in the morning, I remembered he'd also touched her door handle when he questioned her days earlier.

Exhausted, I selected a new cleaning cloth from the airing cupboard and retrieved the bleach from the bathroom. I stumbled to her bedroom and used the cloth to open the door. Julia's floral scent hit me like a wave, introducing a longing into my soul, which I had never previously acknowledged. She'd left a yellow sticky note on the back of the door, just a few centimetres above the handle. '*Already done it*' she'd written in her cursive scrawl.

The closed door had trapped a chill in the room and I shivered. My hair, still damp from another shower, created a cold cap which exacerbated the sensation of icy fingers scraping the back of my neck. Julia's carpet resembled the texture and colour of desert sand, and I stepped across it without turning on the light. Her bed called to me and I missed her with a palpable physical ache. Not willing to disturb her neat pillows and unleash another round of frenzied tidying, I curled up on the rug next to the bedside table, which contained her spare underwear and night clothes.

I woke to the dawn chorus. The heat pump in the kitchen had obeyed its timer and activated, sending warm air through the lower level to filter up the stairs. Julia's open door had allowed it a tentative entry, beating back the chill which woke me. I laid on my back and kept my eyes closed, listening to the sounds of the floorboards clicking and settling as daylight spread its grey digits over the house. Turning on my side, I spread my fingers through the sand-coloured carpet and thought of the desert. It should have affected me more, the grit which got into my clothes, my underwear and even my food. But it was uniform and everywhere, varying little in colour and definition. Perhaps my brain treated it like water, flowing, cleansing and expunging all traces of our war crimes.

A brown woollen blanket dangled from the side of the mattress, thrown there with Julia's staged artfulness. I tugged at the nearest corner, gathering its weight into my fingers until it tumbled from the bed and covered me with a whoosh of perfume and softness. My mind convinced me it was okay because it accidentally fell on me. It absolved me of responsibility and control, ensuring I could place it back on the bed without concern. I pulled the blanket over my shoulders and dozed, relying on an army skill learned from exhaustion, which meant I could sleep anywhere.

"Jacques!" Julia's voice rose in my sleep and I dreamt she shook my shoulder. I lay on my back in the funeral home with my hands clasped over my chest and a sheet drawn up to my chin. "Jacques! What are you doing?" Julia's tone held a hysterical quality and fabric fluttered across my face. My nose twitched with the static which tickled over it. Fear burst into my chest as my dream self decided it didn't want to be cremated.

I sat up with a giant exhale, pushing my fists out in front of me in self-defence. A woman gasped and her frantic leap backwards covered me in more static and the scent of Julia's perfume.

"Jacques!" She said my name again, temper behind it. "What are you doing?"

I ran my hands across my face and scratched the sleepy dust from my eyes. "I don't know," I answered truthfully.

Julia exhaled and sat on the end of her bed. "I phoned you and then I drove here and searched the house for you."

I blew out a breath and yawned. My limbs demanded release, and I stretched, involving as many muscles as I could manage. My feet poked from the bottom of the blanket and I glanced up at Julia, imagining she felt anger at my appropriation of her room and her possessions. "Sorry. I'll wash it."

She rose, her long skirt swishing across my toes as she moved to the side of me. Then she sat down next to me and crossed her legs. I examined the line of navy buttons which ran from her slender waist to the hem of her skirt. It rose and dipped as it traversed the shape of her body, creating a valley between her groin and the curve of her bent knees. "Are you all right?" she whispered.

I shook my head and then nodded, the movement creating a peculiar circular effect. The muscles on either side of my neck bulged as I prevented myself from repeating the motion and beginning another habit I couldn't fight. I relaxed as her cool palm cupped my shoulder, a tentative touch which increased in pressure when I didn't react. "You're right," I concluded with a sigh. "It's getting worse." A mental dictionary appeared in my mind's eye and I scrolled through it for the words I needed. "It's not you, it's me."

Julia snorted and her irises danced. Her chest caved as she laughed and her breasts bounced behind the lacy fabric of her blouse. "I think that's a what-do-you-call-it?" She snapped the fingers of her other hand and her chin bobbed.

"A cliché. But the world has borrowed the word from French, meaning to click." She snapped her fingers again and her sharp features softened. I shook my head without understanding and she nodded. "It's okay, Jacques. I don't believe it's you or me. It's many things. We've both seen enough horror to give us nightmares and now your mother is also gone home. We've spent the last eight years hiding behind our relationship and it's taken a toll on both of us." She squeezed as much of my shoulder as her tiny hand could manage. Then I held my breath as she knelt up and wrapped both her arms around my head. Her scent enveloped me. Jasmine, lilies and safety.

⋈

"Have you ever considered you might have PTSD?" Julia stroked my hair back from my forehead and kissed the space it revealed. I tensed, liking how we'd come to rest in the wide bed and not wanting her to move and break the spell of peace which engulfed me.

"No," I whispered. She cradled my head against her chest and her nakedness muffled the word, sending it ricocheting around my brain. The heat pump clicked off in the kitchen with a sigh, as though to punctuate the moment with a full stop. I tensed and Julia's finger stroked my ear.

"Maybe we could see someone together?" She rested her chin on my crown and I exhaled. I imagined someone trying to pick through the debris in my brain and even the mental image exhausted me. "A counsellor," she suggested.

"A personal organiser," I breathed. "For my mental hoard. In a hazmat suit and respirator."

Julia's third rib dug into my cheek as she snuffled with a soft laugh. "You're funny," she concluded. "And more than a little irresistible." My head bounced to her shoulder as she shimmied down the mattress. Her fingers spread across the plates of muscle encasing my stomach and then dropped lower. "You're my secret addiction, Jacques Alexander Jethro." Her irises glittered and her soft lips curved upwards into a lopsided smile. My body stirred with interest, but I held my breath at the frown lines which bisected her forehead. "It's only you, Jacques," she whispered. Her kiss removed the answer I didn't have, anyway. She pulled back to stare at me. "There's nobody else. Do you understand?"

I nodded and saw the moment she believed me when her pupils dilated. My acknowledgement held importance for her and the dictionary scrolled, providing no useful list of ready words to reassure her of my fidelity. Too late, I realised I didn't need any. It wouldn't be clever sentences that inured us against the world, but our actions and our bodies. We were both too damaged to draw anyone else into our lives. They wouldn't understand the delicate battle lines or the rules of the game which kept us sane. Or at least the version of sanity which passed for normal in the crowd of denizens beyond my front door.

Julia scooted close enough to press her body against mine. Her roving hands continued their work, and the narrators stopped screaming in my head.

Or perhaps I just stopped listening to them. My fingers dug into Julia's hair as I rolled on top of her, and my kisses smothered her groans.

30

De Stijl:

A circle of Dutch abstract artists who promoted a style of art based on a strict geometry of horizontals and verticals

Julia prepared breakfast while I showered and dressed, navigating the even numbered steps to the ground floor and kitchen. A bowl of rice pops sat on the counter with my favourite spoon by its side. I frowned and peered at the layout and then paused to watch Julia finish fixing a mug of coffee. She turned and handed it to me. "I've counted them." She jerked her head towards the bowl. "You can add milk if you wish." Her lips pursed, and I sensed her wanting to ask me something and waited. "Did you buy the flowers for your mother?"

I shook my head. "For you."

"Right." She glanced at the wilting lilies and her cheeks grew pink. "Thank you." She reached for the makeshift vase and topped up their water.

I settled on a stool and stared at the bowl she'd set aside for me. The narrators in my head shouted at me, urging me to recount the tiny rice balls in case she'd added them up wrong. I realised as I pushed the narrators away and lifted my spoon, that I never worried she'd lie to me, only that she might make a mistake. Her body dipped as she leaned forward to run a damp cloth over the counter, her capable fingers collecting stray rice pops within its cotton folds. It didn't matter that she'd handled each of the balls as she'd allocated it a number. The realisation drilled itself deep into my core. She'd touched them and I didn't mind. Julia had slid inside my circle of intimacy without me noticing.

"Ugh!" She dumped the cloth in the washing-up bowl and stared down at her blouse. "I fastened my buttons wrong." She spun to face me and I stared at the line of marching circles as they twisted the collar higher. I pointed my spoon towards her belly.

"It starts there." My lips creased into a smile. "Seven from the top."

I crunched through three spoon's full of my dry rice pops before pausing for a slug of coffee. Julia slid onto the stool next to me, a glass of water clasped in her left hand. She took a sip and tutted as though considering her next sentence with care. "The funeral home contacted my friend yesterday. He's the politician who interceded in your mother's case." She added the last for clarity and then continued. "They were concerned about payment when you left without speaking to their trainee. He phoned me and I grew worried when I couldn't reach you." Julia set her glass on the counter and rested her fingers over my forearm. "That's why I'm here, Jacques. I know it's not about the money. I spoke to the funeral director before I made the journey and assured him of payment. He accepted my credit card as a deposit. I couldn't answer his questions about burial locations or a funeral service. What do you want for her, and how can I help you?"

A buzz grew in my head to obscure all thoughts of Mother. Other matters poured from my lips instead, meant to buy me time but only causing confusion. "We can't divorce until you have citizenship. We can fill out the forms online before you leave. Your documents should hold for now, but we can't risk leaving it too long in case the officials paid by Grey leave the service." I choked on a stray rice pop and my eyes widened in fear of a repeat of the breakfast drama at the hotel. "Or die." I coughed.

Julia's grip on my forearm increased. "Did you hear what I said about your mother's funeral details?"

I nodded and my spoon clattered against the side of the bowl. The sound reverberated around my head and made me want to smash the dish on the floor tiles and stamp the remaining rice pops into oblivion. "I'm not hungry." My teeth ground in my jaw. Mother's face drifted past my inner vision, kind eyes and swathes of brown curls. She hadn't deserved the dementia or the stroke. She hadn't asked for the beatings or for prison. I cleared my throat. "But she liked prison." I continued as though my inner conversation had occurred out loud. "They planned to release her next month. An early release for good behaviour and because she no longer remembered why she went there in the first place. Do you think I could scatter her ashes there somewhere? Inside the prison."

Julia's jaw tightened and her lips formed a line. "I don't think so, Jacques. What about somewhere pretty?"

"France? She visited there once on holiday." My mind performed a leap frog onto another track, desperate to avoid thoughts of Mother's lopsided face and how my efforts with the wipes had stripped her complexion back to a waxy grey. I spun on my stool. "We need to go there, remember? You can't pretend to be from Paris if you've never been. We were meant to get your citizenship and visit. Together." I shook off her grip and lurched backwards off the stool. The rice pops seemed to rattle in my chest and stomach like peas in a tin. "I made a mess of her face." The narrators tried to hold the words in, but I managed to sneak them past, hurling them into the silent kitchen like missiles.

Julia rose and her features softened. "It's okay," she whispered. "The funeral director told me. I can repair it. Let's deal with one thing at a time." She ventured closer and fixed her hands around the caps of my wide shoulders. Her grip felt firm for such tiny, slender fingers. She breathed out, the scent of lemon flavoured toothpaste washing over me, and I held onto the fact that it went unnoticed by the compulsions. They didn't react, still running around my brain and rambling about Mother's face.

"She told me she loved me." The words spilled out and the sense of loss poked its tearful face from the locked box in my chest. If I let it escape, then all the other grief and regret would spill out after it, a tsunami of destructive hurt. "She's the only person who ever loved me. Every phone call and every visit, she'd say the words. She forgot why she went to prison, but she always remembered me. Thursday at ten o'clock." My fingers twitched. "What will happen if she doesn't phone at ten o'clock this Thursday to tell me she loves me?"

"Nothing will happen." Tears pricked behind Julia's eyelids and one spilled over in the shape of a light bulb to break apart on the fifth button of her blouse. She gave my shoulders a shake. "It will just hurt." I knew she spoke from experience and I trusted her.

***

Julia drove to the funeral home in Huntly in her Mercedes, leaving me to collect myself enough to follow.

My fingers itched to paint away my emotions, funnelling them onto the canvas and exchanging my agony for cold, hard cash. But Julia texted after my third shower, promising she'd fixed Mother's face and urging me to show up to meet the concerned funeral director. So, I wrapped the lavender scarf around my neck and drove there, taking the longer route through Ngaruawahia. I stopped at The Point to check the state of the grass and the bench across the river. It still looked a mess after a day's growth and I snapped a photograph on my phone. Brown streaks showed where the mower wheels had slipped on the wet slope and exposed chunks of earth. My loose sketch on the canvas had smoothed out the grass beneath the bench and added a soft shadow. I wanted the photograph for reference, but also to tell the hidden truth. Painting the idyllic scene had already demonstrated my tendency to sanitise the world with smooth lines and gentle tones. The churned sod and stringy grass offended me and I couldn't replicate it even if I'd wanted to, not that anyone would buy the truth. No one wanted the truth, not on their TVs and not on their walls. They wanted the lie as much as me, the irony painful. My birth was a product of a lie; my mother's affair with a married man. She'd been his dirty secret, kept a prisoner in his penthouse suite where she raised me on the broken glass of arguments. Until the day she'd chosen to end the charade.

I ignored the next text from Julia and drove to the funeral home, parking in the same spot as last time. The front door creaked like old bones as I pushed it open and Leoni's eyes widened behind the counter. Her lips curved upward in a smile of acknowledgement until Julia rose from a visitor's chair and eclipsed her in a single, elegant movement.

"I thought you had left the country." Her joke held the bite of sarcasm and Leoni's gaze tracked from me to her and back again. "Come." Julia held out her hand to me and I frowned before taking it, feeling the softness of her skin beneath my fingers. Leoni clattered a clipboard onto the counter and raised an eyebrow at Julia. I sensed the continuation of a discussion they'd shared before my arrival.

"We should finalise arrangements," Leoni offered, venturing from behind the counter. She ran her finger along a list. "We can fit you in at nine o'clock on Tuesday or eleven o'clock on Thursday."

Julia cocked her head to study my reaction and a dark curl tumbled forward over her shoulder. It covered the buttons of her blouse and introduced a lop-sidedness to her appearance. My fingers twitched around her hand, desperate to correct the symmetry.

"Jacques?" she pressed. "You have something important on Tuesday night, so let's choose the Thursday at eleven." Her teeth gnawed on her lower lip. She didn't know how to broach the impending doom of Thursday at ten o'clock when Mother didn't phone me from the prison booth in D wing. Perhaps she hoped to keep me busy, though eight years of experience told her a different story.

"Tuesday at nine o'clock," I said, my tone determined. The split decision brought a rush of relief. "I have a lawn to mow on Thursday at eleven. Cremation. No service. Her friends are still incarcerated and won't come."

Leoni gulped and attempted to cover it with a cough. "What about a nice oak casket?"

I shook my head. "Cardboard. With sunflowers."

"Right." She shot Julia a look of mute appeal.

"You're able to organise such a casket?" Julia cocked her head and Leoni nodded. "Good. Then I will take care of the flowers." She tugged on my hand and turned her body towards the corridor. "Come, Jacques. She is ready for you."

"Open casket or closed?" Leoni skittered around the jutting counter, still clutching her clipboard. Julia groaned and her shoulders slumped. I sensed her tension heighten through the grip.

For her sake, I stifled the scream in my head and answered. "Closed." I offered no reason for my conclusion and they didn't request one. Military funerals always involved closed coffins, and I'd been to enough of those. I'd carried eight good men and Captain Grey on my broad shoulders, knowing only fragments of them nestled within the silk folds of the lining. Sand or dust had buried the other parts. A good sandstorm took care of everything.

Julia led me to the chapel where Mother laid, standing back so I could admire her skill with cosmetics. A soft knock sounded at the door as I gazed down on my mother and Julia spoke to an older man, their voices hushed in reverent whispers. "Jacques," she called in a gentle voice. "This gentleman is the funeral director."

I found it difficult to tear my gaze from Mother's face. Julia had used her own expensive makeup to give the wizened features a healthy glow. The familiar mahogany lipstick matched and turned the thin lips into beautiful bows. Mother would have approved. I turned my feet and my body followed, facing the portly man sealed into his black suit like a sausage. With his straight back and lifted chin, I recognised his military bearing and relaxed. He didn't offer a handshake, but gave a gentle smile instead.

"Is everything to your satisfaction?" he asked. His head cocked a little to frame the question.

"Yes, thank you." My gaze flicked to Julia, including her in my appreciation.

"So, Tuesday at nine o'clock, here in our parlour? Do you have a list of guests? We can make the invitations for you if you have phone numbers."

"Nobody." I shook my head. "She has no friends down here."

"What about you?" His brows narrowed. "I'm sure you have others who'd like to support you."

I shook my head again with less surety. "Roddy, maybe." I wrinkled my nose. "He didn't know my mother." He'd never met her, but he'd heard her voice. Thursday mornings at ten o'clock coincided with some strange times while on deployment. She'd navigated the extra codes required to contact my satellite phone, and the defence force gave me permission to receive the calls. Using a toll-free number meant I paid the fifteen dollar a minute bill instead of her, but the call didn't always connect. Roddy liked to bunk with me because I picked up after him, but the downside was often a disturbed Wednesday night in our time zone. The routine hadn't seemed as desperate to me back then. I wasn't sure what had changed.

"Nobody," I reiterated. Grappling in the right pocket of my jacket, I closed my fingers around the tangled ribbons and pulled them free. Brass jangled against silver as my medals tumbled into my other palm. The East Timor Medal bounced against the carpet and the funeral director bent to retrieve it. His brows drew into a line. "Mother can take these with her." I bunched the remainder in my fingers and held them out to him. Three campaign medals and a New Zealand General Service Medal clinked against the one already in his hand.

"Okay." He didn't question it, but I sensed Julia wanted to by the way her lips drew into a line. Her mouth opened and closed, but she silenced herself, shuttering her eyes and turning away from me.

The funeral director gathered the medals like unwanted children against his smart navy jacket. "Would you like to stay with her until the service? We have facilities available for people to sleep next to their loved one."

"No, thanks. She'd hate that."

"That's fine then." He stepped sideways as I made a bee line for the doorway. My feet kept walking, avoiding the odd floor tiles on my walk along the corridor.

Julia followed me out into the car park, her long skirt billowing in the breeze which contained a nip from Antarctica. I halted next to my truck and blew out a ragged breath. "You are who you are when you're alone," I whispered.

31

Cadavre exquis:

(Exquisite corpse) is a collaborative drawing approach first used by surrealist artists to create bizarre and intuitive drawings

I shouldn't have been surprised to find Henare parked outside my gate. Julia led the way back from Huntly, checking her rear-view mirror on Hakarimata Road before indicating right to enter my driveway. She tapped her brake lights and then, noticing the parked patrol car, sped up, driving past and using the nearest neighbour's wider entrance to turn around and backtrack. I followed, despite the temptation to just keep driving.

Julia used her remote to unlock the gate, and the patrol car shuddered ahead of her. I waited at the bottom until I estimated their snail's progression had reached the top, before blasting through the hard turns and arriving just as Julia parked her Mercedes on the grass beneath the lounge window. I stopped my truck in its usual place by the garage door before the danger hit me like a sledgehammer.

"Shit!" The swearword burst from my lips as I struggled to exit the vehicle. My seatbelt became entangled around my arm and held me up as I dragged it free. In my peripheral vision, I saw the disaster unfold like a film reel and, for once, the narrators in my head grew silent as Roddy stared at the girl he'd abandoned in Iraq.

Julia barrelled across the grass, heading for Henare like a missile. "Why do you not leave my husband alone?" she demanded, shouting at him before she'd reached the patrol car. "We just viewed his mother's body and yet, here you are again."

I wrestled myself from the truck, my soles slipping on the damp runner board. Julia halted as though she'd run into a wall at waist height, and her colour faded to a deathly white as she spotted Roddy.

"Mrs Jethro." Henare slammed the passenger door, his gaze on the ground as he bent and picked up an object at his feet.

Roddy stood by the patrol car, his lips moving but no sound emerging. He stared at Julia with a heady mixture of dread and guilt turning his brown irises to pinpricks of coal.

"Is this yours?" Henare held out his palm to reveal the brass-coloured Gallantry Medal which must have fallen from my pocket on my way out earlier. The purple and white striped ribbon fluttered and danced in his hand.

"Yes." My voice croaked, but I made no move to reclaim it.

"Wow." Henare sounded cowed. "What did you get that for?"

I swallowed and willed myself not to draw his attention to the standoff between Roddy and Julia. "My captain lost his leg below the knee. I carried him to safety, but he died, anyway."

"Right." A frown etched a deep line into his forehead. "I'm sorry about your mother." He cleared his throat and looked across the roof of the patrol car to where Julia and Roddy stared at each other. Julia remained rigid, but Roddy clutched his chest.

"I don't feel so good," he groaned.

Henare's eyes widened. "Then sit down, man!" he growled. He rounded the vehicle and forced him onto the porch steps. His fingers fumbled at the phone in his hand as my medal tumbled forgotten into his pocket. "I'll get an ambulance."

"No! No." Roddy flung his left arm out and pushed at Henare's shoulder. "I'm fine. Just give me a minute."

I glanced up at Julia to find her jaw working against her cheek. Fire back lit her mahogany irises. The wind seized the hem of her skirt and swirled it around her knees, revealing the scars on her ankles created by shackles. I strode across to her, putting my body between her and the police officers. "Go inside," I whispered. She fumbled in the handbag draped across her arm and her shaking fingers dropped her key into the folds. "Take mine." A slick movement passed my door key from my pocket into her hand and I gave her elbow a gentle shove.

Then I returned to Roddy and his penchant for the dramatic. I stopped in front of him as he loosened his shirt collar and slipped off the Kevlar vest.

"I still think you need an ambulance." Henare frowned at the green pallor around Roddy's eyes.

"He does," I agreed. "But they won't find us here. Take the patrol car to the bottom of the driveway and turn it around. Park in the gate so it doesn't close, and flag them down when you see them on the straight part of the road."

"Good idea." Henare darted to the car and slid into the driver's seat. It took him a moment to push the seat back after Roddy's short legs. After a painful twelve-point turn, he set off, and I darted through the front door and locked the gate open, hoping the fool's errand delayed the detective for long enough for me to deal with Roddy.

"I don't need an ambulance." Sweat beaded on Roddy's forehead as he made the announcement.

I crouched on the ground in front of him and peered into his face. "Yeah, you do," I confirmed. "Your lips are grey." I leaned closer after glancing at the open front door. "But if you don't keep your mouth shut, you'll need a mortician."

Roddy's chest heaved, and he clapped a hand over his mouth. Tears brightened his eyes like glitter. "You got her out." He stumbled over the words. "I begged him not to ask you." Spit covered his hand, and he dipped forward. "We couldn't do it. We let him down. All these years I thought she died." His other hand pressed against his chest. "The stuff they did to her. The guilt has ruined my life."

I watched him struggle and an overwhelming sense of deja vu overlaid the scene with images of war. Roddy's face merged with the wreckage in my mind. He groaned and dipped forward again, fear and adrenaline coursing through his body like the product of a burst dam. "You're not suffering heart failure." My tone sounded cold, even to me. "It's a panic attack, but it feels fatal."

"You have them?" His voice rasped, emerging from his lips with spittle that pooled beneath him.

I frowned and listened to the echo of Henare's timidity as the engine took the downward slope in first gear. He still hadn't reached the road, and I had no idea how he'd turn the vehicle around at the bottom without killing himself on the bend. "Yeah, I have them," I admitted. "Julia helped me through the worst."

"Julia?" He glanced up at me from beneath his brows. White knuckles clutched at his shirt. "Is that her name now?"

"Yep." I watched as she emerged from the front door, a paper bag in her outstretched hand. Her fingers shook as she released it and it fluttered towards me. I pulled the edges apart and stuck it in front of Roddy's face. "Breathe into this for a minute. Stop panting." When I looked up, Julia had slid inside and closed the door behind her.

The brown bag extended like a balloon and then deflated as Roddy breathed. The sweat dried on his skin and his complexion lost its waxen hue. He clutched at the fragile sides of the bag as though it contained his life force, which I guess it did for that moment in time. He spoke from within it and the paper and his rasping breaths muffled his words. "The things they did to their women won't leave my head." A tear rolled down his cheek and his eyes glazed as memories like mine filed past his inner vision. I disassociated from them, hurling myself away as though pushing off from the side of a swimming pool.

"She's good now," I offered. "If you say nothing."

Roddy gave an exaggerated shake of his head. "I won't, I promise." He kept the bag closed around his mouth with his left hand and reached out his right to clasp my wrist. "You're a brave man, Jethro. I'll do whatever I can to help. It's the least I can do."

I flattened my lips and nodded. "You can verify her documents for the citizenship application."

"Anything." He gave an emphatic nod and his head bounced. "Anything."

His breathing sounded less shallow, and his cheeks had become ruddy. He needed to drop the paper bag, but the wail of an ambulance cut through the bush and drifted upward to the house. I imagined Henare leading them up in first gear, with the paramedic cursing behind him. If the ambulance climbed that slowly, it would end up going backwards.

"You should stop breathing your own carbon dioxide now," I advised. I reached for the bag, but he turned his body. Like a marathon runner who wears their survival blanket home, the shock made him reluctant to release it. The paramedics would replace it with an oxygen mask. I glanced sideways at the driveway as a petrol engine whined and a diesel followed it with a low rumble. "Why is Henare here again?" I demanded.

Roddy unfolded his torso enough to look up at me. Both hands gripped the paper bag as he blew out and inhaled the fourth-hand air. As he spoke, his chest heaved a little less. "He thinks you killed Nathan," he rasped. "He just can't prove it. Yet."

32

BITUMEN:

BITUMEN IS A NATURALLY-OCCURRING, NON-DRYING, TARRY SUBSTANCE USED IN PAINT MIXTURES, ESPECIALLY TO ENRICH THE APPEARANCE OF DARK TONES

The paramedics took Roddy to the hospital. His eyes watered from over the top of an oxygen mask. He yanked it from his face to whisper an apology to me and I jerked my chin upward in acknowledgement, offering peace but not absolution. Only God could give him what he required. He snagged my sleeve and hauled me closer, and my body tensed. Henare's gaze burned the back of my head. "Don't let her divorce you until she gets citizenship," he rasped. "Does she know the truth?"

I winced and shook my head. Henare appeared at my side as though a sixth sense had warned him of our conspiracy. "What's wrong?" His blue eyes narrowed and their gaze slid from Roddy to me.

Roddy gulped oxygen from the mask before tugging it from his face again. "It reminded me of Helmand

Province," he said, his voice wavering. "I got shot in the shoulder and needed a medevac."

"Helmand Province." Henare rubbed a hand over his chin. The action ended with a scratching motion, and I imagined flakes of his skin fluttering onto my driveway. I took a step back and my upper lip curled in distaste. He jabbed a finger at me. "I thought you served in Iraq? Peace keepers."

Roddy closed his eyes and his lids fluttered as though water boiled beneath their surface. "We went everywhere." His reply ended in a cough. "Who told you the New Zealand army were peace keepers?" He gave a rueful shake of his head and his dark hair swished against the plastic wrapped pillow.

"Are you coming?" The paramedic lined the gurney up with the runners in the ambulance and gave a shove. Its legs collapsed and Roddy disappeared into the interior. The second medic walked through from the front seats and lifted Roddy's wrist to check his pulse.

"Me?" Henare tapped his chest as he framed the question.

The paramedic frowned. "Yeah. Aren't you his boss?"

Henare gave a flap of his hand towards Roddy's prone figure. "I'll make my own way to the hospital in the patrol car."

"Okay. We need to leave. We've got more calls than ambos." He spun away, slammed the rear doors, and climbed into the driver's seat.

Henare stared at me and raised his left eyebrow. "Don't you need to open the gate for them?"

I took the porch steps in two strides on my longer legs, still careful to avoid the odd ones. Julia met me inside the front door and shook her head as I darted a look at the electronic panel on the wall. "It's okay," she soothed. "You locked it open with the remote. I'll see them out." I blocked the doorway to Henare as I hopped on one foot to remove my boots, frustrating his view of Julia waiting for the gate to close before pressing again to open it. The gate camera flickered to life as the ambulance slid from the driveway, presenting a grainy image on the tiny screen of it passing out of view.

Henare stood on the door mat and his gaze gravitated to the picture of Julia. He looked from it to her and then back again as though reaching for conclusions like threads of fog in the air. I saw her swallow before she stepped forward. "You like the painting?" Her eyes danced with the thrill of danger. "Jacques thought she looked like me. He purchased it from my gallery in Auckland." She cocked her head. "I can ask the artist if she has others if you'd like to give me your contact details?"

"She?" Henare's head jerked backwards on his neck. "Oh. How much would something like that retail for on the open market?"

Julia cocked her head to one side as though the question caused offence. She frowned to make her point. "True collectors don't worry about the numbers, Detective. What is ten thousand or a million for the chance to own something beautiful? When we set our sights on a work of art but don't obtain it, doesn't it remain etched inside our lids each time we close our eyes? We will continue to see it and wish we had acted. It will become a regret, will it not?"

Henare gave a shallow nod. He drank in her explanation like a man thirsting for significance. It showed me why Julia sold more paintings in a week than Gordon could in a month. She understood the sting of missing an opportunity. I wondered if she regretted missing out on the life her parents intended for her. My shoulders slumped. Of course she did. She'd been shackled, beaten and abused by rebels because they could. Faith or religion hadn't even come into it. Just plain old wickedness. I'd shot her alleged husband through the eye with a single tap of the trigger and covered her nakedness with a torn curtain. We never spoke about the life ordained for her and the sister who died shackled next to her. Grey had liberated her because she was still pretty. He'd left many others like her to find their way through the repatriation system. We'd got too comfortable with our secrets and our safe, prosperous lives. Roddy was right. She needed to know the truth. I'd got slack and I couldn't let her divorce me yet.

Henare's presence whittled away at my nerve endings. A slight, bony man, he seemed to occupy the entire house with his air of chaos and suspicion. Julia sidled next to me and wrapped her fingers around my bunched left fist. She wriggled her thumb into the hollow and tickled my palm with her nail until I relaxed. When the rigid joints released, she linked her fingers through mine and held on tight. "Will your sergeant be okay?" she enquired, speaking to the back of Henare's head.

He stepped away from the painting with reluctance. I saw his lips twitch as though wanting again to test its provenance, but Julia's reputation stalled his doubts. "I hope so." He flapped his left hand in a gesture which demonstrated he didn't really care. "I'll check on him soon."

"They'll take him to Hamilton, to the Waikato hospital?" Julia cocked her head and narrowed her eyes. "It is half an hour away from here." Her tone suggested a rebuke, as though she thought he should leave right then in order to support his fallen colleague.

Henare nodded. "In good time." He jerked his head towards the lounge and I heard the groan leave my throat. Julia looked up at me, her irises dancing with amusement.

"Would you like tea?" she asked him and he blinked in surprise. She squeezed my hand and her nails grazed my palm with more bite. "Or coffee? Jacques makes a good espresso."

I swallowed to avoid the tart reply. The coffee machine required a cistern of water and a capsule filled with fail safe coffee to perform its duty. She knew that. Her raised eyebrow told me she'd provided my escape from Henare.

"Yes, I'd welcome a coffee." His shoulders relaxed, and he eyed the sofa and bobbed his knees.

"This chair is comfier." Julia pointed towards a leather recliner situated in the bay window. "You can admire the view while we chat." She took him by the elbow and steered him towards the chair, standing close until he'd seated himself with a sigh. I watched from the doorway and she winked at me, communicating her complicity in pointing him to a chair I could wipe clean. Folding herself into its matching pair, she released the laces on her boots, kicked them onto the floorboards and drew her legs beneath her green skirt. Its hue matched the tones in the wallpaper. "So, what brings you back here today?" she asked with a smile.

Satisfied I wouldn't need to vacuum the sofa again, I responded to the warning flare in Julia's eyes and left the room. The gentle cadence of her chatter reverberated through the kitchen wall as she lulled Henare into a trance with her musical voice. The coffee maker hissed and burped, producing two perfect espressos which I laid out on a tray with sugar cubes and tongs. I reached my arms over my head to stretch my muscles and shifted my head on my neck until the small ligaments crackled. Then I blew out a breath and seized the tray in fingers infused with determination. Julia's laughter heralded my return.

"I engaged a Japanese artist skilled in Kintsugi. She fixed the broken pieces of the vase together with lacquer dusted with gold. The delighted potter sold his piece for enough to cover the Kintsugi and the original price by three hundred percent."

"A happy accident." Henare bowed his head, and it bobbed on his neck with appreciation for Julia's story. His eyes narrowed at my return, but he accepted the coffee and added three sugar cubes. I kept my gaze fixed on Julia's curls as he used his fingers instead of the tongs, resisting the urge to smash the tray over his head. It seemed impossible to discern whether he goaded me on purpose or just happened to stumble through life as a natural infection source.

"Merci Jacques?" Julia scrunched up her eyes, her lashes swishing across her cheeks as she acknowledged my extreme self-control. She took the handle of her cup in delicate fingers and sat back in her chair. "Detective Sergeant Henare was just asking about your gymnasium." Her eyes flashed, and I received the warning loud and clear. "He expressed his surprise about how long you spend exercising each day."

Henare glowed beneath Julia's inclusive warmth, blossoming like a bud beneath the first rays of watery spring sunshine. He sipped his coffee, peering over his cup at her beautiful face as a sudden shower pounded on the window behind her. The water droplets refracted the light and my fingers itched to paint her as she rested in her curled position in the chair. Her outward guise exuded a sense of safety, but I recognised the twitch between her brows, which signified fear. I admired her ability to keep the monster under control, her soul drowning beneath its sinister threat even while her lips smiled above the water's surface.

The need to protect her drove me to set the tray on the floor and take a seat on the arm of her chair. I rested my wrist along its leather back and encompassed her in a wall of muscle. Her eyelashes fluttered, and she offered me a conspiratorial smile. The coffee remained untouched in her hand, a mere prop for our subterfuge of domestic bliss.

Flung back to the outside of the circle, Henare cleared his throat and remembered his mission. "Mrs Jethro explained, you don't hear the gate buzzer when you're in the gym."

Julia spoke for me, resting her left hand on my thigh. "They only wired the buzzer into the lobby. And Jacques doesn't take phone calls either when he's exercising. He plays Beethoven loud to get himself into the zone." She dragged out the word 'zone' and lifted her hand from my thigh to produce air quotes before resuming her contact with me. I tuned in to the soothing motion of her finger pads as they shifted against my trouser leg. I realised in that moment how much she grounded me, her understanding completing my electrical circuits and earthing me.

"Why do you exercise for so many hours each day?" Henare's questions caused me to blink in surprise. I floundered, no ready answer presenting itself. He sipped his drink and then pushed further, edging his way into my psyche with a sledge hammer. "Are you a professional athlete?"

"No." His question threw my habits out of balance. Why did I spend so much of my life lifting weights, running on a treadmill or sweating on an attack bike? What purpose did my activity serve? My lips moved, and I stared at the tufted rug which butted up to the hearth. My mind recited the diameter of the room and ran through calculations to produce the percentage of the floor area occupied by the rug.

Julia sniffed, and the sound brought me back to the conversation and the unanswered question still floating between us like a black spectre of possibility and danger. "It's common for ex-servicemen to maintain habits they relied on during deployment." She answered for me. Henare's head jerked back as though he didn't believe her, and she continued. "Jacques is neat to the point of fastidiousness. He lives as though ready for a parade at any moment." She jerked her head towards the ceiling. "They teach servicemen that beds are for sleeping. Jacques never just lies on his bed because he can." She shrugged and took another sip of her coffee. "Exercise is great for venting excess energy."

Henare set his cup on the floorboards next to his foot. I closed my eyes to avoid running the various scenarios of him knocking it with his shoe and spilling the brown liquid. Julia's fingers tapped a three-beat on my thigh as though reading my mind. Pages rustled as he drew his notebook from his inside jacket pocket and clicked the ball of the pen to extend the nib. "I wanted to ask you about work, but I see here that you both co-own the art gallery in Auckland." He clicked the pen three more times, and I reasoned I could live with that. Four clicks in celebration of an even numbered day. When he clicked it again, Julia drew circles on my thigh with her index finger. I shelved the urge to snatch it from his hand and shove it through his eye socket. He waved a hand towards the window and the view distorted by sheets of rain. "Why keep a house here in Ngaruawahia?" he asked. "Don't Aucklanders like beach houses and boats for their escapes?"

Julia wrinkled her nose and stepped into the breach again. She handed me her coffee cup, and I dipped to place it on the tray. "I don't like wide expanses of water," she stated, her voice tight. We'd never spoken about the six-week voyage encompassed in her multi-transport journey to Australia. Trains, planes, automobiles and fishing vessels. Grey organised them all before his death. Roddy's words returned to me like a distant echo. '*Does she know the truth?*' I forced my mind to tune back in to Julia's lyrical accent. "I get sea sick just looking at the ocean." She laughed, a hollow, false sound to my ears. "Auckland is too busy. The traffic is heavy, and it takes hours just to drive along the street." She sighed and stared up at me, appealing for assistance in her desperate monologue. "It's lovely to visit the country and just relax for a few days."

Henare frowned. "And you're getting a divorce." He framed it as a statement rather than a question, and a single voice screeched a fear response in my brain.

33

Curator:

A person whose job it is to research and manage a collection and organize exhibitions

"No." My answer sounded short and filled with venom. "A misunderstanding."

Julia stared up at me, and her irises sparkled. The circular motion of her fingers against my leg became a squeeze. "Yes," she agreed. I studied her face for signs of distress or regret and watched the glitter form into tears. "We're stuck with each other, Jacques and me. No one else will have us."

The truth hit me like a freight train. It ran over me, a warm whoosh of diesel filled air making it hard to breathe. She was right. The only thing that waited for us on the other side of a divorce was loneliness. Julia would never expose her body to another, and I couldn't tolerate the sassy hair and attitude which any other relationship threatened.

"How did you meet?" Henare dipped forward, his nose forming a beak beneath his dirty blond eyebrows.

I tensed, but Julia relaxed into her greatest role. She tossed her long curls and smiled. "We both love classical music," she said, shooting me a look of gratitude. "We bonded online over an appreciation of Beethoven's *Moonlight Sonata*. I arrived on a holiday visa, and we married almost straight away." She closed her eyes and squeezed her face into a look of pleasure. "Jacques worked his way out of the army and we settled here. I've always loved art, and we purchased our share of the Auckland gallery six years ago. Then, we bought a house there, and I split my time between both locations."

Henare flicked a page back, and it curled over his knuckles. I tasted danger in the air. "Dexarn." He stressed the latter part of the word and created a jolting effect, as though his tongue struggled with the name. "That's the trust which owns this property." He lowered his notebook and stared at me from beneath his eyebrows. "I've already linked that trust to you, Mr Jethro. What does the name mean?"

Julia released a snort of laughter and my eyes widened. She squeezed my thigh. Hard. "Jack asked my opinion, and I wanted to acknowledge the name of my jeune fille." She looked to me for help, though she didn't require it.

"Maiden name." She forced me to translate to hide my redundancy in the conversation. We'd learned French together from online courses after she arrived in New Zealand. Julia found its similarity to Persian heartening. I'd sucked up the dictionary with limited interest.

"That's right." She smiled at me. "My maiden name is Arnot, meaning little eagle. I love the numero ten. Jacques named the company Dixarn, but an administrative error made it, Dexarn." Her shoulders shook with the vibration of her fake laugh. "How crazy is that?"

"Right." Henare closed his book with a snap. Whatever thread he'd hoped to pull had been shut down hard enough to trap his fingers. When his gaze flicked to the open doorway into the lobby and the far left corner of Julia's portrait, I knew he didn't seek the skinny kid's killer, but pursued 'X' with a relentless hunger.

"Why are you here?" I couldn't tolerate the thought of his endless returns, the notion hanging over me as a black cloud. My teeth ground in my jaw. "You can't keep invading my privacy because it suits you."

Henare rose and tucked his notebook back into his inside pocket. "Ah, but I can, Mr Jethro. A young man is dead and the only clue I have is that he argued with you on the night of his death."

"Was he an argumentative man?" Julia cocked her head. She withdrew her feet further beneath the folds of her skirt as though in hiding. "Did he fight with others?"

Henare blew out a breath of exasperation. Rapid blinking betrayed his discomfort. "Yes," he replied after wrestling with the revelation. "But his partner stayed at the women's refuge where Mr Jethro took her. Refuge staff verify she didn't return to Ngaruawahia until after his death." His shoulders slumped. "Nathan Watson sold drugs for a local gang and that's the first community we checked. But they travelled north to another member's funeral and didn't return until the next day. The bar manager signed him into the RSA, but he shouldn't have gained access because he wasn't an ex-serviceman. His presence there was a total fluke."

"Had you ever met him before, Jacques?" Julia gave me a tiny smile of encouragement.

"No." I shook my head. "Never. He accused me of hitting on his girlfriend and I didn't know who he meant at first."

"Because you gave her a ride to the women's shelter?" Henare squinted and his officious manner eased as he sensed my cooperation. "So, someone saw you and informed him?"

"Must have. I told no one."

"Not even me." Julia blinked up at me. She pursed her lips and offered Henare enough to send him away satisfied with his expedition to the top of my mountain. "Jacques spent some of his childhood in a refuge with his maman. You must know this?"

Henare nodded. "I did some background research on Alexandra Jenssen's case. She stabbed her lover through the eye with a kitchen knife." He swallowed. "And killed his wife."

I schooled my face into an impassive mask, a reflex action when someone mentioned the reason for Mother's incarceration. There was only so much a person could take in the way of systematic beatings, and she'd drawn the line when he attacked me. A spindly boy of eleven, I'd made the mistake of coming to Mother's rescue, yanking his head back using a hank of dark hair. I'd paid for my stupidity. My throat constricted beneath the memory of his huge hands. Mother had dragged his attention away from me, receiving a backhander for her sacrifice.

My fingers moved to my larynx, feeling the ridges beneath the softness of her lavender scarf. She'd placed ice over my throat, collected the kitchen knife into her handbag, and kissed me on the forehead. '*Back soon,*' she promised as she stepped into the lift. '*Things will be different.*'

"Mr Jethro?" Henare's lips moved as he spoke my name, and Julia slipped her fingers beneath the wall of my bunched fist.

"Detective Sergeant Henare offered his sympathy on your maman's death," she said, her tone soothing.

I nodded and rose, determined to end the conversation. The narrators in my head clamoured for attention, and only my weakening resolve muted their cacophony of fear.

Without speaking, I pulled my phone from the front pocket of my trousers and searched for the number for the hospital. I called it and lifted the phone. Julia's brow furrowed as I stuck my index finger into my other ear. "I'm enquiring after a friend," I said when the switchboard operator answered. "Roderick McAllister. Sergeant McAllister. He would have arrived by ambulance a few minutes ago. Can you tell me how he is?" I strode away from Julia and Henare, my call a direct rebuke to the latter. He might not care about Roddy, but I realised I did. Captain Grey had stressed our battle brotherhood until we believed him. Roddy and I had shared bunkers and food, but never a toothbrush.

I paced while the operator's fingers tapped a keyboard, grateful that she didn't fill my left ear with mouth noises or heavy breathing. My antsy feet took me out into the lobby. Other voices murmured in the background, continuing their one-sided conversations with callers. The operator cleared her throat but did it away from her microphone. "Hello, sir. Can I ask about your relationship?"

I paused and imagined my life without Roddy's thorn in my side. It left an emptiness, like the lost familiarity of a healed scab. "My brother," I replied. Not shared blood, not DNA, but brothers by experience and trauma. I allowed myself to wish he would be recover enough to sit next to me at the RSA on Monday, Wednesday and Friday nights for the foreseeable future.

"Thank you, sir. Sergeant McAllister has just arrived and is undergoing triage. If you could phone back later, there will be more news then."

"Thank you." I remembered my manners and killed the call. Then I sat on the second step from the bottom and absorbed the safety of its evenness. Henare's soles scraped against the floorboards of the lounge as he rose. The chair creaked as though celebrating his imminent departure. Julia's voice murmured, and they appeared in the doorway, her long skirt brushing her pink painted toenails.

"Detective Sergeant Henare would like to see your gym." Julia widened her eyes at me and issued the silent command. "Then we should return to the funeral home to sit with your maman for a while."

My chest caved in on itself and I struggled to fill my lungs. I didn't want to return to the gurney containing the shell of my mother. It wasn't her. She hadn't crouched beneath that tent-like body since the day she sent my father's innocent wife to her grave.

34

—·—

DAGUERREOTYPE:

A PHOTOGRAPHIC TECHNIQUE INVENTED BY LOUIS-JACQUES-MANDÉ DAGUERRE IN 1839

Julia returned to the lounge for her boots and directed Henare's attention away from me as she slipped the gym key from the dresser and tucked it into her pocket. He waited with patience while she chased her boots around the floorboards and drew the laces into a loose bow at her insteps. She pulled one of my jackets from the cupboard beneath the stairs and swaddled it around her lean shoulders. I watched her from my step, noting the grace with which she performed even the most mundane of tasks.

Their exit admitted a sharp breeze, which swirled around my cheeks and nipped at the ends of my fingers. The door closed with a snap.

I groaned and let my chin sink onto my knees. My fingers reached involuntarily for the scarf at my throat, and the soft fabric soothed my shattered nerves as I plucked at it with gentle strokes. Julia seemed determined to take care of Henare, and it turned our relationship on its head. I'd been her gladiator, her knight, providing all the protection I never managed to give my mother. "Sorry, Mother," I whispered into the echoing lobby. My gaze tracked to Julia's portrait, her frightened eyes regarding me from beneath the shadowy folds of her hijab. The slight uplift of her lips offered me salvation. Restoration.

Redundant and lost, I started counting.

Six hundred seconds later, the patrol car's engine started with a guttural cough. I exhaled with relief. Six hundred made itself divisible by twelve. Fifty times. Twelve, the number of completion.

"Brrrrr!" Julia slipped through the narrow gap she opened in the front door and stamped her feet on the mat. "It's freezing out there." Her teeth chattered, and she closed it before drifting to the gate panel and activating the camera view. She pressed the button twice to lock the gate open, and a long one hundred and eighty seconds later, Henare passed across the camera lens in his police car. "He's gone," she advised, crossing her arms over her chest and rubbing her hands up and down my jacket sleeves. "Please, can you light a fire in the lounge? I've brought my laptop and need to send some emails."

"I want to paint." My knees locked, and I shot upright from the second step like a marionette. My mind filled with an image of the pthalo green and cadmium yellow tones of fine, lush grass beneath a freshly stained bench.

Julia blinked up at me. "Okay." She exhaled, and a knot appeared in her brow. "He noticed nothing amiss in the gym." She rolled her eyes. "He asked about the chemical smell and I said you just painted a wall. I think the exercise equipment impressed him. He wished your friend exhibited similar tendencies." She wrinkled her nose. "He has an affinity for fast food, apparently."

I tapped a three-beat against my thighs with both index fingers. One, two, three. One, two, three. "He got married. His wife had two sons. She slept with his brother. She left him. The second son's parentage is in doubt."

"Oh." Julia nodded. "So, he has no one to cook for him at home then."

"No."

"Would you like to invite him for dinner?" She cocked her head, and a smile lit her lips as she answered for me. "No. That's fine. You paint this afternoon and I'll do some work." She swallowed. "I'm thinking from your earlier reaction that you don't want to visit your mother?"

I jumped from the second step without answering and fetched wood from the shed behind the house. Collecting it into a bucket, I cursed the pain still present in my middle right finger. Henare hadn't noticed it, though my sleight of hand had kept it hidden from his gaze behind Julia's head. I didn't want him to draw wrong conclusions about how I'd acquired the injury.

Julia sat on the cream sofa next to the dead fire, a laptop open by her side. She still wore my jacket, and I liked the idea of wearing it and having her floral scent surrounding me. She spoke to me as I scraped the poker through the debris left in the grate. "Jacques, I fear Henare suspects you're 'X'. What do you think?"

I glanced back at her and nodded. "You're right. He does."

She blew out a breath and folded her legs beneath her. The laptop tipped on the cushion. "I think he visited the gallery a while ago. Maybe two years. We ran the exhibition of your work and I remember him from that. A woman accompanied him and a teenage girl."

I frowned, not sure how to process Henare's dislike of Jack Jethro alongside his reverence for 'X' and my alter ego's skill with a paintbrush.

"Would he recognise the landscape depicting the gate?" Julia tapped her top teeth with a fingernail. "I might remove it from the gallery website."

"No. I changed it."

"Changed it? Changed what?"

I used the shovel and brush to clear up the mess beneath the cast iron rungs of the grate, irritated as always by how the brush spread more than it collected. A fine grey layer covered the tiles. "I replaced the wooden gate with a metal one and sprayed the weeds. He wasn't aware of the track until we talked last time.

Julia tutted. "Still, be careful, Jacques. Paint nothing local for a while. Anyone acquiring your work puts photos online and I suspect he's keeping up to date with what you produce. I'm afraid he might recognise something."

My mind skipped back to the half-finished landscape in the basement of my gym. Anyone familiar with Ngaruawahia might recognise the location I'd painted it from. Julia must have seen the guilt in my expression, because she narrowed her eyes. "What are you working on now, Jacques?" I cringed, and she settled her hands over her hips. "I see you squirming and I know you can't lie. What are you painting?"

"A garden." I blew out a breath and gazed through the lounge window. Light came from behind Julia and lit her silhouette as though she wore the halo of an angel. I closed one eye and squinted the other, lifting my thumb to assess the perspective.

"No!" She slammed her feet onto the tufted rug and reached me in three huge strides. Her fingers closed around my raised wrist. "No more pictures of me. A journalist from the Herald keeps calling the gallery for an interview. New Zealand is desperate to discover your identity and as your only contact, it's just a matter of time before someone starts following me.

"Did you speak to the lawyer about a divorce?" I framed the question to make my reluctance to end our charade clear. If she'd phoned him, she'd know I intended to end the trust's partnership with Gordon and give the gallery to her as part of the settlement.

"No." She swallowed and lowered her arms. She dropped my wrist and returned to her seat. "I've ordered the spray paints you asked for and they're due to arrive at the gallery tomorrow. Mandy will take delivery from the courier and store it ready for Tuesday night. I'll move them to the hotel myself. Are you prepared to wow Auckland?"

I didn't know the answer to her question. My art emerged from my soul like a butterfly freed for its rudimentary fourteen days. What happened to it after that gave me no concern. I would never understand the craze for 'X'. He used my hands to wield the paint, but his occupancy ended there. I was not him and he was not me.

The paper caught in the grate and the fledgling flame licked at the kindling. I stole a glance at Julia and found her gaze resting on my moving fingers. But her eyes appeared vacant, as though she chased her mind across a different continent. One with endless dust and wicked men. "I need to tell you something," I began, the words sticking in the back of my throat. Her irises flickered to life, her soul summoned back to my lounge and the strengthening fire. She smiled at me with encouragement and I focussed on the flames and picked my words with care. "I assumed you'd got your citizenship when I spoke of divorce at the hotel in Auckland." I wanted to lock in the moment by listing the date and time, hours, minutes, and seconds. It unravelled like a film reel in my head, when I'd said it, how I'd said it, why I'd said it.

"It's okay." She reached for her laptop, gripping the side of the keyboard in anticipation of hauling it onto her knee.

"You don't understand." I rested my index finger over my top lip before realising I'd spread soot across my face. My lips opened and shut as I drew my hand away and inspected the mess. "I got too comfortable and forgot the risks. It might not be possible."

"What?" Julia's spine straightened as she unfurled her legs. The laptop remained on the cushion. "Why? It was always the plan, wasn't it?" Suspicion laced her tone, making the consonants harder than they deserved.

I nodded. "It was the plan. My plan." I closed my eyes to deaden the impact of my words. Not to avoid the effect on myself, but on her. I was about to make the last cut in her battered heart, and I wasn't sure she could recover. My mind ran through the potential scenarios for once I'd launched the incendiary aimed at her soul. "Captain Grey organised your passage to New Zealand, but I picked up the responsibility after he died." I opened my eyes with a snap, realising good manners meant I needed to get eye contact with her to deliver the blow. My fingers shook, and I eased myself onto my bottom without touching the rug with my sooty hands.

"Just say it, Jacques," she breathed, her voice almost inaudible.

I swallowed and forced myself to keep facing her. Perhaps I could absorb some of the shock. It occurred to me that my eight-year silence had been an attempt to do that already. "Captain Grey was under investigation. He trafficked women from war zones to Oceania. You were bound for a brothel in Wellington. I intercepted you at Sydney airport and brought you straight to New Zealand before your handlers could miss you. A man on the inside of Grey's organisation helped me for a payment." The effort cost me in exhaustion. I realised I had nothing left.

"Captain Grey had a wife and three children." Julia's voice held notes of strain. "And a dog, and a cat, and a budgerigar called Fred."

"And that." I nodded, relieved at having told her part of the truth. Unable to lie, the half-told tale had robbed me of my sanity. Honesty caused a catharsis, which made me want to run on the treadmill until my legs collapsed.

Julia released a low breath, which emerged as a snort. "You think I didn't know, Jacques?" she whispered. "You truly believe I wouldn't recognise cruelty when I saw it. And wickedness? Did you think I travelled first class or enjoyed a luxury cruise? They herded six of us onto fishing boats and packed us into rusty vehicles. Moving, always moving." She swallowed. "I know of the man who helped you and your influence stretched across the continents. I can look back and recognise the moment you got involved. He was afraid of you and told me in Baghdad I was bound for somewhere special. I did not expect a nervous man in an army uniform to meet me at the airport. A man with my new name inscribed in perfect calligraphy. A man, and not another monster." Her lips stretched into a smile. "You've asked so little of me, Jacques Alexander Jethro. You bought my life and I will remain grateful to you for as long as I live."

I watched her unblinking as she rose. She dipped at the waist and her soft palms cupped my cheeks. Her warm kiss seared its brand onto my forehead.

35

DER BLAUE REITER:

FORMED IN 1911 IN MUNICH AS AN ASSOCIATION OF PAINTERS AND AN EXHIBITING SOCIETY LED BY VASILY KANDINSKY AND FRANZ MARC

Her nimble fingers loosened my scarf, the sensations erotic as she tugged the knot free. She batted away my sooty fingers when they twitched to reciprocate. Bending, she kissed the hollow at the centre of the ugly scar at my throat and settled herself across my thighs. Her skirt swished against my trousers and static crackled between us.

It reminded me of the first time we ventured into intimacy, the snapping sticks in the grate evocative of that afternoon eight years earlier. Julia started it. Julia always started it. I'd expected nothing from her after the abuse she suffered and besides, a fake marriage didn't require consummation. It began when she accidentally dropped a sheet of pasted wallpaper worth a hundred dollars onto my head and ended with us naked on the hearthrug.

Eight years, ten months, six days, two hours and twenty seconds ago. All even numbers. I smiled.

The growing flames burned our skin, but we didn't notice, satiating ourselves with the safe familiarity of our lovemaking. Afterwards, Julia fetched a blanket from the nearest sofa and swaddled us both beneath it. I'd failed to add the meatier logs to the fire, and it died down to a few flickers as it lapped up the last of the kindling. She rose onto her knees and sprinkled more kindling onto the smouldering orange and umber tones. Streaks of soot left shaded tracks along her olive thighs, a darker patch over her ribs. I closed my left eye, squinting to reduce her to a shimmering mirage of shadows and highlights. I painted her in my mind, reproducing the delicate imprint of my fingers over her ribs.

"Stop!" She jabbed my collarbone with the square end of a stick. Her lips curved into a smile as she reached for a heftier log. Sparks flew from beneath it as she dumped it onto the resurrected flames. She brushed her hands together to dislodge the splinters and snuggled back under the blanket. "It's warmer in Auckland," she said with a sigh. "As much as two degrees. You should come." She forced her head between my chest and shoulder, her fluttering eyelashes like butterfly wings against my skin. My nose wrinkled on one side and she sighed again, though I know she hadn't observed the gesture of discomfort.

"I like it here," I concluded. "It's peaceful."

Julia snorted. "Really?" She pushed herself up on one elbow. "I hadn't noticed."

I frowned and let my mind sift through the events of the last few days. It stuttered over Wednesday of last week. The skinny kid stood at the apex of my troubles. He'd caused me grief at the RSA and continued to do so even from the mortuary. I shook my head. "I have the gym and the studio. Everything works for me."

Julia laid her head against my biceps and her teeth ground in her jaw. "And you don't like change." Disappointment laced her words, causing the narrators in my head to surge back with their ready quips and unhelpful comments. What more did she expect from me? I wasn't sure I had anything left to give.

Her right arm stretched around my waist and tightened. "It's okay," she whispered, as though she'd heard my thoughts. "I'm happy with what we have now."

We relaxed for a while, in as much as I ever released control of anything. The room grew warmer, but the space in front of the fire became too unbearable to remain. The heat from the burning logs prickled our skin and caused rashes of red to bloom across exposed body parts. We fled from the lounge on Julia's count of three, running through the chill of the hallway with her shrieking. I took the stairs two at a time to avoid the odd ones, and she scampered behind me with laughter and chattering teeth.

Julia accompanied me into the shower and most of the day disappeared from beneath us. I activated the wall heater in my bedroom and we lay on the mattress wrapped in our towels. Julia yawned. "You wear me out, Mr Jethro," she said, covering her mouth with her hand.

I turned my head to smile at her. "You distract me from my painting."

She shrugged. "You seemed distressed. I don't trust you not to wreck things when you're upset."

I stared at the ceiling and thought about her words. A replica Monet floated past my vision. I'd used it as a practice piece when I first started painting on canvas, finding the lost essence of myself in the intricate mixing of colours. The acrylic medium failed to counterfeit the original, but it wasn't my intention. I favoured Monet's technique for *Woman with a Parasol* and liked what I produced. When I didn't answer, Julia nudged my hip. "Remember when we had the disastrous meeting with the immigration officer? You smashed a canvas on the ground and then burned it in the fire."

"I remember." My nose wrinkled and my upper lip curled back in disdain. "I liked the picture. Destroying it didn't have the desired effect."

"No." Julia exhaled and rested her cheek in her cupped hand. Her expression grew gentle. "Are you sure you can finish the wall at the docks in one night? I'm worried about you, especially after your mother's funeral in the morning."

As I turned to face her, the damp patch on the pillow from my hair felt cold beneath my cheek. "I've never been more ready for anything in my life," I promised. The tick of excitement began a steady beat in my chest, releasing an unexpected flush of giddiness.

Julia groaned and rolled onto her back. "This has disaster written all over it. You realise he will come after me when he can't find you?"

My teeth ground together and I stared at her with intensity, wanting to score the truth into her mind. "Then he'll wish he hadn't."

"Jacques, no." She cupped my cheeks in both her palms and kissed my forehead. She ran her left hand across my shoulder and along my arm until she reached my fingers, dragging my hand to her lips. I winced in pain at the grinding of the bones in my sore finger. "You think I didn't notice?" She placed a gentle kiss over the bruise. "You broke Gordon's tooth. He spent yesterday afternoon at an emergency dental appointment." She kissed the joint again and sought my gaze. "He called me about your lawyer's offer. Are you serious about buying him out?"

An involuntary twitch in my left cheek preceded my reply. "Yes. I don't want to talk about Gordon Rossie."

"Okay." Julia drew back and inspected my finger. "I need to strap this or it will hinder your painting. Why don't we delay the docklands job?"

"No." I pulled my left hand from beneath me and twinkled my fingers. "This one is still good."

Julia smiled and shook her head. Her hair moved on the pillow like pools of darkness on an angry sea. "The haulage company will deliver the scissor lift tonight and the client has organised a scaffold with plastic sheeting for installation at the same time. He's planning a big reveal on Wednesday and doesn't want anyone to see it until they have champagne in their hands."

"What's the weather forecast?"

Julia reached backwards and snatched her mobile phone from the bedside table. Her towel slipped to reveal a tantalising corner of her rounded breast. The bone in my finger smarted as I reached out and smoothed my hand over the softness, closing my eyes to map the swollen contours. Julia gasped as I nudged the towel aside and continued my examination. "The weather for Tuesday night is calm and clear," she breathed. Her eyes widened and her breath caught in her throat. "No rain."

"No rain," I repeated. I edged closer to her, leaving my damp towel behind on the mattress as my hard muscles pressed against her inviting softness. Her phone made a dull clunk as it fell from her hand and bounced against the rug.

36

DESIGNER:

A PERSON WHO CONCEIVES AND GIVES FORM TO OBJECTS USED IN EVERYDAY LIFE

Despite Julia's efforts to persuade me to visit Mother, I resisted. To escape her dismay, I locked myself into my studio, barring the gym door with a bolt at ground level so she couldn't follow. I tensed behind my barricade, waiting for her steps to patter across the drive and experiencing a wave of disappointment when she didn't even try to challenge my obstinacy. The emotion confused me as I hadn't realised I cared what Julia thought.

I changed into my paint speckled overalls and folded my discarded clothes, laying them neatly on a chair. The bench painting called to me and I remembered the photograph I'd taken at The Point. I retrieved my phone from my trouser pocket and refolded the clothing before unlocking the screen. The image appeared before me; the moment preserved as a snapshot in time. I held the screen in front of my left eye, allowing me to observe both images at once.

Experience meant I'd replicated the perspective of the slope and the proportions of the garden with accuracy, but my obsession with the bench and the grass beneath had blinded me. I'd missed the presence of two tall birch trees at the water's edge and the way they framed the bench. Somehow, their towering height made it seem even more isolated than my rough draft had captured.

The extractor fan whirred on the wall, swapping the chemical scent for fresh mountain air, but I tugged at the collar of my overalls as though suffocated. The smooth green layers beneath the bench in my painting disguised the mess in the photograph. And as I stared at my version, I realised it had lost something important. The painting held perfection, but the photograph oozed life. I realised with the force of a body blow that I couldn't have both.

I stepped back four hours later, tired, hungry, but still not satiated. Creativity had poured from me like a snaking river, but I wasn't finished yet. Unable to vent the catharsis in my soul with brushes, I'd resorted to using my fingers and the cuff of my overalls. My favourite brushes lay on the concrete floor, paint hardening in their bristles. I should have cared because I always cared, the cleaning and protection of the delicate hairs my usual priority. But something had changed, a subtle leakage of emotion turning my processes upside down and throwing me into confusion.

I exhaled and took a step back, staring at my stained fingers in surprise. The palette clutched in my right hand wore a covering of disorder and violence, the colours mixed in fury like the aftermath of a bomb blast. Maroon nestled beside cyan to overlap and touch. Forbidden lovers in the colour wheel. Painting the truth exhausted me, and I had nothing left.

I lifted my phone from the ledge of the easel and wiped the screen on the thigh of my overalls. Paint smeared it again, and I reactivated the sleeping device while I caught my breath. The photograph bloomed to life, its contours and tones as familiar as my palm. I'd learned the intimacy of how the filtered light licked the slats of the bench and replicated the pattern of the scattered grass beneath its feet. Like the face of my mother, the photograph reached out and touched the protected parts of my soul with a sense of belonging. I knew it and had learned to be unafraid by the notion that it knew me.

The phone vibrated in my hand and I jumped, almost dropping it onto the concrete. Julia's number flashed on the screen and I jabbed at the call button. "What?" My tone sounded snippy and unaccommodating.

"Jacques?" Her soft tone slid over my skin, a soothing balm over a sore. "I made dinner." She didn't say that she'd called me five times, perhaps sensing I already realised as I'd sent her to voicemail each time. She didn't mention that she'd knocked on the outside door and that I'd ignored that, too. I heard her inhale. "Is something wrong, Jacques?" When I didn't answer, urgency replaced concern. "Open the door to me or I'll call the fire brigade and they'll break it down!"

I sensed she meant it.

The ladder to the gym groaned beneath my weight as I clambered up, using both hands and feet. A strange weakness entered my joints, giving my limbs a leaden quality as I strode across the familiar room. My fingers fumbled as I drew back the bolt and unlocked the door. I stood back and waited as Julia pushed it open, her face awash with highlights and shadows from a waxing moon. Frigid air surged past me on its mission to infiltrate every available corner of existence.

"Jacques?" Her eyes widened, and she stepped across the threshold. She reached for the door without looking and closed it behind her. The cold created puffs of condensation as she spoke. "Your friend phoned. The hospital released him and he's fine." She swallowed and lifted a hand as though to touch me before taking it back. "What happened?" Deep furrows marred her brow and her neck jerked as she searched me from head to toe.

"What?" My voice croaked, no energy left for talking.

Julia touched the cuff of my sleeve and shook her head. "You have painted yourself?" The Persian accent sneaked free from beneath her surprise.

I shook my head. "That would be stupid."

"No." Her hair swished as she shook her head from side to side. "No, not a portrait. Your actual self." She made a motion in the air as though stroking a cat, meant to encompass my dishevelled appearance.

I stared down at my overalls, met by a cornucopia of earth tones. "I'm working." My lips pursed together as an uncharacteristic giggle fought to free itself.

Julia's eyebrow rose in question. "Does the concept of working include rolling around in your paint palette?"

Exhilaration bubbled into my chest and masked the exhaustion. "It felt like flying." My fingers twitched of their own volition. "Like a superpower."

"I want to see." Before I could stop her, Julia jogged across the gym and descended the ladder. I followed, worry stamping its boot over its compatriots and dulling the effects of my creative ecstasy.

I forgot about not touching the odd steps, lunging down after her and landing almost on top of her as she gaped at my afternoon's work.

Paint covered the floor in wide sweeps of mess. I peered down at my bare feet and lifted the left one to peer at the sole. "No!" I breathed at the green tone covering my heel and the ball of my foot. A perfect left print tracked from the painting to the ladder, blobs of winter green spread over each rung. Julia turned over her hands and stared at her palms. She held them out to me and twinkled her fingers. "We match," she said with a smile. She pointed at the painting. "This is beautiful. It's so different." She took a step back and cocked her head, looking through the eyes of an acclaimed connoisseur. "I love it, Jacques. I could sell it fifty times over in the gallery."

My lips twisted. I hung my head and stared at the floor. The impressionist work depicted a winter garden, rough, textured grass, and towering trees. But the bench just left of centre formed the perfect base of a scalene triangle. The trunks of the birch trees contributed to the outer angles, the baton picked up by the ridges of the mountain and culminating in an unseen point near the top of the canvas. My house. The apex roof peaked above the white glare from my bedroom window, hidden within the smudges and textures of the native bush. I knew it was there, but doubted anyone else would realise to search for it. The focus of the painting began and ended with me.

Julia frowned and dipped forward to look at the mess on the floor. Her fingers twitched as though she wanted to touch the canvas but couldn't cross the moat of chaos at her feet. She turned to me, guileless and unblinking. "Can I sell it?" she asked.

I swallowed. "No."

"But it's beautiful. It's raw and open. The critics will lick the paint from the canvas."

"No." I turned my back on her, walking on the side of my left foot to avoid spreading any more paint. Hot water gushed from the sink in the corner and I folded my knee and jammed my foot under the tap. I stripped out of my overalls and balled them on the floor inside out. Then I ran more water into a bucket and liberated a mop and cleaning fluid from a cupboard. Julia remained in front of the painting, her lips moving without sound and her gaze raking every inch of the canvas for clues.

The acrylic smeared beneath the mop, creating a montage of colours which mixed into a muddy brown. I used a cloth to remove it from the ladder. I worked in my boxer shorts, mopping a circle around Julia's feet and taking my obsessive cleaning activity upstairs to the gym. I'd tracked it as far as the door and then back again, finding it easier to remove upstairs in the colder atmosphere.

Julia turned to me as I clattered down the ladder with the mop. I remembered the need to avoid the odd steps and slid the last three, saving the bucket but not the mop.

"What have you called it?" Julia seemed not to notice my impromptu cleaning spree or my state of undress, still fixated on the painting. "Does it have a name?"

I retrieved the fallen mop and looked at the riot of colour and texture. The drying paint acquired a matte quality, ridges in the paint creating shadows and giving it a life of its own. "I don't think so," I admitted. "Perhaps it doesn't have one."

37

PHOTOGRAVURE:

A PRINTMAKING PROCESS IN WHICH A PHOTOGRAPHIC NEGATIVE IS TRANSFERRED ONTO A COPPER PLATE

I spent Monday finalising the plan for the commissioned mural. Julia snuggled beneath a blanket in the lounge, using her laptop and making phone calls. The weather brightened and a weak sunshine peeked from behind fleeing cumulus clouds as I remained sequestered in my underground studio.

Once I was satisfied with the sketch, I turned to mathematics for my solution. Using my favoured technique, I created a grid over the page and numbered the segments. I discovered the method when I replicated the Monet, dealing with each square as a separate entity while laying the base coat, in order to maintain both perspective and proportion. For the smaller works I'd carried out in Auckland while home on leave, I'd spent hours creating detailed stencils from light plastic. It sped up the spraying process and reduced the likelihood of getting caught when I could roll up my tools and shove them into a rucksack.

These antics carried out in my twenties provided stress relief after the continual deployments. The long, boring hours between patrols allowed me to plan and reproduce my ideas, bound only by the limits of my imagination. Back on home soil, I'd rented a storage unit near the army base and spent hours sketching and practising my craft. It was there I taught myself how to paint landscapes, buildings and portraits, buying every book I could find on the subject and studying each online video repeatedly until I knew them by heart. It wasn't enough to have natural talent; I needed to excel.

Over the years, I set challenges with myself, working to improve both my speed and skill. The storage unit became littered with practice canvases, which leaned against the walls and reduced the floor space to a narrow passage. Julia later sold all of them, using Gordon's store front as a venue. Overnight, she raised the few thousand needed to purchase the thirty percent share of his business and enshrined the gallery within the Auckland art scene. I'd been an anonymous street artist regarded as something of a novelty, but Julia turned my brand into a sensation. The little Persian girl had a gift for event management and her passion for my craft created an immediate buzz as she advertised 'X' as New Zealand's very own Banksy. The concept caught fire, and she basked in the glow, a butterfly released from her cocoon.

I traced the outline of my sketch onto clear plastic using a permanent marker pen. The sheet fitted into a rough projector I'd made many years earlier from a cardboard box. Masking tape fixed it in place. Once stiff and upright, the box had grown tired and curled. It wobbled on its frayed edges, needing books on either side of it to prevent its collapse. The light from my phone cast the image and I got to work, replicating it onto a sheet of plastic pulled from a roll and pinned to a blank wall.

"Jacques?" Julia's voice called from upstairs as I sketched onto the plastic. I contorted my body to avoid obscuring the reflection, replicating the image with a series of dashes to indicate areas needing to be cut.

"Yeah?" I put the finishing touches to an arm and stepped back. "Don't come down."

"Oh." She crouched at the top of the ladder and peered through the gap at me. "Can't I see it?"

"No." I blocked her view by climbing half way up and poking my head through the hole into the gym. "You need to wait."

Her nose wrinkled, and she clutched one of my coats to her throat. She'd borrowed it from the cupboard under the stairs and I knew it would smell of her perfume for days after she returned to Auckland. "How far did you get? Will you be ready?"

"Yep." I nodded and used my left hand to brush my fringe from my eyes. I'd spend all night preparing if I needed to.

Julia reached for my right hand and I let her examine the tape she'd used to strap the knuckle. She frowned. "I'll do this again when you've showered. What if you need both hands tomorrow night?"

I pushed myself through the gap and sat on the edge, my legs swinging below the studio ceiling. "I'm fine." Squeezing my fingers into a fist sent a dart of pain into my wrist, but it ached less than when I'd done the injury. I imagined Gordon's face hurt a lot more. I hoped so, anyway.

"How far did you get?" Julia rose and backed up until she could sit on the edge of the weight bench. She pulled the coat tighter around her shoulders like a puffy shawl.

I used the knuckles of my left hand to scrub at my eyes. Tiredness descended over me like a shroud. "I enlarged the sketch and traced most of it."

"You're stencilling?" She cocked her head in surprise. "I thought you weren't."

I shrugged. "Too risky. I'll cut out the stencil for the basic outline and spray the rest free hand." I yawned and covered my mouth with my forearm.

"Everything is in place. I've seen a photograph, and they made it appear as though there's construction on the site. No one will notice what's happening from beneath the plastic sheet." I nodded and rubbed my eyes again. Julia tutted. "You didn't turn on the extractor fan, Jacques." She flapped a hand in front of her face. "It smells like a chemical soup even up here. I'm surprised you're not high." She shivered and eyed my thin tee shirt and jeans. "And it's freezing. How do you not have frost bite?"

"My overalls are warmer." I pursed my lips and remembered her taking them from me the previous day. She anticipated my question before I asked it.

"They're still drying. I can carry a portable heater from the house?"

"No. Thanks." I squeezed my eyes closed to avoid the urge to rub them. "Just a couple more hours." My stomach whined and a covert glance at my watch showed I'd missed lunch. The thrill of creation could do that to me, plunging me into a pit of obsession where nothing else mattered but the satisfaction of finishing.

Julia smiled. "I can make you a sandwich."

I blinked up at her, wanting to tell her she didn't need to mother me, while enjoying how those minor acts of service seemed to press warmth into the shadowy corners of my psyche. Nodding and shaking my head at the same time created a strange circular motion, which made my neck crack. She laughed and pushed herself upright, hauling the coat tighter around her shoulders. A shiver rippled through her body at the thought of going back outside. "You need a tunnel to the house," she remarked.

Her gaze tracked back to mine, and she shook her head as a light flicked on behind my eyes. "That was a joke, Jacques. Don't begin digging until you've finished your preparations for the commission."

I nodded and peered down at the concrete floor of the studio. My legs and dangling feet created a frame for the paint spattered surface and I imagined painting the view. Instinct told me it wouldn't look right. Sometimes the natural world created scenes for the eyes only.

Julia returned an hour later with a ham sandwich and left it at the top of the ladder. She placed a bottle of water next to it. I thanked her but didn't stop to eat or drink. She waited for a while, watching as I crawled around the plastic sheet with a craft knife, cutting out the sections which would form the outline of the stencil. I didn't notice when she left.

The sun had already set when I staggered back to the house with the empty plate in my hand. The bottle balanced on top of it with dregs sloshing around the bottom. Julia met me at the front door after hearing me lock up the gym. "You haven't drunk enough today," she advised, cocking her head. "I worry about your kidneys. There are links between dehydration and declining cognitive function."

"Don't." I shook my head in dismissal, fearful of a lecture about my health while my mother reclined on a gurney in a funeral parlour. I doubted whether gallons of water drunk over an entire lifetime would have prevented her decline. It seemed more likely that serious and prolonged bangs to the head might bear more responsibility. At the thought of my father, my fists curled and my right hand complained.

Julia's shoulders slumped, and I sensed her disappointment.

"Thank you for my lunch." I infused my words with enthusiasm, but produced something more akin to mania.

"You're welcome." She yawned and covered her mouth with the blanket shrouded around her shoulders. "Your overalls should be dry before we leave for Auckland tomorrow. Mandy has readied the four colours we ordered and plans to deliver them to the site before we arrive. I ordered extra of each just in case." She raised an eyebrow. "We don't need to worry about Gordon's interference this time because he's having a dental procedure in the afternoon."

I cleared my throat and smothered a smile by turning away from her. Sometimes fortune really favoured the brave. The contact between my fist and his mouth couldn't have come at a better time. The gallery owner had muscled his way onto a previous site along with an unknown number of his cronies. They'd bullied the security guards into giving them access, Gordon fancying himself a celebrity and worthy of meeting 'X'. Their plan ran aground when they encountered Julia at the bottom of the scaffold. She'd threatened to stop the job, and the client lost his temper with Gordon.

The chatter in my head sounded tired as it began repeating the phrase. *'Fortune favours the brave. Fortune favours the brave.'* Reluctant to let it take hold, I rose and staggered towards the stairs. "Going for a shower," I muttered. "Then I need to get to the RSA."

38

PICTOGRAPH:

AN IMAGE OR SYMBOL REPRESENTING A WORD OR A PHRASE

I parked in my usual space across the street, relieved to see Roddy's personal vehicle dumped in the car park. A mural of a poppy field produced by the local primary school smiled down on it, the bowed petals of a giant red flower kissing the flaking paint on the roof. I stepped through the front doors as my watch showed the allotted time for entering the bar.

Comfort surrounded me and soothed away the compulsions as we slipped into our routine. We exchanged the familiar grunts of greeting and I pulled cash from my pocket for our beers.

"No." Roddy flapped his hand. "Not for me."

The narrators in my head silenced before releasing their clamour of panic. Every other thought in my brain screeched to a halt. The air molecules clanged together in the pause between realisation and acceptance. Even the barman stopped wiping the glass in his hand. Roddy swallowed, aware he had the attention of every patron in a twenty metre radius. "I'm okay. The hospital visit was just a warning. The doctor took bloods and my liver is in trouble. I'm making changes. I wanna see my kids grow up and then maybe my grandkids."

The barman's bushy eyebrows disappeared into his fringe. He plonked the glass on the counter and reached for the jet containing the watery soda, which no one ever asked for. Air bubbles and spray gushed from the pipe in response to his finger on the trigger. He set it in front of Roddy without comment and walked back to his glass-shining activity. Roddy reached for his drink and sipped the brown liquid. His nose wrinkled, but he didn't change his mind.

"What are you having?" He blinked up at me and jerked his head towards the barman. "Come back, Ted. You didn't serve my mate."

I stared at Roddy's glass and then at him. My fingers tapped aggravated beats of seven on the smooth edge of the bar as the narrators in my head tried to sort out the calamity. "I don't know," I whispered. He'd turned my routine upside down. I bought beer because he drank it, only taking a single sip before leaving it for him. If he wouldn't drink it, I couldn't buy it. *People will notice. People will notice.*

Roddy squinted up at me and then frowned. He leaned closer to the bar to speak to Ted. "Jack will have the same as me," he said. "And he's paying."

Ted glanced at him and then back at me. "What are ya, drinking twins?" His tone held enough snark to grind the gears in my brain. My trigger finger twitched on the bar. *One, two, three. One, two, three.* He poured me a cola and dumped it on a beer mat next to Roddy's.

"When is your ma's tangihanga?" Roddy changed the subject, but my agitation increased. He'd made it worse, forcing me to think of Mother. "You need another pall bearer?"

I shook my head, unable to remove my gaze from the offending drink. "No. Thank you. Tomorrow morning at nine o'clock. They're cremating her."

Roddy's head shot back on his neck and his eyes bugged. "No tangi? What about people paying their respects?"

I shrugged. "There's no one." My hand shook as I reached for the glass. I sipped the remaining bubbles from the top of the liquid and felt the faint oxygenated spray tickle the underside of my nose. The narrators debated inside my head. '*This is a new routine. He could take three sips instead of one. Or twelve. Twelve sips. Twelve sips. Twelve sips.*'

I didn't want twelve sips, and I wanted nothing to change. My life had tilted on its axis since the skinny kid's accusation. I clung to my snowball of routine and habit as it plummeted downhill, unable to change course and unwilling to release my grip.

Roddy glanced around the room and focussed on the old soldiers in the corner. A line of dominoes skittered onto the faded table and the owner of the bench in my painting rose and ambled towards the bar. He gave me an upward jerk of his head in acknowledgement, and I returned his gesture. "Three pints, Ted," he barked at the barman.

"You've lost to Pete again, Sammy?" The barman reached for a glass and rested his hand on the beer tap.

The old man nodded and dug in the front pocket of his trousers for a handful of loose change. I turned back to face Roddy and recoiled at finding his nose inches from my cheek. "You didn't go straight home, did you? That night when Nathan picked a fight. You didn't go straight home."

I looked around me in the bar, suspicion in my eyes. Any sensible answer dropped through a loose cog in the back of my brain and was lost forever. "Go home," I repeated. My gaze tracked to the door, the path of yellow and blue carpet squares offering an early release. "Go home."

"It's not a trap, I promise." Roddy leaned closer, dipping his head after a glance at the barman. His breath smelled of sugary soda instead of beer. He blinked and his fringe bounced on his eyelashes. "I can't help you if you don't tell me the truth." He reached for the glass of brown liquid on the bar. It sat in the same place his pale beer usually rested. This was a different version of Roddy, a stranger. His sobriety gave him an honesty I found difficult to process. My lips formed nonsensical words, and he sipped his cola and shook his head at me. "I bloody knew it, Jack!" he hissed. "You did that thing, didn't you?" He lifted his left hand and his index finger performed a circle. "You drove home and back until you'd cancelled out the thing with the kid." He stated it as a fact, not framing it as a question.

I gave a shallow nod in reply, more like a jerk of my neck. Roddy swore. He forced a smile onto his lips as the barman glanced our way. "How many times?" he demanded as someone called for a refill and distracted Ted from his studious glass cleaning.

"Seven."

His eyes bugged. "Geez man! I didn't know he upset you that much!"

The hands of the clock above the optics hadn't moved. Panic started as an itch in my chest. I pointed to it with a shaking finger. "The clock stopped."

Roddy glanced up at the white face and the huge numerals. He shouted to Ted. "Hey, change the battery in the clock, will ya?"

Ted wrinkled his nose and resumed wiping the inside of a pint glass with his cloth. It left damp streaks on the inside, which refracted in the light. "It stopped over the weekend," he muttered. "I'll get to it."

I tried not to think about his hand in the glass and the greyness of his cloth. My fingers tapped a beat of three on the bar as I struggled to calm myself. My delicately balanced world slid sideways as the local police sergeant stared at me through unblinking eyes. "Jack! Get it together," he snarled. "No wonder Henare fancies you for Nathan's killer." He shook his head. "You drove home and back seven times. That's what, five minutes each way?"

"Seventy minutes in total."

Roddy closed his eyes. "Jack, Jack, Jack." He murmured my name with exasperation. "There are no cameras on the road between here and your place if you didn't go near The Point. Could anyone have seen you? A dog walker or someone else driving home."

"I saw no one walking a dog. No other cars."

"Is that why Henare became obsessed with your gate camera?" Roddy's eyes widened. "If it has a motion sensor, it would pick you up each time." He tapped his front teeth with his fingernail. "Do you turn around at the bottom of the driveway?"

I blinked. "That would be stupid. My gateway is on a blind bend."

"Stupid?" Roddy's eyebrows disappeared into his fringe. "Mate! Don't make me explain what stupid looks like because right now, I'm looking at it."

I edged backwards around my stool and checked my watch. Another fail. I hadn't even sat down on it. And I'd stayed too long. *Monday. An odd day.* I liked them even less than Wednesdays. "Julia's at home."

Roddy stared at me. "I know you didn't kill Nathan," he whispered. "But your gate camera is causing Henare sleepless nights."

"It broke." I looked at him without blinking. "Power outage. Something hit the box on the road and the power company fixed it the next morning."

Roddy cocked his head and gave a slow nod. "Good," he concluded. His Adam's apple bobbed as he swallowed. "I don't want to know anything else." He jerked his head towards my bruised finger. "Find a way to hide that too. I don't care how it happened."

I nodded and pushed my stool beneath the overhang of the bar. Roddy shoved his cola away with the slightest wrinkle of his nose. "Jack," he murmured, "I've got your six."

"Thanks." I planned my route to the doorway over the minefield of garish colours and odd steps. "But I don't need it."

39

PLANE:

A FLAT OR LEVEL SURFACE

Tuesday dawned bright and clear. Julia stirred in the wide bed and I heard her yawn and turned from the window to observe her stretch. Her arms reached above her to touch the wooden headboard and the sheet rode down to reveal the swell of a breast. Her creamy olive skin contrasted with the starched white of the bedding, and I closed my left eye and lifted my right thumb in front of my face. I longed to push the events of the day aside and just paint her. My thumb provided perspective and allowed me to place her on an imaginary canvas. I hadn't understood the concept of beauty until I'd painted Julia. The narrators in my mind mumbled to each other, knowing they couldn't challenge her. They cowed before her and gave me a moment of peace.

"Big day today, Jacques." She leaned up on one elbow and flattened the fingers of her other hand across the space

I'd vacated hours ago. The coolness of the mattress gave away my angst. "What time did you get up?" she asked, a frown lining her forehead.

I twisted my lips and turned back to the window. "0400 hours," I told her. The narrators started their endless chatter. '*And twelve minutes and thirty-three seconds. Tell her the truth. Tell her the truth.*'

The sun rose higher, a yellow dome which seemed to rise from the old soldier's roof. I couldn't see the bench from my window, but I imagined the light hitting the rickety legs and casting long shadows behind it. My fingers twitched, and I ached to jump into my truck and drive to The Point to witness the march of the sun across the grass for myself. I looked down at my boxer shorts and bare feet and regretted the compulsion, which would drive me in and out of the shower for long enough to miss the spectacle. "I hate it!" The words spat free, drowning out the alarmed cacophony of murmuring in my mind. I spun to stare at Julia, wanting something from her she couldn't give. Sanity.

"I know." She inhaled and stepped from the bed. Her soft skin rode across the curve of her ribs and stroked the gentle slope of her hips and buttocks. She leaned forward and snatched up my folded shirt from the previous day. The fabric crackled with static as she shook it loose and shrugged it over her shoulders. My lips parted at the snapshot of her which my mind snatched and held like a still. Naked Julia caressed by the highlights and shadows of my dress shirt, her long dark ringlets scattered over her shoulders like a niqab. A breast poked from between the buttons as she wrestled the fabric into place. The years had changed her body as it had mine. Her hips and breasts appeared fuller, a glossiness adding a sumptuousness to her skin. I lifted my thumb again, and she spoke without looking.

"Stop it, Jacques. No more pictures of me."

My hand dropped to my side, and I turned back to the window. The full sun marched upward, following its well-worn track to heaven. The moment for recording shadows and highlights had finished. But I didn't want the day to start.

"Will you have breakfast before we leave?" Julia lifted her watch from the bedside table and peered at the analogue hands. The pink leather strap curled over her fingers like a caress. "I ordered flowers from town, so I'll need to leave here by eight o'clock. I think you should travel with me, mon chéri." She glanced at me from beneath her lashes as she dropped the watch onto the mattress and fastened the shirt buttons over her cleavage. "Do you agree?"

The fingers of my right hand tapped a seven beat against my thigh. My middle finger ached, and I forced it to bend. The resulting pain distracted me from her question. I didn't know the answer. What difference did it make whether I travelled to the funeral alone or with Julia? Mother still lay on the gurney, still dead, still lopsided and still destined for cremation.

I jumped as Julia's light touch dragged me from my confusion. I hadn't noticed her weave a path across the discarded bedspread on the floor. "Stop," she whispered. Her hair tickled my arm as she reached for my right hand and uncurled my fingers. She rested her cheek against my shoulder. "I will drive us," she said, removing my options. She shifted in front of me and placed a kiss over my heart. "I don't trust you to turn up." Another kiss. "Get ready, Jacques." She quirked her left eyebrow upward, which indicated command before sashaying from the bedroom in my shirt.

She clattered around in her bedroom next door and a while later, her bare feet pattered to the bathroom. The shower cubicle closed with a click and water gushed free to slap against the tiles. She'd started off in her bed the previous night, slinking through to my room when she heard me pacing the floor. We'd worn each other out and she'd slept as though in a coma. I'd snatched a few hours but woken with a sense of doom resting on my chest. Its weight set me pacing again until the magnificent sunrise transfixed me.

Julia kept me moving, sending me into the shower and busying herself by the sink while I washed three times. She stole covert glances at me as she glossed her lips and teased her eyelashes into curls with a mascara wand. "Come on, Jacques," she urged. "Trois is a good numero for today. Perhaps because Tuesday is an odd day." Her reflection smiled at me, her irises sparkling with flecks of green and hazel.

"It's an even day." My tone sounded sullener than I intended but I'd spoken through gritted teeth.

Julia's frown refracted through the water-speckled glass. "You changed it?" Hurt blossomed in her eyes as she tucked a stray curl behind her ear. "I don't understand."

I shrugged and turned away from her to pump more shower gel into my hand. "It moves. Seven isn't divisible by two."

Julia's swallow held a hiss of exasperation. She collected her makeup into a patchwork case which looked second hand but probably cost a fortune. "You used to make it work."

"I let the narrators choose on Sundays." I licked my lips and kept my head bowed. The shower gel slipped across my chest. "But now they don't want to. Sometimes I know what day it is and they change it half way through just to fool me."

"The narrators?" Julia stopped clattering at the sink. "The people who speak to you?"

I nodded and the shower jets dulled her next comment. She'd given them the name and I'd kept it. She shouted over the sound of the splashing water. "We leave in half an hour. Will you have breakfast?"

I shook my head and wiped the droplets from the glass of the shower cubicle. Sickness roiled in my stomach to create a fathomless pit.

After seven washes, I turned off the spray and stepped from the shower. Julia handed me a clean towel. A tailored jacket flared at the waist and met the pleats of her skirt. She'd knotted her hair into a loose bun at the back and tendrils hung down over her shoulders. I wrapped the towel around my waist, but as I tucked the end in on itself, I caught my stomach with the fragile knuckle. Pain blossomed outward, and I bent double with a groan.

Julia's palm rested on my forehead and she pushed my damp fringe away from my eyes. "It's okay," she soothed. "In a few hours it will all be finished."

I fixed on her words and banished the nausea with mathematical equations. Thirty minutes until we left, ninety minutes until the funeral, a few minutes to say goodbye, and then I would need to formulate new patterns and routines for my life. "What about Thursdays at ten o'clock?" The tiles swam before my eyes, my toes multiplying and swelling in my blurred vision.

"Today is Tuesday." Julia tugged on my forearm and forced me to stand. "We'll use Tuesday's energy for Tuesday and Thursday's energy for Thursday." She raised the cuff of her jacket to mop at my sweating forehead. "One day at a time, Jacques. One day at a time."

She'd hand washed and pressed Mother's lavender scarf and tied it around my neck. My fingers shook as I fastened the buttons on the double-breasted suit jacket.

"Perfect." She stepped back and cocked her head to admire her work before running her fingers through my long fringe and pushing it back towards my crown. "It will flop down anyway," she mused. "I don't know why I think it will stay, but it's what gives you the devastatingly handsome appearance." Her upper lip quirked upwards on the right, as though she regretted her sentiment. She used her thumb to wipe an imaginary smudge of toothpaste from my chin and gave me a rueful smile. "Come, Jacques." Her palm pressed against my spine and she sent me through the front door to wait by her Mercedes. My fingers itched to carry the keys and to lock and unlock the front door, but she absolved me from the responsibility. Like a mother hen, she twittered behind me until I'd complied with her wishes and climbed into her passenger seat. She started the engine while I fastened my seat belt. My knees banged against the dashboard and I lacked the energy to alter the angle of the seat.

Julia drove the winding route downhill with care. But she glanced at my long legs and frowned. "There is a switch at the side," she said. Her index finger stabbed at the remote to open the gate before we reached the last bend and the camber of the driveway forced my knees against the plastic until it hurt. Instead of altering the seat, I kept my hands writhing in my lap and focused on the pain. The gate eased sideways and, for once, I didn't see Henare lurking outside it.

"Just change the seat, Jacques." Her tone sounded snippy, and she tutted as I ignored her. "It's still set as the manufacturer left it. Nobody rides there but you." She sighed. "I am always alone."

Always alone. Always alone. The sentence reverberated in my head like a series of separate conversations. Julia slammed her foot on the accelerator and steered the Mercedes across the centre lane and onto the right side of the carriageway. I turned my head in surprise to stare at her.

"Do you always do that?" I demanded. "A truck could come flying around the bend and kill you." I imagined her vehicle slamming against the bank to her right, her body twisting and breaking against the impact and the noise of tearing metal reverberating around my head. Worse. She could end up in the river. My fear was all for her, with none left for me. "Don't do that again!" I snarled.

She didn't answer, but her jaw showed through her cheek as a hard line. I released a ragged breath and realised the chatter had stopped in my head. The shock subsided to leave a strange lull, as though I floated on a wide sea beneath the eye of a storm.

Julia's lips tightened into a wooden smile. "Be careful, Jacques," she warned in a whisper. "I might start to believe you care."

40

PLASTIC ART:

A TERM BROADLY APPLIED TO ALL THE VISUAL ARTS TO DISTINGUISH THEM FROM SUCH NON-VISUAL ARTS AS LITERATURE, POETRY, OR MUSIC

Leoni waited for us outside in the car park. She grinned at me before Julia's expression wiped the smile off her lips. "These are for the casket." Julia dumped the bouquet of sunflowers and greenery from the florist in Leoni's arms and took my hand as we crossed the threshold. Her gaze as she glanced back at the girl held a predatory note of warning.

Mother waited in the chapel for us, encased in an eco-friendly casket. I froze in the gap between two rows of chairs as the finality hit me like a freight train. No more advice. No more calls on Thursdays at ten o'clock. No more Mother.

Julia tugged me along the carpeted aisle and pushed me into a chair in the front row. The funeral director regarded me with a sympathetic smile which involved his eyes as well as his lips. Leoni tottered in on her heels and arranged the sunflowers in an elegant spray across the yellow cardboard coffin. They made a strange swishing sound as she shifted them around on the corrugated surface.

"Are we expecting any other guests?" Leoni's voice echoed in the empty chapel and the funeral director winced.

"No." I shook my head and my voice creaked at the end of the word. Julia's grip on my hand increased, her nails digging into my palm. I winced in pain and glanced sideways at her, in time to see a fat tear roll down her cheek and bury itself in the dark fabric of her jacket. My lips parted in confusion, as she'd never met my mother. But when she lifted her gaze to mine and more droplets sparkled against her irises, I realised she grieved a different mother. One who received no decent burial or remembrance.

"Please, stand." The funeral director turned his palms upwards and performed an action intended to lift us from our seats. A flash of hairy stomach peeked from beneath both his shirt and waistcoat, seeming as desperate as I felt to escape the formal proceedings. Julia released my hand as we rose, fumbling in her pocket for a tissue. The sudden lack of contact cast me adrift, and it jarred me to realise the difference her touch made to my emotional stability. I held out my hand to her and misunderstanding, she placed a clean tissue into it.

The funeral director opened his mouth to speak, trying to glance at his watch without me noticing. We had ten minutes before the official start time, but I guess he decided not to prolong the agony. Ten minutes early seemed like a fitting number for Mother's dispatch in view of her regimental ten o'clock call on a Thursday. I wrinkled my nose and wished I'd thought of it sooner. Thursday at ten would have been a perfect ending for her had it been available.

Sweat beaded my palms as the funeral director steepled his fingers as though preparing to burst into song. The lavender scarf at my throat tightened to a choke hold, and the tissue disintegrated in my hand and created a carpet of snow on the floor. "Let's take a moment to remember our dear friend and mother to Jack, Alexandra Jenssen," he began.

Air moved behind me as a door swung open and Julia's head screwed around fast enough to give her a neck injury. I turned to follow her gaze and swallowed at the motley crew filing into the chapel.

"Sorry, sorry," Roddy whispered. His eyes widened at the sight of the funeral director getting ready to perform. He slid into the second row on the other side of the aisle and then shuffled along to the end. A group of old soldiers from the RSA filed in behind him and took their seats with creaking bones and grunts of discomfort. The door opened again and another row of seats filled, and then another. The funeral director raised his eyebrows at Julia and her elbow bumped into mine as she shrugged.

Roddy wore his best police uniform, but the soldiers had donned relevant parade attire. Medals tinkled against their breasts and they kept their peaked hats and berets clasped in their gnarled hands. Each of the services bore representation, army, navy and air force. The officer whose lawn I had an appointment to cut wore a major's pips on his arm. He offered a nod of acknowledgement, and my head gave an involuntary bounce in response.

I didn't know what to say, so I said nothing.

The funeral director did his best to put on a show. He'd expected a guest list of two and ended up with thirty-two. I hadn't asked for a service and so he floundered at the front. "Let's sing the national anthem," he suggested after burbling for five minutes about a woman who wasn't my mother. He reached for a guitar concealed behind a flower display.

The old soldiers rose with a rustle of heavy fabric and the clanking of medals against shiny buttons. They put their hearts and souls into the anthem, just like they did every night at five o'clock at the RSA. Desperation induced the funeral director to add the little known verses to the end, and the chorus descended into something bawdier and more like a drunken sing-song.

I couldn't sing and I couldn't move. My lips twitched, but no sound emerged. My chin gained a life of its own, a paroxysm of trembling taking hold as though my body imagined me encased in ice. I focussed on a maroon carpet square and my mind occupied the narrators with whispered counting. *One, two, three. One, two, three.*

The funeral director's feet bisected two squares and rage bubbled into my chest as his shiny shoes straddled the join. Why couldn't he decide on a single square and stand in it? Why occupy both odd and even at the same time? It messed up the pattern, and the narrators stirred, their chatter growing louder as the guitar strummed its muted strains as though under water.

Julia tugged my sleeve, and I realised everyone else had sat down, leaving me like a totem in the gathered men. My knees bent and I sat, my back rigid and unbending. The funeral director placed his guitar behind the flower display again and nodded to Julia. To my horror, she rose and her skirt swished. My eyes widened as dismay percolated through my senses. What would she say?

Julia clasped her hands in front of her stomach and I noticed they shook. Her posture relaxed as she got into character and the art expert emerged from her cocoon to wow the crowd. "I did not get to meet Jacque's mother," she began. Heat budded at the base of my spine as the muscles complained at my rigidity. I dropped my gaze to my shoes and focussed on a blade of grass which had dared to ride on the right toe. My fingers itched to flick it off, but Julia kept talking. Talking. Talking.

"I have much to thank Alexandra for," she said. I glanced up to find her gaze fixed on me. "She raised a beautiful son. The legacy she left for me will be greater than the sum of her life. '*Put me like a seal over your heart, Like a seal on your arm. For love is as strong as death, Jealousy is as severe as Sheol; Its flashes are flashes of fire, The very flame of the Lord. Many waters cannot quench love, Nor will rivers overflow it; If a man were to give all the riches of his house for love, It would be utterly despised.*'" She smiled at her rapt audience, seeming to consider each of the upturned faces in her spell. "I quote that passage from the bible, from the *Song of Solomon*." Laugh lines showed at the corners of her eyes as she turned and bowed to Mother's casket. "Thank you, Alexandra," she said. "You have given me the riches of your house."

I slid my gaze sideways to regard Roddy. He squirmed in his seat, turning his hat in a circle in his fingers as though to distract himself from his guilt. I hated that they'd all known about Captain Grey's other role. It left me out of the circle of confidence and I realised I'd spent my entire life looking through a window at the rest of humanity enjoying their feast. But it explained why they hadn't wanted to help Julia. It also accounted for the speed with which the unit pulled out of the raid, and left Captain Grey unguarded and alone. I switched my gaze to Mother's gaudy casket and sighed. They'd done it on purpose. They'd killed Captain Grey.

My shoulders slumped. Roddy and Mother were more similar than I ever imagined. She served prison time. He carried a life sentence of guilt. But they'd both committed murder.

Julia's skirt swished as she stepped in front of me. I hadn't listened to the end of her speech, but forced my lips into a tired smile of acknowledgement to reward her efforts. She slumped against me and her fingers clasped mine and drew my hand into her lap. Tissue fibres scattered over the rustling fabric like snowflakes. I tried to count them but couldn't concentrate.

The funeral director cleared his throat to punctuate an awkward silence. He spread his hands in a gesture of generosity. "You're all welcome to retire to our reception for refreshments."

With grunts of appreciation, the old soldiers rose as one and filtered through the rear doors in search of the promised food. I followed the military stampede and hung in the doorway, not knowing what I'd expected from Mother's funeral. I was a rudderless ship and but for Julia, would have sunk Mother's final send off by accident and omission. "Thank you," I managed to say, dipping forward so only Julia heard. She slipped her arm through mine and smiled.

Leoni dropped into the role of waitress, providing tea, coffee and biscuits from a secret stash they would probably invoice me for later. The old soldiers milled around, straight backed and shod with shoes shined for the occasion. Julia drew them like paper-clips to a magnet while I returned to the chapel and cleaned up the tissue mess on the carpet. The funeral director drove me away by producing a hand-held vacuum cleaner.

The soldiers stayed, they commiserated, and then they left, clambering into the RSA mini bus and a few private vehicles. The major gave me a nod and waved his hat in my direction. "See you on Thursday," he said, his tone filled with command. "You're right, soldier. It looks shit under that bench."

Roddy hung back, mopping his brow with a grey handkerchief and shooting wary glances at Julia. He waited until the funeral director engaged her in conversation before lurching to my side. "Ted's opening the bar early," he whispered. "First round is on you. I said you were good for it and you'd settle up on Wednesday night."

I nodded. "Thanks." I watched over Roddy's tousled head as Leoni and three other people wheeled Mother's casket away from the chapel on a trolley. The gnawing began in my stomach again and acid burned my throat. My knees let me down first, a tremble beginning in the tendons until the vibration involved my thighs and ankles. A wail started in my head, an awful, primal roar which threatened to burst from behind my teeth and lips and split me in half. It occupied all thought, rising to fever pitch and forcing me to close my eyes to remain upright. I needed to tell her about the skinny kid.

"Jacques." Julia gripped my elbow and held on, digging her nails through the jacket and shirt until they bit my skin. "Jacques." She said my name again, her soft Persian accent cutting through the melee and forcing the wailing to divide around it. "It's okay," she whispered. "It will pass." I kept my gaze fixed on her and gave a jerky nod. Roddy faded away in my peripheral vision. My heart raced in my chest and I focussed on my breathing. In and out, in and out. My chest rose and fell until the lightheaded sensations dispersed. When my blurred vision corrected itself, I realised the flower display also hid a door at the end of the chapel. Mother and her sunflowers had gone.

41

PLIABLE:

CAPABLE OF BEING SHAPED, BENT, OR STRETCHED OUT

"Put on your mask." Julia pulled over in a layby just before the viaduct. She tapped her fingers on the steering wheel in irregular beats which ground on my nerves. I'd spent the afternoon preparing for the job and trying not to replay the scene of Mother being wheeled away for the last time. Julia had forced me to call in at the RSA and pay the bill for the soldiers' early tipple. She'd cocked her head as I'd counted my steps to the bar and back.

"Are you ready?" Her irises glinted, reflecting the light of the overhead street lamps.

I didn't know the answer to her question. A knot of pain throbbed in my chest, and I shrugged. I slipped the mask over my face and pulled goggles over my eyes to protect me from the aerosol fumes. The black Moldex fitted the contours of my cheekbones and jaw to create a seal. I closed my eyes against a moment of claustrophobia.

Explosions and battle sounds echoed in the recesses of my memory. I blew out a rugged breath and settled, forcing my fingers to unclench.

"Do you have enough filters?" Julia leaned across and straightened the black woollen hat around my ears as I nodded. "And your finger is okay?"

I wanted to tell her not to worry, but knew from experience the mask muffled my voice. I nodded instead.

She dropped her hands into her lap. "Be careful, Jack." She sighed. "I'm sorry now that I considered the commission. I'm even sorrier that I passed it on to you." She shook her head and lifted a hand to run delicate fingers over her nose and mouth. "Forgive me?"

I forced a smile from behind my mask, which she didn't see. The effort required to remove it negated the potential benefit now I'd achieved a decent seal. Julia forged on, like she always did. "Just a few more hours and today will be over." I nodded, and she patted my thigh. She drew an invisible circle in the air between us. "The mask makes you look like an insect."

"Mandible." I said the word which best described my alien appearance. She dipped towards me with a frown and I realised she hadn't understood. It wasn't worth repeating.

"Are you sure you're ready?" she asked after a long pause.

A smile broke out upon my lips, which she also didn't see. I was more than ready. I'd been preparing for this moment my whole life.

Julia switched on the engine and the Mercedes purred beneath her confident handling. I closed my eyes and leaned my head back against the seat, counting my breaths to centre myself. My fingers twitched of their own accord as I imagined the feel of the spray can and heard the whoosh as the nozzle expelled the paint at my direction. The thrill of a new mission coursed through my veins, spreading adrenaline to my organs and causing my body to tremble with anticipation. This time, it wasn't my life on the line, but another's.

The mask and filter created a rubbery scent which I detested and my jaw line prickled where I'd shaved before Mother's funeral. *Mother's funeral.* It came again, the overwhelming rush of loss and sickness. And guilt. I should have done more, but the narrators' accusations didn't include what actions would have satisfied them. I'd left her alone on the gurney when the funeral director expected me to stay with her as a vigil of respect. Throughout my life, I'd relied on others to direct my emotional responses to events, unable to wade through the levels of appropriateness for myself. Having missed his gesture of surprise, I'd left it too late to remedy my mistake.

'*Perhaps not,*' the narrators whispered. My fists balled and the middle finger of my right hand released a sharp stab to remind me not to do that again. I glanced over my shoulder at the art folder lying on the back seat. It contained the sketch for the mural. The cardboard roll next to it held the stencils. I blew out a breath and Julia shot me a worried look. "You sure you're okay?" she said. I shook my head in response, wishing I could just tell her what she wanted to hear. The fingers of her left hand reached for my thigh and she squeezed it through the heavy fabric of the navy overalls. She drove one handed, making the turn onto Quay Street and slowing as she looked for a place to park.

A line of orange and white road cones cordoned off a block just before the Maritime Museum. The streets around the harbour had emptied like a drain after rush hour, and those heading for dinner wandered past the construction signs without interest. Julia reached her arm into the back seat and her fingers rested on the art pad. "Can I see now?" she whispered.

I shook my head and burst from the passenger seat. She blinked in alarm as I hauled open the rear door and snatched up the folder before she could stop me. She exhaled and climbed from the vehicle, speaking to me across the roof as I retrieved the cardboard roll and rose. "Please, don't ruin me, Jacques," she begged.

I pursed my lips behind the mask and didn't answer. Assurances formulated like written sentences in my mind, but the narrators swept them away. I couldn't lie, and she knew it. Her shoulders lowered, and I watched dread spread across her features like paint spilled in water. "Sorry," I whispered, but she didn't hear.

Julia walked up the steps and into the reception of the five-star hotel on the waterfront. I leaned against the Mercedes, clutching my sketch and the cardboard roll to my chest. She emerged with a porter and a security guard. "The paint is already in place." She spoke to me, though her tone sounded clipped and terse. Her brow knitted with a frown. "We can access the work area through the back of the hotel. The scaffold is sheeted from all sides and the scissor lift operator can take you to the first level." She pressed a button on her key fob and the Mercedes boot lid rose to reveal my harness and the ropes I'd use to secure myself to the scaffold. The porter jumped forward to grab it in his arms, his pristine white uniform stark against the paint-stained nylon webbing and the dirty ropes. He snatched up a plastic bag containing other equipment, and it dangled from the index finger of his right hand. I gave him a nod of thanks, but he refused to look at me, his movements filled with nervous jabs as he gathered my safety gear and set off walking.

"It's an honour to meet you, Mr 'X'." The security guard pushed his right hand forward before withdrawing it at a shake of Julia's head. I figured she'd told them not to bother. He stared at my hands, the only exposed part of my body. His gaze fell on the empty ring finger of my left hand and he made his incorrect deduction about my marital status. Julia wore an expensive ring, but my simple gold band resided in a wooden box in my bedroom. I'd removed it after Julia qualified for her residency, having never got used to its restrictive presence while painting. Our five years of marriage had come and gone without me realising she hadn't yet applied for citizenship. The oversight might prove our undoing.

Flakes of colour had collected beneath my wedding ring as a daily reminder of the germs which attached themselves to my body. I blinked in surprise as the narrators whispered in my ear, telling me they wished I'd worn it more. *We would have exempted it,*' they promised. *'Like we exempted her.'*

Too late. Everything seemed too late. As Julia, the porter and the security guard stared at me in expectation, I quantified my regrets. I wished I could return to last Wednesday night at eleven minutes past nine and ignore the skinny kid. Julia's lips parted, and she paused, forcing herself not to say my real name. "We must begin," she said instead. "Let's go inside."

The side lights of the Mercedes blinked as she activated the central locking. She handed the key to a man waiting by the front doors of the hotel and he nodded and set off back down the steps. The lights blinked again as he reached the vehicle and I stopped to watch his movements as he hauled open the driver's door.

"Focus!" Julia hissed. She used her elbow to jab me, aiming for my ribs but getting me in the stomach as I turned. She covered my grunt of shock with a loud cough.

The security guard led us to an elevator and used an access card to take us downstairs. My stomach lurched at the sudden downward jolt and I held my breath. After a few seconds, the doors opened onto a bar area. Darkness shrouded the room, the light from the lift casting shadows across the deserted tables and chairs. Place settings intensified the sense of confusion, as though the napkins and cutlery held its breath in expectation of visitors who wouldn't come.

The security guard turned to Julia. His gaze coasted across my face and he looked away as though my mask and goggles made him uneasy. "The hotel manager will meet you in a moment. The bar is closed for tonight." He set across the carpet on rubber-soled shoes and Julia followed.

Floodlights flicked on and the sudden illumination cast an eerie glow across a patch of concrete slabs. Stacked tables and chairs occupied one corner of the space. Beyond it, the reflections of moored boats twinkled like stars in the harbour.

A man wearing an expensive black suit pushed the door open from the outside and smiled at Julia. Both of his arms lifted, and he embraced her, adding an air kiss to either cheek. "Welcome, Mrs Jethro," he said with a formal bow. "And Mr 'X'." Sweat beaded around my nose as his piercing gaze bored through the safety goggles and connected with my soul. I experienced a moment of extreme nakedness, as though his perception had stripped me to the bone. My heart thudded in my chest and I used the beats to regain my rhythm. The narrators whispered to themselves behind a veil, which muted their words. Julia's ears twitched as though she wanted to look at me but resisted.

The man introduced himself without removing his gaze from my face. He didn't offer his hand or attempt to give me air kisses. "My name is Paul Raines. I manage this hotel and another also owned by our chain." He gave a grunt of amusement. "My father chose this location as it has a blank wall above the bar and beneath the fifth-floor windows." His pointed nose wrinkled. "The wall is wasted real estate, really. Waterfront views make the money, but the space behind it is a fire egress and the heritage people won't let us bash the building around anymore." He sighed as though wishing he could take a sledgehammer to it himself. He flapped a hand towards the door he'd left ajar and through which a sea breeze intruded. "We'll access the mobile elevated work platform from the veranda and the scaffold will block any views from the water. Only the platform operator will go up with you and if you need to go higher, you can use the scaffold boards. The electric knuckle boom was the only type of scissor lift we could fit around the side of the building and it reaches as far as sixteen metres. We blanked the windows on either side of your work area from the outside after those guests left this afternoon."

"The rooms are definitely empty?" Julia cocked her head and narrowed her eyes.

"Yes." Paul Raines gave an emphatic nod of his head. "My security team is guarding both ends of the relevant corridors and I can guarantee the rooms were vacated." He gave a watery smile. "One cross I bear is health and safety. The last thing we need is paint drift and lawsuits from idiots inhaling it."

Julia cleared her throat. I turned my gaze on her, watching the signs of her floundering and unable to offer assistance. "We're more concerned about spectators using adjacent windows to watch 'X' work," she concluded. Nervous tension stretched out the vowel sounds of her fake Parisian accent to betray the Persian undertones.

Raines shook his head. "The rooms are locked," he promised. "It won't happen. We've even ensured there won't be any unplanned photos or video footage by confiscating the operator's phone. He has a two-way radio, but no other mobile device." He clicked his fingers, and the guard scurried forward to hold the door open so we could proceed onto the veranda. Tall and straight backed, he eclipsed Julia, but not me. He held himself with an erectness which came with the confidence of a never-ending supply of money. *'Paul Raines. Paul Raines.'* The narrators' voices buzzed in my head and I overlaid their sounds by humming the melodic strains of the *Moonlight Sonata* under my breath. The floodlight picked out the highlights of Raines' dirty blond hair and he smiled at Julia, though the expression didn't reach his blue eyes.

She gulped and glanced back at me. I stepped out behind her, and the security guard closed the door and stood in front of it. He spread his legs and clasped his hands behind his back, a stance I knew well.

Julia didn't look at me as I inspected the boxes of spray cans already loaded onto the platform of the scissor lift. I tucked my art folder behind one of them and stuffed the end of the cardboard roll into another open box. It took five minutes for me to get into my harness and allow Raines to inspect the safety of the *Bowline with a Bight* knots I'd used. I kept my face averted as he lifted the rope and tugged on the carabiners. The way his fingers moved conveyed his inexperience and highlighted the depth of his pretence. I could have tied a bow and he would have accepted it. My safety wasn't his primary concern but the prospect of adverse publicity and legal action if my blood decorated his concrete pavers. He needed to show he'd tried to save me. I understood the sentiment. More than he would ever know.

"Will your father join us tonight?" Julia framed the question with skill, adding just the right amount of indifference.

Paul Raines shook his head. "He sends his apologies. He'll fly home tomorrow in time for the celebration and reveal party tomorrow night. There's a big vote taking place in parliament and the prime minister is counting on him."

"Of course she is." Julia pursed her lips and stared out at the boats in the distance. Lights twinkled off the water like a star burst.

"You need a safety vest and a hard hat." Raines jerked his head towards the operator but spoke to me. The man faltered, his eyes widening beneath his white hat. The orange of his overalls and vest matched the lurid tangerine and yellow of his machinery.

"We're good." Julia held her hand out to the porter, and he released the plastic bag to her. She dug inside and pulled out my orange vest and white hat, both stained by paint drift until they'd become works of art in their own right.

I refused the operator's offer of assistance as I clambered onto the platform of his scissor lift. Already upset, the narrators wouldn't cope with any more contamination. I secured the carabiner from my safety rope to the rail and grasped the smooth metal in my fingers as he started up the motor. The machine jerked to life, the electric less noisy than the diesel ones I'd ridden for other commissions.

Julia offered a watery smile as the boom lifted me above her head. The goggles and the refracted light sources distorted her lips, but I saw the words in her eyes. "Sorry," she mouthed. "I'm so sorry."

42

POSE:

THE WAY A FIGURE IS POSITIONED

The hard hat fitted over the thin woollen one which hid my ear buds. I tightened the chin strap as the scissor lift jerked to life under the direction of the operator's skilled fingers. Being encased in my protective gear gave me an illusion of safety, despite the growing distance between the platform's non-slip surface and the concrete slabs of the veranda. I looked over the rail as we cleared the top of the bar's high doors and continued to the level of the first-floor windows. Blue tarpaulin flapped in the breeze sweeping from the ocean and the platform rocked with the motion of the boom as it extended. I'd studied seaward photographs of the building and knew the proportions. I'd start at a height of six metres, continuing to just beneath the fourth-floor windowsills at sixteen. High enough to die from a fall but nothing compared to parachuting over a battle field attached to a flimsy piece of silk.

I smiled behind my mask as I remembered my squad's first free fall together. Roddy scarfed a burger and fries before the flight and threw up at two thousand metres. I'd had the foresight to jump before him, but he managed to cover most of those following. It earned him the nickname Ruaki, which was Māori for vomit.

The chassis levelling stabilisers gave the platform a solid foundation, and the operator shot frequent glances in my direction. His lips moved as though he wanted to speak, but knew I wouldn't hear him over the hydraulics. I lifted both hands and showed him six fingers. He gave an enthusiastic nod and a thumbs up. At exactly six metres, he drew the platform to a halt and spun it horizontally ninety degrees. I released my carabiner from the rail and hooked it near the gate. The chugging of the hydraulics faded to an even hum, and the operator stopped the platform level with the first of the scaffolding boards.

"You good to go?" His brow furrowed as he passed me and unlatched the gate. A newer safety harness kept him tethered to the rails of the platform, and the metal hooking points jangled together as he moved. His rope swept over the boxes containing my gear and dislodged the cardboard roll. I caught it as it bounced free and hit the floor of the platform. "Sorry." His nose wrinkled and his shoulders slumped in defeat. I watched him from behind my goggles and mask, wondering if his head contained narrators to berate him. I had no interest in reassuring him and besides, he couldn't see my face even if I smiled.

When the shopping mall at Sylvia Park commissioned a landscape for the side of the food court two years earlier, I'd faked a Scottish accent for my scant replies. The news media went mad, forging links with the kilted country and making up stories to fit their agenda. It amused Julia, but she told me not to do it again. The honorary degree which Edinburgh university offered 'X' a month later embroiled her in a tough conversation. I exhaled a sigh into my mask and rolled my head on my neck as the operator pushed the gate open and stepped back.

'*Show time,*' the narrators giggled. They repeated the word numerous times, but I blocked out their gibberish. The operator helped me to drag the cardboard boxes onto the scaffolding. It involved squeezing through a slit in the tarpaulin, which hid my work from view of the water. The extensive sheeting created a micro climate of its own between the plastic and the building, but the crack of the sheet in the breeze disturbed the false sense of peace.

I unhooked my rope from the platform and frowned as the operator did the same. I shook my head to indicate my displeasure, but he shrugged and winced. "Sorry. I must stay nearby. Health and safety." He pointed to the radio attached to his belt. "I have to get help if you fall."

I snorted in my mask at his politically correct reply. If I fell from a height of sixteen metres, he wouldn't need his radio. Julia would know about it pretty fast and Paul Raines would pick bits of me off his veranda for weeks afterwards. I tapped my mask and goggles to indicate he needed the same, and he gave a definitive nod. "On the platform. I'll get them."

He turned away, and I capitalised on his temporary absence to start work. Shoving the art pad in my teeth and tucking the cardboard roll under my arm, I strode along the boards to a ladder at the end of the first run. Then I began my climb, zigzagging to a height of sixteen metres before the platform operator reappeared.

I emptied my hands and took a step back, taking a second to calm myself. The handling of this moment could make or break my creativity. I breathed in and out seven times, holding each breath for three seconds as it came and went from my lungs. Dragging my phone from a pocket at thigh height in my overalls, I pulled up Beethoven's *Moonlight Sonata* and waited for the Bluetooth to connect to my ear buds. I wasn't stupid enough to play it so loud that I couldn't hear warnings, but I needed it at a volume high enough to cover the frequent crack of the tarpaulin. The carabiner clanked against the metal scaffolding rail as I secured myself to it.

The structure shuddered as the operator moved down below, and I hoped he wasn't tasked with standing over me as I worked. His head didn't appear at the top of the ladder and so I began, popping the lid from the cardboard roll and withdrawing the three plastic stencils I'd created in my studio. Julia had organised for bricks to be left at the sixteen-metre point, and I used them to hold each figure as I laid them flat across the boards and waited for the plastic to relax.

A trip back to the bottom involved unhooking and hooking the safety rope as I moved through the levels and I found the operator waiting near the platform. He shifted from foot to foot, radiating a mixture of fear and boredom. I dragged a hammer and a pot of thin nails from a box and snatched up a can of black paint. All three went into the pockets of my overalls and I set off back to the top.

The building owner hadn't asked for rudimentary details about my work, and it proved a good thing. I used the nails to hold the stencils in place and hoped he didn't mind the liberty. It took an hour and a half for me to position them where I wanted them, crawling along the boards at each level and securing them to the brick. The mask heated my skin to create a prickling sensation, and I wished I could slip it off for even a moment. The operator moved around below, his footsteps sending a low vibration through the metal, and I couldn't risk him seeing my face.

Beethoven soothed my soul as I unhooked the carabiner and headed up to the sixteen-metre point. The can of black spray waited for me where I left it and, with a deep breath, I seized it and began shaking the paint. The ball bearing inside rattled more as the paint loosened, hammering the interior of the can. Julia had ensured Mandy spent her afternoon softening the paint inside the cans, shaking each in turn to ensure the liquid didn't settle. I wondered which of Paul Raine's employees had continued the task after she dropped the boxes at the hotel and took her aching arms home for the night. Someone had done a good job because it took less than a minute for the paint to reach the right consistency. I turned over my sketch and sprayed a burst onto its rear. Dots of inky black loosed on the thick watercolour paper before the nozzle behaved. I used a stray brick to secure the paper and rose, a light headed sensation blurring my peripheral vision.

A lone piano vacuumed up the remnants of a movement as Beethoven's crescendo waited above my head. It descended with a burst of furious notes as I resecured my carabiner to the rail and stepped forward, spray can clasped in my left hand. I wanted to howl as the first paint hit the sides of the stencil and left a sheen across the brick. My whole life had led to this moment, and the narrators silenced in my head.

Only one set up a faint whisper beneath the rousing piano and I pushed it aside, though my soul heard its cry.

'Sorry Julia,' its voice wavered. *'Sorry Julia.'*

43

PRIME:

TO PREPARE A SURFACE FOR PAINTING BY COVERING IT WITH PRIMER, OR AN UNDERCOAT

It took two hours to complete spraying the stencils with their striking black outline. I ran up and down the ladders, working methodically to fill the gaps before moving to the next level. Twenty-three empty spray cans littered the boards, spread around like the spent cartridges of bullets. A chemical haze hung around within the tarpaulin, drifting beneath the watchful glare of the floodlights. I sat on the boards in front of the detailed outline of a man's head and paused to catch my breath. The heady scent of toluene seeped beneath the mask and I frowned. Each filter had an eight-hour lifespan in an environment such as the one created within the tarpaulins. I used my fingers to search around the edges of the mask, discovering where sweat had broken the seal with my face to allow seepage.

Claustrophobia bit at my psyche, urging me to rip the goggles and mask from my face. I resisted, not trusting

Paul Raines and not willing to compromise my anonymity if he'd secreted cameras around my workspace. The knuckle of my middle finger ached. I'd needed to alternate the use of my hands in order to give my trigger fingers a break. Rolling up my sleeves, I checked the digital display on my watch. My back twinged from the constant stretching as I contorted myself to join up the painted areas from one level to another. The *Moonlight Sonata* began from the start and I forced myself to a standing position. The next part of the process involved less running up and down the ladders and I rotated my right arm in its socket in celebration.

Thankfully, the scissor lift operator helped to carry more paint to the upper levels. He held the box at one end of each section while I deposited the relevant paint colours in front of the image. His lips moved as I took the last canister from the box and I paused as his voice cut through the piano music. "I'm gonna tell my grandchildren about this," he repeated, raising his mask to make sure I heard.

I backed away from him and almost tripped over my trailing safety rope. My frantic activity had silenced the narrators, but his sentiment woke them. They rattled around my head with a heightened sense of anxiety but offered nothing helpful in reply. Not that I could speak to him if I wanted. Julia's orders.

The sketch came into its own with its grid as I filled in the wide spaces with colour. Black faded to navy, overlaid with highlights of white. A man emerged from the brick, dressed in smart business attire. Highlighted white flecks demonstrated the shine on his black shoes. A woman cowered on the next level of the scaffold, shielding a young boy with her body. She crushed him against the side of a kitchen cupboard, the counter overhanging his downy head. Highlights and shadows carved a paroxysm of fear into his features, and a small hand clutched his mother's upper arm.

The man appeared so average and just as I remembered him. Tall and imposing, but loved by many. His relaxed posture gave nothing away. Viewed from behind his back, it could have been just an ordinary man looking in a shop window.

The woman made the picture come alive. The balling of her fists displayed her resilience and willingness to fight for her child. She wore the white skirt with its black polka dots for him and not because she liked it. Later in life, she would prefer the dowdy prison green and wear it with a strange kind of pride. Her calm face channelled determination and courage. Rosebud lips parted in a threat and I heard her promise echo in my head. *'Touch my son and I'll kill you.'*

Mother commissioned me to paint our story where those who made the decisions would see it. She paid me five dollars because it was never about the money. It was about the plight of women like her, invisible until she blinded him. Then the entire nation believed it knew the truth, but it didn't.

It was about New Zealand's pitiful statistics as having one of the highest rates of domestic violence in the developed world. Just over a year ago as parliament sat for the first time since the election, I'd chosen a location as close to New Zealand's seat of power as I could get; the Beehive in Wellington.

I'd hit him where it hurt. For her.

But it hadn't hurt him enough. He'd used his influence as a member of parliament to ensure a happy accident saw my work obliterated beneath the nondescript cream paint on the side of the citizen's advice bureau. He'd removed my statement from opposite the parliamentary building. He'd wish he hadn't done that.

I finished my masterpiece after eight more hours. The lift operator slept on the bottom board of the scaffold, his mask askew on his face. He'd watched me start the free hand lettering to finish the piece but keeled over in the fumes. Reluctant to touch him, I'd pulled open the slit in the tarpaulin and wedged it apart using a spare carabiner poked through the plastic. Fresh sea air poured through the gap and swirled around my legs as I worked.

I figured the operator would wake with one hell of a headache, so set about clearing up my mess. The empty spray cans went back into the boxes, along with anything else I didn't want to leave behind me. Julia vexed herself worrying about fingerprints and DNA and I knew she'd ask me about my rubbish afterwards. I stashed everything on the platform of the scissor lift and then kicked the operator's foot to wake him.

My back ached, my shoulders ground in their sockets, and my finger throbbed. If I didn't get the mask and goggles off soon, I'd explode.

Pleasure thrummed in my chest as I considered my art. The final touch had involved a metre high 'X' at the bottom right-hand corner below the boy's bent knees. I'd saved the last of the navy colour for the flourishing signature.

I was done. Finished.

The pianist completed Beethoven's final flourish, as though he shared my ecstasy. I wondered if he ever approached the keys again after such an outpouring of emotional baggage. The narrators chattered in muted voices, which I could ignore. They had no words and nor did I.

The operator struggled to his feet and hauled his mask over his head. He blinked and shook himself like a dog. "Bloody mask," he said with a sigh. "I feel as high as a kite." His fingers clasped the rail as he shuffled towards the slit in the tarpaulin. He frowned as he noticed how I'd pinned it back to allow an increased air flow. "Are you gonna tell?" He swallowed and his fingers twitched on the left filter of his mask. I shook my head, knowing I wouldn't speak to anyone except Julia. I glanced back at my huge signature and smiled behind the rubber which shielded my expression. The mural did my speaking for me.

The operator touched my arm, and I jerked away in shock. "Sorry," he gushed. "Sorry." He licked his lips and paused. "I have to seal that tomorrow. They want to preserve it." His gaze slipped back to the hem of Mother's skirt showing beneath the next floor of the scaffolding. "My dad beat my mum." He lifted the hand containing the mask and the rubber strap shivered in his grip. "It looks like her."

An uncomfortable prickle began in my stomach and pressed into my heart. I froze in place, staring down at him as he wrestled with his confession. He ground his teeth and made a decision. "I'll take care of it. I'll find a way to stop Raines seeing it before the big reveal." A smile of complicity spread across his face. "I'll make sure the guys seal it so well that he'll have to sand it back to the support beams if he wants to get rid of it."

He raised his right hand to me in a gesture of solidarity. The narrators held their collective breaths as I took it, my paint-stained fingers closing around his in acceptance of our shared confession.

44

PROFILE:

A SIDE VIEW, USUALLY REFERRING TO THAT OF A HUMAN HEAD

The scissor lift jerked as the operator lowered it to ground level. Exhaustion and dehydration laid claim to my body, and I squatted on the platform with my head leaned back against the rail. Unused bottles of water nestled in another box near the operator, but I hadn't wanted to lift my mask to drink. I craved whisky on the rocks and focussed on the memory of how it would crackle in the glass as the liquor hit the ice. The journey down took longer as the operator messed with the controls.

Julia appeared on the veranda with Raines as the platform cut out two metres from its resting point. "What's wrong?" she demanded. Her gaze flicked to me and a tired furrow appeared between her brows.

"We almost didn't make it down," the operator lied. His expression showed no discomfort.

"What's up with it?" Raines' heels struck the hard surface with staccato beats. His lips straightened into a line of annoyance. "I need to go up and see the mural."

"Sorry boss, no can do." The operator shook his head and feigned regret. "This is buggered. I'll get the engineers out first thing and we'll get sealing the mural." He glanced at me and gave a lopsided smile. "It's fantastic."

Raines relaxed, though his teeth gnawed at the inside of his top lip. "What time will the engineers get here?" He shot a glance at the first floor of the scaffolding above and the fingers of his right hand tapped a beat against his crisp pants leg. Julia appeared frayed around the edges by her long wait, her curls hanging from the neat bun and clinging to her jacket. But Raines looked as though he'd woken from a refreshing sleep. His suit remained crisp, hugging his body like a sleeve and not a single hair rose in the sharp breeze coasting across the harbour. He checked his watch. "Can you call them now?"

The operator gave a snort of mirth. "Not a chance, boss. They don't work nights. I'll call them as soon as the service coordinator starts in the morning." He turned his wrist over and waggled his bushy eyebrows. "That's in four hours' time."

Raines released a huff of disgust. "This is typical!" he spat. He jerked his head towards the scissor lift as the operator released the gate latch. I unhooked my safety rope and scooted to the edge of the platform. The short distance to the ground felt like a free fall sky dive as I swung my feet towards the pavers. I landed heavily and listed to one side.

"Good job, Mr 'X'." Raines frowned, his expression scrunched and pained by his blocked goal. He wanted to see what I'd done and couldn't. He offered me his hand to shake, and I ignored it.

"Let's go." Julia gave me a smile marred by the lines of exhaustion. She rubbed at an ache in the hollow of her spine where her flared skirt met her blouse beneath the jacket. A different man appeared wearing a porter's uniform, and Julia gave him a list of instructions. She held out the key of the Mercedes and my left hand ached as they fell into my palm. "Everything is packed?" She raised an eyebrow at me and I nodded. "Good." She turned to the porter and he stepped underneath the platform. She half turned her body back towards me. "Open the boot. I'll oversee the retrieval of the rubbish."

Raines led me back through the darkened hotel and opened the front door. He stared at me, trying to find distinguishing features behind the mask and goggles. Our shoulders were at equal height as I paused to unlock the car. The boot rose in a gentle motion in response to my press of the remote. I wished Raines would leave, his continued presence making me agitated. The narrators woke, setting up a cacophony of warning, but I didn't need their advice. Ignoring his attempt to make small talk about the sudden clap of thunder in the distance, I pushed my way into the passenger seat and sank into the soft folds of the leather interior.

Julia's heels echoed on the pavement in the hushed street. The porter followed behind, loaded with boxes so he couldn't see over the top. I closed my eyes and leaned my head against the seat, desperate to remove the goggles and mask. A rubbery scent through the filters turned my stomach as it merged with the smell of my sweat. The skin beneath the seal of the goggles itched as though biting ants crawled across my face and forehead.

The porter returned for the rest of my gear and I heard the cardboard roll thud onto the floor of the boot. Julia slammed the lid, and I watched through the wing mirror as she shook hands with Raines. He leaned in and kissed each of her cheeks, lingering over the action. His brow furrowed in disappointment as she pulled away and swung towards the car. The driver's door slammed behind her and she eyed the keys I'd dumped in the cup holder. "Let's get out of here," she hissed as her index finger jabbed the ignition button.

She didn't speak again until we reached the outskirts of the business district. I grappled with the goggles and she reached across and stayed my hand. "Not yet," she advised. "I don't trust his father not to access the traffic cameras."

I groaned and suffered the sense of desperation for another ten minutes. My skin prickled, and I forced my fingers beneath my thighs to prevent me from venting my agitation and ripping off the mask and goggles. At the sign for Mission Bay, Julia relaxed and gave a definitive nod. "You can remove them now."

I hissed in pain as I pulled the mask away from my face. Julia's perfume hit me like a wall of flowers. I hauled the goggles off and dropped them into my lap with the mask, scrubbing at my sore face with my palms to get the blood flowing again. I saw Julia wince as she glanced sideways at me while steering around the gradual bend of the headland. "That looks painful," she commented. "A hot shower will help."

She drove me back to her house overlooking the sea. Seven showers later and a heat haze rose off my broad shoulders and steamed up the bathroom mirror. I wondered what it felt like to feel really clean. I used my wrist to clear the condensation and peered at my distorted reflection through the water droplets. The skin rose in arcs where the equipment had cut into my face. Red welts wound around my eye sockets and continued along the side of my cheeks to meet beneath my chin. The door clicked and Julia's reflection appeared behind mine. A fluffy white towel wound around her, knotted above her left breast.

"How is your face?" she asked. She clasped my biceps in warm fingers and turned my body. A clip held her wet hair on top of her head. She frowned at the raised skin. "I'll put aloe vera on it." My gaze studied the folds of the towel and she smiled. "I grabbed a shower in my ensuite in case you used all the hot water." She dropped her left hand to cover her yawn. "What took so long with the painting? I assumed you'd be a couple of hours as usual."

I licked my cracked lips and shook my head. "Not this time."

Julia exhaled and moved towards the door. Steam billowed out ahead of her as she walked onto the landing. "Come to bed, Jacques. And you need to drink. You look dehydrated."

"Whisky." I gave a definitive nod. "On the rocks. To celebrate."

Her eyes narrowed, and she half turned and cocked her head. "Water first." A damp curl sneaked forward over her shoulder and nestled against the fluffy towel at her cleavage. "What are we celebrating?"

I swallowed and pursed my lips, the action painful.

She gave a slow blink and sighed. "I guess I'll find out soon enough."

I nodded at her retreating back, noting the gentle curve of her shoulder blades and the elegant way she glided down the stairs. Lifting my thumb, I assessed her perspective against the dimly lit hallway and hoped she didn't hate me tomorrow.

45

PROP:

AN OBJECT USED TO AID OR ENHANCE A STORY OR PERFORMANCE

We got little sleep. Julia left the sumptuous curtains open as a storm attacked the coastline. Lightning arced through the black sky to touch the water in angry forks as thunder rumbled overhead. She covered my abrasions with aloe vera and my face stuck to hers as I kissed her beneath the exhilarating flashes of light. We rolled in her giant bed until dawn sneaked through the darkness. Exhaustion hung over us both as she rose in time for work.

"Use your key to lock up when you leave," she said, leaning over the bed to kiss my forehead. "Your face looks much better this morning. Perhaps wear a baseball cap and don't shave your beard today."

I nodded in agreement, blinking as she placed another kiss on my lips. She paused, and I sensed her wanting to quiz me about the mural. Wise to my resistance, she alluded to it via another angle. "I wonder if the tarpaulin survived the night." She threw her handbag on the bed and dug through it until she found her favourite colour. I studied her movements as she spread the red hue over her rosebud lips. "Will it be okay if the rain wet it?"

I nodded, no longer caring. I doubted my work would survive the week.

Julia jerked her head upwards and shrugged. "It doesn't matter. He paid in full and the money is in our account."

A bowl in the kitchen contained one hundred and forty-four rice pops. I sat at the counter and ate them dry, choking on the remnants but reluctant to commit them to the waste disposal. I'd deviated from my routine and used Julia's shower gel and conditioner during the last of my three showers. Her scent hung around me in a floral haze and I caught myself smiling as I crunched the rice pops.

My phone rang as I pushed my feet into my shoes by the front door. Julia's number strobed on the screen and I lifted it to my ear.

"Check the news." Her tone held urgency and a hint of excitement.

"I'm going home." I held the device between my chin and shoulder and continued to tie my laces. My fingers ached from holding the spray cans and behaved like two bunches of bananas. I hissed in frustration. "My laces won't tie."

"Check. The. News!" Her voice rose. "Just do it, Jacques." A door slammed in the background and I heard heels tapping against a wooden floor.

"But I have my shoes on now." I turned with the phone in my hand and strategised a route along the hallway to the lounge. It looked possible if I skirted the rug. Or took my shoes off. I wrinkled my nose and peered down at my toes. I was stuck, my process disturbed, and my systems cast asunder.

"Jacques?" Another door slammed, and the echo subsided. She exhaled, as though calming herself. "Take off your shoes and jump from the rug in the hallway to the carpet in the lounge. *Tap. Tap. Tap.* Her nails on a surface restored my equilibrium. I did as she asked, kicking off my shoes and entering the lounge.

A chill air stirred in the wide room as I counted my steps across the carpet. A cupboard hid the TV screen from view when not in use, and I pulled open the doors and used the remote control to activate the screen. I flicked through the channels. As though reading my mind from afar, Julia said, "Channel three. Breakfast news."

My fingers coasted over the raised buttons on the remote, aware that Julia had been the last person to touch them. It seemed a lifetime ago that she'd nestled on the sofa in my house, hidden within the folds of a blanket and watching pointless movie images scroll across the screen.

"Are you looking?" *Tap, tap, tap.* Her fingers moved faster this time. "I'm streaming the broadcast on my phone."

"Yes." I frowned as an image of my mural flashed on the screen. The newscaster sat in a studio with it emblazoned behind him. I inspected the remote and turned up the sound as his lips moved again. The screen capture of my mural switched to a live feed from a windswept blonde woman reporting from a boat in the harbour.

"A local boat owner moored in the harbour last night took this footage." A grainy image occupied the whole of the TV screen. "He believed he saw vandals entering a construction site at the Eden View hotel on Quay Street in Auckland. Police contacted the hotel owner in response to his call and Richard Raines MP confirmed his staff were carrying out routine maintenance." The screen cut back to my mural and a smile spread across my lips. The female reporter's voice continued over the view of the flapping tarpaulin, which had obliged the harbour users with an early preview. "New Zealand has woken up to this," she said with a flourish.

A man appeared next to her, his face lined with the rugged map gained from hours on the water. He smiled to reveal a missing front tooth. His eyes crinkled at the corners, wisps of white hair flapping in the breeze. Turning sideways, the reporter stuck a microphone under his nose. The boat listed and her eyes widened. The seasoned sailor grabbed hold of her elbow and stopped her from pitching backwards into the harbour. "Mr Salter, you are currently the first member of the public to have filmed 'X' at work.

How does that feel?" Her voice wavered with adrenaline from her wild ride.

"Grand." His beaming grin indicated his thrill at the attention, but the blank quality in his eyes discounted him as an art lover.

"Are you familiar with work by the artist known as 'X'?" the reporter continued.

Mr Salter's smile wilted. "Na." The sea made another valiant attempt to dislodge the TV crew from his boat. The screen cut back to the newscaster, who finished the item with a steadier hand and a tad more professionalism.

"Last night's storm tore the plastic sheeting from one part of the scaffold and allowed an early view of what will surely become a beacon for New Zealand's art critics. A hotel spokesman has confirmed commissioning 'X' to paint the mural in celebration of its one-hundred-year anniversary." Behind him, workers dressed in orange overalls swarmed from the platform of the scissor lift. The newsreader frowned and cocked his head to listen to his ear piece. "I understand the work is being sealed, ready for the celebration event this evening. Tune in to tonight's broadcast for an update. Richard Raines, the Minister of Parliament for West Auckland, is expected to fly in from Wellington following his party's loss of a vote last night. Raines has been outspoken in his dismissal of paid leave for victims of domestic violence."

Then my father's face filled the TV screen. I took an instinctive step backwards and my calves tangled with a coffee table. The remote control flew from my fingers, the batteries skittering free as the plastic casing hit the floor. Julia's voice piped from the phone still in my hand. "Jacques? Jacques!"

I lifted it to my ear and swallowed before replying. "I broke the remote."

"It's okay," she soothed. "I'm sorry. It didn't occur to me they'd show his image, but of course they would." She exhaled. "Stay there. I'm coming home."

I pulled the phone away from my ear and stared at the face of my father on the TV. A blue eye patch covered the mess my mother made of his right eye when she ambushed him with our vegetable knife. Genetics had given me his features and a height which put me over six feet in my socks. His parliamentary photograph showed a smiling, generous man, but the sentiment didn't reach the single cold eye which glowed like ice water.

The newsreader's voice droned on as I dropped to my haunches and covered my ears with my palms. The phone thudded onto the carpet. I knew they'd show his wife's photograph next, the woman whose death had tainted Mother's claims of battery and hardship. Court records showed she'd stepped in front of Mother to protect her husband, and the downward trajectory of the blade nicked her jugular. Instead of halting her revenge mission, Mother stabbed my father in the eye and left him unconscious before returning home to me. The media branded her a lunatic and social services slid me into the anonymous care of the state.

The sound of sloshing water filtered beneath my palms and I forced my eyes to open. Mr Salter's gnarled fingers showed at the bottom of the shot, holding onto the female reporter as she roiled in the boat. The mural looked stunning, even though the scaffold still bisected its full glory. My signature appeared small compared to the other wording next to it. I read it aloud, along with the steady voices of the narrators in my head. '*For the 12*,' it said. '*2019*.' The twelve women who died that year, victims of intimate partner violence. I knew there were men who died too, but the mural was a tribute to Mother. I'd repeated the smaller work my father forced the city of Wellington to deface and I'd done it on his own building. Adding the statistic proved an afterthought and gave it a severity the original didn't have.

I didn't hear the words of the news reporter as the sea tossed her around in the harbour. My gaze shifted to the windows of the penthouse far above her as they reflected the scudding clouds. Our penthouse in the Eden View.

Mother's and mine.

46

PROTOTYPE:

AN EARLY SAMPLE BUILT TO TEST A CONCEPT OR PROCESS

Julia flew through the front door half an hour later, finding me laid on the bathroom floor. She complained about the rush hour traffic and covered me with a scratchy blanket and her apologies. I'd thrown up the rice pops and my stomach ached.

"I'm so sorry, Jacques," she whispered, her arm stretched around my shoulders. She sat on the side of the bath and pressed my cheek against her thigh. "I wanted to talk to you when we got home last night. It seemed too hard to form the words, and we distracted each other." She gave a giant swallow. "Your brother is an asshole."

I exhaled and sat up, wiping my hand across my nose. Military deployment had made me a silent witness to death and atrocity, but it hadn't scored the memories into my soul the same way as the experiences of my childhood. Julia's ring tone echoed from the hall downstairs. She glanced at the door and her lips flattened into a wince. "He keeps calling." She lowered her voice, her tone halting, as though not sure if she should continue.

I clambered to my knees and reached for her toothpaste tube. It reminded me of the consistency of oil paint as I squeezed a line onto my finger and watched it balance there. Julia rose as the trilling stopped and then began again. Her fingers closed around the door handle and then dropped to her side, her reflection in the mirror betraying her divided loyalty. I used the toothpaste and fresh water to swill out my mouth. Washing my face in cold water restored my stoicism. The phone rang again. "Just answer him." I rose and rested my hands on either side of the sink, watching the water from my chin dribble into the plughole. "Half-brother. Not brother."

Julia swallowed and her boot heels dragged across the floorboards. "It's not Paul Raines," she whispered. "It's your father."

I turned, adding a slow nod and a shrug to the movement. Julia's hazel irises appeared too large for her olive features. She stepped in front of me and wrapped her arms around my waist.

"It's okay," I whispered. My biceps ached as I lifted them and held her. "You can talk to him. My anger is gone." I said the words before hearing them, and the startling revelation almost rocked me off my feet. The narrators whispered among themselves, as though afraid to intrude upon the thoughts in the forefront of my mind. It felt different. They'd never cared before, running roughshod over me without regard. "Talk to him." I dropped my arms with a sigh. "I did what I came to do."

Julia nodded and offered me a wooden smile as she responded to the next round of ringing. I sat on the edge of the bath and listened to her conversation. She said very little after the initial greeting, but a rasping male voice drifted up the stairs, the words broken and indistinct. It only halted as she cut across it with a loud exclamation. "There's nothing in the contract about a theme." I sensed her land on more certain footing. We'd both inspected the legal documentation. The male voice barked something, but Julia countered. "I'm sorry, Mr Raines, but that was not part of the contract. 'X' had free rein to paint, and that is exactly what he did. If you wanted an appropriate nautical theme, it should have been documented. I suggest you return to the agreement signed by myself and Paul Raines for clarification." She ended the call as the male voice rose. A beep sounded as she turned off her phone and ran back up the stairs.

"Nautical theme." I squinted and a deep furrow rooted itself between my brows. "He wanted a nautical theme?" I snorted and covered my mouth with my hand. Julia's face creased into a grin, and she nodded.

"A nautical theme." The way she said the word made it sound like 'naughty' and set me laughing. When one of us calmed, the other would say it and set us both off again. Julia blinked back tears as we stopped, as though by mutual ascent. A subduing blanket settled over our hilarity.

"Maybe your half-brother isn't such an asshole after all," Julia whispered. "He gave you a blank canvas."

I shook my head. "He doesn't know who I am. He gave someone a blank canvas."

Julia slid her fingers through mine and perched next to me on the side of the bath. She rested her temple against my shoulder. "My phone is blowing up with calls from journalists and potential clients. Te Papa Museum is interested in a mural for their war exhibit. Does that interest you?"

I wanted to say no, but shrugged, no longer sure of my answer. "After last night, I wanted to retire 'X' forever." I ran a hand over the bristles on my chin. "But today, seeing my work on TV fired up my creativity, so I'm uncertain. I'll still paint on canvas, but no more walls for a while."

"Okay." Julia reached up and placed a kiss on my cheek. "Scarcity is the secret sauce, anyway. Less is more."

I smiled and stared at my toes, their outline creating ridges in my socks. Julia mangled both cliches, and the narrators repeated them in the dark recesses of my mind. I sighed. "I must get home."

Julia nodded. "It's RSA night, isn't it?"

"Yes. RSA night."

She blew out a breath through her nose and pursed her lips. I studied the curves and recesses of her face and ached for my fine oil brushes. Her smile appeared forced. "I'll drive down later this week. We have things to talk about."

I blinked. "You spoke to the lawyer?"

"He phoned me last night. You purchased the building, Gordon's seventy percent share of the gallery and two properties on the other side of the road."

"An art district." I closed my eyes and pictured the facades of craft shops with high-end artists working in view of the public. It seemed ironic for a man who painted in secret beneath the cover of a single alphabet letter. The narrators whispered perhaps I envied them their exposure. I silenced them with seven dull beats of my fingers against the side of the bath.

"It sounds amazing." Julia studied me from beneath her long eyelashes. "A community of potters and painters, writers and sculptors. You could allocate studio spaces for them to work and sell their products." Her eyes glinted with pleasure, and she pressed her free hand against her chest. "I'm so excited, Jacques." The fingers of her other hand squeezed mine. "Shared spaces mean individual artists can afford the rent." She flapped her free hand. "I can fill them ten times over just from my contacts list."

I uncoupled my fingers from hers and rose with a nod. "Good," I replied. "It's all in your name."

"My name?" Julia's mouth opened and closed. Her fingers smoothed the silky fabric of her skirt. "But why?"

I closed my eyes and rubbed at the space between my eyes. "Roddy told me that Henare believes I killed the skinny kid. It's only a matter of time until he finds a reason to arrest me."

Julia hissed. "That detective is like a wasp. As fast as we shoo him away, he comes back again." She rose and her feather light touch caressed my elbow through my shirt. "Whatever you need, Jacques, just ask for it." Her gaze misted as she stared at the sink. I'd placed her toothpaste back in the exact spot I found it. "This is so unfair," she breathed. "So unfair."

47

ROCOCO:

A STYLE, PARTICULARLY IN ARCHITECTURE AND DECORATIVE ART, THAT ORIGINATED IN FRANCE IN THE EARLY 1700S

The uneventful drive down the motorway gave me time to think. Julia took twelve more calls before I left, all from news reporters and hopeful clients wanting more of 'X'. Richard Raines didn't phone her again, and I rolled my shoulders as I drove. I knew first-hand how he dealt with women who didn't meet his exacting expectations. It pained me I'd allowed Julia to wind up in his crosshairs. *Tap, tap, tap.* My fingers drummed the steering wheel.

I'd used every weapon allocated to me during my time in the military, from heavy guns, grenades to a deadly knife I rather liked. My father's face had overlaid that of my opponent every single time until I'd killed him more than proved healthy for my mental state. If he touched Julia, I'd do it for real.

Once home, I sequestered myself downstairs in the studio. I ramped up the heat against the bitter cold, but removed my overalls later when it grew hot enough to make me sweat. I imagined Julia rolling her eyes and asking why I didn't turn down the thermostat, while admiring me painting in my boxer shorts.

The picture of the bench stood before me, the colours rich and inviting. The finishing touches added a chaotic realism. Blades of green grass thickened with gesso created the mess beneath the wooden legs. Burnt Umber and Mars Brown mixed with a little Bordeaux Red to create the clumps of soil intermingled with the debris from the weed eater. Titanium White and Cold Gray created the microscopic glare from my bedroom window as it stared down blindly at the scene. The red roof of the major's house obscured its view, as it did in reality.

Exhausted, I sat in my paint-stained leather armchair and looked at my work from the more distant perspective. The strapping Julia placed over my knuckle looked like I'd used it to paint. I unwound the bandage and rolled it into a neat, multicoloured sausage, ready to go into the dustbin. The black bruise had faded from my finger to surround just the joint. My biceps ached and my hands curved into crab claws after spraying the mural and then continuing with the intricate detail of the bench.

I spoke the name out loud, allowing the art to breathe from the canvas. "You are *The Bench*," I said to it. My gaze slid to *The Woman in the Garden*. I rose and pressed my finger to a petal near the bottom of the oil painting. It didn't give way to the pressure, and I pronounced it dry enough to varnish. I oiled out her surface with linseed, which gave the colours an even tone. "Just a few more days," I told her. Adding a thin layer of Gamvar varnish would complete her and Julia would transport her to her new owner.

I'd just finished in the shower when a dull knocking seized my attention. Slipping a clean towel around my waist, I stepped from the bathroom into the gym and paused to listen. It came again, the strange rapping, and I cocked my head, not wanting to process where it came from.

"Mr Jethro!" A raised voice accompanied the next series of knocks and I swallowed. My tongue swelled in my mouth to prevent me from answering. "I can see the light, Mr Jethro! Open this door!"

My footsteps faltered as I walked across the gym and unlocked the door. A blast of freezing air whipped around my bare skin. Henare strolled across the threshold as though he hadn't just hammered loud enough to disturb most of Ngaruawahia.

"It's freezing out there!" he exclaimed. A ski jacket covered his torso and hiking boots encased his feet. Loose soil and grass clippings sprinkled the door mat, and he made as though to move further into the room.

"No." I held up my palm in protest and jerked my head towards his feet. "Don't walk your crap into my home again."

His lips parted in surprise at my assertion he'd done it previously. But he had. Twice. He remained on the door mat, clods of earth dropping from the grips in his boots. Despite his preparedness, the idiot wore jeans which had absorbed the cold. Scuffs on both knees showed where he'd fallen as he'd used the bush trail to access my home from its less protected rear. "Wait there!" I ground out the words and turned, not wanting to face him without clothing.

My fingers tingled as I strode across the floor, and my chest tightened to restrict my oxygen. I'd fixed the cupboard back into place over the ladder to the studio, but not secured it. Henare's feet shuffled on the mat and my ears twitched as he swore at the marks on his jeans. I couldn't use the coin without him noticing.

Deciding to distract him seemed like a good idea at the time. I dropped my towel as I reached the cupboard and gave him a full view of the physique I'd worked hard to maintain since my army days, and which Julia appreciated with abandon. If he enjoyed seeing my muscular buttocks shrug into a clean pair of boxer shorts, he made no comment. I took my time, adding socks, sweat pants and a tee shirt and hoping it intensified his discomfort. Roddy wouldn't have cared. He once sat on my bunk buck naked and only the force of the rest of my squad stopped me punching him into the next century for leaving his ass germs on my sleeping bag.

I faked a light stumble as I clutched the middle shelf of the cupboard to push my left foot into my trainer. The unit shuddered, and the narrators celebrated at the satisfying click it gave as the mechanism connected. I slipped the jacket I'd arrived in over my tee shirt and strode towards the door.

A heavy line bisected Henare's brow, a lump in his cheek showing where he'd pushed his tongue against it. I waited for him to pull the door open and step outside, determined not to overlay my hand over anything he'd touched. He set off towards the darkened house and I used my sleeve to pull the door closed and lock it behind me. His boots clumped up the porch steps, and he turned, one eyebrow raised in expectation. "It always smells of fresh paint around here," he commented.

Knives of cold attacked my wet hair and pressed their icy blades against my cheeks. I forced myself to lean against the balustrade and fold my arms, holding my muscles rigid to disguise the shivering. "You're trespassing," I snarled. "What do you want now?"

Henare dug his hands into his jacket pockets and blew out a white cloud of condensation. "I'm walking. My route just happened to cut along the boundary of your property, so I called in on the off chance of seeing you." The cerulean hues of the sky threatened to progress to a deep ultramarine blue. Instinct told me it was almost time for me to drive to the RSA. The edge of the balustrade cut into my hip as I shook my head and sighed.

"Why are you here, Detective?"

Henare stepped in a circle on the porch, causing the motion sensor light to activate. He'd highlighted a massive fault in my security and the narrators chattered to themselves in the back of my mind. The sudden burst of light picked up all the clods of soil from his boot grips. They reminded me of *The Bench*.

"I wanted to update you on the investigation." Henare's teeth chattered. The woollen hat pulled over his ears made him appear like a boiled egg hiding beneath a knitted cozy. The turtle neck of his ski jacket completed the effect of the ceramic lip of an egg cup. I didn't paint caricatures otherwise, it would have amused me. Instead, his presence on my property heated my chest from the inside and I imagined all the various ways to dispose of his body in the bush behind my house.

I released a tired sigh. The resulting cloud obscured his arrogant smile. "I don't care about your investigation. It has no relevance to me. Please leave."

Henare frowned and his head jerked backwards. His rapid blinks revealed he'd expected a cheerier reception. His scrawny neck proceeded high enough from his ski jacket to ruin the image of the boiled egg. "Nathan Watson drowned, but he suffered a broken neck moments before he hit the water. I've been a detective for a long time, Mr Jethro, and something about this stinks. He boasted in the RSA after you left about getting a big pay out from somewhere. He spoke of knowing something about someone which they wouldn't want made public. I think that someone might be you."

I released a snort of disgust. "That kid wore Velcro trainers because he couldn't tie his own laces. The only thing in his head was a ball bearing which rattled when he opened his mouth." I tensed my leg muscles and pushed off the balustrade. "Leave me alone, Detective. Get off my property. This is police harassment."

I unlocked my front door and ignored his protests as he stepped out onto the porch. Condensation billowed from his mouth in the plummeting temperatures. He paused and a furrow appeared in his brow. "I wondered if you knew anything about a local run cannabis growing operation up near the track? It's beneath the ridge. You wouldn't find it unless you knew it was there."

I released a grunt of annoyance and slammed the door in his face. Kicking off my trainers, I jogged upstairs and somehow managed to miss out the even numbered steps without breaking my neck. Henare hammered on the door downstairs, and I groaned at the prospect of something else to sanitise. "Mr Jethro!" His voice changed to placation as I sat on the end of Julia's bed. "Could I at least use your driveway to get back to town? Can you let me out of your gate?"

"No, and no," I whispered to the satisfaction of the narrators. Dipping forward, I rested my elbows on my knees and waited for him to leave. My breath exhaled as a whoosh five minutes later when he clattered down the porch steps and scrunched through the gravel at the side of the house.

My watch hands crawled towards the time when I'd need to climb into my truck and head to the RSA. Bouncing on my heels as I waited only seemed to intensify my anxiety. With ten minutes left to spare, I rose and walked to Julia's bedroom window overlooking the rear of the property. Relief caused my breath to exhale as a soft moan at the sight of a thin beam of light spreading across the tufted paddock grass towards the bush. The mountain rose like an indigo warrior against the sky, a head and shoulders guarding my secrets. The light jerked as Henare slipped and I almost wished he'd hurt himself. Then the narrators intervened. *'He'd blame you for that too,'* they said.

48

SECONDARY COLOUR:

"Hey, bro. Did Henare find you?" He pushed his glass away and called to the barman. "Get me an orange juice, please, Ted. This cola tastes like a dog's armpit."

I repositioned my stool, not wanting to sit next to him if he'd been doing weird stuff again. Roddy had perfected the art of getting his kicks in the oddest of ways. Sniffing a dog's armpit wasn't beyond his repertoire of strange behaviours. "Yes, he found me," I replied, answering his question once I'd settled. "He walked up the mountain and accessed my property from the rear." I sipped the cola Ted set in front of me and almost vomited. The dog's armpit description held a certain degree of truth. Not that I'd ever taken the time to sniff one.

"Where is he now?" Roddy glanced towards the door as if expecting Henare to step through it in his filthy boots.

I shrugged. "Walking back the way he came."

Roddy blinked. "But that means he'd need to climb uphill and then find his way onto the track. How far is it from there to the old reservoir?"

I closed my eyes and pictured the route. "Two point six kilometres to the summit and then another two kilometres down if he uses the stairs at the southern lookout."

Roddy turned in his seat to stare at me, a dimple showing in the centre of his rounded chin. He'd shaved for once, giving him a less unkempt air. "It's dark."

I screwed my neck around to look through the slatted windows near the ceiling. "So, it is," I confirmed.

"Man, you've got big kahunas," Roddy breathed. "He'll come after you for sure now."

I used my index finger to trace a line of condensation trailing down the side of the glass. The one sip rule gained a blessed relevance of its own. I didn't even want to take another. Ted dumped Roddy's orange juice on the counter and removed the cola. He took a slug and shook his head. "Tastes fine to me," he grumbled, though his grimace said otherwise.

"He's coming after me, anyway." My shoulders slumped, and I stared at the clock. Ted had replaced the batteries, but it ran a minute slow. I could live with that.

Roddy jerked backwards after tasting the orange juice. He released a low whistle. "Man, is this stuff made from real oranges or what?" He closed his eyes and shook his head. "Nearly blew out my eyeballs." He wiped his mouth with the back of his hand and turned to me. His eyes darted left and right as he assessed an internal dilemma. "Look," he whispered, "I'll help a brother out just this once. Henare thinks you have a secret. He believes you're shady and wants to get to the bottom of it." He tapped his chest. "I know you didn't kill Nathan and Henare probably knows it, too. But he wants it all, man. If you're hiding something from him, he'll find it."

I gave a slow breath in through my nose and counted to three before releasing it. Roddy had said nothing I didn't already suspect. Protecting 'X' was drawing the detective like a wasp to sugar. It wasn't about the skinny kid. It had become about 'X'. "He said the kid drowned with a broken neck." I drew an 'X' in the condensation on the glass before realising my error and rubbing it out so fast, I almost upended the drink. Glancing sideways, I saw Roddy still recovering from his fruit hit with the juice. His eyes watered as he took another slurp and reacted the same way.

"Yeah." His voice sounded strained, as though the orange had purged his vocal cords of years of beer and cigarettes. "Post-mortem report came back. A line of bruising across his right ribcage is consistent with the top rail of the Waipa Bridge. Someone broke his neck and pushed him over. Pressure spots under his chin and finger marks on the side of his head show the killer knew what they were doing."

"Right." I sighed. "Hence his interest in someone ex-military."

Roddy blew air into his cheeks and shook himself like a dog. Then he flapped his hand at the dimly lit bar with its regulars lurking in corners. "It could have been any one of us, mate." He jabbed a finger towards the domino players. "He insulted every soldier at that table the night he died. And he called me a fat, useless plod, which I must admit was partly true. I am fat and a copper but I'm not useless." He shrugged. "That all happened after you left. He had mud on his arse where you pushed him over, but he was walking and talking and complaining when Ted threw him out half an hour later." He lifted one nostril in disdain. "Shouldn't let jerks like that in here. It's for soldiers, not losers. We earned the right to drink discounted beer." He stared at his foaming orange juice, and I sensed him weighing up another part of his life's rituals. If he didn't drink the beer, how long would it take for him to stop visiting the RSA at all? The narrators panicked behind the veil of my mind at the thought of losing another pattern. They hurled abuse at the skinny kid, whose challenge on an ordinary Wednesday changed everything.

I frowned and pushed my fingers beneath my thighs to suppress the urge to count the tapped beats twitching in my joints. The bruise on my middle knuckle sent out a blossoming dart of pain which helped to ground me in reality. "Do you think you'll find out who killed the kid?" My voice shook with unusual emotion.

Roddy shrugged and pushed his drink away. He leaned close enough for his shoulder to touch mine, and I forced myself not to recoil at his sharp, fruity breath. "Don't really care. He dealt drugs, beat his woman and his kids, ran with the gang and was a legend in his own head. Henare has so many suspects, he's started a new notebook."

"Beat his kids?" I whispered the words, and the narrators paused their clamour to listen.

Oblivious to my horror, Roddy continued. "Yeah. The wee boy got it the worst. Not just hitting, if you know what I mean." He tutted and surveyed the bar, his gaze drifting towards the optics as though spirits might provide a better solution to his need than the beer he'd forsaken. Pulling his gaze away, he turned to me. "See, I'm in no hurry to find his killer. Unless it's to give him a medal." He stepped backwards off his stool. "I'm gonna head off now." He raised his voice to Ted. "Hey, get some of that kombucha stuff, will ya? It's meant to be good for the liver."

Ted gave an upward jerk of his head and returned to wiping the same glass he'd been working on since I walked through the front door.

With a hearty slap of my shoulder, Roddy walked across the bar and left, just like that. He stepped on every square without regard. *Blue, yellow. Blue, yellow.*

I envied him with every fibre of my being as he destroyed my Wednesday night pattern for the second week in a row.

And left me floundering.

49

SITE-SPECIFIC:

DESCRIBES A WORK OF ART DESIGNED FOR A PARTICULAR LOCATION

Exhaustion caught up with my body, but not my mind. I roamed the house until the early hours of the morning, vacuuming, dusting, and scrubbing until the cream cleanser wore away the skin from my finger ends. The narrators screamed their cacophony of doom in my mind until I couldn't think straight. I scoured everything Henare had touched during his visit seven times and still didn't experience any sense of closure. *'It's a mess! It's all a mess!'* the narrators cried.

And it was.

Though my house gleamed like a show home, my inner turmoil muddied the view like the ground beneath the bench in my painting. I fell asleep on Julia's rug again, her blanket pulled over my head like a bivouac of safety.

I slept late, waking with a start at the realisation I'd drifted into Thursday without concern.

Thursday. An even day. Without Mother's phone call.

I sensed a crisis looming and attempted to stave it off by removing my watch and leaving the house. Fog swathed the mountain as I ran to the summit, passing lines of skinned earth where Henare slipped and slid the night before. He'd left a decent chunk of his expensive ski jacket on the barbed wire fence bordering my property, and I plucked the fluttering fabric free and released it into the wind.

The southern lookout towered over the bush, offering a view of the winding Waikato River and the outskirts of Hamilton in the distance. I bent at the waist to catch my breath at the bottom of the stairs, the exposed skin of my limbs mottled against the cold. My breath created furls of white as I rested my hands on my thighs.

Girlish laughter and French accents forced me to rise, my heart beating with more than exhaustion at the thought of Julia. Even before the tourists clattered down the steps, my mind had already reasoned it made no sense for her to be up there. Snuggled in heavy coats with woolly hats pulled down over their ears, the two young women stared at me as they reached the bottom of the lookout.

"Bonjour," they chorused, their brows furrowing at my inadequate clothing of a thin tee shirt and stubby shorts. I hadn't expected to see anyone on such a miserable day, and their combined gaze coasted across my many battle scars. I offered an upward jut of my chin just to show politeness and jogged past them up the wooden steps to the platform. They spoke in French, but I understood their whispered conversation. "Did you see all those scars?" one said to the other.

"It looked like someone slit his throat, didn't it?"

Resting my elbows on the rail, I closed my eyes against the magnificence of the craggy slopes and dipped at the waist, pressing my lips to my right forearm. I wanted to scream, to hear my agony echo across the valley and disturb Ngaruawahia township as it nestled like a chick in the crook of the mountain's wing. My mother died. How could it not feel my pain?

As the numbness faded and grief filled the remaining corners of the void, the narrators sifted the rubbish in my soul. *There's no wonder you're a mess,'* they rebuked. *With an animal for a father and a killer for a mother, what did you expect?'* They stood in judgement but didn't offer to absolve me of my crimes. Only God could do that and while I believed in his deity, I wasn't ready to pick through the debris and hold up each item for his consideration.

Not yet. Not at almost ten o'clock on an even numbered Thursday.

Despite having no watch or phone with me, my shadow collaborated with the weak overhead sun to tell me, anyway. I sat on the wooden slats and leaned my head back against the rail, closing my eyes against the inevitable passage of time as ten o'clock arrived and left without hope of a phone call from Mother. Discovering late the significant difference between freedom and aimlessness, I realised I'd lost my rudder. I'd always had a leader, someone to follow with my relentless blind devotion. Mother, the social worker, then Captain Grey. My faulty examples had led me to this point and abandoned me there to find my own way home.

Mother, the murderer.

The social worker, who went to jail for selling dope to minors.

Captain Grey, taken out with the trash by the army.

My head hung between my knees as I stared at my hands planted on the wooden floor of the platform. Paint clung to the grooves on either side of my fingernails, betraying my creativity like DNA. My whole life had led to this moment, honing and driving my skill into something in a prime position to repay my father for his violence. Yet, I felt nothing.

"Enjoy it, New Zealand," I whispered. "He'll set fire to the building before he leaves it there to condemn him."

I closed my eyes and remembered the effort required to create the statement piece. My ears heard the muted hiss of the spray beyond the strains of the *Moonlight Sonata*. My index fingers twitched against the ache caused by hours of depressing the nozzle of the many cannisters Julia had ethically disposed of. I knew Raines would destroy the painting as fast as he could, but hadn't factored in the pain it would cause me. The creation process had always been enough before and I picked Payne's grey paint from beneath my thumb nail and realised it wasn't. Not anymore.

For the first time in my life, I wanted to build something lasting.

Running down the steps to the road used up the next half an hour. The mental reordering of my priorities and plans occupied my mind and banished the sense of loss amid a flurry of purpose. Jogging past the water works and onto Hakarimata Road brought the Waipa Bridge into view and Roddy's words returned as a faint echo. *'A line of bruising on his right ribs is consistent with the top rail of the Waipa Bridge.'*

I waited for a car to pass before jogging across the wide mouth of the road and stepping up onto the narrow section of concrete which rose above the asphalt. Too thin to walk on even single file, it encouraged pedestrians to use the other side of the road, which the council had equipped with a metal barrier and moderate pavement. I walked to the centre of the bridge and stopped to stare at the rail. White dust coated it, though the rain had caused the fine forensic powder to congeal and spread like thinned paint. I shook my head at the spot where the markings intensified, thinking how unfair it seemed that even the skinny kid left a legacy. My memory recalled the silent child in the back seat of my car and my vision blurred. Like me, he'd gained a dreadful inheritance from his forebears.

Turning, I left the bridge where Nathan Watson met his painful, protracted death. The swollen depths of the river meant he'd had a quick drop into the taniwha's embrace, not long enough to count his blessings or to atone for his wrongs.

Me however, I still had time for both.

50

SETTING:

THE CONTEXT OR ENVIRONMENT IN WHICH A SITUATION OCCURS

Managing to fit in only one shower, I towed the trailer down to the major's house just before eleven and parked in his driveway. My sophisticated yellow mower coiffed the steep slope of his river facing garden with the skill of a hairdresser. Neat lines gave the grass a symmetry which fulfilled my need for order.

The major brought me a mug of coffee as I drew level with the bench and I dismounted and used one of the stripes to walk back to the house. "Drink that," he commanded. His tone of voice offered no room for disobedience and I closed my eyes and lifted the hot drink to my lips without question. If I didn't look, I wouldn't notice the chipped rim of the mug or the floaty bits on the surface of the coffee. I'd lacked blind obedience and relaxed beneath its welcome safety.

"She'll give you trouble," the old man warned. He settled into a stained deck chair to enjoy the show. "I hope youse got gloves, kid, cause she'll eat ya alive."

I looked to where he pointed and viewed the rear aspect of the bench. It seemed childish to admit I'd saved the conundrum to last, hoping to draw energy from fixing the problem.

"She'll be right," I breathed, using the Kiwi expression to negate all emotion concerning the issue.

The major turned his rheumy gaze in my direction. "My wife liked that bench," he commented with a sigh. "Sat there every morning to drink her coffee and watch the brown trout jumping for bugs on the water." I lifted the left side of my lips in an awkward smile to acknowledge his sentiment. He leaned back in his deck chair and the wispy hair at his crown rose with static. "Many a time, I've felt like smashing the bugger. It just sits there, reminding me of what I've lost and giving me splinters when I haul it out of the way to mow the damn grass."

"Thank you for the drink, Sir." I placed the empty mug on a low wall next to his chair and followed the mowed line back to my silent vehicle.

My experience with the painting gave me an affinity for the bench. It represented me and the obstacle I'd presented to so many others who'd failed to nurture me or accept my faults. Only Julia had ever taken me at face value, tolerating the splinters and handling me with dignity.

The old man watched from his chair as I clipped the neat lines on either side of the bench. I estimated it would take three perfect stripes to mow beneath it and join up the pattern. I finished the sloped garden and raised the blades, before parking the mower on its ultimate turn before beginning my actual mission.

Approaching the bench involved ultimate concentration. I counted seventy steps before reaching it, extending my stride in the last few metres to ensure I landed on a number divisible by seven. Grey clouds drifted overhead, interspersed with pale streaks of perfect blue. Mother promised me once that the sun always shone in the sky, but the clouds obscured my vision. *'It's always there,* she reassured my infant self. *'It never leaves. Like God. He's always there too. You just can't see him because of the clouds.'*

I stepped around the front of the bench and inspected it. The chipped varnish and faded stain revealed neglect. A harsh New Zealand sun destroyed everything from plastic to metal. The major could have treated the wood last year or ten years ago. Unless I asked, I would never discern the answer. Ragged wood and splinters protruded from the seat and the rugged arms which ended in neat carvings, like the paws of a lion. I drew my gardening gloves from my pocket and pulled them over my fingers.

Then, I dipped, put my weight into my legs and lifted the bench into the air as though all my training had led to this moment.

"Just drag the bugger!" the old man shouted from his chair.

Every tendon and sinew in my body stretched as the heavy bench rose from the jagged grass and mud beneath its legs. I walked it forward and sideways, my stomach tense enough to eject the coffee. The hard edge of the front plank rested against my thighs as I crab walked it to the nearest mowed stripe and set it down on the ground. A white cloud of condensation exited my lungs from the exertion and I straightened my back and rolled my shoulders. Then I walked seventy steps back to the mower, climbed onto it, and completed the remaining three stripes. The ground beneath the original bench site appeared less churned as grass clippings scattered over it to cover the mess. I finished my task at the river side of the garden and raised the blades, driving back to the top. The bench slotted back into place with the same degree of energy, leaving several spiteful splinters pushed through the fingers of my gloves.

A sense of satisfaction created a natural high as I surveyed my work. I wouldn't know the extent of my success until I viewed it from The Point across the river. Distance offered a clearer perspective sometimes, and might reveal a wonky stripe or a place I hadn't reached. Having secured the regular gig, I could improve it next week or the week after that.

I parked the mower by the gate, already itching to get home and hose off the machine. The old man rose as I eyed my trailer, backed up ready. "That's a grand job," he acknowledged, his eyes watering. "See you same time next Thursday?"

I jerked my head in a nod, which seemed too wooden. He swallowed and cleared his throat. "I always wondered why that idiot Roddy called you *The Concierge*." I blinked in surprise and a frown drew in my brows and narrowed my eyes.

"Not to my face."

"No." The major shook his head. He flapped an arthritic hand towards the bench. "I thought it was because you liked things tidy." His bushy brows knitted to cover his eyelids. "But it wasn't, was it?"

I shook my head, but the single word required got lodged in my chest. It wasn't the reason for the nickname. My single minded, emotionless performance built on numbers and mental challenges meant the squad always sent me in first. Captain Grey called it 'clearing up' and I did it with skill and precision. The scoreboard in my mind kept track, and I treated killing flesh and blood with the passivity of a video game I could exit at any time.

Until we found Julia.

"Thank you for your service," the old man whispered, and I held my breath. My organs squirmed in my chest as I reeled with discomfort at the unexpected praise from a superior.

"See you next Thursday," I replied, my voice gruff. I didn't look at him as I opened the gate and drove the mower onto my trailer. My mind whirred with possibilities and by the time I'd hauled the trailer up the steep drive to my house, I'd already planned the restoration of the bench and sanded and stained it in my mind.

I couldn't allow it to remain in its broken state. Despite my own faulty nature and the loose threads in my personality, I still believed that everything could be fixed. If I didn't give it new life, then no one would.

I knew I couldn't watch it decay week after week.

It deserved better.

We all did.

51

SELF-PORTRAIT:

A REPRESENTATION OF ONESELF MADE BY ONESELF

The weekend passed without incident and I regained some of my equilibrium. My days stretched into their comforting rituals and the knotted tension in my chest relaxed.

Until Julia arrived on Sunday afternoon without warning, bringing with her a frightening cloud of doom which engulfed me in uncertainty and fear.

"Hey." She used her key and clattered over the threshold. The door clicked shut behind her and I studied the overnight suitcase as she wheeled it across the floorboards. Its presence suggested she intended to stay, and I held my breath, not wishing to destroy the momentary hope. I lurked at the bottom of the stairs in my socks, hiding my fingers behind my back as I tapped out a series of three-beats against the left leg of my shorts.

Julia parked the suitcase beside the lounge doorway and cocked her head. "Going for a run?" Something like the twang of disappointment laced her tone, and I didn't know how to answer. If I confirmed her assertion, it meant leaving her at the house alone. Her presence indicated she'd driven down to see me, but my legs tingled with the expectation of blowing off some energy.

'*You promised, you promised, you promised!*' the narrators cried in agitation.

I nodded and shook my head at the same time, creating a circular motion. Julia smiled and sat on the bench to remove her boots.

"That's okay. I fancy a walk to the lookout. Why don't you run ahead and I'll change my clothes and follow you? We can meet at the top in about an hour."

The narrators settled, and I released the held breath. Julia always found solutions. I unclenched my tapping fingers and gave her a smile which attempted to convey my gratitude. She wheeled her suitcase across the lobby, her steps light and bouncy, before pushing the handle towards me. "Please, can you carry this upstairs for me, Jacques?" She nudged past me onto the bottom step and paused to press a kiss to my cheek. Her lips carried the sting of the outdoors and the faint scent of strawberries.

She'd already begun undressing by the time I arrived upstairs with her suitcase in my arms. Lacy black underwear defined itself against her stunning olive skin and I set the case on the bedside rug and stopped to watch her striptease. The swell of her breasts and the soft curve of her stomach caused the promise of the run to fade in importance. The narrators clamoured with indignation, knowing they couldn't overrule Julia.

She strode to the wardrobe on her slender legs and threw open the doors. Reaching inside, she hauled a sweatshirt and jogging pants from a shelf and turned to face me. Her lips parted in a lascivious smile. "Behave, Jacques," she rebuked. "I can read your mind. Exercise first, bed later."

I shrugged and my nose wrinkled. "It's exercise."

Her sharp laugh split the peace as she shrugged into the sweatshirt. "I agree. But with you, the afternoon will disappear and the sun will set on our good intentions." She flapped a hand in my direction. "Go now. I'll lock up the house. You have time to run to the reservoir and back to the lookout before I reach the track."

I halted in the doorway and turned to face her. "Run. You can keep up with me."

She tugged the jogging pants over her hips and shimmied against the stretch of the waistband. "Not today, Jacques. I'll see you at the top."

The sense of doom followed me to the lookout. Though the blue sky shimmered over the green hues of the bush, it did little to remove the knot of doubt in my mind. Even the narrators silenced, unable to second guess Julia any more than I could. I didn't run to the reservoir but waited on the platform, a knot in my gut not caused by exertion.

Sunday afternoon roused the families, parents herding their overweight offspring up the steep steps from Hakarimata Road. A tracksuit top zipped up to my chin prevented the stares, but caused me to overheat in the sun.

The teenagers clumped onto the platform and sulked at the view, killing time until they could return to their screens. Their constant chatter rattled my brain, and I descended, chased from my safe place by their complaints.

I ran a kilometre along the track, which led away from the reservoir before halting without warning. Another runner cursed as he dodged sideways to avoid hitting me. The leads from white ear buds trailed across his chest and a rucksack containing a water bladder betrayed his intention to keep going long after I stopped. He hurled a swear word behind him but didn't slow, the green of his baseball cap swallowed by the hues of the bush.

A sense of deep unease engulfed me. The lack of a watch had suited my need for freedom, but it worked against me as the sun dipped lower in the sky. My stomach roiled beneath my ribs and I sensed more than an hour had passed. I hadn't felt a portend of doom this strong since the night Captain Grey died.

Turning a full circle, I ran back to the southern lookout to wait for Julia's arrival.

Half an hour later, she strolled along the track to the platform. I saw her coming from my high vantage point, my restlessness chasing away all other prospective tourists.

She climbed the stairs with a steady gait. "It's busy on the track, but not up here." Her gaze took in the platform's emptiness. She looked at me and frowned, correctly surmising the reason people would slog to the top of the mountain and then avoid enjoying the view. Me.

I gripped the top rail of the wooden balustrade and stared at her, reading her expression and body language as though searching an ancient document containing the secret to eternal life. "Why are you here?" My question emerged with more force than I intended. Instead of giving an instant answer, Julia rested her chin on her forearms and squinted down at the town.

"Have you seen any of the news about your latest work?" She avoided using my brand name or making any direct referral to the mural on the Eden Hotel.

"No." My body stiffened as I watched her, the narrators waiting for her to say the words. I knew my father itched to destroy it, but not before the nation committed its image to photograph and video.

Julia's smile stretched across her lips. "Richard Raines MP is in hot water." She stood up straight and turned her back on the majesty of the shadows cast by the lowered sun. It settled behind the mountain, leaving a yellow glow peeking over the summit. She folded her arms across her chest. "The Eden Hotel is a heritage property. It seems you can't change the facade of a listed building without permission. That includes adding a mural."

I shrugged. "He must know that."

Julia rested her teeth over her lower lip. "Yes, but he thinks of himself as above the rules for ordinary mortals. And now, he has a notice of prosecution from the council."

A frisson of sadness flickered through my heart, pressing my chest inward until my shoulders curved to protect its fragility. "So, now he has an excuse to destroy it. He must be thrilled." I'd painted the mural with no hope of its survival, yet learning of its certain defacement gave me cause for unexpected regret.

Julia reached out and her fingers closed around my biceps. She moved to stand next to me with her thigh touching mine. "That's where it gets interesting, azizam."

I frowned and glanced around at the empty platform. She'd used the Persian term of endearment without thinking. She leaned close and pressed a chilled index finger over my lips. "The foundation of local artists knows about the art district you've proposed. They've appealed to the council to have your work considered nga taonga, a national treasure. Haven't you seen the argument playing out on the television? A group of protesters set up camp outside the Eden Hotel on Thursday after the council issued their notice." She leaned closer and kissed my arm through the sleeve of the tracksuit. "Jacques, you have started a war."

I exhaled, long and slow. "I don't want any part in another war."

"This is a good war," she promised. "Your mural hit the world media and I've spoken to journalists from Canada to Britain. Everyone has seen your painting. New Zealand has remembered your mother and her claims about Richard Raines."

"What about his hundred-year celebration last Wednesday?" I'd imagined his horror at seeing the mural but expected him to spin it as his own idea. His parliamentary speeches contained the slick application of a seasoned politician.

"He tried to cancel."

I frowned at her statement and the narrators tittered among themselves. "It affected him?" I slipped an arm around her shoulders and tugged her closer. I rarely initiated physical contact, but the urge to keep her safe overwhelmed the warnings of the narrators. "He'll come for you now."

Julia exhaled. "He tried to cancel the party, but Paul Raines denied receiving the call. It went ahead as planned. Your father didn't attend. He has more to worry about than identifying 'X' or coming after me. The police in Auckland and Wellington have received reports from multiple women claiming your father has assaulted or abused them." She rested her cheek against my shoulder. "Your mural gave them courage, Jacques."

A lump worked its way up my throat, cutting off any words I might have spoken. The mural had a name in my head. I'd spoken it as I finished the flourish of my signature and gazed on it before waking the scissor lift operator. I'd named it under my breath. *Her Quiet Legacy.*

We watched in silence as the sun disappeared behind the mountain, leaving in its wake a wash of Payne's grey and Prussian blue. Julia stirred first. "We should get back to the house before it becomes too dark to see." She tugged a bunch of keys from her jacket pocket. "I left the paddock gates unlocked."

I nodded, though the presence of the keys surprised me. She jumped or clambered over the gates with ease just like I did, her wiry frame and lack of bulk dealing with the obstacles without breaking a sweat. She never unlocked the gates. Usually. The sense of doom descended back over my head, sinking like a hood to cover my eyes. "Why are you here, Julia?" I whispered. "Why are you really here?"

52

REPLICA:

A COPY OR REPRODUCTION

I left Julia standing at the lookout, my head fizzing with the heaviness of her revelation. Mother's disapproval followed me down the mountain and I ran without checking my footing on the loose gravel tracks.

The terrifying downhill slalom removed the skin from my knees in falls I barely noticed. Blood coursed through the wounds. Threats of disaster screamed in my brain, the seriousness of Julia's condition rising like spikes of pain in my head. A miserable childhood at the mercy of ill-informed opinion and an equally lonely adult life had spurred my decision to never have children of my own. She knew that.

The thought of passing on the unnamed strangeness in my genetic code roiled my stomach. I never wanted to watch Julia defending her child with the expression I'd witnessed so often on Mother's face. It mingled like spilled paint filled with equal measures of defensiveness and agony. They both deserved better.

My blind run had taken me away from the track and forced me to breach my physical defences against the curious. I clambered over the barbed wire fence into the paddock at the back of my property, forgetting Julia left the gates unlocked. Metal barbs snagged against my bare skin, leaving bleeding welts as I yanked my limbs free of its clutches. My fingers balled into fists and I bent double on the front porch of the house, my chest heaving with repressed emotions. I couldn't decipher one from another. They filled the cavity behind my sternum with wads of cotton wool formed by an unseen hand into plugs of tangled, scratchy wire.

Guilt blossomed like black tracks of unguided paint through the mirage of angry reds. The responsibility rested on my shoulders as much as on hers, and I'd never given it a second thought. Julia's assumed barrenness had played into my desire for safety and I'd nurtured its existence, toying with the risk and ignoring the potential consequences.

"Stupid!" I brought my fists up to my face, not caring that my knuckles clattered with my eye sockets. Pain offered an outlet for my grief, but nothing satisfied the bubbling anger.

Like a switch flicking in my head, I inhaled, recognising one thing which might ease the terrifying escalation of raw emotion. If I couldn't force it back into the box, I could exorcise it, letting it run riot until it grew tired enough to cast me aside.

I jerked to attention and dragged the spare front door key from the hidden pocket in my shorts. A warning bleat from the house alarm showed me Julia had armed it in obedience to my rules when she set off to find me. The anger boiled again like lava in my stomach. I wanted to hate her for always complying, for fitting into my sterile life without complaint. I hated her for belonging with me as I deactivated the keypad with a stabbing motion.

The bunch of keys containing the one to the garage tinkled against my fingers when I lifted them from the bureau. I progressed as far as the kitchen, where I snatched up a butcher's knife. The front door hit the wall behind it and I shoved it aside. My clattering footsteps on the porch echoed off the dark mountain. The door slammed behind me, but I didn't lock it, my mind already focussed on the object of my anger. I didn't bother turning on the lights in the gym as I traversed it, dodging the stationary equipment. My usual safety blanket of numbers fled before me, turning their backs and refusing to assist my desperate need for calm.

I dropped the coin twice before managing to press it into the slot at the side of the cupboard. The mechanism moved faster than I anticipated and the front corner of the unit slammed into my foot, jabbing my toe through the cloth of my training shoe. I hissed through my teeth and lifted my foot from the floor, bowing my head and closing my eyes while the pain subsided.

A cursory glance at my foot revealed the blood on my legs, and I turned my hands over to inspect the sticky redness coating the delicate webs between my fingers. The stainless steel of the knife glinted against my palm. The anger toned down a notch, but it still burned my insides, needing release and craving a violent outworking. For once, the narrators remained silent like spectators before the start of a cage fight.

I hobbled down the ladder, curses fuelling my progress. My fingers twitched with the need to destroy something priceless and beautiful. But my breath stilled in my chest as I gulped air and halted.

An empty easel stood where *The Woman in The Garden* had hung. I spun in an arc, confusion overshadowing the rage. *The Bench* and even the unfinished seascape weren't there.

The knife skittered against the floor as I traversed the ladder back up to the gym. Blossoming pain from my various injuries slowed my progress, and I reached the house on steps made more tentative by my toe's refusal to bend. The front door pushed open at my touch and I stared at the vacant space on the lobby wall. Blind panic had shrouded the absence of Julia's portrait and instead, a rectangle of darker paint occupied its former position.

I slid down the plaster until my bottom hit the floorboards. Turning my palms over, I examined the blood ingrained into the lines of my skin. At least this time, it was mine and not someone else's. I leaned my head back against the wall and closed my eyes, listening to the sound of my heart hammering in my eardrums. The chaotic beats refused to group into numbers, jumping around like the evasive clicker beetles which invaded the bush each summer. They resisted sevens, but as I calmed, I found safety in fours and then eights. Blood snaked down my shins and soaked the socks pushing from my training shoes. Winter stole through the open front door and inspected my home in a rare opportunity to sneak through the rooms without opposition.

"There you are." Julia stepped over the threshold in a haze of grey light and closed the door behind her. "It's freezing in here." She leaned her palm against the wall to slip off her muddy trainers. Her brow furrowed at the gravel and grass clippings spread through the lobby and as far as the kitchen doorway. "What happened?" Her voice caught in her throat and she exercised caution as she crouched next to me. Tentative fingers touched the tip of my shoulder.

My gaze tracked to hers and I found myself without words. She read the angst in my eyes and it proved enough for her. "I'll clean you up," she said with a sigh. Her socks padded her to the kitchen, the route jagged as she dodged the clods of mud and grass deposited by my careless feet. She returned with a first aid kit and knelt on the floor next to me. I clutched my knees to my chest and shrank away from her, chagrined by the way her eyes flared and she covered her stomach with a proprietary hand. "I'll leave it here then," she concluded, rising to her feet.

She busied herself repairing the damage I'd done to the house. I watched through the corners of my eyes as she fetched a broom from the hall cupboard and swept up the mess. The dustpan clanked against the floorboards as she removed the small pile of debris. She swept in strokes of three and I wondered if she did that naturally or if my proximity influenced her actions. When she disappeared into the kitchen and didn't return, I leaned sideways to see where she'd gone.

Victory flashed in her eyes as she peeked around the door frame and caught me looking. Her lips straightened into a line. "Now, can I clean you up?" she demanded. Her hand flicked towards the floor beneath me. "You're making a terrible mess."

I shifted my feet and instead of grass clippings, sand surrounded me in a visual mirage of insanity. Sand and blood, body parts and brain matter covered my inner vision. I listed sideways and covered my head with my arms.

"Jacques!" Julia squeezed my shoulder between her fingers. Her nails dug through my tee shirt and into my skin. I gulped and clamped my hand over her wrist to make her stop. Smooth, delicate skin met my fingers, the roughness of her sleeve creating a textural reference point. I lessened my grip but kept my hand there, counting the gentle beats of her pulse through our combined touch. Seven. Julia's heart beat in sevens.

"You have a heart defect." I sniffed and wiped my nose across the back of my hand.

"So do you." Her eyes smiled at me, though her lips remained pressed together. "But your daughter has a perfect heart, with racy two-beats." Her irises sparkled. "I've heard it and counted for myself."

She knelt on the floor and picked up the first aid kit. Her fingernails dug into the groove to release the catch. If she noticed the tears of frustration pooling on my lower lids, she chose not to mention my weakness. The saline proved ineffective against the many cuts and scrapes and she climbed the stairs to fetch a packet of wipes from her suitcase. I rejected the offer of multiple plasters. "I need to shower."

Julia sat back on her haunches and raised an eyebrow. "Now you tell me! You're an impossible man! I swear you just pretend to dislike my affections."

I wrinkled my nose and pursed my lips. "Where is *The Woman in The Garden*? And *The Bench* and the seascape?"

Her low chuckle induced a sugary taste at the back of my throat. "They're safe from your anger for now." Her gaze flicked to the blank space above my head. "And so is your other potential victim. I arrived at the top of the mountain late because I spent time saving your daughter's legacy." Her delicate lips grunted as she settled next to me, her thigh touching mine. She leaned back against the wall and sighed.

53

RELICS:

BODY PARTS OR PERSONAL BELONGINGS OF SAINTS AND OTHER IMPORTANT FIGURES THAT ARE PRESERVED FOR PURPOSES OF COMMEMORATION OR VENERATION

I sat in my truck and licked an ice cream cone, wincing against the pain in my front teeth from the chill.

The supermarket car park buzzed around me as shoppers pushed empty trolleys through the automatic doors and emerged with enough packages to pollute the Waikato River while feeding our small town. A man wrestled crates of energy drink into the boot of his car and I closed my eyes and pictured the effect of the drink on his arteries. Suicide by mouth. An interesting concept.

He grunted as he hefted the last carton onto the back seat and slammed the door. A half effort of returning his trolley involved walking across the car park and shoving the handle so that it skittered ahead of him and rammed into the metal rails of the enclosure. Unashamed, he turned his back and strode to his car. The trolley ricocheted off the rail and plotted its own journey, making a gentle arc towards a dip in the asphalt and parking itself there in a silent protest. Seconds later, another shopper claimed it, spinning it back through the automatic doors.

I ate my cone from the bottom, tempting the ice cream to dribble onto my fingers. A pleasurable emptiness filled the space in my brain as I exerted the tiny rebellion. The chatter would return, but I'd foxed it for a moment.

The energy drink addict popped the opener on one of his many cans and tipped his head back to drink. His Adam's apple bobbed in his throat and I wrinkled my nose, realising if I continued to watch him, I wouldn't be able to finish my treat. I ate too fast, and a pain bloomed across my forehead, forcing me to squeeze my eyes shut. When I opened them again, the man had driven away, giving me an unobstructed view of the police station car park.

The woman from the reception desk had arrived just before eight o'clock, parking her car nearest the building. I imagined Henare would drift in much later. He hadn't struck me as a respecter of time or rules. A courier van spun into the car park and slewed to a stop, the sliding door visible from my vantage point. The driver left the door open and the engine running as he sped into the police station with the package clasped under his arm. The front door gave him enough difficulty to summon the receptionist, and she helped him wrestle the package addressed to Detective Sergeant Henare inside.

The painting contained enough of my DNA to draw the detective back to me, but I didn't care. I knew he wouldn't bother proving my identity. The canvas bore the familiar 'X' signature and a label from Julia's gallery verified the provenance from the rear of the wooden frame. I sensed he'd use the phone number printed at the bottom of the sticky tab.

He arrived twenty minutes later, breezing from his car with the tail of his jacket stuck in his belt and one of his trouser legs longer than the other.

Five minutes and twelve seconds later, my mobile phone rang. "Jethro."

"Hey." Julia's tone held tiredness. "The detective just phoned me."

"Yep." Satisfaction budded in my chest. It gave me pleasure to find others as predictable as myself.

Julia paused and then continued when she guessed I wouldn't fill in any gaps. "You gave him the painting of the bench."

"Yep."

"I covered for you. Told him the artist wanted him to have it in appreciation of his interest."

"Thank you." My fingers felt sticky after the ice cream, and I frowned. "Did he ask for the value or for any other documentation?"

"No." Silence filled the space between us and then Julia gave a hiss of acknowledgement. "Ah. He doesn't intend to declare it to his employer as a gift."

I smiled to myself as the front door of the police station opened and Henare reappeared, hefting the canvas with both hands. The bubble wrap hung loose, the string having lost the precise tension I gave it when I secured the knot. He stared at the back of his car for a moment with his head on one side before opening the rear door and sliding the painting behind the driver and passenger seats. After closing the door with care, he stared around the car park with his hands on his hips.

"Jacques?" Julia nudged me back towards the conversation. "What is happening?"

I sniffed and waited until Henare hauled open his driver's door and slipped behind his steering wheel. He'd checked the car park and the street, but not thought to cast his gaze as far as the supermarket. I gave a slow exhale. "He's taking it home."

"I could have sold that for you at the gallery." Pique entered her tone, and she dragged out her words. "You could have created a series of alternative works."

I wrinkled my nose. "Maybe."

"He asked if 'X' painted it. I said I would verify the provenance if he needed me to do so. He didn't ask me anything about you."

"Good." I started the engine and the Bluetooth snatched Julia's reply and echoed it through the speaker.

"You wanted him to know?"

"I wanted him to leave me alone." I waited for a vehicle to pull alongside me before driving out of the parking space. "Now, he will."

"How do you know?" Julia's voice rose with the strain. "He could ruin everything."

"He won't."

"You just bought a cop with a one-off, priceless piece of art?"

The notion made me want to yell through my open window. If I'd had a gun, I would have let loose and peppered the sky with my elation. I grinned so widely, it stretched my lips to an uncharacteristic thinness and hurt my face. A laugh bubbled up from my chest and I caught the tail end of Julia's sigh.

"Just when I think I understand you," she said. "You've become a secret rebel."

"All art has a story." And I liked the story of this piece. *The Bench* had begun as an exorcism and become my salvation.

"Do you think he'll display it in his home?"

"I don't know." I didn't much care, either.

"It will cost a fortune to insure." She tutted. "Do you think he'll insure it?"

"No." I imagined Henare stashing the canvas in his attic and visiting it on special occasions. He would own it but never enjoy it. The manner of receiving the gift had ruined it for him, while at the same time fostering a secret addiction that would permeate his life.

I should have felt guilty, but I didn't.

"Are you going somewhere nice?" Julia must have looked at a clock, causing me to glance at the digital display on my dashboard. She exhaled. "Sorry, Jacques. I didn't mean to remind you of her loss. I thought perhaps you'd found a diversion."

The hour when Mother usually rang loomed in the distance, foreshortening my day with the effort of clambering over the habit.

"I'm okay," I told her, realising as I said the words that I spoke the truth. "I'll finish the kowhai and seascape painting this afternoon. But I have an appointment at eleven." My fingers itched with the prospect of improving on the major's grass from the previous week.

"Keep safe, Jacques." Julia ended the call, and I wondered if she'd left three beats after my name on purpose so as not to spoil my mood.

I turned onto Hakarimata Road and jammed on the brakes. The wide road had narrowed to a thin stream as cars struggled to park on either side of the street. They mounted curbs and stopped on the grass verge, slowing commuters to a crawl. Roddy directed traffic, wearing his best uniform despite the jacket tugging across his belly. He offered a wave as I edged my way along the street.

I braked again as a woman stepped out in front of me. She carried a wreath of flowers in her arms, her shoulders heaving with the force of her sobs. Two small children trailed behind her like ducklings crossing a perilous road. I held my breath until she reached the other side and a woman met her on the verge. Neither the women nor the girl child noticed me, but the tiny boy stared at my truck and then at me.

I gave him an upward jerk of my chin in acknowledgment before shoving the gear lever into first and setting off home.

Roddy stepped in front of the truck as I entered the first bend. I'd only reached third gear, but I slammed on the brakes to avoid hitting him. He wore his best uniform, the trouser creases sharp as knives against his chunky thighs.

"Slow down, dude," he rebuked. His dark brows knitted into a line. Then he laughed, the severe expression gone. "Just kidding." He slapped the side of my truck. "Road traffic has a stop-go system outside your place. There's a memorial for Nathan Watson starting at half-past nine. Wanna come?"

I shook my head, my expression impassive. "No, thanks."

As though answering an unasked question, Roddy tapped his chest. "Henare's meant to do this gig. Something urgent came up with his family. Says he's putting in for a transfer. Auckland somewhere."

Nodding, I kept the inner smile from leaking into my face. "Right."

Roddy wrinkled his nose and tapped the decorative buttons of his jacket. "Look, I got my old uniform out. The one I wore to your mum's funeral hung off me. I couldn't fit in this rig two years' ago. It just goes to show what good living does for ya." He bent his knees and sank his weight into them as though about to sit in mid-air. He winced. "It was touch and go for a minute there. Good job we're standing and not sitting."

Another truck pulled up behind mine and the driver gave a tap on his horn. Roddy jabbed a warning finger towards the road tax sticker in his windscreen, and I glanced in my rear-view mirror to see the man slump lower in his seat. "See you tomorrow at the RSA?" I framed the statement as a question as doubt crept into my mind.

'He'll be there, he's always there,' the narrators promised.

Roddy wrinkled his nose. "I dunno, mate." He patted his stomach. "Not the same now I can't drink beer. The missus said I can have the kids every other weekend if I stay sober. I'm fetching them after my shift tomorrow."

"Okay." The word escaped as a hiss. A lack of control swirled around me, sucking me into quick sand. The skinny kid had changed everything.

And then I remembered.

My shoulders relaxed, and I shrugged. "I might not get home in time, anyway. I'm meeting Julia in Auckland."

Roddy's eyes crinkled into a smile. "Nice, dude. You doing anything special?"

My head jerked into a reluctant nod and the driver behind pushed his luck with a strangled toot of his horn. "Antenatal appointment," I stammered.

Pushing the gear lever into first, I took off up Hakarimata Road with enough speed to take Roddy and the other driver by surprise. I glanced in my rear-view mirror to find Roddy still standing in the middle of the road, his mouth hanging open like a carp out of water.

54

·—·

BAUHAUS:

GERMAN SCHOOL OF ART AND DESIGN SHUT DOWN BY THE NAZIS IN 1933

I watched from the edge of my lawn as Talia knelt on the riverbank, the left knee of her jeans pressed into the orange mud. The heel of her other foot slid against the greasy surface and her arms splayed wide to save her, like a ballerina entering a pirouette.

An older woman waited behind her, clutching the hands of two small children. Skinny versions of their father observed Talia's shaking fingers through wide blue eyes as she laid the bouquet next to the lapping water. The current licked at the bank with a lazy tongue, snatching her offering before she'd even dropped her arms.

The gathered mourners wore black. Roddy clutched his hat to his chest. I watched his shoulders move, knowing the words issued from his lips didn't match the ones in his head.

Talia rose, and her shoulders slackened. I dared to believe she sampled the first heady draughts of relief beneath the obvious grief. Nathan was a lousy partner and would have made a violent and abusive husband. His selfishness and aggression would have escalated with every passing week until she became a limp punch bag, unable to lift herself or her children from his web of control. I'd saved her the trouble.

Disappointment locked my chest as she lifted mud-streaked palms to her face. Her lips parted to release a wail of utter misery. My brain fired, beginning its familiar loop of searching for answers, unable to let the anomaly rest without explanation. I'd taken a risk, allowing myself to imagine she'd see his death as an escape.

My stomach roiled at the realisation that her grief was no less painful than mine. I mourned an excellent woman, a mother who'd defended me from her brutal partner, and paid the ultimate price. Talia grieved for a man who'd given her black eyes and a cut to her lip which would scar.

The older woman released the hands of the children to wrap her arms around Talia. Their tiny wrists showed at the ends of their sleeves before they dropped their arms to their sides. Like little flecks next to the raging river, they remained standing, their hands loose and their gaze impassive. Talia thrashed and wailed less than a metre from them, but their disconnection frightened me. They became ornaments at the scene, bystanders in a theatrical display which would shape the rest of their lives.

I balled the front of my shirt in the tense fingers of my right hand as I wrestled with the pictures in my head. Willing Talia to cease her wailing and take the hands of her flotsam children didn't work. The images receded as I withdrew the binoculars from my eyes and dropped them to my side. I would never understand people.

Nathan was trash, and I had taken him out for her. Why wasn't she grateful?

A glance at my watch showed the hour approaching ten. I picked my way through the shrubs and dead leaves to crunch towards the house. Concrete seemed to encase my boots as I lifted my feet onto the porch steps. I sat on the bench in the lobby to remove them, placing the binoculars next to me on the wooden slats. Then I waited for a call which would never come.

Habit dictated I sit by the phone, anyway, imagining Mother's voice against the backdrop of slamming metal doors and the hum of prison life. Last week's avoidance hadn't released me and I'd lived with the nagging pain ever since. Ten thousand and seventy-eight minutes of guilt. Two more still to go.

I dug in the case belonging to the binoculars and found a soft cloth. It glossed across the lenses in a circular pattern, giving my fingers something to do while I considered my situation. I'd found them in a junk shop in Ngaruawahia, perhaps discarded by the executors of an opera goer's estate. They pre-dated the second world war, manufactured by Leroy in Paris. The brass and metal housing gleamed from hours of polishing and I'd repaired the original leather case. I stroked the smooth domed surface of the glass and wished it had witnessed a better performance than Talia's futile thrashing.

When the handset of the landline rang, I jumped. I hadn't expected the call to come from beyond the grave. The cloth fluttered to the floorboards. I lifted the receiver and gave a slow exhale. "Hello?"

"Jacques?" Julia's gentle tone caressed my ear drum. "I didn't want you to be at a... what do you call it? A loose end?" Something crashed in the background, followed by a swear word. I recognised the sound of wood on wood, the impact deadened by canvas and bubble wrap. Julia sighed. "I love you, Jacques. I wanted you to know that."

She didn't give me the opportunity to respond, ending the call at nine fifty-nine and twelve seconds. I stared at the handset for a moment before placing it back on the receiver.

A clock ticked in the lounge, its beat offset by one in the kitchen. Julia had set them running again and one of them ticked fast enough to cause a mismatch in the joint record of seconds. They beat together as one and then diverged, making their own time line in glorious oblivion of each other.

Like me.

I ran at my own speed, creating my individual pattern for life and oblivious to the beat of others.

Except Julia.

At ten o'clock, I checked my watch and lifted the receiver again. The dial tone sounded, and I drowned it out with my words. "Hello, Mother," I said. "I need to speak to you about a skinny kid who abused his girlfriend." I rushed on, not wanting the surge of disappointment to derail me when she didn't answer. "He reminded me of my father and I had to reset seven times." I sighed. "I went the wrong way home and met him on the bridge after he got thrown out of the RSA. He stepped in front of my truck and when I stopped, he walked to my open window and spat in my face." I closed my eyes against the mental image of flecks of his spit on my sleeve. Moonlight gave them a shimmering appearance.

"He'd planted cannabis in a grove beneath the mountain track and needed to make sure I didn't find it by accident. So, he'd spied on us, Mother. Julia didn't know he watched her undress when she last stayed at my house. He'd been waiting for her to return." My fingers shook on the receiver and I steadied them, calming myself through a sheer act of will.

"His breath stank of beer and sickness and his neck snapped like a twig. I shoved him over the Waipa Bridge." I tapped out three lazy beats against my knee as I recalled sabotaging the electrical power box with a swift kick to the plastic casing. It always knocked out the gate camera while leaving the mechanism working on its own backup battery.

I hadn't lied to Roddy when I claimed a seventy-minute round trip home. He'd estimated each journey as five minutes when it was only four minutes and forty-five seconds. He'd also allowed for fourteen trips and I'd made only thirteen. One disastrous trip and twelve more to correct it to total seven complete cycles.

It took two minutes for me to realise money wouldn't silence the skinny kid and three more to despatch of him. Two minutes and fifty-eight seconds accounted for the damage to the power box.

Seventy minutes.

I wouldn't split hairs with Roddy over two seconds.

My nose wrinkled in confusion as I returned to my one-sided conversation. "But I don't understand why his partner is crying. What is that, Mother? Is that love?"

Like Japan's Otsuchi 'wind telephone', the one-way conversation gave me an odd kind of peace. I chatted to my mother's spirit as though I'd acquired an acute case of verbal diarrhoea. I told her about the mural, about Julia's pregnancy, and our joint plan for the future. My wife had promised to help me raise and love our daughter within my own safe parameters, and I trusted her.

Sudden freedom of speech loosened my tongue and Mother's expectations tumbled to the floorboards beneath my feet. Nobody argued with her in the background to hang up the phone. No prison doors echoed with their metallic clang as they trapped her in someone else's pattern.

She was free at last.

And so was I.

DEAR READER

I hope you've enjoyed *Her Quiet Legacy*. I would be grateful if you would take the time to leave a review at your usual retailer. You can do that at ktbowes.com. I often feature snappy review comments on my covers. My work is also ranked on reviews and your comments will allow me to reach a wider audience.

It doesn't have to be an essay - I will be grateful for a few words.

Thank you for doing this for me.

About the Author

K T Bowes is a bestselling teen and women's author.

Her novel, *A Trail of Lies*, was the winner of the genre award for Author's Cave in 2014.

Phoenix Du Rose was considered for the prestigious Ngaio Marsh awards for 2021.

K T Bowes is an Englishwoman in exile in New Zealand, swapping rugged cosmopolitan for mountain ranges and terrifying rivers. She loves Māori culture and has learned to weave flax using traditional methods. Her other passion is Rongoa Māori, which involves creating medicines from native plants. She is a student of Te Reo Māori.

You can find her hanging out on social media in the following places.

Check in and say hello. Maybe suggest she gets back to writing and stops watching cat videos.

FACEBOOK

https://www.facebook.com/NZauthorKTBowes/

TWITTER

https://twitter.com/ktboweswrites

INSTAGRAM

https://www.instagram.com/k_t_bowes

PINTEREST

https://www.pinterest.nz/hanadurose/

Phoenix Du Rose

******

The Calculated Risk Series:

The Actuary

The Actuary's Wife

The Actuary in Trouble

The Heart of The Actuary

******

Troubled series for teens

Free from the Tracks

Sophia's Dilemma

A Trail of Lies

Gone Phishing

******

New Zealand Soccer Referee series

All Saints

******

Escaping the Back Country NZ series

Pirongia's Secret

Deleilah

****

A Keeper's War Fantasy Trilogy

Perpetual Winter

The Bee Queen

Hive

****

UK based mystery/romances:

Artifact

Demons on Her Shoulder

****

The Curly Fan Club

Dead Straight

Bad Hair Day

Side Parting

Take a look at all K T Bowes' novels at ktbowes.com

Disclaimer

This novel is a work of fiction, entirely the product of the author's imagination. Any similarities to actual persons, living or dead, businesses and events are purely coincidental.

All rights reserved. No part of this book may be reproduced in whole or in part without the express written permission of the author. This work is the intellectual property of the author writing as K T Bowes.